# JANTHINA

Also by Diana Bachmann and published by
New English Library:

BEYOND THE SUNSET

# JANTHINA

## Diana Bachmann

New English Library

Copyright © 1987 by F. Beerman B.V.

First published in Great Britain in 1987 by
New English Library, Mill Road, Dunton Green, Sevenoaks, Kent.
Editorial office: 47 Bedford Square, London WC1B 3DP.

Typeset by Rowland Phototypesetting Ltd,
Bury St Edmunds, Suffolk

Printed and bound in Great Britain by
Biddles Ltd, Guildford and King's Lynn

**British Library C.I.P.**

Bachmann, Diana
  Janthina.
  I. Title
  823'.914[F]       PR605Z.A2/

  ISBN 0-450-39944-3

*To my family*

# CONTENTS

# PROLOGUE

BEAR FOOT was her friend – had been for as long as she could remember. When she was tiny she used to watch him chop logs for the fires, long sinewy wrists protruding from ragged shirt sleeves. He always wore a hat, a stiff felt mildewed with age, a miscellaneous collection of chicken feathers stuck in the discoloured band, and Janthina marvelled that no matter what he was doing or the angle of his head, the hat never moved. When he wasn't chopping wood he wore a black coat, once kept very smart, pressed and brushed for Papa to wear to church on Sundays; but the elbows had been worn through on the hymn-book shelf in front of their pew, and not even Papa, scrupulously careful with his money and insistent on every economy, would consider wearing patches on his Sunday coat.

Papa's trousers would have wrapped round Bear Foot at least twice. Despite his austere habits, Papa had developed a prosperous girth and the Indian, not having been dealt so kind a hand by Fate, was lean and bony. So with the discarded church coat, Bear Foot wore narrow canvas trousers . . . and shoes.

Janthina had been five years old before she plucked up courage to ask him why he wore shoes when his name was Bare Foot.

'My name not Bare Foot, missy,' he explained. 'My name Bear Foot,' which didn't help at all until he drew something vaguely resembling a bear in the yard dust. 'Bear tread soft and gentle. Bear claws sharp and strong. My papa name me for foot of bear. Is good name, huh?'

The little girl had solemnly agreed.

Ten years later, she was still attempting to teach him how to pronounce her name correctly.

'Janty . . . Jan-e-tee . . .' he stumbled.

'No. Jan-tee-na,' she repeated.

'Janty.'

'No, Bear Foot, no.' She shook her head.

'Janty. Is good. Plenty good enough for you and me,' he said, finally.

They were sitting together on the edge of the water trough, out of sight of the parlour window – Mama would not approve if she saw – in the leafy shade of a cluster of birch trees, growing slender and graceful in the centre of the yard. August was hot this year. Even the

ix

hens sat motionless in their dust baths, waiting for Bear Foot to scatter their evening corn.

Janthina was bored. She had so longed for her fifteenth birthday, to be grown-up enough to wear a long dress like Mama and Ruth, but now, after only two weeks, the novelty was wearing off. It wasn't so much the new dress itself, which, in pale green watered taffeta scooped up at the sides, with bows, nipped waist and frilled cuffs and collar, was very beautiful and suited her pale sandy hair and green eyes; but rather it was the corsetry, six petticoats and decorum, all part of the new image, which irked. Now, even when the dress hung in her wardrobe and she wore, instead, one of her old, calf-length dresses covered with a frilled pinafore, Mama insisted that she must walk, just so, sit, just so. No longer might she ride her pony astride, or scramble over walls scuffing her boots; from now on she must behave like a young lady.

Ruth, two years her senior, was in the parlour with Mama right now, handing buttered scones and little iced cakes to the minister's wife and to Mrs Grant, Chairwoman of the Church Ladies Bible Study Group. Dear Ruth, she loathed these tea parties as much as Janthina herself, but knowing how much they meant to Mama, and loving Mama so, Ruth would always play the demure, dutiful daughter, just to make Mama happy.

Janthina could not accept that anyone should waste a whole afternoon being 'seen and not heard', bored to tears simply because it pleased Mama. If Mama enjoyed her tea parties, let her have them; but why should she inflict them on her daughters? It wasn't fair.

Instead of going upstairs to put on her new dress, Janthina had crept out through the dairy after luncheon, run down the hill to the stables to saddle Pickle, and galloped away along the river to her secret hideaway where she could lie and watch the wading herons feed.

Mrs Grant's pony and trap was still in the yard when she returned, so she had stayed down by the stables to talk with Bear Foot, a far more interesting person to her mind.

Bear Foot looked at her, sideways, with a puzzled frown. 'Why you people don't have names that mean something?' he asked. 'Like Bear Foot and his people.'

'I don't know. I think your names are lovely. But you know, my name does mean something.'

'Janty?'

'Yes. Janthina is a kind of shell.'

'Shell? What shell?'

'Ummm . . .' she looked around for a snail shell but saw nothing, then glanced cautiously up at the house. 'Wait a minute, Bear Foot, I'll fetch them,' she said, and jumped off the trough to run up the tree-lined path, frilled petticoats bouncing to reveal the starched legs of her pantaloons, pigtails swinging across her back, until she disappeared behind the rhododendrons.

Bear Foot pressed a plug of tobacco into the bowl of his long-stemmed clay pipe as he watched her go. He liked young Janty best of all this family, but he considered she should have been born a boy; he couldn't ever imagine her becoming womanish. She was too bright and strong, always laughing – except when in the company of her parents, particularly her father. Strange man, that: stern and fierce, always speaking words from the black book he carried to church on Sundays.

Janty skipped back down the path, covering her boots in another layer of thick dust. 'Look!' she called. 'These are Janthina shells. Aren't they pretty?' She was swinging a string of pale purplish snail shells, threaded like a necklet. Hitching herself back on to the edge of the stone trough beside him, she dropped them into his lap.

Bear Foot was intrigued, turned the shells over and over. 'I see plenty these shells in your Mama's garden, but not pretty, so. Where you get them?'

'My uncle, Mama's brother, is in the Royal Navy. . . .' She saw a look of total incomprehension on the face of her audience. 'I mean, he works on a boat in the big ocean.'

Bear Foot nodded, sagely. He had never seen the ocean, but he had heard tell of it. Some said that it was bigger than Lake Superior, as these strange people called it, but he found that hard to believe.

'Well,' Janthina continued, 'he found these shells in the tropics. They float on the sea on masses of air bubbles, and when there are storms they are washed ashore. Uncle William brought them with him when he came to visit Papa and Mama fifteen years ago. When Papa heard the name "Janthina", he said he would call his new daughter by it, because she had arrived late and slow like a snail, only that very day. I don't think it is very nice to be named after something that is late and slow, do you?'

Bear Foot looked horrified. Like all Ottawa-Algonquin Indians he knew how important it was to have a good name – a name to give encouragement, dignity and self-respect – and the thought that this young woman had been burdened with a name which gave her such a poor self-image was appalling. Again he reflected on the attitude of these parents, who seemed determined to make their children into frightened, submissive creatures, instead of wanting them to be bold, courageous and serene – able to handle all the conflicts they must face throughout their lives with dignity and fortitude. The older brother and sister both seemed frightened of their father. Joseph, the eldest, seldom smiled, laboured long hours on the farm, and, like his father, neither smoked nor drank strong liquor, and solemnly carried his black book to church. Simon, the younger boy, was different. Bear Foot smiled to himself. Though he too was submissive, the Indian had often seen anger and resentment in the boy's face, and knew that it was only a matter of time before he rebelled.

The other girl, Ruth, now she was different. Tall and beautiful, quiet and obedient, she never voiced her true thoughts to anyone. But he, Bear Foot, guessed. He sensed the strength behind her soft voice and mild manners; knew she watched her father's determined efforts to dominate his wife and children with secret disapproval. Very secret, because she was clever enough to know that revealing her thoughts would only bring more anger and disruption to the lives of her family as well as her own, and achieve nothing.

Hamish Curran McKenzie was not a man to tolerate anyone's opinion if it varied from his own. He alone was always right, unquestionably. Bear Foot suspected it all had a lot to do with the black book and the terrible Lord he so often quoted and visited on Sundays.

So was young Janty to have the laughter crushed out of her soul before she had had a chance to blossom into womanhood? She lacked the wisdom and serenity of her sister; her spirit would be broken like her mother's. They were both too loving and sensitive. How could such a child remain unaffected, retain her confidence and independent spirit after all the angry shouts and beatings her father employed to discipline her into submission?

Bear Foot's big, calloused fingers toyed gently with the string of delicate shells, and the thin line of his lips, which reflected the anger in his soul, softened into a smile. 'Janty! Why no one ever told you the story of the shells – how they came into being?' he asked.

The girl gave him a puzzled stare. 'They told me only what I have just told you. Why? Is there more?'

'Yes. Much more. I tell you.' He held up one shell. 'See how it twists round and round to a tiny point in the middle?'

'Ye-es,' Janthina nodded, still frowning.

'That little point is how the snail started life – so small you wouldn't see him in the water; just a helpless, baby thing like us, when we are born. But he was clever. See how he made his shell bigger as he grew, ridge after ridge, round and round, changing the shape to suit the way he must live? Just as a child, growing up, must change his thoughts and himself, to suit the world in which he lives so that he may live a good, successful and contented life, no matter the trouble and pain and injustice he must bear. See,' he held up another, 'the shell is shaped so wide and yet so light.' He weighed it in the palm of his hand. 'So that it can float easily, survive the storms and winds and waves, live out its life span.' Solemnly he looked at her. 'They gave you a good name; means you grow here. . . .' He tapped his head. 'Wise and strong. You float always, never drown, as long as you remember your name.' He sighed. If only she understood Algonquin, the language of his tribe, he could explain much more, help more. . . . He saw that she was smiling to herself. Perhaps she had understood.

Janthina took the string of shells from him and dropped them over her head; lifted her pigtails out so that the string hung properly on her neck, letting the shells lie over the front of her pinafore like a necklet of huge beads. 'Thank you, Bear Foot.' She stood up, squared her shoulders, tilted up her chin. 'I'll always remember the meaning of my name. I wish I'd known before what a good name I have.' She pirouetted in the dust.

'Janthina!' A voice called from the house. 'Janthina, where are you?' It was Ruth.

'Here, down by the stables,' the younger girl shouted back.

Her sister appeared round the rhododendrons. 'What are you doing, Jan? Mama has sent me to find you. She says you must come immediately.'

Bear Foot watched the shoulders droop and the smile fade as Janthina followed her sister back to the house, dragging her feet along the path.

He sighed again.

She had forgotten already.

# PART ONE

## *PAPA*

### 1898 – 1901

'Be good, sweet maid, and let who will be clever;
Do lovely things, do not dream them all day long;
And so make Life, and Death, and that For Ever,
One grand sweet song.'

'A Farewell', Charles Kingsley

# 1

JANTHINA LOOKED at her reflection in the maple-framed swivel mirror on the chest of drawers, and, turning her head to one side, tried to tuck the stray wisps of sand-coloured hair into the large knot formed by her twisted pigtails, pinned up in the nape of her neck by Ruth.

There were so many damp spots on the mirror that it was difficult to see anything properly, and they made all her freckles look much worse. She gazed angrily at the little brown marks clustered on her nose, forehead and cheeks and even on her chin, causing the full, soft lips to pucker tightly across her wide mouth, and her green eyes to darken under their long, brown lashes.

The white cotton, tuck-stitched blouse fitted beautifully, and Ruth had tied the sash of her skirt in a perfect bow at the back – but Janthina couldn't see it. In fact, she could hardly see any of the blouse and skirt below the little gold-set cameo at her throat. The mirror was too small and too high. It was a great pity she and Ruth couldn't have a full-length mirror in the bedroom. She had dared to suggest, one day, that she could be much neater and tidier in her dress if they had one on the back of the door, but Papa refused to consider the idea. 'Certainly not,' he had said. 'At your age? You would be wanting to spend far too much time in front of it, primping. It would encourage you to become vain, and vanity is a sin. Ungodly.' And, as always, that was the last word. Ungodly. Like most of the things she wanted to do or have. Too many layers of frills and lace on one's petticoats and dresses were ungodly. Ringlets, riding astride one's pony, running so fast that too much length of pantaloon could be seen, any form of activity on Sundays – apart from preparing food, going to church and Sunday school, or sitting reading the Bible – all angered the Lord, according to Papa. He took religion very seriously and administered chastisement, in the Lord's name, with a cane kept in his study for such transgressions as lateness for meals, clumsiness, or tearing one's dress.

Papa was actually a rather terrifying person, but nevertheless Janthina loved him, desperately wanted to please him, to draw from him a smile or, on rare occasions, a word of praise. The trouble was there were so many pleasant things which were forbidden, or she

3

guessed would be were they known, so that even if she wasn't caught she sometimes felt sick with guilt, terrified that, as the Lord could see and hear everything, He would know and punish her even if Papa didn't.

Mama almost seemed to sympathise, flashing a warning look or giving a surreptitious shake of the head behind Papa's back; but she never argued with him, always nodded in agreement when one of the four brothers and sisters was punished. Only very seldom had she shown anger, like the times when Janthina did not appear in the parlour to help entertain church ladies at Mama's prim tea parties.

'Janthina, aren't you ever coming down?' Ruth called from the bottom of the stairs.

'Yes. At this very moment,' she called back, and checked with the mirror that she was absolutely presentable before running down the stairs.


Ruth sighed with relief as her sister came down. Papa had frowned at his pocket watch twice already, and she dearly hoped Janthina wouldn't get another scolding.

She had loved her little sister from the day she was born, helped Mama tend her, rocked the cradle and played with the fat, baby fingers, although she herself was only two years old. Janty's first steps had delighted her; she had held her little hand, helped her up when she fell, and later taught her her alphabet and numbers. When Janty was old enough to go to school, Ruth had held her hand all the way.

The sisters had always been good friends, and Ruth had taught Janty everything she herself had learned – save for one thing. Ruth had discovered very early, certainly by the time she was six years old, how to avoid Papa's wrath; no matter how boring, one should never do anything that might dirty one's dress or boots, but sit quietly stitching for hours, always remembering to keep one's back straight and knees and ankles together, while the grown-ups talked. Children should be seen and not heard, was Papa's motto. Not that she had ever dared to do otherwise. Papa's raised voice frightened her, made her shake, paralysed her brain so that she lost control of her limbs; so much so that when she was little she would stand in horror, feeling hot liquid running down inside her pantaloons and into her boots, to create a tell-tale pool at her feet . . . which had always resulted in Papa fetching his cane and, purple with rage, ordering her to bend over and be whipped for this 'deliberate act of insolence'.

Oh, yes, she had learned quickly. Learned to hate both the beastly man and the vengeful Lord he claimed to serve, in whose Name he made miserable the lives of all his family.

Naturally her hatred, all her secret thoughts, caused frequent waves of guilt to sweep through her body, as now. She looked at him, through the open front door, standing beside the pony trap, impatiently tapping his foot on the ground. His coat was open, a thumb hitched in the armhole of his waistcoat, while the other hand held the reins. Lamb-chop side-whiskers framed the narrow, drooping mouth and deep-cleft chin, and his pale eyes, with almost invisible lashes, were overhung with long, thick whiskers growing from his brow. The man who was always right. Because all he did and said and thought was in the Name of the Lord, to uphold the Word.

How she hated him. Not with a passionate, burning anger, though. Oh, no. Hers was a cool, calm, controlled hatred, even when he was striking her darling little sister, and remained so despite the pounding of her heart, the pain in her chest and head, the nausea in her throat caused by each shout, each blow.

Little did Hamish Curran McKenzie realise, as he exchanged a smile with his elder daughter who, with her black hair drawn tightly back into a knot and big meek brown eyes, reminded him so much of her mother years ago, that he was looking at two people. Those meek eyes were not, as he thought, admiring the man who had turned his Scottish immigrant father's smallholding into a large, prosperous dairy farm; the man who was a much sought-after benefactor in their community, who made large donations to the hospital in Kingston and fiercely struck the pulpit on Sundays as he tried to lead the misbegotten herd back into the way of the Lord. He never suspected that this beautiful, biddable young woman whom he was proud to introduce at receptions in town as his daughter, despised him as a callous tyrant, unloving and unloved.


But Adeline knew. Could a mother who loved and understood her daughter so well and was so loved in return, not know? Yet no word had been spoken between them about the man; that would have been most unseemly. Only by an occasional movement, a glance, a touch, did they convey their understanding. She admired the girl's courage and control, wishing she herself had had the strength to survive marriage to this man unscarred, without losing her nerve, her ability to create an independent thought. The silky blackness of her own hair was grey and dull now, like her face, her dress, and her soul.

*       *       *

5

Winter fodder for the cattle was a very important matter in the farming area where the McKenzies lived, and hay was a vital factor. When the snows were melted and the early sun warmed the grass to grow long and lush, the cows were allowed to graze only in limited areas where they could obtain all the nourishment they required to produce plenty of good quality milk and healthy calves, without damaging growth in the vast areas of grassland intended for hay. When each farmer mowed his hay in turn, and it had had time to dry in the sun, his family gave a hay picnic. All the local farming families were invited and while the men of the host family were joined by the visitors, wielding long, two-pronged pitchforks, raking and pulling the hay into long rows of haycocks between which the horse-drawn haywains could pass to be loaded, the ladies of the host farms piled the results of several days' preparation and baking into a pony trap, to be taken into the hayfields and laid out on linen cloths for the workers.

The McKenzie women loved the haymaking season, never quite able to decide whether they preferred their own picnics, with all the cooking that was involved, or those of their neighbours, where they worked with pitchforks, raking, lifting and stacking the cocks for the men to collect in huge forkfuls and throw up onto the passing haywains.

Janthina, especially, loved the picnics: the cooking of pigs' heads for brawn to spread on fresh-baked bread; kneading out the round yeast biscuits, crisp on the outside and soft when you cut them in half to butter each side; the mouth-watering smell of steaming hot fruit cake as it came out of the oven. It was exciting taking pans from the oven to turn out the layers of chocolate sponge to cool, before sandwiching them together with cream and jam; and last, but most important of all, the trifles made with jellied sponges and fruit, vanilla custard and cream.

Everyone brought their own plate, cup, knife and spoon, and the hostesses would walk amongst the picnickers with jugs of tea and lemonade, encouraging people to return again and again to help themselves to the fare laid out on the cloths.

Ruth loved the picnics too, partly for the happy atmosphere but also because it seemed the only time of the year when Mama really came alive, the dullness in her eyes washed away by the activity and excitement. Haymaking was the highlight of her year.

Papa was better humoured too. Preoccupied with the refilling of haylofts and the siting of outdoor ricks, he forgot to watch or criticise his family on the usual daily basis. He did little wielding of pitchforks, but instead strode up and down supervising until it was time to return to the house to fetch the women and the prepared food.

6

Now his tongue clicked behind his teeth as he forcefully assisted his daughters up beside their mother, took his place behind the pony, and flicked the reins.

Each year the McKenzie ladies set their food out under a group of pines which offered welcome shade for the workers. Today, when everyone was seated with loaded plates and mugs of tea, Hamish, who never ever sat on the ground, cleared his throat.

'Almighty God, we thank Thee for the bountiful mercies Thou hast heaped upon us, Thy humble servants.'

Ruth caught her brother Simon's eye as they both smothered the smiles which always threatened to betray their secret laughter at their father's repeated use of this blatant piece of hypocrisy, wondering again if he really considered himself one of the humble.

'We thank Thee that in Thy great mercy, despite the sinful wickedness of our minds and bodies, Thou hast seen fit to grant us once again a plentiful harvest.' He closed his eyes and paused before continuing. 'Oh, Lord, bless this food before us and bless all who are gathered here, and forgive them their . . . ahem . . . forgive us our trespasses. We ask this in the name of Thy beloved Son, Jesus Christ. Amen.'

When she looked up, Ruth saw that her brother Joseph's eyes were still devoutly closed, his lips moving silently under the sparse whiskers on his face, made longer and thinner by the already receding hairline. One had to feel sorry for his obvious confusion between honest-to-God love and religious obsession. Thank heavens there was no chance of the fun-loving Simon suffering the same problems; but he would have others. Though two years younger than Joseph, he was already showing signs of rebellion which frightened Ruth. . . .

'You young ladies go and join in the fun,' Mrs Callaghan, round, dumpy and beaming, told Ruth and Janthina. 'I'll help your mother clear away the remains of the food into the trap.'

Janthina's eyes lit up. 'Ooh, thank you. Are you sure?'

Ruth's eyes strayed around the field, searching for Papa, but realising he must be back at the barn, she allowed herself to be persuaded to join her sister wielding the pitchforks, stooking with the other women but without joining in the laughter. Janthina laughed constantly. It was a deep-throated, burbling laugh, infectious to those around her. Tall for her age, and strong, she worked competitively, teasing the others good-naturedly, swinging the fork, gathering, piling. The smell of fresh hay was delicious, and she was unable to resist the temptation

7

to 'fall' onto the stooks with other girls, tangling haystalks in her hair and smothering her skirt with bits, happily thinking that haymaking would always be the highlight of every year – all her life.

Ruth, meanwhile, watched from a distance, indulgently but fearful.

Of course all the farmworkers and their families were expected to join in, not only on their employer's farms, but on those of their neighbours as well. It was during the picnic, when everyone was eating, that Janthina saw Luke Callaghan. She hadn't noticed him at first; she was preoccupied unloading the trap and placing trays of food on the cloths, while he was busy at the far end of the meadow standing on a haywain distributing the forkloads of hay evenly to be sure the final immense load would not tip off on its journey back to the lofts. Nor did she see him collect his plateful of food, along with everyone else. Not until she was handing out extra slices of chocolate cake was her eye drawn to the quiet youth with tanned skin and straight brown hair falling over his brow.

Shyly he had thanked her as his long, brown fingers carefully removed a second sticky wedge and later, when she returned with a bowl of trifle, he tilted his head slightly so that he could look up and give her an equally shy smile.

Later in the afternoon, they worked together building haycocks, timidly exchanging polite conversation. Janthina learned that he was a year older than herself, lived in a cottage with his parents on the McKenzie land, and had, in fact, attended the same school as herself until he left at the end of the summer term to come to work for her father.

Whenever they attended hay-picnics together, thereafter, they gravitated towards each other to work side by side, often in companionable silence, though he was never so bold as to sit beside her to eat.

Sundays were boring, even in summer. There was little to do but attend church in the morning, eat lunch after suitable prayers, and attend Sunday school in the afternoon. Except that one was allowed a sedate walk, trying not to dirty one's best buttoned boots.

Janthina stood on the riverbank, watching and listening to the shallow water burbling round the rocks and stones, and the roots of trees whose branches dipped to touch the surface of the water, making magic reflections. Oh, if only she had her sketch pad with her . . . but it was forbidden on the Sabbath.

A sudden splashing up river caught her attention, and for the first time she noticed Luke standing in the shallows, fishing. He had a fish on his line and, forgetting decorum, she held her skirts and ran along the grassy bank to watch the young man land his catch.

'Oh, well done!' she exclaimed. 'What a beauty.'

Luke smiled shyly. 'Yes, he's a fair size,' and added even more shyly, 'would you like to have him?'

'Thank you very much, but he's yours. You should eat him for your tea.'

'I've four others in here.' He indicated his basket.

Janthina stepped forward to peer into its depths, and soon the two were engrossed in discussion on the finer points of angling. Not that she understood all he said – the subject was not of particular interest to her – but his enthusiasm was infectious and his fishing stories made her laugh.

'Janthina!'

The boy and girl sprang up and turned to see Hamish McKenzie glaring at them from a short distance away. Janthina flushed, murmured a hasty goodbye, and hurried with fearful tread to join him.

'What do you think you are doing?' her father demanded.

'I was just admiring Luke's catch,' she answered, heart pounding.

'You mean you arranged to meet down here secretly and fishing was his excuse. Don't deny it.'

'Papa! I must. I had no idea he would be here, I promise.' Tears stung her eyes at the injustice of his accusation.

'Very well. But just remember in future that I won't have you consorting with hired hands. That boy's father is my herdsman.' His fingers dug painfully into her arms as he led her away. 'We don't associate with them socially.'

The McKenzie farmhouse was large and rambling, the parlour and dining room low-ceilinged but spacious and the limestone-floored kitchen large enough to accommodate a ten-foot long scrubbed table at which Adeline presided each afternoon, a lace cap pinned on her hair and a tired but sweet smile on her face, to pour tea from a huge pot for all the farmworkers. Most, except for the Callaghans and the more senior men, were Indians, and, along with Papa and the boys, they scraped their boots and shoes on the iron bar outside the scullery door, before trooping through for their afternoon break, sitting on benches which lived under the table when not in use.

Built in limestone blocks weathered to a rich cream and timbered in Canadian pine, the house was entered through a modest porch. The hallway was long and at the far end, past the parlour and the dining room, were doors to Papa's study and a cloakroom on one side, and on the other to the kitchen, through which one reached pantry, scullery, dairy and outside, in a separate building all on its own, the wash-house. Although the bedrooms were not large, three were fair-sized and there was also a dressing room for Papa, a sewing room for Mama and a storeroom. Another room which had once been a small bedroom had recently been converted into a bathroom, with piped water to the lavatory, wash-hand basin and bath, all three of which were made in porcelain and painted with garlands of blue flowers.

Janthina thought it the most beautiful house in the world, and dreaded the thought of spending three school terms away in Kingston in Aunt Mary's cramped little house, but next year, once she had outgrown the local school, Papa and Mama insisted that she should attend Kingston Ladies' College for a year, as Ruth had just done, to complete her education as a young lady.

Young lady. She wasn't sure she liked the term, not if it meant snubbing nice people like Luke, and that she refused to do. In the months that followed the incident beside the river when Papa had told her not to associate with the boy, she had disobeyed several times. They both loved the untamed rivers, lakes and forests and had met, accidentally, wandering over grass, rocks, and thick beds of pine needles as she sought vantage points for sketching, he, good fishing areas. They had watched and admired each other's skills, and Luke had learned to relax and overcome some of his shyness in her company. Sometimes they forgot the time, and suddenly noticing the dipping sun, she would hastily and indecorously lift her skirts and throw a leg over Pickle's bare back and gallop back through the trees to collect the dreaded side-saddle, buckle the girths, and ride sedately back across the meadow in full view of the farm, for, as Papa had repeated on several occasions, no decent young lady rode astride.

Janthina did miss her rides out alone on Pickle, her meetings with Luke, her sketching – but not as much as she had expected. School was fun, her cousins were sweet and good company, and she learned to develop her art beyond mere sketching, into the use of water colours and even oils. And she was more than artistic. The headmistress was a progressive woman, anxious that 'her' girls should go out into adult life well equipped to stand on their own two feet, understand business and, if necessary, earn their own livings. So that when Janthina's teacher discovered the girl's ability in mathematics, she encouraged her to learn book-keeping and the basic principles of commerce.

Janthina enjoyed manipulating figures as much as she enjoyed oil-painting and browsing through the school library, which was filled with books by famous explorers, historians and novelists.

The autumn term passed quickly and though it was wonderful to return home for Christmas, she found herself genuinely looking forward to going back to school for the spring term . . . which passed even faster than the first.


Easter was damp and overcast.

When they were not busying themselves in the kitchen, Adeline and her daughters sat by the parlour fire stitching, talking or reading. Janthina had brought home with her some books, recommended by her English teacher, for holiday reading, on one of which she would have to write a précis on her return.

One afternoon, only a week before she was due to leave, when Mama and Ruth were in the kitchen together, she sat alone by the fire engrossed in the book.

Papa strode in, frowning. 'Those men out there! They cannot be relied upon for a minute. Have to be constantly supervised,' he growled, holding his hands to the fire.

Janthina politely set aside her book. 'Papa, you look quite frozen. Would you like me to make you a hot drink? Tea, perhaps, or chocolate?'

'You might as well make yourself useful, I suppose,' he replied ungraciously, pulling an armchair towards the heat. 'Tea, I think.'

She went out to the kitchen and moved the kettle from the hob to the hot end of the range, over the fire, where it immediately started to sing. Mama was rolling pastry while Ruth opened a bottle of fruit, preserved last summer. A cosy domestic scene.

When she returned to the parlour, bearing the tea and a plate of biscuits on a tray, her father was standing in front of the fire, his back to the door.

'Here you are, Papa. I'll put it on this table beside your chair,' she said, and crossed the hearth behind him to return to her own chair.

'What's this?' Hamish rounded on her, brandishing the book she had been reading.

'*Wuthering Heights*, Papa. It's a charming book written by a lady who was only thirty years old when she died. Her name was Emily Brontë.'

'It's rubbish, ridiculous rubbish,' he snarled. 'Where did you get it?'

It was on the tip of her tongue to tell him the truth, that she had

11

borrowed it from the school library, but she stopped herself, fearing the possible repercussions. Supposing he decided that a school which permitted a book he disliked so much was no longer a fit place for his daughter? Might he ban her from returning for her last term?

Praying that he would not see the school label inside the cover, she replied, 'I bought it at a shop in Kingston.'

'So that's what you spend your pin money on, is it? Something to fill your head with a load of wicked trash. Well, that's all it's good for.' He threw the book onto the back of the fire.

'No!' she squealed. 'Papa!' And went down on her hands and knees, fire tongs in hand, desperately trying to pluck the book out of the flames.

'Confound you, girl.' Hamish's hand struck the side of her face and sent her crashing across the hearth. 'How dare you try to remove it?' He hauled her to her feet, shaking her, like a dog with a rabbit.

Janthina screamed.

The long, high-pitched yell reached the kitchen. Ruth and Adeline looked at each other in alarm, then fairly flew down the hallway and flung open the parlour door.

Hamish held a rag doll between his hands, and as he shook it, its head flopped back and forth, arms swinging at its side.

'Hamish!'

'Papa!'

The women shrieked and dashed across the room – too late. At the sight of them Hamish let go of the girl and strode from the room, leaving Janthina a crumpled heap on the floor.


Sick and dazed, Janthina lay on her bed unable to think, speak or eat. The left side of her face was swollen around the cut where her cheek had struck the leg of a chair as she had rolled across the hearth.

Ruth and Mama crept in and out of the room in turn, offering kisses and comfort – but she was unable to respond.

Hamish, Joseph and Simon sat alone in the dining room that evening, serving their own food; the women were too horrified to eat – too angry to sit with the men. They were dumbfounded that a man who could enact the role of loving father, gracious husband, landowner, public benefactor, who was so looked up to in the community and could stand in the pulpit on Sunday preaching the word of God, could suddenly, without warning, become so savage and violent.

Even Hamish could only peck at his food and Joseph was frowning as he ate, unaware of all that had happened, yet strangely disturbed.

That night, for the first time since before Christmas, Joseph heard his mother cry out from the next room. In shame and horror he hid his head under the pillow.

# 2

SPRING GAVE way to summer-like warmth early that year. The rivers slowed from angry torrents of melted snow to benign mirrors of crystal, reflecting puffs of pure white cloud which changed shape as they chased each other across the deep blueness of the sky, between tall, majestic pines.

Baby calves frolicked in the fields while red cardinals and Boston orioles flew busily from dawn to dusk, collecting and delivering food for their young. Long grass grew in the meadows and soon it would be haymaking time again.

Janthina pictured it all as she lay in bed savouring those precious, cosy moments before stepping out into the May morning to prepare for school. She was sad, in a way, to be missing it all, yet happy to be where she was, experiencing life in Kingston for a year with her cousins, enjoying school. She would return to the farm next month, too late for this year's haymaking, but she would be there for the next, and the next. And what after that? She was going to miss her aunt and cousins, dreadfully. Papa would never let her return to Kingston to earn her own living, as several of her schoolfriends intended. She would probably marry a nice young farmer and have lots of children and a lovely limestone house. She'd stay out in the beautiful, wild country, might even be able to do more painting – possibly sell them. The only trouble was she didn't know of any nice young farmers as prospective husbands. The only nice young man of her acquaintance was Luke. It would be nice to see him again, watch the squirrels together, as they flew through the air from tree to tree, to see the beavers working industriously at their dams.

It was Joseph who came to Kingston to bring her home. As they sat in the train together he told her that Simon had left home to join the Merchant Navy. The younger boy had never accepted his father's strict discipline, and though life below decks would doubtless be equally strict, at least he would be sailing the seven seas, free. Joseph seemed

14

uncharacteristically pensive as he spoke. He went on to talk about this year's calving, the latest batches of cheese and a neighbouring farm which had sold for a huge sum of money. He seemed a far more relaxed and natural person when he was away from home.

Ruth was thrilled to have Janthina back, hugged her and exclaimed how grown-up she had become in the past term. Mama and Papa looked happy too, and Papa was especially lavish in his congratulations on her prizes, the unpleasant incident of Easter forgotten.

It was comparatively easy to fall back into the routine of house and dairy work, far easier than all the school work Janthina had done each day, yet somehow, less stimulating.

Pickle had grown fat and lazy in her absence, his only exercise rolling in the paddock and, occasionally, in mad moments, galloping, bucking and kicking his way round the perimeter.

Bear Foot caught and saddled the skewbald pony for Janthina to go out and explore the farmland, gave her a foot up into the high-pommelled side saddle.

Passing out of the immediate farm area into the surrounding meadowland she heard pounding hooves behind her and turned to see that the men had released a herd of cows from the stables after morning milking and the excited beasts were stampeding, jumping, trying to mount each other and heading directly for her. To a city-dweller it would have been an awe-inspiring sight and he might well have been excused for turning tail in terror. Janthina slipped off her riding jacket and kicked Pickle into a canter, straight at the leading cows, waving the jacket and shouting at them. The animals checked a moment, their followers bunching up behind them, then came on again – but only for a few moments. The shouting and waving was too daunting for the timid beasts, who turned to wander off in search of the day's best grazing.

The forests were still, brilliant patches of sunlight clearly etched against pine needles and rocky outcrops. A pair of little grey squirrels played chase along the branches overhead, and Pickle obediently paused to allow his mistress to watch the game.

They emerged onto a rock-strewn area dotted with sparse scrub, beyond which was a small lake.

Janthina dismounted and led Pickle to the water's edge to allow him a few draughts – he definitely was not as fit as he used to be – then hitched his reins to a bush. The crystal clear water was too inviting to resist so she slipped off her boots, stockings and pantaloons, feeling confident that it would be safe to do so at this long distance from the house.

15

In fact, there was no reason why she shouldn't bathe!

Shedding her remaining garments she stepped out up to her thighs with a shiver, ducked down, careful to avoid wetting her hair.

Directing Pickle back through the forest at a sedate walk, Janthina rode straight-backed, head high as her spirits, whistling. Papa could not possibly hear her out here.

And that was the answer to her problem.

Here she was free. Free to whistle, sing, bathe; remove the cumbersome saddle, swing a leg across Pickle's bare back as she had done years ago when she was small, and ride free as the wind, legs gripping hard against the soft brown and white coat, feeling the rippling muscles. She could even bring books to read, the kind banned by Papa, and, of course, her sketch books and paints.

Yes. This was the answer. Whenever the strictures and inhibitions of home built up oppressively, she could come out here, away from it all, far from Papa's bigotry and limited horizons. She would find release in the wild with the squirrels, cardinals and orioles, watch beavers work and the silver salmon leap.

Papa smiled benevolently as his younger daughter approached across the meadow. She looked magnificent sitting tall in the saddle, back straight, head high, hands low and, as she came within earshot, he could hear her singing, softly, 'Now thank we all our God.'

He nodded his approval.


Home life lacked the joy and laughter of the Kingston household, and Janthina was constantly aware of the tense atmosphere, particularly when Papa's footsteps drew near. She resented the perpetual need to guard her thoughts, words and actions, to ask herself, 'Will this please or anger Papa?'; 'Is there any way he might misconstrue my intention?' However, she managed to avoid upsetting him more than to draw an occasional sharp word or frown, and as time passed there was a noticeable easing of tension amongst the three women.

Household duties and dairy work she had always found tedious and boring, but she realised that now she was at home permanently she must shoulder her full third share of the work. She rose early each morning to assist with breakfast, then, with Ruth, checked temperatures in each section of the dairy store to ensure steady maturing of the cheeses. They set aside the soft, white, uncured farm cheese which all the family loved with fresh oatmeal biscuits for breakfast. The wide shallow pans of milk which had been simmered and allowed to cool the day before, had to be skimmed of the thick, creamy skin, some of which would be whipped for serving with fruit tarts and the remainder churned to butter.

A task the two sisters really enjoyed was the weekly wash. In the centre of the wash-house, out in the paved yard behind the house, a large copper boiler stood built in with bricks, an open space underneath for a fire, and a brick chimney to carry the smoke out through the middle of the roof. Bear Foot's first duty each Monday morning was to fill the copper with water and light the fire so that as soon as breakfast was finished the housemaid and mistresses could melt the soap and put the first load on to boil, covered with a copper lid. They collected all the sheets and pillowslips, towels, tablecloths and napkins, antimacassars and doyleys, petticoats, pantaloons and shirts, and carried them to the wash-house to be sorted into suitable loads.

When each batch of linen was boiled clean it was dug out of the copper in a steaming tangle on the end of an old, scrubbed broom handle, and slopped into waiting tubs. There was a long, wooden table along one wall at the end of which was a water pump. Each tub was lifted onto the table and pushed under the pump-spout for one girl to work the pump-handle while the other waited until the cold water had cooled the scalding cloth and she could start disentangling and rinsing. Then every item was fed through the mangle and, except for the towels, everything went back to the table to the tubs of cornstarch which had been prepared in different strengths – stiff for table linen, less so for clothes (though the girls often complained that their pantaloons had been put in stiff starch, causing the seams to scratch and chafe their legs), and quite mild for bedlinen.

The best part of all was pinning the washing out on the clothes line so that the wind filled the sheets like sails and the pillowslips and underclothes ballooned out, thrumming, tugging at the lines. The clever part was to unpin each item at exactly the right moment – not too wet but certainly not too dry, otherwise one had the trouble of spreading them on the table and sprinkling them with water before they could be folded and rolled into neat sausages to retain their dampness – and laid in laundry baskets to await ironing.

Lace doyleys were the nicest to iron. Janthina and Ruth loved taking the damp cotton balls, pinning them out on the thick white cloth covering the kitchen table to obtain a perfect shape, then, with one of the irons hot from the kitchen range, pressing from the centre out to set the hissing stitches into stiff points.

But oh, those endless sheets! How they hated them.

Exercising Pickle became an important part of Janthina's routine. By hurrying with her chores she was able to leave the farm at least two or three times each week and canter away through the forest where she would pause to remove the cumbersome saddle, pull the pins from the severe knot behind her head, and gallop bareback, along the river bank, hair flying in the wind.

There were so many routes to take leading to river, lake, woodland and, further, to where great majestic pines had thrust their roots down through the rocks and boulders, and their needled branches high into the sky.

Quite often Janthina allowed Pickle to choose their direction; wherever they went she could relax – feel free to sing, wade, sit and dream or read a smuggled book; lie on her back and watch the birds and squirrels.


Luke had appeared only a few days after her return from Kingston. He was walking along the riverside, carrying a rod and fishing basket.

Janthina had reined in her pony. 'Hello, Luke! Going fishing?'

'Yes, miss.' He nodded shyly.

'Do you mind if I come along to watch? I'll keep very quiet.'

Of course he had accepted her company, and she had sat, intrigued, as he took a hook decorated with bits of feather from his basket and attached it to his line, rolled up his trousers and, kicking off his boots, waded out into the shallow-running stream to cast.

Two trout and one small salmon.

That first day he had offered a trout to her, but much as she would have loved to accept, especially now that Simon was no longer supplying fish for the table, she declined. The fish would only betray where she had been, and with whom.

They had met quite often since that day, talking little but sharing the peace, beauty and solitude, enjoying the presence of a kindred soul.

The meetings ceased to be accidental. Janthina soon realised that she liked Luke's company, and deliberately set Pickle's head towards the young man's favourite fishing grounds.

Luke gained confidence after a while, even agreeing to call her by her first name. One day, after landing a large trout, he built a fire, spitted the fish, and cooked it for them to eat with their fingers.

Another day she led him up stream to the place where she knew a pair of beavers were building their lodge. They lay in the long grass side by side, watching in fascination as the two animals gnawed away

18

at the foot of a sapling till it was felled, then dragged it into the stream, floating it between them as they swam, propelled by their flat, scaly tails and webbed feet, towards their new home.

Two days before her seventeenth birthday, Luke had greeted her with a posy of wild flowers. 'You can pretend you picked them,' he said, knowing, without ever having been told, that their friendship was never mentioned to her family. 'They're really for Thursday, but I don't expect you'll come out here on your birthday.'

Janthina buried her face in the fragrant cluster. 'Luke! They're lovely. But how did you know it's my birthday on Thursday?'

'Aha,' he teased, grinning.

'Come on, you beast! Tell me,' she demanded.

'Surely you can guess who would know and who talks to me.'

Standing there beside him, racking her brains, she had been aware, all at once, of his quiet masculinity. Slim, no taller than herself, trousers supported on braces worn over his check shirt, he had none of the handsome appeal of some of the young men in Kingston, aroused no desire in her to be taken into his arms and kissed, but she did feel a bond of friendship for him and . . . yes, affection, too. She grabbed his arm and shook it. 'I don't know. Come on, tell me.'

'Bear Foot.'

'Oh, of course.' She released him. 'He knows about everything and everybody on the farm. He's a very wise old bird, you know.'

'Yes,' Luke nodded, solemnly. 'I do know.'

The flowers had lasted well, set in a posy bowl in the centre of the dining table for her birthday tea.


Autumn was late and warm and Janthina was glad. She dreaded the curtailment of her escapes into the wilderness which the snows of winter would enforce, and made frequent trips away through the forests knowing that any day now, the gathering clouds would darken as the Arctic sent icy fingers of wind south, to encrust the lakes and rivers, harden the earth before blanketing it white, and driving much of the wilderness into hibernation.

The pommelled saddle had been discarded one day as usual, and she cantered out of the trees onto the verge of grass between forest and river, eyes scanning the bank ahead for a glimpse of the brightly coloured check shirt Luke usually wore. She hadn't seen him for over a week and half hoped he would be there, fishing. On the other hand, she wouldn't mind too much if he was not. She was reading Jane Austen's *Pride and Prejudice*, and hoping to finish it before the snows

19

kept her indoors; the book was bouncing in her pocket against the pony's flank.

'Jan! Janty!'

She heard his voice faintly but could not see him. 'Luke,' she called back. 'Where are you?'

'Across here, on the island.'

The shallow rivers were frequently divided by islets, some nearly half a mile long, others no more than a heap of rock which vanished under the spring torrents of melted snow.

She saw him kneeling on a little island which boasted a few trees and patches of grass. Drawing level she dismounted, hitched Pickle's reins to a fallen tree branch, and scrambled over the rocks towards the water.

'What's the matter?' she shouted. 'What are you doing?'

'There's a beaver here, caught in a trap. I can't free her alone. Can you get over here and help me? The water's not deep.'

'All right. I'm coming,' she replied, then wondered how it could be achieved. Shallow as the water might be, it was still too deep not to soak her dress, petticoats and pantaloons – but she couldn't be stupid and girlish just because of that, and possibly leave the beaver to die, poor thing. And Luke would have a pretty poor opinion of her if she refused.

She removed her boots . . . then looked across at the young man. His back was turned towards her as he bent over the animal. Quick as a flash before he turned round, she whipped off her pantaloons and stockings, placing them on a rock with the boots weighting them against the wind. Then she gathered up the back of her skirts, pulling them forward through her legs and over the front, tucking the back hem through her belt to form baggy trousers which reached to her knees.

Wading across was not easy. The stones under her feet were slippery and uneven, and the pull of the current was enough to unsteady her. Teetering, arms outspread to keep her balance, she progressed slowly, watched anxiously by Luke.

The beaver was petrified, cringing away from the rescuing hands, vicious teeth snapping if they came too near.

'You're bleeding.' Janthina looked at Luke's hand. 'What happened?'

'She bit me. That's why I need your help. Fortunately she's only a young 'un. If it was an adult male I doubt if we would get near him. Look, if I hold her down, can you prise open the trap?'

She looked at the cruel-toothed iron jaws doubtfully. They were quite large and held closed by a strong spring. 'I'll try,' she said, and knelt beside him, holding her breath as he grabbed the beaver by the scruff of its neck, pressing its chest and forepaws into the grass.

Janthina squeezed her fingers cautiously between the jaws close to the bleeding hind leg, and pulled. The jaws wouldn't move. Again and again she tried, and each time the beaver screamed and wriggled in agony.

'Never mind,' Luke said, aware of her distress. 'We'll swop. You hold the poor little beast down like this. Put all your weight on her, though; she's very strong.'

She grasped the furry scruff firmly.

'Press down hard,' Luke commanded. And she obeyed. The animal heaved, tried to turn its body to fight her. Bite her. Fear lent her strength.

Meanwhile Luke wedged a strong piece of wood in the ground beside the trap, pushed his fingers between the jaws, and with a grunt of effort managed to pull them apart. Gently, with his bare toes, he lifted the mangled leg and webbed foot free of the jagged iron buried in the flesh.

'Don't let her go!' he ordered as the animal screamed again. His face was red with the effort to keep the jaws apart until he manoeuvred them over the waiting piece of wood which would prevent them closing on himself.

'Ugh!' he gasped as he withdrew his white, distorted fingers. 'No wonder you couldn't open it.'

Janthina continued to hold the beaver down while Luke examined and massaged the injured leg.

'Are any bones broken?' she asked.

'I don't think so. I'll take her from you now, and put her straight in the river.' His strong fingers grasped the animal by the scruff and lower back, and, holding her well out in front of himself, he stepped cautiously down to the water and threw her in.

The freed animal streaked away almost without a ripple.

Luke returned to the heavy trap. 'I'm going to get rid of this beastly thing; throw it into the deepest part of the river. Dear God, how I hate those trappers.'

When the instrument of torture had been disposed of, they sat talking, jokingly speculating on Little Beaver's reception when she arrived home to her anxious parents.

They laughed, pleased with their successful rescue.

'Better had be getting home, I suppose,' Luke remarked, looking up at the sky. 'I think it's going to rain.' He got up and helped Janthina to her feet, picked up his rod and basket.

21

'The water's getting jolly cold, isn't it?' Janthina shivered.

'Yes. And it's very slippery. Here, let me take your hand.'

Gratefully she grasped the outstretched fingers and groped with her toes for firm footings. 'Thanks,' she panted as they reached the dry rocks near the edge . . . then gasped in horror.

Papa and Joseph were sitting astride their horses, watching the pair wade ashore hand in hand.

The watchers sat in silence as the youngsters left the water.

Picking up her boots and garments, Janthina subdued her panic with the thought that Papa couldn't possibly be so cross with her this time; she had a perfectly good reason for taking her things off. She released the hem of her skirt and walked barefooted up to her father, smiling. 'Hello, Papa. Luke found a. . . .'

He ignored her and walked his horse to where Luke was standing a few respectful yards away. 'Damned scoundrel!' he roared. His riding crop hissed through the air and struck Luke's cheek.

'Papa, don't!' Janthina screamed. 'Why are you hitting Luke?'

'It's not what you think, sir,' Luke pleaded, backing towards the rocks.

Hamish followed and the crop caught the boy again, this time on the shoulder.

Suddenly, for the first time in her life, Janthina was furiously angry with her father. 'Papa!' she shouted. 'Will you stop that! You are behaving like a raving madman. Luke,' she called, 'you'd better get back into the river until he comes to his senses.' She ran towards her father, not caring that his next blows would strike her. 'What's the matter with you? Why don't you listen. . . . Agh!' She reeled as the crop struck her, but she grabbed it and hung on, trying to force him to hear her explanation. 'I told you, there was a beaver caught in a trap over there, and we released it. We were saving the life of one of God's creatures, do you hear?'

Hamish tugged the crop from her grasp and swung it across her shoulders. 'I don't wish to hear your lies, you wicked, deceitful brat . . . !'

She ducked away from him. 'It's not lies! It's the truth. Why do you say we're wicked? What on earth do you imagine we were doing?'

Luke was angry, too. 'Obviously he imagines we were . . . well, making love,' he finished, mumbling.

'What?' She swung round to Joseph, who was still sitting, tight-

22

lipped, saying nothing. 'Do you really think we were over there . . . kissing?'

'I'd like to think that's all you were doing,' he replied, scowling.

'What on earth do you mean?' Janthina's eyes betrayed her total ignorance.

'There,' Luke shouted. 'You see? She doesn't even know what you're talking about.'

'Be quiet, you cur,' Hamish roared back. 'Why don't you come here and take your punishment like a man?'

'Stay where you are, Luke!' Janthina ordered. 'Don't listen to him. He's mad!'

'No, he's not!' Luke shouted back. 'Just evil-minded. And he's going to be in the bloody pulpit on Sunday, preaching as though he were a saint. He's nowt but a bloody hypocrite. . . .'

'Be quiet!' Joseph rose in his saddle. 'How dare you speak to your employer like that?'

'Because it's the truth, that's why. I'd never have believed it, but for seeing it with my own eyes.'

'Damn you,' Hamish growled. 'Damn you, damn you! Well, let me tell you, I'm no longer your employer. You're finished. And your parents, too. When you get home you can tell them that they have until this time tomorrow to get out of that cottage and off my land.'

The three young people were struck dumb by his words.

Joseph was the first to find his tongue. 'Papa, don't you think. . . .'

'Quiet, Joseph,' Hamish snapped, and turned to Janthina. 'As for you, you wicked, ungrateful creature, get on your mount and go home, immediately. I'll deal with you later.'

Janthina squared her shoulders. 'No, Papa, I will return home in my own time, when I am ready,' she said softly.

'What!' Hamish almost screamed with rage, leapt off his horse, and advanced on her, crop raised.

'No, Papa,' Joseph cried in alarm. 'No, please.'

'Don't worry, Joseph,' his sister called back, her breath coming in angry gasps, her face scarlet. 'Let him hit me all he likes . . . and I'll make sure that all the congregation see what a foul beast he is, on Sunday.'

'Not where I'm going to tan you, they won't,' Hamish said, grabbing her. With one strong arm he pinned her across his thigh, raised her skirts, exposing her bare buttocks, and lashed, again and again, with his crop.

'You sadistic beast!' Luke shouted at him, coming back towards them. 'Me and my family have got more pride than ever to take another penny off you.' And in a blind rage he plunged his hands into the water, bringing up stones from the river bed to fling them, wildly, at Hamish's back. The missiles all missed their target, but one caught Hamish's horse on the hind fetlock. The animal squealed, reared, and bolted away through the trees.

Hamish flung the girl aside and rounded on Luke. 'That's it! I'll see you gaoled for that.' He turned to Joseph. 'You saw! You were witness to what he did!'

'Yes, Father.' Joseph was white and shaking. 'And I also saw what you did,' he replied, accusingly. He looked at his sister, who was leaning, panting, against her pony, angrily gritting her teeth against the insistent tears she would not allow to fall. 'Come, Janthina, you can ride my horse. I will shorten the stirrups for you so that you can stand in them. You won't be able to sit in the saddle. I'll ride Pickle for you.' He dismounted as he spoke, and undid the buckles under the saddleflaps. 'I don't know what you have or have not done, but I think we should hear what you have to say before you are punished like this.'

Hamish stood agape, purple in the face. 'Joseph? Are you out of your mind?'

'Perhaps I'm in it for the first time in years,' Joseph muttered.

Hamish advanced once more on his children. 'Look here . . .' he started.

'No,' Janthina interrupted. 'You look here.' She held up the hand she had just slipped under her skirts to touch her painful weals. It was smeared with blood. As he came up to her she wiped it across his white shirt front, and before he could mouth his renewed fury she stepped up to Joseph's horse. With great difficulty, despite her brother's help, she heaved her weight up onto the stirrup-iron, swinging her leg over the saddle.

Only Joseph could see the immense pain in her face and her struggle not to weep. He straddled Pickle and unhitched the reins.

'Just a minute, boy!' Hamish shouted. 'I haven't got a mount. You'll have to. . . .'

'You'll have to walk home,' Joseph called over his shoulder. 'It will give you time to cool off.'

Janthina cast one long, last, miserable look in Luke's direction, gave a brief wave, and rode off with her brother into the forest, neither of them giving a backward glance at their father.

Neither was aware, therefore, that he had fallen.

# 3

THERE HAD been years of torment, anger, frustration, to prepare Ruth for what had happened, but nothing could have prevented the shock and renewed bitterness, followed by alarm and confused emotions, which beset them all that fateful September afternoon.

Ruth doubted if she would ever erase the memory of Joseph lifting the weeping Janthina from his horse and carrying her upstairs, laying her gently, face down, on her bed. Red spots of anger burned in his white face as he said, 'Father has done it again. Have you some ointment?' And suddenly he sat down at the top of the stairs and wept.

Joseph wept! He, who had retreated from all emotion years ago, put his head in his hands and sobbed aloud.

Ruth and Adeline ran to Janthina, and saw the blood on her petticoats before they found the open weals and bruises. And they, too, wept.

Bathing and salving the wounds, Ruth's anger and hatred pounded in her chest as never before, and once again she wondered if it would be right to kill him. Should she go down and load one of the hunting guns from his study and shoot him down as he strode, all puffed up with self-righteousness, into the house?

'It's all my fault,' Adeline cried. 'I'm entirely to blame. I've known for years that your father had this . . . this weakness. Oh, my poor baby.' And she smoothed the hair back from Janthina's forehead.

'We've all suffered, haven't we?' Ruth said quietly. 'But you have had to bear the greater burden.'

Her mother looked up, quickly, staring at her, open-mouthed.

'Yes, Mama, I knew. I tried to tell you so many times.'

'I never realised. . . .'

'No. Somehow I never managed to say it all. You were being so brave, trying so hard. I couldn't bring myself to . . . oh, dear God. And now this,' she sobbed. 'Darling Janty, my poor little sister.'

'Hush, Ruth, don't take on so,' Janthina had murmured. 'It's all over and it won't happen again. . . .'

'Of course it won't, dear,' Mama said. 'We will have to. . . .'

'We will have to go away and leave him, all of us.'

Ruth and her mother gazed at each other, and shrugged. It was a thought which had gone through all their minds – but now was not the time to discuss it.

Nor did they ever.

A few moments later there was a clatter and slamming of doors in the kitchen and a voice calling, 'Mrs McKenzie, ma'am? Miss Ruth? Master Joseph? Are you there?'

They left Janthina and rushed downstairs to find Luke Callaghan standing in the hallway in his singlet, his shirt missing.

'It's Mr McKenzie, ma'am. He's had a fall, out by the river near Pine Rock. You know, Master Joseph, where we. . . .' He stopped, his face turning scarlet.

'What happened? He was all right when we left.'

'You weren't out of sight when he fell. I thought for a minute he had just sat down. But when he didn't move I come out of the water and he couldn't get up. I yelled after you, but you'd gone. Can you come with me, Master Joseph? Bear Foot's harnessing one of the horses to a wagon and me dad's sent me brother for the doctor. I'm afraid his leg is broken.'

'Good thinking. Thanks for your help, Luke. It's more than he deserves,' Joseph said, his mouth a grim line. 'Justice is mine, saith the Lord. Hm? Of course I'll come.' The two young men hurried away.

'I wonder what happened to Luke's face?' Mama asked after they had gone.

'Papa slashed it with his riding crop.' Janthina was standing at the top of the stairs, leaning heavily on the newel post.


Adeline and Ruth stood at the bedroom window watching as the wagon came up the drive from the farm. The men carried Hamish McKenzie upstairs and laid him on the bed, leaving the women to tend him till the doctor arrived.

Joseph waited with the men in the kitchen, where Luke took it upon himself to brew a large pot of tea. 'Hope you don't mind me doing this,' he said to Joseph, kettle in hand.

'Good idea. Make yourself at home.'

'Bit late for that, I reckon,' the boy remarked.

Joseph looked up. 'Oh, don't worry. Forget anything my father said this afternoon . . . if you can, that is.'

Luke stared at him and flushed. 'I suppose it did look a bit suspicious to you, what with me holding her hand and all. . . .'

'Yes. Very.'

Luke looked around. The other men were over by the table, their backs turned, talking. 'Well, like Jan . . . your sister said, you see, I'd found this young beaver kit, with its leg caught in a trap, over on that island. I tried to free it but when I put my hands on the trap she turned and bit me . . . see her teeth marks?' He held out his hand, the neat row of puncture wounds quite clear amidst the blood. 'Then I saw Jan . . . your sister, riding along the river and I called and asked her to come and help. I was forgetting she'd have to fix it so as her clothes didn't get wet. Got a lot of spirit, your sister. She tried hard to open the trap while I held the beast, but she couldn't move it. So she held the kit while I did it. No wonder she couldn't open it; it was darned strong. We'd put the poor little devil back in the water and I'd thrown the trap into the deepest part and we started wading back. . . .'

'Yes. I see.' Jospeh nodded.

'You do believe me, don't you?' Luke peered at him.

Joseph stared at the anxious face for a moment, then said, 'Yes. Absolutely.'

Luke gave a sigh of relief.


'It's concussion,' the doctor had announced. 'Fairly mild, I think. He's able to speak, now, and move about. He has a broken ankle. I'll have to return and set it in plaster of Paris. He must stay in bed for a few days.'

He left some laudanum with Adeline, and Joseph saw him out before returning to the kitchen to tell the men the doctor's diagnosis and thank them for their help.

He held Luke's arm, detaining him till they were alone, then said, 'I'm sorry, Luke, about what happened this afternoon, and I reckon it was very Christian of you to do. . . .'

'Forget it, Master Joseph. I only did what anybody else would've. I hope he'll be all right, though I have to say he brought it on himself. But. . . .' He hesitated. 'Jan . . . Miss Janthina. Is she . . . I mean. . . .'

'She'll be fine. You'll see her again in a day or two.' Joseph realised that the boy had been in Janthina's company on occasions prior to this day and wondered if he should say something . . . but decided this was not the time. Instead he went on, 'Don't worry. I promise I won't let that happen to her again. To either of you.' He held out his hand.

Luke suddenly shivered. His trousers were still wet to the thigh, knees muddied and the shirt he had removed to place under Mr McKenzie's head was presumably still upstairs and he hadn't liked to ask for it. He smiled and grasped the hand Joseph offered. 'Thanks for

27

saying that, and thanks for believing me.' He took a deep breath. 'If you don't mind me saying, Master Joseph, I think your sister's the loveliest young lady I've ever met, and not just to look at. We've met up a number of times, out there, just to watch the beavers working or the squirrels building their winter stores and such like, you understand. But I know my place, sir, and I'd never lay a finger on her. She's not for the likes of me.' He released Joseph's hand. 'Reckon I'd best get home before I catch me death of cold.'

Remembering the anger and hatred she had felt for her father when she saw what he had done to Janthina, and the murderous thoughts which had gone through her mind, Ruth wondered if perhaps she had caused him to be struck down, with her death wish. Overcome with guilt, she prayed fervently for his recovery – until after the doctor assured them that Papa was in no danger.

Then the worry returned – what would happen now?

Mama insisted that only she should attend the invalid. She spent most of the next few days in their bedroom while Ruth herself prepared the meals, and Joseph went out to the farm.

Janthina walked stiffly around the house from time to time, to relieve the pressure of bed on her painful sores. Her anger had given way to despondency, and Ruth knew her sister was suffering more from mental than physical anguish.

Apart from Adeline, no one saw Hamish until five days later when Joseph told the two girls they were both to go to his room.

Papa was sitting in a chair by the fire, dressed, and appearing quite normal – apart from the plaster on his foot, the expression on his face and the tone of his voice.

'Now are you satisfied?' he growled. 'You could have killed me with your wickedness.' He glared at Janthina.

'That is enough of that.' Joseph stepped between father and daughter. 'Your fall was caused by your wicked imagination and uncontrolled temper. We all know that's the truth, and that Janthina was perfectly innocent.'

Adeline stood beside Joseph, pale and nervous, but determined. 'Yes, Hamish, Joseph is right. . . .'

'What?' He threw aside the rug which had been wrapped about his knees, stood up, and hobbled towards them. 'Have you taken leave of your senses, the pair of you?' His face was only inches from Joseph's, his hand raised ready to strike . . . but the young man grabbed his wrist, so he began to raise the other . . . which was seized by Adeline.

'Sit down, Hamish,' she ordered with unaccustomed force. 'Control yourself! We've all had enough from you, more than enough.' And between them they pushed him back into his chair.

Hamish tried to fight back, but Joseph held him down. 'Listen, Papa, sit still and listen. If you don't, so help me God, hurt as you are, I will strike you.'

Ruth felt a surge of hope as she saw the glances between Mama and Joseph. They had planned this confrontation. They were actually doing something, at last!

Janthina stood rigid, quivering, her teeth clenched and her mouth a thin, hard line.

The enraged man just sat opening and shutting his mouth, speechless with surprise.

'Hamish.' Adeline dropped her voice. 'We think you are more sick than you know. We hope so, because you are either a sick man . . . or a sinner.'

'You're mad. . . .'

'Whichever,' she ignored his interruption, 'you are responsible for your own wicked thoughts and behaviour.'

'You're all mad! Bewitched by that little she-devil,' he shouted, as Adeline crossed the room to fetch her Bible from beside the bed and returned to stand in front of him, holding the book in both hands.

'I hereby swear by Almighty God,' she spoke with eyes closed, 'that if you, Hamish McKenzie, ever again raise your hand against anyone, your children, your wife, or any employee, I will enlist the help of the minister and elders of the Church and of doctors too, to have you committed either to a prison for your violent sins or to an asylum. We have all suffered enough.'

Before Papa could recover from the shock, Joseph had taken the Bible from his mother and repeated her oath, word for word.

Hamish sat clenching and unclenching his hands on the arm of his chair, his colour turning from purple to white. He looked from one face to the next, shaking his head. 'I cannot believe it,' he whispered. 'You too, Ruth? *All* of you have turned against me?'

'Father,' she replied, resolved to show her approval of Mama's and Joseph's stand, 'You, our dearly loved father, have beaten and abused us – abused your authority as head of our family, to give rein to your evil, sadistic violence. In the name of Jesus Christ you have perpetrated the work of the Devil. You have driven Simon away and caused me to hate you – you and your religious hypocrisy. No one, knowing the way

29

you have treated your family, could feel anything for you but disgust.'

She was trembling, shocked by the words she had dared to speak.

They were all shocked, most of all Hamish. Suddenly he clutched his head, eyes wide and rolling horribly, mouth opening and shutting, lips moving . . . yet uttering not a sound. Then he lolled back in his chair, unconscious. Together they stood round his chair in horror, before half lifting, half dragging him onto the bed.

The doctor confirmed their fears. Hamish McKenzie had had a stroke, causing what they hoped would be only a temporary paralysis.


Adeline made a decision. 'I think you two girls should visit your grandparents in Scotland. Joseph agrees that a year in the old country will be very good for both of you.'

Ruth and Janthina looked at each other wide-eyed, neither daring to speak.

'I would like you to leave for Kingston next week, where you can stay with your Aunt Mary while your passage is arranged and a letter is sent to my family to forewarn them. Your aunt will assist you in purchasing all you need for the voyage.' She spoke quickly and almost sharply, and then hurried out of the room.

'It's not fair!' Janthina exploded when the door closed. 'We haven't done anything wrong. She said I was not to blame and Joseph told Papa I was innocent. Yet we are the ones who are being sent away!'

'But aren't you pleased?'

'Pleased? Why should I be pleased? I don't want to be forced to leave home. It's Papa who should go, not me!'

'Don't be so stupid and childish!' Ruth was exasperated by her attitude. 'You were the one who said we should all leave him, the day he beat you. Well, now we're going. This is Papa's home, forever, and we are the ones who would leave, anyway, when we were old enough, or married. I agree with you, he is the transgressor, but . . . between us we did cause his stroke. . . .'

'But I don't want to go. I only meant we would go and live in another house near here. Not leave Canada. It's different for you, you've always wanted to get away. You've never loved the country and the wilds as I have. Why should I leave it? I'm going to speak to Mama. Anyway,' she added, 'I honestly think he brought the stroke on himself.'

Ruth had followed her out of the room and into the kitchen where their mother was preparing a tray for the sick room. Janthina launched straight into her complaint while Adeline continued her task, setting a plate, knife and fork on a clean white cloth.

When Janthina was finished, her mother looked up, her face a mask of misery, and for the first time the girls saw that she was silently weeping. They ran to her and the three clung together until Adeline was able to speak. 'Please, Janty, my love, please do as I ask. Don't make it harder for me. There is little hope of your father's temper or condition improving if you stay. He is my husband, remember – I don't want to be forced to have him committed. Anyway, there's nothing for you here; little social life and few nice young men for you to meet. You must go and learn about real life and real, warm people. Normal family relationships. . . .' Her words were choked off by tears and she clung to them again, whispering, 'My darling girls, my darlings.' They both realised that the last thing in the world she wanted was to send them away, that she considered her decision to send them to Scotland to be the only possible solution to the problem.

So Janthina never protested again, only wept silently in the night.

Hamish's condition did improve. Before they finished packing the things they had decided to take, and tidying away the clothes they would not require until their return, he regained the use of his left hand and foot and there was even some movement in his right limbs. But he still could not speak, so that when they went to say goodbye to him he was unable to express the anger they could still see in his face. For which they were not sorry.

Saying goodbye to Mama was different. Even Janthina, who still seemed distressed by their departure, found herself trying to console her mother, whose eyes were red in her deathly white face. 'Don't cry so, Mama. The year will pass in a flash, like the year I was in Kingston, and we'll soon be home again.'

Words intended to comfort, but they only seemed to distress Adeline the more.

Years later, Ruth would cast her mind back to the bubbling excitement she had felt as they were driving down to the station, and remember her impatience with her sister's misery. The girl's tears, as they left the farm – she had even kissed Bear Foot at the station – and sobs in the pillow at Aunt Mary's at night. She had presented a long face and listless inattention when Aunt Mary was helping her buy a trunkful of clothes in Kingston, and shed more tears as she hugged each of her cousins goodbye before they left for the Kingston railway station.

Janthina wept again as they crossed the Canadian border into the United States, and even more, four days later as they stood together

31

looking back over the stern of the *Campania* until the bright lights of Manhattan disappeared over the horizon.

It never once occurred to Ruth at the time that her sister might have had a premonition.

# PART TWO

## ROLAND, GRANDFATHER AND ANTHONY

### 1901 – 1902

'Yet mark'd I where the bolt of Cupid fell:
It fell upon a little western flower,
Before milk-white, now purple with love's wound. . . .'

*A Midsummer Night's Dream*, William Shakespeare

# 1

A LONE passenger paced the wind and spray swept decks of the SS *Campania*, wrapped in a thick cloak and with a shawl held tightly over her head. The late autumn storm had passed on its trek northward, leaving only a strong southwesterly to hasten them across the Atlantic.

The wind was bitterly cold, and the ship heaved over the long swell, keeping those passengers of uncertain stomachs in their berths, and even the hardier ones in the warmth of the saloons – all except for Janthina McKenzie. She had quickly discovered she had good sealegs, and the turbulent ocean had not worried her. The worst part of the journey, as far as she was concerned, was Mrs Abercrombie.

It had been obvious from the start that two young girls could not be sent away on a long train and sea voyage unchaperoned. Aunt Mary had made some enquiries the day after they had arrived in Kingston, and discovered that Mrs Abercrombie and her daughter were leaving Canada in just over two weeks' time, to visit relatives in England. They had passages booked on the Cunard liner *Campania*, leaving from New York, and the large woman declared herself delighted to have Ruth and Janthina join them.

'Don't take on so,' she admonished Janthina, seeing more tears spill as the train pulled away from the Kingston station. 'A year will pass very quickly. I well remember when I was a girl . . .' and the three young ladies were subjected to endless, boring reminiscences.

Janthina's tears had been stemmed more by irritation with the monotonous monologue than through any soothing words Mrs Abercrombie might have uttered. But now she felt sorry for the overbearing woman and her daughter; they could barely lift their heads from their pillows, except to be terribly sick, and in fact it was the nauseating smell in their cabin which had driven Janthina out, lest she, too, be overcome.

Ruth was not ill-affected either, and was, at the moment, ministering to the stricken pair. Janthina had already taken her turn in the night, and would again, later, giving her sister a chance to come up on deck to the fresh air.

The clouds thinned, allowing a watery sun to cast a little warmth on the starboard side, and Janthina paused a moment to lean on the rail and watch veins of foam spreading away from their bow wave. After weeks of worry and tension she was beginning to relax.

Dark, blue-green waves; as far as the eye could see in every direction, nothing but waves surging with immense power, sometimes cresting with long overfalls, frightening, thrilling. Janthina stood facing the bow, feet placed squarely on the deck, knees flexing with the pitch and roll of the ship, clothes pressed hard against her back and billowing before her with the force of the following wind, her hair blowing wildly about her face. This tremendous new experience was at last banishing her depression. The responsive motion of the ship to the sea, like perfect dancing partners, the steady vibration of the engines, even the smoke which swirled forward with the gale, and the taste of salt on her lips were irresistibly uplifting, exhilarating.

She was smiling to herself, eyes closed against the whipping of her hair, when the voice spoke.

'Obviously you are not troubled by *mal de mer*!'

'Oh! I didn't realise I was not alone,' she stammered, blushing at the sight of a tall young man, standing hunched in a thick overcoat, smiling at her.

'Sorry if I startled you. You looked such a picture standing there smiling and swaying with the deck. I hope you don't mind my talking to you. My name is Roland Burrows.'

Janthina took the proffered hand and shook it briefly. 'No, not at all. I'm Janthina McKenzie. There are not very many people on deck, are there?'

'No. A few are in the saloon but I think most passengers are finding the sea rather too boisterous. It doesn't seem to worry you?'

'No. I don't feel the least bit upset.' She turned to the rail. 'Beautiful, isn't it? Quite majestic.'

'Yes, wonderful.'

They stood side by side, a little apart, watching each wave surge by, clashing with the great wash that curled away from the ship's side as the bow sliced through the water.

Later, they promenaded the deck, occasionally lurching against the rail or each other, laughing.


'You were out on deck a long time,' Ruth remarked when they met in the saloon later. She had done all she could for Mrs Abercrombie and her daughter and left them, white and groaning, in their stuffy cabin.

'Yes. It was lovely. And . . . dear sister, I met a charming young

man out there. We walked right round the deck together – twice.'
Janthina peeled off her gloves and scarf. 'I think I had better comb my
hair, don't you? I'll be back in a moment, and we could share a pot of
tea, perhaps?'

Ruth was sitting behind a tray of tea when she returned. 'How did
you come to meet this young man, Janty? Who introduced you?'

'No one. We introduced ourselves. There was no one else on deck.'

Ruth raised one eyebrow above twinkling eyes, but said nothing.

'It's all right, senior sister!' The younger girl laughed. 'I'm a big girl
now, you know. I can look after myself. He didn't try to be over-
familiar. He was just polite and very nice.'

'Like Luke?' Ruth asked, then wished she hadn't.

Janthina's face clouded for a moment. 'No, not the least bit like
Luke. He was taller, older, and . . . well. . . .'

'Far more sophisticated?'

'Yes, but in a very nice, natural way.' Roland entered the saloon
before they had finished, and Janthina presented him to her sister for
inspection.

'You're right,' Ruth agreed when they rolled back to the dreaded
cabin. 'He is very nice.'

Thereafter, mysteriously, whenever Ruth was busy on her turn of
'duty' with their useless chaperone, Janthina would chance to meet
Roland. They continued to promenade together, sat drinking tea, and
even played a few hands of rummy, which he taught her quite quickly.

She realised she was looking for the tall, broad frame whenever she
left the cabin, and her heart pounded as he loomed into view. It was
a strange, new sensation, pleasant, not to say exciting – but quite
frightening, too.

They spoke about themselves. Janthina was shy at first but Roland
was so relaxed and easy to talk with that soon he was hearing about
her beloved Canadian wilds, the beauty of it, and the wildlife. 'My
father is a dairy farmer, and we live about sixty miles west of Kingston,
towards Peterborough, near the River Severn.'

'Severn? There's a Severn River in the west of England, close to
where I live in Gloucestershire.'

'I've heard of it. I believe many of our places are named after places
in England. We have lots of French names in Canada, and Indian ones,
too, like Ottawa, for instance.' She hesitated, then asked, 'What do
you do in Gloucestershire?'

'Well . . . I got a law degree at Cambridge and was working in my
father's practice in Gloucester when I decided to enlist and went to
South Africa. Then my wife died, and they shipped me home. I had

contracted malaria out there and had a bad attack in England. A rather bad period of my life, I'm afraid. When I was fit enough to travel, I was sent to recuperate with my elder brother in Connecticut for a few months.'

'Oh, I am sorry. How terrible for you. Had you been married very long?' Janthina felt shocked and saddened.

'Barely a year. My wife died giving birth to our son. My mother is looking after him.'

'What will you do now?'

'I don't know. I'll have an army medical and see if they'll have me back. When the war is over, I'll go back to law, I suppose.'

'Is it very interesting? It seems such a vast subject.'

'I enjoy it. But I'm particularly interested in commercial law. I would like to specialise in that subject.'

'Will you continue to work in Gloucester?'

'Probably not. There'll be more scope in London.'

'But what about your son?'

'He'll remain with his nanny in my parents' house until I sort something out.'

Janthina sighed. 'I'd love to visit London. I've seen lots of photographs and paintings of it.'

'It is a wonderful city,' Roland agreed.

'Better than New York?'

'Oh, yes. Far more beautiful.' The sadness left his face, and the deepest-grey eyes glowed as he spoke, making her tingle – all over. She admired the way his brown, wavy hair grew back from his forehead, his very broad shoulders and his height. It was rare indeed for her to meet a man taller than herself and Roland actually looked down at her. He was very handsome.


'I thought you were going to keep that gown to wear in Scotland,' Ruth remarked as they prepared for their third dinner in the ship's dining saloon.

'My brown is so little-girlish and boring.' Janthina strained to see herself in the tiny cabin mirror. Would he notice, she wondered? He was so much older and so sophisticated – why, he must be at least twenty-three – there seemed little chance that he would regard her as more than a schoolgirl. But he might. Ruth watched as her younger sister brushed her thick hair up into a chignon, making herself look much older.

'I don't know how you girls can bear to think of food while the ship is rolling so dreadfully,' Mrs Abercrombie moaned. 'Have you ordered some bread and milk for us from the steward?'

'Yes, nearly half an hour ago. It should be here any minute.' Ruth had already told her twice.

'Oh, Mama, do we really have to have bread and milk again? I'm sure that's what makes us feel so ill.'

'Rubbish. Best thing for you. Do stop whining.'

Reeling towards the dining saloon after settling the sickly pair with their awful supper, Ruth took Janthina's arm in a friendly squeeze. 'Janty, dear, don't let yourself get too involved with Roland, will you? Remember it's a chance in a million that you will ever see him again after we dock at Liverpool.'

'I can't help liking him an awful lot. Don't you think he is very good looking – and nice?' Janthina's eyes sparkled and she skipped a few steps, nearly causing them to tumble. 'Isn't it sad about his wife?'

Ruth nodded. 'Yes, very sad. I do think he's gorgeous, but don't tell him I said so.'

'I certainly won't. If he knew you liked him he would turn his attention to you immediately. You're so much more grown-up than I am, and beautiful.'

Roland didn't mention her dress that evening after dinner when he asked the sisters to take coffee with him in the lounge, but Ruth couldn't fail to notice the interest in his eyes and voice every time he addressed Janthina. It seemed such a shame that nothing could come of their friendship; but there would be others.

Janthina found herself waking earlier each morning, forcing herself to stay in her bunk until a reasonable hour, and not hurriedly dress and dash out on deck in the hope of an early morning stroll with Roland. She hugged herself under the blanket, dreamed of him perhaps holding her arm, or even her hand, as they paraded their beat together. But he never did, except to assist her on or off the companionway and guide her through a door. She wondered why.

On the last morning the temptation to get up early was too great to resist. Well wrapped against the intense chill, Janthina strode rapidly round the promenade deck – and then walked around more slowly, her disappointment at Roland's non-appearance matching the dull grey skies.

# 2

THE SOLITUDE during the comparatively calm passage through
Liverpool Bay and into the Mersey gave Janthina a chance to think.
The pressing sense of unease she had suffered before the voyage had
lifted, due largely to Roland, but she had not yet attempted to understand the recent past events or to anticipate the future – after their
return from Scotland.

Perhaps she hadn't really analysed the situation relating to Papa and
so had not understood the extent to which he was distorting the lives
of everyone around him, inhibiting them, angering them, forcing them
to think only within the narrow channels to which he had been confined
for so many years. Ruth's hatred of Papa had shocked Janthina for a
long time, but since that horrible day when he had beaten her raw and
lashed out at Luke she had felt only an immense fury against him,
certainly no love and no sympathy, even when he lay speechless and
paralysed. So wasn't that as bad as hatred?

She had to admit that Ruth and Mama and Joseph had been right; it
would be best for the two of them to have a year away from Papa –
to break the pattern of his violent outbursts. She had defied him in her
attempt to give herself more freedom; now, at last, she would have
all the freedom she wanted, depending of course on how much liberty
Mama's elderly parents would allow. But despite her determination to
look forward to enjoying their holiday in Scotland and to take every
opportunity of experiencing all the fun they had missed throughout the
years with Papa, she found it hard to shake off the persistent, depressing idea which had plagued her from the moment Mama had suggested
this trip: an idea that still brought a lump to her throat and caused the
corners of her mouth to droop, that she and Ruth might never return
. . . never see Mama or Canada again.

Standing beside Ruth as they entered Liverpool harbour and the
tugs manoeuvred the *Campania* to her berth, she resolved to put the
silly notion out of her mind and enjoy the coming year to the hilt,
positive that when it was over they would return home, to dear,
beautiful Canada and Mama, refreshed and better able to prevent any
more disastrous confrontations with Papa.

The arrival of a passenger ship, no matter how small nor how short and frequent its journey, never fails to create an atmosphere of excitement and bustle, the more so if she happens to be the world's fastest, largest liner drawing alongside after a trans-Atlantic crossing. With much shouting between ship and shore the massive warps were hauled up the dockside by their casting lines and looped over the bollards while crewmen worked the capstans fore and aft to winch the pride of Cunard Shipping, the SS *Campania*, into position where the waiting gangways could be hauled up and disembarkation commence.

After breakfast, Ruth and Janthina were both caught by the excitement and exchanged broad smiles and waves with strangers in the crowd below them. Suddenly Janthina was aware of someone standing the other side of her, very close. It was Roland.

'Good morning.' He smiled down at her.

Her mouth was too dry to speak and she wondered if he could detect the rapid beat of her heart through all the layers of clothes.

'Good morning.' Ruth responded for her. 'You must be glad to be home again.'

He grimaced. 'I enjoyed the crossing so much I would have been quite happy for it to have taken a few more days.'

'I think Janthina and I would have enjoyed it more save for the indisposition of our so-called travelling companions. I think I had better go and see that they are getting themselves dressed and ready for disembarkation. For in case I don't see you again, Mr Burrows, I'll say goodbye. It was a great pleasure meeting you.'

'Thank you, Miss McKenzie. I assure you it has been splendid for me to have the pleasure of your company and that of your sister on the voyage. I do hope you enjoy your visit to Scotland.'

When Ruth had gone, Roland took Janthina's arm and led her to the far side of the ship, where all was quiet. 'Dear Janthina,' he murmured, retaining her hand in his.

She looked up at him, wondering what he was thinking – whether she disturbed him as much as he did her. Was that possible? She held her breath.

'I am feeling very sad,' he went on. 'We have only just met and now it seems we must part. I should hate to think we might never meet again.'

She nodded vigorously. 'Yes, I agree.'

'Would you think it very forward of me to ask for your address in Scotland? I would very much like to write to you.'

'Not forward at all. I have it written down here somewhere.' She hunted through the tapestry bag she carried and drew out a small bundle of papers, cards and photographs tied with ribbon. 'Can we go inside out of the wind or everything will blow away.'

Despite the shelter of the saloon, her nervous fingers dropped a cascade of papers onto a table and some fell to the floor. 'Yes, here it is. Do you have a pencil to copy it down?'

'Mmm,' he responded distantly. He was gazing at a photograph of herself taken at school in Kingston. He looked up and grinned. 'Do you think I could possibly keep this?' he asked.

She smiled shyly. 'If you really want it, but I look awful.'

'You could never look awful, dear Janty.' For a moment she thought he was going to lean forward and kiss her. Instead he took a small gold pencil out of his pocketbook and wrote the address. When he had finished, he tucked the photograph between the pages. 'Are you sure you don't mind?'

'Truly. I'm only sorry I haven't a photograph of you,' she replied, then gasped at her daring.

Roland opened his pocketbook again. 'Will this one be all right? It was taken ages ago with my parents and my sister.' He held out a stiff, sepia print.

Janthina blushed. 'Oh, yes,' she breathed. 'Thank you.' She tied it up in the bundle of returned papers with the same pink ribbon. 'Oh, dear, I suppose I should go now and join Ruth.'

'Yes. You must. But this isn't goodbye, I'm sure, only au revoir.' He took her hand between both of his, looked into her eyes, then leaned forward and kissed her forehead. 'Au revoir, dear, dear, Janty.'

She hurried away before he saw any tears fall.


'There. Thank goodness that's over,' Mrs Abercrombie declared. 'It's to be hoped that my family over here appreciate the suffering to which I subject myself in order to visit them.'

The sisters glanced at each other, rather suspecting that the Abercrombie family might not be as appreciative as she wished.

'There is our steward,' their chaperone pointed. 'We had better follow him so we may see which porter he engages for us. Come, Amelia.' And she led the three girls away down the companionway to the head of the gangway; Customs and Immigration having already been cleared in the upstairs deck saloon.

It had been decided that once she had seen her charges on to the train to Carlisle and thence to Glasgow, and given the guard appropriate instructions as to their welfare, she and her daughter would bid them farewell and make their way to the London-bound train. A cable had

42

been received in Kingston before the girls left, saying that Cousin Ian would meet them in Glasgow and escort them on the remaining journey to the family estates near Pitlochry.

They were installed in a first-class carriage, their luggage stowed in the baggage van, and reservations were made for luncheon between Preston and Carlisle.

'Now be sure you don't speak with any strangers, my dears,' Mrs Abercrombie warned. 'And when one of you needs to leave her seat be sure you go together. You cannot be too careful.' Having said which she swooped on both girls to plant kisses on their cheeks before waving them goodbye, the ever silent Amelia at her heels.

The endless sheds and warehouses which backed Liverpool's dockland were made more drear by steady drizzle. Soon the carriage windows steamed up and the girls turned to the journals they had purchased from a platform vendor when the train halted at Liverpool Central Station. Fresh from the wild beauty of Canada, where a ten-minute ride would transport one into magnificent solitude, it was too depressing to watch street after street crammed with tiny, blackened houses sliding by in the murk, their occupants scurrying along huddled against the cold while in the background huge factory chimneys belched soot into the sky to be carried by wind and rain in a blanket to smother every building and every living thing for miles.

The sky cleared after they left the coast at Morecambe Bay and they enjoyed their first view of really beautiful English scenery from their luncheon table in the dining car, as the train wound its way through the mountains and lakes of Cumberland. In Carlisle, carriages from the Leeds train were linked to their own with much shunting and jolting and Janthina began to feel impatient for the journey to end. She longed for some distraction to take her mind off Roland.

Crossing into Scotland they exclaimed over the magnificent seascape to their left down the Solway Firth, but soon the view was obscured again by sleet and rain.

'I wonder what Cousin Ian looks like,' Janthina said. 'Did Mama describe him to you?'

'You forget that Mama hasn't seen him for nearly twenty-five years. He was only Joseph's age when she left.'

'So he'll be quite old now, and bald and fat.'

'Well, middle-aged, anyway,' Ruth corrected. 'She says he lives in Perth with his family.'

'Oh! Not at Glenfalk with Grandpapa?'

'No, no, he's the son of Great-Uncle Alistair, Grandpapa's younger brother.'

43

'Oh, fiddle! I doubt if I'll ever remember who's who in this family. Well, who does live at Glenfalk?'

'Apart from Grandpapa and Grandmama, there's Mama's oldest sister, Aunt Laura, whose husband was killed in battle very young, and her brother, Uncle Andrew and his wife Meg and their two children,' Ruth explained.

'It must be a huge place.'

'Yes, some kind of castle. Don't you remember Mama's photographs of it in her album?'

No, Janthina couldn't. She had been out in the forests or down by the river with Pickle when Ruth had sat listening to Mama reminiscing and looking at the faded sepia photographs. Scotland had always seemed too remote from their lives to be of much interest. It had never occurred to her that she might one day see the 'old country' of her parents and forebears.

They didn't find Cousin Ian as they alighted from the train at Glasgow – he found them. 'Miss McKenzie!' said a voice, and they turned to see a short, plump man with red side-whiskers doff his hat to reveal a bald head.

'Cousin Ian! How did you recognise us?' Ruth asked, while her sister smothered her amusement on seeing her description of him fulfilled.

'Easy. You're the living image of Adeline twenty-five years ago.' He shook her hand. 'And this must be your sister. My, my! You two are going to set Scottish society by the heels. We never doubted that Adeline would have splendid children, but we were never warned to expect a pair of ravishing beauties.'

The girls laughed at his welcome and followed him, and the porter who was trundling their luggage, across the station to another platform for the Perth train.

Five minutes in Cousin Ian's company was sufficient to assure the sisters that they couldn't fail to enjoy this visit. Laughing, he told them of the excitement at Glenfalk as their arrival date drew near. Their grandmother had had two rooms redecorated especially for them and was busily organising party invitations to launch them into the social scene. 'The only pity is that you are arriving at such a bad time,' he went on. 'November is not the season for one's first visit to the Highlands. You cannot appreciate the view in this weather and it's bitterly cold outside. Never mind. There's a very warm welcome waiting on you up there.'

Unfortunately it was late, dark and wet and both girls were tired and hungry after travelling since early morning, when the carriage which had met them at Perth station finally drew up on the gravelled forecourt beside a pair of enormous, ironstudded oak doors. One of these was opened by a butler who ushered them into a vast hallway where they stood gazing about them in awe. Red Axminster carpets were laid over polished floors; a huge, granite fireplace housed an iron basket of blazing logs; wide, carpeted stairs divided halfway, branching to left and right to the galleries where the portraits of ancestors hung.

A door to their left was opened, and people hurried out to greet them. They were shaken by the hand, hugged and kissed; their cloaks and gloves were taken by the butler and handed to a uniformed maid, and eventually they were led upstairs, breathless, by their stately but agile grandmother.

'I cannot overcome my amazement, Ruth,' said the elderly lady. 'The likeness you bear to your mother is quite uncanny.'

'And she is so like you, Grandmama,' Ruth said. 'But Uncle Andrew and Aunt Laura appear to favour Grandpapa, am I right?'

'Indeed. As Janthina appears to favour Hamish.'

'Yes,' the younger girl joined. 'Simon and I do look more like Papa. Joseph is more like Mama, though he is going bald already.'

'Baldness runs to all the men in my family, I'm afraid. Andrew is fortunate to take after his father.'

They reached Ruth's bedroom first. The bed was a huge brass fourposter with pale blue velvet curtains and valance, gold-tasselled and fringed, matching the window curtains. The walls were white-painted wood-panelling up to the chair-rail, the upper half papered with tiny blue and green flowers. The carpet was pale blue and the furniture painted white, each door and drawer panel etched in gold. There were huge gilded mirrors and on the dressing table, writing bureau and mantelpiece above the blazing fire, stood blue and white porcelain figurines, each one a part of the matched suite.

'It's beautiful,' the visitors chorused.

'Oh, Grandmama,' Ruth turned to hug the delighted woman, 'it's the loveliest room I ever saw in my whole life!'

A maid was already unpacking Ruth's bag on the far side of the room, so Alexandra MacDougall took Janthina's hand and said, 'Come, we'll go and see your room now. Will you come with us, Ruth, so that you'll know where your sister's room is?'

Janthina's bedroom was some distance away, and very similar to Ruth's except that the basic colour was pink and the carpet was patterned with roses. Here, too, a maid was unpacking.

It was Janthina's turn to hug her grandmother. 'It is perfectly gorgeous!' she exclaimed.

45

'I'm glad you're both pleased with your rooms. Now, why don't you quickly freshen up and come downstairs? Don't bother to change for dinner tonight; it's very late and your grandfather's tummy has been groaning this past hour. We mustn't keep him waiting much longer or he'll drink more whisky than is good for him.' And she disappeared with Ruth.

The maid abandoned the unpacking to pour water from the china ewer into a matching, flowered bowl on a marble-topped washstand.

'Thank you,' Janthina smiled at the girl, who was about her own age. 'What is your name?'

'Mary, miss. I'm your personal maid as long as you are here. I'll look after your clothes and help you to dress. I'm pretty good with hair, too. I'll help do yours if you'd like me to.'

'Thank you, that would be a great help. I'm afraid my clothes are badly crushed and there are several things soiled from the sea journey.'

'I've already sorted them out, miss. And I'll be sure to press everything before it goes in your wardrobe.'

What luxury! To have this wonderful bedroom to oneself, and a personal maid.

Janthina washed her hands and face and pulled the pins from her hair. Mary immediately picked up the hairbrush and took over while Janthina sat on the dressing stool watching the expert fingers quickly twist the long hair into a high, soft chignon.

'There, miss, is that all right for tonight? A bit plain, but we'll have more time tomorrow.'

Her new mistress turned her head, this way and that, viewing the result with pleasure. She had never had her hair in such a flattering style. 'Thank you, Mary, it looks splendid,' and tiredness temporarily forgotten, she hastened away to find Ruth.

Donald MacDougall, Laird of Glenfalk, sat at the head of a long, oak refectory table with his Canadian granddaughters on either side. Everything about the laird was huge. His beaked nose was huge over a full white beard. His massive head with its shock of white hair was set on huge, wide shoulders; at more than seventy years old he stood well over six feet tall. With his narrow black trousers and stiff-fronted white shirt he wore a close-fitting green jacket and thin black tie. On Ruth's left hand sat his son, Andrew, similarly attired, an immense replica of his father though his hair retained its MacDougall colour of pale sand, and beyond him his sister Laura, a strangely small person in this family of giants, pretty and bubbling, wearing a light brown dress with much lace around the low-cut neckline and sleeves.

Cousin Ian was placed between Aunt Laura and Grandmama, who

sat opposite her husband, statuesque and sleek, her hair drawn up in a sophisticated chignon, long earrings flashing as she followed the conversation to and fro. Aunt Meg, Uncle Andrew's wife, was blonde, petite and plump, her blue velvet gown straining at its seams when she giggled, which she did frequently. Unfortunately her son, Roderick, took after her rather than his handsome father, excepting that he seldom spoke and then only in very sombre vein. At twenty-five he was much given to poetry and contemplation . . . and little else. In contrast, his sister Elinor was a twenty-year-old giant, bony, flat-chested but, it transpired, with the perfect equestrian seat. Seated on Janthina's right, she soon swung the conversation to horses and was noisily delighted to learn of Janthina's love of riding and quick to assure her cousin that in her opinion fancy side-saddles were only for promenading in parks to show off the latest fashions – not for serious horsemanship. Janthina's spirits rose by the minute and during the second course she was pleased to find that she and Ruth could hold Grandpapa's and Uncle Andrew's genuine interest on the subject of Canadian political and economic growth. When the ladies withdrew to the great hall, leaving the four men with their cigars and their decanter of port, Grandmama, sensing that the McKenzie girls had led an extremely limited social life, steered conversation into comparisons between Canadian and Scottish farming.

'We keep herds of our Aberdeen Angus in the valleys,' she explained, 'and sheep in the hills. I'm sure Elinor will be delighted to take you girls out riding on a guided tour as soon as this beastly weather clears. Have you brought riding clothes?'

'Only habits suitable for riding side-saddle in the park, I'm afraid,' Ruth laughed. 'But Mama . . . er, Papa, has given us an allowance to add anything we need to our wardrobes.'

'Excellent. We must take a trip down to Edinburgh next week. And how many ballgowns did you bring? Christmas will soon be here and there will be a great many parties and balls. Which reminds me . . . we are giving a small party on Saturday evening to introduce you to some of our friends and neighbours. We will serve a buffet supper and open up the ballroom for some dancing. Do you know any of the Scottish dances?'

'I learned the "Eightsome Reel" at my dancing class in Kingston,' Janthina said. 'And "Strip the Willow" and "Petronella" were very popular.'

Aunt Laura eyed the girls doubtfully. 'I think we'll have to take you in hand and teach you some of the basic steps before Saturday; they're very easy. And I suppose you can waltz and polka?' The girls shook

47

their heads, mournfully. 'Oh, well, don't let it bother you. We'll soon put that right.'

Ruth and Janthina could scarcely keep their eyes open when the men finally joined them, and their grandmother insisted they should retire immediately. 'The poor girls are exhausted, we must excuse them early tonight,' she said, and when the round of 'goodnights' was done, the sisters stumbled upstairs to their waiting maids and lovely copper warming-pans in their beds.


Next morning it took Janthina several minutes to remember where she was, partly because the bed still seemed to be rolling. She had slept so heavily that it was hard to recall the names, faces and places of yesterday, and all that had been said; but when it did come back to her it was all good. Fears and torments of the past weeks were forgotten in the excitement of her new surroundings. Stretching luxuriously in the vast bed, her thoughts drifted back to Roland. How dearly she longed to receive a letter from him. Or perhaps he might just come to call instead. Surely she would know within the next week – and then? Would the fondness between them continue? Would it grow? How wonderful it would be if he proposed and they could marry . . . and go back to live in her beautiful, beloved, Canadian wilderness.

Throwing back the bedclothes, she jumped out of bed, opened the curtains to admit the bleak day, and, without ringing for Mary, washed and dressed herself and hurried along to collect Ruth before going down to breakfast.

Later that morning, it was Aunt Laura who lifted each outfit from the girls' wardrobe, held them on their hangers against their owners, and made rapid notes on her writing pad. By lunchtime she had presented her list of necessary purchases to her mother whose only comment was, 'I guessed as much. You'd better start right away.'


'Don't you think it's just like a fairy tale, Ruth?' Janthina asked, whirling in front of her sister's full-length mirror. She was a trifle breathless, being unaccustomed as yet to the corset into which Mary had laced her, tighter and tighter, until her waist was almost as small as Ruth's. It showed off to perfection the full skirt of her cream lace gown and the daringly low-cut bodice above which the mounds of her breasts peeped audaciously. Ruth wondered if the dress wasn't a bit too daring for a seventeen-year-old, but she hesitated to mention it lest her comments be interpreted as sour grapes, being so much less well endowed herself.

Polly, Ruth's maid, was as gifted as her cousin Mary when it came to dressing hair, and had swept her young mistress's heavy, black locks into a smooth chignon, which accentuated her height and fine features. Janthina had a younger style with soft curls clustered from the top of her head to the nape of her neck.

Aunt Laura bustled in. 'Oh, my!' She clapped her hands. 'Don't you both look lovely! Polly, dear, how beautifully you have dressed Miss Ruth's hair. Yours too, Janthina. It suits you magnificently. Come. If you are both ready, I think we should go down,' and she led them out along the west gallery to the stairs, down to the party which was being held in their honour.

It was impossible to memorise all the names and faces, Grandmama's idea of a small party being no less than fifty people. Ruth and Janthina laughed and chattered, and drank champagne for the first time in their lives; they pranced amongst the swinging tartan kilts of the men in the reels and rounds to the wail of the bagpipes; and responded eagerly to their partners' leads in the exciting waltzes and polkas played by a five-piece orchestra. This was far more exhilarating than anything Janthina had experienced at school in Kingston. No matter that there had, as yet, been no letter from Roland; that would come within the next few days she had no doubt, and in the meantime these handsome young men who stood before her arguing for the privilege of escorting her into supper would more than suffice.

Ruth sat across the room at another table forking dainty morsels of food into her mouth and listening with obvious interest to her escort. Perhaps not handsome, he was yet very distinguished looking, tall and broad in a smart green and black kilt, tasselled sporran, lace ruffles on cuff and shirt front, frothing from beneath his short black jacket. His tartan sash was held across his massive chest by a large silver insignia and above it, in the strong face, merry eyes never left Ruth for a moment.

Captain Benjamin Kirkpatrick of the Argyll and Sutherland Highlanders was captivated.

All Janthina's partners seemed charming, though none was particularly outstanding. She enjoyed them all, and felt quite light-headed from the gaiety and the champagne when the guests began to leave. It was two o'clock before the last hand was shaken and the last goodbye said. Mary and Polly were dozing upstairs, waiting to release their young mistresses from their corsets and hairpins. The moment Janthina had tied the girdle of her dressing robe she raced along the corridor

49

to Ruth's room, hair flying, for a post-mortem on the evening. The girls fell into each other's arms with squeals of excited laughter.

'The champagne made me quite dizzy. . . .'

'Didn't you love those waltzes?'

'But oh, those bagpipes!'

'And all those gorgeous young men in their kilts. . . .'

'What do you think they wear underneath them?'

'I can't imagine.'

'Nothing!' Janthina announced.

'I don't believe that!'

'It's true. Elinor told me.'

'Suppose a man tripped over on the dance floor?'

'He would be barely embarrassed, I should think.' And the two of them collapsed on Ruth's bed, laughing until they cried at Janthina's joke.

They were both wide awake and in talkative mood. Janthina rolled on to her back and gazed into space, a dreamy smile on her face.

'What are you thinking of?' Ruth asked.

'What it's like to be married.'

'To Roland?'

'Perhaps. Ruth . . .' she suddenly sat up.

'Yes?'

'How do you get babies?'

'You've seen cows calving, haven't you?'

'Yes, of course. I know they grow inside the mother's stomach, but what makes them start?'

'I don't know. Being married, I suppose.'

'But cows aren't married.'

'No. But that's what we keep bulls for.'

There was silence for a few minutes as Janthina pondered. 'Ruth,' she said thoughtfully, 'why have Simon and I got the same colour hair and eyes as Papa and you and Joseph are like Mama?'

'People often look like one or other of their parents.'

'I can understand them looking like their mothers, but why should they look like their fathers?'

'I don't know. I've never really thought about it. Funny, isn't it?'

'I wonder if when a man and a lady kiss each other on the mouth he passes something to her to start the baby.'

'That's an idea. I expect you're right.'

'I asked Mama about it once.'

'And what did she tell you?'

50

'That is was nothing to do with young girls. The peculiar thing was that she blushed, absolutely scarlet.'

'Poor Mama.' Ruth yawned. 'I think I'm going to go to sleep now. Are you going back to your room?'


It was nearly ten o'clock before either awoke next morning to face the breakfast trays brought in by their maids. Janthina toyed with the solid bowl of porridge and finally abandoned it for a few dainty fingers of toast. From her bed she could look out of the window at the distant snow-capped hills and she thought about home, Mama, Joseph, and Papa. Darling Mama. No wonder she had wanted her daughters to see Scotland before they married and settled down in Canada – it was all so exciting. Certainly the countryside she had seen so far could not compare with the beauty she had left behind, but the homes, the parties, the fun, and above all the smiling faces of both relatives and friends . . . not even Aunt Mary and the cousins had appeared so perpetually happy and contented. And to think how much she had dreaded coming! She had certainly changed her mind very quickly. When she thought of the tense, restrictive atmosphere of her own home, of the times she had deliberately set out to deceive Papa so that she could enjoy the freedom she craved; why, here that freedom was automatic. She was beginning to think she had not been so wicked after all, for the more she saw of other men the more odd, overbearing, and ill-tempered Papa appeared to have been in comparison. She could never imagine Grandpapa or Uncle Andrew or Cousin Ian shouting and hitting anyone with a riding crop. She wondered how Papa was now, and if he was quite recovered.

In ill-fitting, borrowed clothes, the girls rode out with Elinor and Roderick that afternoon to be given an idea of Scottish farming.

Hills! Hills everywhere, smooth-domed in heather with Scots pine skirts and capped with snow. There had been hills north of their home in Canada, but none to compare with these.

'I thought that Canada was all mountains, far higher than these hills,' Elinor replied to their comments.

'Oh, yes. The Canadian Rockies, but they are far to the west of us, and there are the Adirondacks to the east, but Kingston, Ontario, is on the great Canadian shield in between, a vast, low-lying area with thousands of shallow lakes and rivers and hundreds of little islands,' Janthina explained.

'Except for the Great Lakes,' Ruth added. 'They are more like huge inland seas and terribly deep.'

They reined in their horses to watch a herd of stocky-legged cattle grazing. 'Are those the famous Aberdeen Angus?' Ruth asked.

'Correct,' Elinor smiled. 'The pride of Glenfalk. There's some good, firm ground ahead; would anyone like a gallop to blow away the cobwebs from last night?'

'Oh! Yes, please.' Janthina was delighted at the prospect.

But Roderick put his hand to his head. 'I just couldn't take it, sister dear; I think I'll wander slowly back and have a rest before dinner.'

'A good idea. We'll leave the hard riding to the young and strong, shall we?' Ruth laughed, and they watched as Janthina and Elinor dug their heels into their mounts and raced away at full gallop.

The icy wind stung their cheeks red and made their eyes stream with tears. Elinor slowed her horse to a trot, waiting for Janthina to catch her up. 'I'm sorry I chose old Rufus for you, I had no idea you rode so well and was afraid you might get into difficulties on a livelier beast.'

'Rufus is certainly the largest horse I've ever ridden, but he is very docile. I've only been up on Indian ponies at home, much smaller but very agile and independent. I named my pony Pickle because he was so full of tricks. He has a hundred ways to unseat one once he decides it's suppertime.'

At the head of the glen Janthina was fascinated to watch the river cascade over a series of high waterfalls from the hills, way down into the burn below. 'It's beautiful,' she breathed, thinking to herself that even though it was different, it was beautiful enough to suffice until she returned home.

'You've seen nothing yet. There is so much more to show you when we have more time. Brrr,' Elinor shivered. 'It's freezing. Come on. I'll race you home.'


Accustomed to the modest architecture of Kingston, Ruth and Janthina had been quite awestruck by the rearing skyscrapers of New York and the brilliantly lit night skyline of Manhattan, but the nobility and grandeur of Edinburgh, dominated by its magnificent castle, left them speechless.

'Is it possible to visit the castle?' Ruth asked her grandmother. 'I would love to explore it.'

'Yes, indeed. Full of great Scottish history – a very interesting place. But I think you will have to wait. We'll find it difficult enough to complete our shopping list today as it is. We must organise some special visits so that you may tour Edinburgh properly. Perhaps you would arrange that, Laura?'

'Of course, Mother,' Laura replied vaguely. 'Now, here we are in Princes Street, girls. This is where the day really begins,' and their aunt waved a gloved hand and nodded to the smart occupants of sleek equipages of all types driven by liveried groomsmen.

This was a style of purchasing entirely new to Ruth and Janthina. No question of walking through shops looking at goods: they were greeted with smiles and bows, led into private rooms to be offered dainty cups of hot chocolate or glasses of Madeira while models paraded for them and assistants brought selections of undergarments, corsetry, stockings and gloves for their inspection. Nor were they expected to undress to try on the clothes. Instead, two days later, the managers of two emporiums arrived at the castle with fitters and seamstresses and with vast hampers full of dresses for day and evening wear, some severely smart, some covered with lace and frills, bolero jackets with full, puffed sleeves, smart little hats with veils, feathers, bows and flowers and the new 'must' for every smart woman, tall, frilled umbrellas with elegant fancy handles, made in colours and materials to match every outfit.

Alexandra and Laura were in their element, fingering cloth and trimmings and testing the softness of leather boots and slippers. For hours on end the girls stepped in and out of the elegant clothes they had admired on the models in Edinburgh, and Mary and Polly dressed and tidied their hair as the milliner pinned on and removed one after the other of her exotic creations for the ladies to consider and discuss.

'I do believe Grandmama and Aunt Laura think we are their new dolls,' Janthina gasped to her sister as she collapsed on Ruth's bed later. 'I feel quite exhausted.'

'Do remember,' Ruth warned, 'that Grandmama insists on paying for everything herself. I did offer, you know, but she says we must keep our funds for pin money. Though I don't know when we will ever have a chance to spend it.'

'I cannot believe that all the money we brought with us could possibly pay for all the things we have bought today. In fact, I can't imagine when we will have the opportunity to wear them all.'

'I agree. But in Scotland it seems unforgivable to be seen in the same gown on more than one occasion. And to tell you the truth, I've quite lost track of all the items that go together to make up each ensemble. Can you remember which ribbons and gloves and slippers and hats and umbrellas are intended to be worn with which gown?'

Janthina laughed. 'No! I don't believe I can. All I can say is that your Benjamin will be struck speechless every time he sees you.'

'He is *not* my Benjamin,' Ruth retorted with heat.

'You may not realise it, but everyone who saw the doting look on his face on Saturday night knew he was at your feet. I thought he was charming. Don't you like him?'

Ruth's coy smile and shining eyes betrayed the enormous change wrought so soon in the elder sister. The cold anger that had governed her thinking for so long, and determined her against men and marriage lest she find herself tied to a man like her father, was already giving way to a new, soft sweetness, and Janthina could see an increasing likeness in her to Grandmama. Dear Grandmama who looked so tall and autocratic, so proud and dignified, yet who, like Aunt Laura, was really so caring, loving and demonstrative; who hugged and kissed her family in spontaneous bursts of affection and who displayed transparent joy at the visit of her granddaughters.

'If only Roland could see you in your new pink and white ballgown!' Ruth turned the conversation away from herself.

Janthina sighed. 'I wish his letter would come. I wonder if the postbag has arrived yet this morning.'

Ruth pulled the tasselled rope by her bed, and a few moments later Polly appeared.

'Yes, miss? You rang?'

'Polly, has Malcolm returned yet with the postbag?'

'Yes, miss, ten minutes ago. But there was nothing in it for either of you ladies.'

'Thank you, Polly. That will be all.' Ruth nodded in dismissal.

'Anyone would think you'd been pulling bell ropes for your personal maid all your life,' Janthina teased when the girl had gone. 'I still haven't got used to summoning Mary without wanting to apologise for inconveniencing her.'

'Well, don't get too used to it. Remember that it will only be for a year. Then you'll have to run your own errands and probably a few for other people as well.'

Who would mind running errands for Roland, Janthina asked herself, her mind drifting back to her beautiful dream.

Ruth saw the wistful look in her sister's eyes and sighed. 'Janty, dear, I'm afraid you are just going to have to accept the fact that Roland was just a . . . a shipboard romance. I've read about them. People feel very romantic at sea, away from home and the critical eyes of people they know. They allow themselves to become fond of others in a way they would not normally. Then, despite promises, genuine enough at the time, they just forget about each other and go their separate ways. Maybe it was like that with Roland.'

'Maybe,' Janthina said sadly. She could feel the stiff outline of his photograph through the material of her reticule.


There was certainly no doubt in the minds of those who saw them together during the next few weeks, that Ruth McKenzie and Benjamin Kirkpatrick had fallen head over heels in love, and the person who found the situation quite incredible was Ruth herself.

Janthina was delighted, though never missing an opportunity to tease. 'And how did the avowed spinster enjoy last evening?' she would ask. 'Are you just leading poor Benjamin to believe you will be his bride when all the time you intend refusing him because you are convinced that he will turn into another Papa the moment he is wed?'

'Never!' Ruth would flush at the reminder of her old fears. 'Ben would never be like that in a million years. Anyway, since leaving Canada I have realised that Papa is an exception. I no longer believe that husbands and fathers carry on like that normally. I only wish poor Mama could have come with us.'

'Yes, so do I,' Janthina agreed. 'I wonder how Papa is now?'

The news arrived in a letter from Mama a week before Christmas. In it she explained that Papa had been taken to Kingston to be examined by a team of doctors, and she had been assured that he was now perfectly mentally and physically recovered . . . except for two factors. His seizure had left him with only partial control of his right leg, and with total paralysis of the vocal chords. It now seemed doubtful that he would ever speak again.

The postbag had arrived late that day due to snow on the road, and the family were gathered in the Great Hall waiting for the butler to announce luncheon.

Ruth and Janthina sat on a settee reading their letter together and Alexandra looked up from the post as she heard their gasps.

'What is it? Not bad news, I hope?'

'It's Papa,' Ruth explained. 'Apparently as a result of his seizure he may never speak again.'

'Oh! My dears, I am so sorry, how terrible. You must be devastated.'

Janthina glanced at Ruth and saw the old familiar mask close over her sister's face for a moment, the cold anger which had frozen the girl's feelings for so many years.

'No. Maybe Jan is, but I'm not. I believe it is God's judgement on

55

him for his wickedness.' Ruth sat erect as she spoke, flames from the burning logs in the fireplace reflecting in her eyes.

'Wickedness?' Alexandra spoke softly, frowning. 'What wickedness?'

'Vicious verbal and physical abuse which he has heaped on us all for years,' Ruth replied.

The room remained silent, until her grandmother stood up. 'I knew it. Adeline never told us a word, but I knew. Her letters became dull, lost the great joy with which she had started her life in Canada.'

The laird sat upright in his chair, a scowl forming on his usually cheerful face. 'Ach! I tried to discourage her from marrying one of those McKenzies; I knew Hamish's father many years ago. A hard, cold man. Made himself unpopular wherever he went. I always thought that was why he emigrated to Canada.' He shook his white head. 'But I doubt if he made any more friends there than he did here. A geographical change won't reverse a man's character.'

'You don't mean that he actually . . . beat any of you?' Alexandra probed.

The girls looked at each other and it was Janthina who answered. 'The scar on my shoulder was not really an accident. That was a lie, I'm afraid. It was actually a cut from Papa's riding crop. As are the scars on . . . here.' She spoke very quietly, and touched her posterior with her hand.


Christmas presents made a large hole in the McKenzie sisters' pin money. They spent a whole day together in Perth discussing their respective gift lists, worrying over them, yet caught up in the festive atmosphere: brightly lit shop windows displaying gifts, tinsel and holly; Christmas trees decorated with guttering candles and imitation snow; and groups of carol singers at the street corners. Malcolm traipsed behind them through the slushy snow on the pavements carrying their parcels while the girls hurried from shop to shop, far too preoccupied to notice their soaking hems and squelchy boots. They had declined Cousin Ian's invitation to lunch, knowing that unless their visit to his home was offensively brief their shopping time would be so reduced as to require another trip into town before Christmas. Instead they had allowed themselves to pause at a charming little tea-shop where they ate thin sandwiches and iced cakes while Malcolm took his morning's load back to the carriage. And in fact he looked by far the most tired of the three, when they eventually drove back to the castle that evening.

'Oh, look, Ruth,' Janthina gasped as they rolled up the drive. 'Doesn't the castle look beautiful?' She was right. Outdoor lanterns lit the snow-covered ground, against which the dark stonework of the castle walls stood in stark silhouette, crenellated towers reaching up into the moonlit sky. It seemed that every window in the castle was glowing with the warmth of Christmas candles and even the vast, forbidding oak doors each bore wreaths of holly and mistletoe.

'Obviously a home full of love and laughter, not a fortress full of soldiers,' Ruth remarked, and both girls were secretly aware at the same moment that this was also a home into which one could slip joyfully unrestrained, without fear of facing angry criticism and retribution.

Next day was spent with pretty paper and ribbons parcelling their purchases and penning loving messages on pretty labels.

'Oh, dear! I knew I'd get in a muddle,' Janthina moaned. 'Look, I've bought these lace handkerchiefs for a non-existent aunt and I have nothing to give Cousin Ian.'

'Don't worry, I've made the opposite mistake,' Ruth laughed. 'You give him these cigars and I'll give Aunt Meg the handkerchiefs.'

When their task was finished they carried all the parcels downstairs to the huge, gaily decorated Christmas tree in the Great Hall where they were piled amongst all the other exciting looking packages to await Christmas Day.

The church, festooned with holly, ivy, mistletoe and flowers from the conservatories of Glenfalk, was filled to overflowing on Christmas morning with worshippers.

For the first time she could remember, Janthina was filled with such gratitude for the birth of the Babe born to bring love and hope to the world, that her eyes glistened with tears as she sang His praises . . . and she wondered why? Could it be, perhaps, that subconsciously the Wrath of God had been miraculously transformed for her into a message of love and joy for mankind? That the interpretation of the Word of God imposed by Papa on his home and family for so long had so oppressed her that only now, released from that oppression, could she understand the true meaning of her religion?

Suddenly she was aware of two conflicting emotions: one created by the continuous happiness she had found here in Scotland amongst her mother's family, which stretched out through the coming year to next Christmas, when they would be back in Canada, her beautiful, beloved Canada . . . and the other, a mixture of fear and horror, centred on the stark picture of sitting in the farm parlour on Christmas

57

afternoon with Papa furiously silent, grasping his walking stick like an offensive weapon, glaring at her, daring her to lift her needlework or open her box of water colours or read anything but her Bible. And Mama, weary, ageing, flesh as grey as her hair, sitting motionless, hands folded in her lap, dreaming the dreams of 'might-have-been' behind the image of her misery.

The congregation were rustling the pages of their hymn books. No, no, it would not be like that; she would not let it be. She would enjoy this year, every day, every minute, every second, to the maximum. She would absorb the joy, love and laughter and take it back with her to the farm, transform the misery there to happiness; love Papa and make him aware of all the sweetness in life he had denied them. She would bring colour back to Mama's face, cause Joseph to throw back his head in mirth . . .

The last exultant chorus of 'Once in Royal David's City' rang through the church rafters as the jubilant members of the congregation and choir stretched their lungs to the maximum, faces red with effort, before kneeling for the Blessing. There was handshaking and kissing in the churchyard as they emerged into the pale sunlight. Every villager wanted to shake the laird's hand, and get a view of his bonny, Canadian granddaughters – though they saw them every Sunday, Christmas Day was special. Joining the greetings and good wishes, Ruth and Janthina were well aware that their grandfather had not bought this affection with largesse, donations to education and medical facilities, but with genuine concern and caring. The villagers, everyone who knew him, loved him – and he loved them.

Only one sad thought loomed on Janthina's horizon as she walked back up the lane from the village with the Glenfalk churchgoers: there had still been no letter from Roland, and as each day passed her reasons had turned to excuses and now the excuses had run out. The leaden ball of disappointment in her stomach told her that there would never be a letter, now. Perhaps Roland had found a new love – certainly he no longer cared. She sighed. She would keep the photograph of him as a perpetual memento of her first love.

Having changed their church clothes for more festive gowns, with dry hems, and their boots for soft kid slippers, the clan gathered in the Great Hall to await the Christmas luncheon feast. The girls were introduced to more MacDougall cousins, aunts and uncles who had arrived during the morning, before the butler led the party to the dining hall where the table had been extended to accommodate every possible chair. Festive paper crackers were pulled immediately every-one was seated, paper hats arranged over curls, and silly conundrums read out while the butler supervised the serving of wafer-thin slices of smoked Scotch salmon. Soup followed and then Malcolm and one of the grooms, both in their Sunday best, with hair greased flat to their scalps, carried in a vast tray bearing two huge turkeys, a fresh-baked ham and a long rib joint of beef – all magnificently garnished. The laird, Andrew, Malcolm and the butler stood at the sideboards to carve whilst maids hurried the plates of meat and tureens of steaming vegetables to the diners.

Flaming Christmas pudding followed with mince pies and brandy butter. White wine in crystal goblets was served with the salmon; sherry with the soup and a heady Burgundy accompanied the main course. Later, with the petits fours and crystallised fruit, they sipped a cool Château Yquem.

It was four o'clock and already quite dark when the sound of carols reached them. 'Come, let's go and greet them,' Grandpapa said, pushing back his chair, and the family hurried from the table into the hallway where the great doors were thrown open to admit the church choir, together with the minister and his family. All were ushered into the Great Hall where Aunt Laura sat at the piano to provide an accompaniment and everyone joined in the singing.

'Mr Cameron, I have to congratulate you and your choir,' Grandpapa said. 'I swear your performance improves every year and how, I fail to understand, for I never can detect any room for improvement. And I see you have your eldest son back with you from South Africa. How are you, James?'

'The better for being home for Christmas, sir,' James Cameron replied.

'Are you quite recovered from your wounds?'

'I believe so, sir. But unfortunately I'll not be able to take up my duties again with the Highlanders. They say I canna march with a gammy leg.'

Despite his apparent politeness to the laird, Janthina suspected a cockiness about this stockily built man with straight brown hair greased flat and over-large side-whiskers. Compared with his father his clothes appeared almost flashy. He caught her eyes on him and gave her a smile which made her feel quite uncomfortable.

'So what are you planning to do now?' Grandpapa continued.

'Having been in the army for eleven years, I'm afraid I have no other professional training, so I suppose I must go into trade. I am currently acquiring some experience in that direction in Perth.' Which sounded a good deal better than admitting, either to his audience or himself, that he was currently a grocer's shop assistant and delivery boy.

'Good for you!' The laird clapped a hand on his shoulder. 'I wish you every success, and I'll be interested to know how you go on. There is nothing wrong with a man taking an honest trade. And you, Mrs Cameron, must be relieved to see your son back with no worse than a gammy leg.'

'That I am,' the minister's wife agreed, bouncing the feathers up and down on her best hat. 'I am sure we are very lucky indeed. The Boers have claimed the lives of so many of our brave young men, and South Africa is a very long way from home when you are wounded. I believe a number of soldiers died before they could be given the medical attention that would have saved them.'

There were more carols and a hot, fruity punch was handed round before the singers went on their way.

'You certainly made a hit there,' Ruth commented to her sister. 'James Cameron never took his eyes off you.'

'I know. He made me feel most uncomfortable,' Janthina scowled.

'Oh, come, it's Christmas Day. Poor man has been so starved of feminine beauty all these years. . . .'

'I wouldn't wager anything on that!'

'Let's all open our presents, now, shall we?' Grandmama suggested in a loud voice. 'Everyone come and sit down, and Anne can distribute the parcels.'

Anne was Cousin Ian's daughter, just twelve years old and the youngest member of the family. She read out the message on each gift before handing it to the recipient amidst clapping, oohs and aahs. The ceremony took a long time, and when the last paper and ribbon had been discarded, the last kisses and 'thank yous' exchanged, Grandmama stood up. 'I'm going up to my room for a wee rest,' she announced, 'and I recommend that you, Donald and Alistair, do the same, or you'll not remain awake till suppertime.'

In fact there was a general exodus, everyone agreeing with Grandmama's suggestion . . . which gave the maids time to clear away the piles of torn paper and ribbons and straighten the room before the evening activities commenced.

It was the opportunity for which Ruth and Janthina were waiting. They dashed upstairs to ring their respective bell ropes and to hand prettily wrapped gifts to Polly and Mary, who hurried away in delight to display their delicately lacquered pintrays and boxes in their own rooms.


Party followed party that week.

Soon Ruth and Janthina became accustomed to falling into bed at one, two, or even three o'clock in the morning, and not rising until ten or eleven; to being pampered by their maids, bathed, dressed and coiffed ready to step down to the morning room to discuss the previous or coming evening's events over dainty cups of chocolate.

The biggest excitement of the holiday season was Hogmanay – New Year's Eve. Glenfalk was to host a party to see out the Old Year and bring in the New, and trestle tables were erected in the ballroom to seat all the extra diners. Ruth and Janthina assisted their aunts in arranging fresh garlands of greenery and in placing namecards before each chair in the dining hall so that correct protocol might be observed amongst all the older generation; the younger people would be allowed to seat themselves where they pleased in the ballroom.

The Canadian girls wore their very best gowns that evening. The styles were similar in design, but totally different in effect. Janthina's consisted of palest coral pink satin cut to fit smoothly in bodice and skirt down to the knee, where it billowed into tier upon tier of frills and lace which dipped at the back to sweep the floor as she walked. Two tiers of matching frills and lace trimmed the low, off-the-shoulder neckline forming tiny cap sleeves and the very deep sash fell in folds across the front of her skirt from her hips like an apron, to be scooped up into a frothy bustle and fall again to rest on her train. The lower edge of the sash was trimmed with more matching frills and lace, and edged between satin and frills with slightly deeper coral velvet ribbons, matching the bows on her gloves and the thin band fastened high around her throat. Her fan was of white lace decorated with tiny coral rosebuds.

Ruth had chosen white. Panels of scallops and pleats alternated round the skirt, and the frills which edged her sash and neckline were fewer but deeper, while the velvet ribbons at her waist were of deep blue as were the bows on her wrists and the band tied round her throat with the ends trailing down over her bustle. Her fan was white lace ribbed in matching blue. And above all, pinned from shoulder to hip and carefully avoiding breaking the fashionable lines of their dresses, both girls wore a sash of the McKenzie tartan.

Aided with pads and pins and curling irons, Mary and Polly had surpassed themselves, crowning their creations with coral and white silk flowers for Janthina and blue and white for her sister.

Guests who lived any considerable distance from Glenfalk had been invited to stay overnight at the castle, and all the unused bedrooms had been opened and cleaned and had fires lit against the cold. These guests had arrived earlier in the afternoon and many were already assembling in the main hall, listening to the musicians playing from the west gallery, when Ruth and Janthina stepped down the stairs in their coral and blue slippers. There was a sudden hush followed by many exclamations and comments as people, gentlemen in particular, pressed forward to greet them.

Janthina always wondered, afterwards, why she was immediately aware of one face in the crowd. He was standing back near the fire watching her, his slim, black-clad figure motionless, flames giving a reddish glow to his pale blond hair. Caught up in the crowd of new friends and relatives she lost sight of him, greeted each of the new arrivals, and with Ruth played the charming hostess alongside her grandparents, aunts, uncles and cousins.

The noise was tremendous, everyone speaking loudly to be heard above the orchestra. Grooms and maids dressed as waiters and waitresses moved among the crowd with trays of glasses and canapés; some people drifted into the Great Hall in groups. The Canadian girls were asked a hundred times if they liked Scotland and how it compared with Canada.

As the grandfather clock in the hall chimed the half hour after seven, the butler struck the big brass gong at the foot of the stairs until everyone was hushed, including the musicians. 'My lords, ladies and gentlemen, pray silence for Donald MacDougall, Laird of Glenfalk,' he announced, and the laird trod two steps up to look down on his guests.

'My friends, in accordance with the Hogmanay tradition at Glenfalk, we ask you to select your partners for the Treasure Hunt. Many of you will remember the rules, but for those of you who have not been with us in previous years let me explain. Our good friends William Shakespeare and Rabbie Burns have, as usual, collaborated to provide us with clues and these you will find cunningly placed throughout the castle. They are all indoors, clearly visible without lifting or removing any item; they are numbered from one to twenty-five, and each pair must write down the missing word from each quotation on the notepad with which you will be provided. Try not to let anyone see you reading a clue as this will reveal its hiding place. Each clue will lead you to the next and the first couple to bring me the correct list of twenty-five missing words wins first prize. However, no one should give up as there are many runners-up prizes. Now, as soon as you are all paired and have your pads and pencils, John will ring the gong again for you to commence.'

His audience clapped and cheered as he stepped down and the waiters reappeared with stacks of notepads and pencils.

Janthina looked about her, wondering whom she might partner, saw

Ruth and Benjamin smiling together – and several young men she had already met at parties advancing towards her.

'Miss McKenzie?' A voice spoke shyly at her shoulder, and she saw the fair-haired young man she had noticed earlier. 'I regret that we have not been introduced. May I present myself – Anthony Mears, at your service.' He bowed, took her gloved hand, and touched it with his lips.

'How do you do, Mr Mears,' she murmured, noting the deep blue eyes with unusually long dark lashes for one so blond, and the small moustache curving over his lips. He was not so much handsome as utterly beautiful. She felt strangely dizzy, her heart banging wildly as he smiled, still holding her hand.

'Do you think it would be overly bold of me, having enjoyed your acquaintance for only one minute, to ask if you would consider taking me as your partner for the Treasure Hunt?' he asked.

'Oh, yes . . . I mean, no, er, no, not at all too bold,' Janthina stammered. 'I would be pleased. . . .'

'Thank you, Miss McKenzie.' He bowed again. 'Shall we claim a notepad and pencil?'

When the gong was struck again there was a great hustle and bustle as all the guests headed in various directions after their clues. 'Come, follow me, Miss McKenzie,' her escort instructed, taking her hand to draw her along in his wake.

'I think it will be most tedious to use our surnames all evening, don't you?' she panted, wishing her corset was not pulled quite so tight. 'Please will you call me Janthina?'

'I would be honoured, providing you will call me Anthony.'

They sped down a corridor to the morning room and walked around it examining every item for clues.

'Here, look!' Anthony exclaimed, pointing to a neatly penned card which was pasted beneath a painting of flowers, over the title panel on the gilded frame. 'It's number five, and reads: "I know a bank whereon the wild thyme blows, Where ox-lips and the nodding violet grows, Quite over-canopied with lush. . . ." There's a gap there and it goes on, "With sweet musk roses, and with eglantine." '

'*A Midsummer Night's Dream*, and the missing word is "woodbine",' Janthina said, writing the word on her pad. 'I would guess the next clue will be in one of the conservatories, probably on or near a climbing plant, don't you think?'

'Oh, yes. Clever girl! Which conservatory do you think it might be?'

They found their next clue pasted on the back of a name-tag on a vine, and this time Janthina read it out, ' "What's a' your jargon o' your

. . ." then the blank, "your Latin names for horns and stools; if honest Nature made you fools, what sairs your grammars." That must surely be Robert Burns, don't you think?'

'Undoubtedly. But I'm dashed if I can think what the missing word might be. I suppose it will have to rhyme with stools and fools. Pools? Ghouls?' A pucker formed between the deep blue eyes. 'Wait! I have it. "What sairs your grammars?" So what about schools?'

'Yes, yes, that must be right. The old schoolroom! Come on, it's upstairs. We'll take the back staircase by the Servants' Hall,' and this time it was Janthina who grasped her partner's hand and led him towards their next clue.

The trail led them up and down the old castle past couples hastening in the opposite direction or standing in despair frowning at their pads. Twice they simply listened as others read the quotation they had found out loud, keeping their guess at the missing word to themselves. The ancient walls echoed to the shouts and giggles of nearly sixty couples hunting and probing for clues which were staring at them from clearly visible but unlikely places, and as the notepads filled excitement grew; voices became more urgent, and prospective winners raced full tilt around corners into their close opponents.

And all the time they ran, Janthina was aware of Anthony: the warmth of his hand, the brush of his sleeve against the bare flesh of her arm, his cool breath as their two heads bent to read. There was also the disturbing feeling that he was as aware of her closeness when, from time to time, he would gaze at her, his eyes seeming to penetrate past her conscious thoughts into her secret feelings. Yet she was not embarrassed that he should know . . . what? That a strange goblin was turning cartwheels under her bodice? She had no idea what caused the disturbance within herself, the little shivers of excitement which momentarily raised goosepimples on her flesh – followed by a flush of heat and quickening heartbeat; the spasms of weakness in her legs from groin to knee.

They did not win the Treasure Hunt, but were close runners-up, rewarded with a thick cashmere scarf for Anthony and a hand-embroidered Chinese silk stole with a long fringe for Janthina – taken from Grandpapa's big, oaken treasure chest. Ruth and Benjamin came sixth, still high amongst the first twenty couples who received prizes.

Waiters and waitresses reappeared with more trays of glasses, and at a quarter to nine the great gong boomed again signifying that dinner was about to be served. Automatically Anthony drew Janthina's hand through his arm and they drifted into the ballroom together, sat together talking, oblivious of the noise around them. They seemed

64

unaware of the early courses of the banquet, Janthina's plate being removed scarcely touched . . . until the highlight of the occasion. They heard the plaintive wail from a distance growing louder and nearer.

'What on earth . . .?' Janthina started.

'The haggis,' Anthony chortled. 'It's the haggis. They're piping in the haggis,' and he started to clap rhythmically, joined by others around him until the whole place was resounding as the piper entered the ballroom followed by the butler and Malcolm, each bearing a large silver dish on which sat a weird, steaming object.

'What on earth,' Janthina repeated, 'is a haggis?'

'A sheep's stomach filled with minced heart and liver, onions and oatmeal, which has been boiled like a pudding,' he explained.

'Ugh! How perfectly revolting.' She shuddered in mock horror. 'We surely don't have to eat it?'

'Ssssh!' Anthony warned. 'Such remarks are sacrilege north of the border! They've burned people at the stake for less. But really, you must taste it; it's not half as bad as it sounds.' With which she had, eventually, to agree.

After dinner the ladies retired, first upstairs, and then to the Great Hall. The men also vacated the ballroom, mostly joining their elders in the dining hall, whilst the waiters and waitresses cleared away the trestle tables to make way for dancing.

Anthony claimed the first waltz with Janthina, whirling her around at arm's length but sometimes drawing her perilously close, almost into an embrace, swamping her with such feelings that she swayed dizzily. But she did not forget her duty to the other young guests, and when the orchestra changed the tempo she excused herself to mix with the young crowd and be claimed, again and again, for reels and rounds and polkas. But as if by magic she was always aware of where he was dancing, and the magic was enhanced by the constant meeting of their eyes. So that when midnight struck he was at her side.

'Happy New Year, Janthina,' he whispered, and kissed her ear. Everyone was kissing and embracing amidst the flying paper streamers, and in the excitement of the moment she leaned towards him and kissed him gently on the mouth.

She was totally unprepared for the reaction in them both. Gently he returned her kiss, his lips soft and caressing, moving over hers, moist and inviting. They might have been standing alone at the top of a mountain or on the sands of a tropical beach; there might not have been another soul within a million miles of them. She was aware only of rivers of sensation which, starting at their mouths, ran through her

65

body to her toes. Her lips parted and his tongue found hers, stroking. And hers stroked back. All the time their eyes were locked, speaking a new language, though no other part of them touched.

They sprang apart as the orchestra struck a loud chord and everyone drew back, crossing arms and holding hands for 'Auld Lang Syne'.


Slipping into her warm bed hours later, Janthina was still lost in the disturbing sensation of that kiss – and of the look in Anthony's eyes. Vaguely she recalled the ringing of the great bell beside the front door – for the First Footing; the dances with innumerable handsome young men; the champagne breakfast at two o'clock followed by more dancing. She remembered standing stiffly in the hall shaking Anthony's hand as he said goodnight, a disturbing message still in his eyes.

Is this love? Is this how it feels? Is this how Ruth feels? I must ask her in the morning.

She fell asleep, unaware of just how far the morning had already advanced.

# 3

'NEW YEAR'S Day, 1902. I wonder what this year will bring.' Janthina was reclining on the chaise longue in Ruth's bedroom while Polly finished dressing her mistress's hair.

'The end of the Boer War, I hope, and it won't be a minute too soon. Every day I'm terrified that Ben will receive embarkation orders.'

'You're both very much in love, aren't you?'

Ruth smiled at her sister's reflection in the mirror. 'Do you think I am quite out of my mind, to have fallen so soon after our arrival here?'

'On the contrary, I think it's absolutely wonderful. Tell me what it feels like.' She so wanted to compare Ruth's feelings with her own, to know if the palpitating heartbeats, breathless giddiness and turmoil in her stomach which she experienced every time she saw Anthony also amounted to love.

'I doubt if I could possibly describe it. It's a kind of warm, exciting sensation whenever Ben is with me, and an urgency for the hours to fly when he is not.'

'There, miss, is that all right?' Polly stood back to cast a critical eye over her handiwork.

Ruth picked up the hand mirror and turned to see the back of her head, while Janthina watched, aware of the great change in her sister in so short a time. It wasn't simply the elegant clothes, or the fact that her almost blue-black hair was now always swept up into shining, sophisticated chignons, nor even the way that the hard, angry set of her jaw had relaxed, the thin line of her lips fallen into a soft bow; no, it was more than that. Ruth had always been beautiful. Her dark blue eyes, shaded like Mama's by long black lashes, black arched eyebrows, high cheekbones, small, pointed chin and almost transparent, ivory skin, together with her height and slim gracefulness, had always drawn attention and comment. But now there was something more, a blend of joy and serenity which seemed to radiate from her, forming a halo of happiness to enhance her beauty. Was this the effect of being in love? If what she felt for Anthony was also love, then had she, too, developed a similar glow? Oh, if only Polly would hurry so that they could talk in private.

'That's lovely, Polly. Thank you.'

Polly responded happily to Ruth's smile and asked, 'Will that be all, miss?'

'Yes, thank you. You may go.' And the maid picked up an armful of discarded clothes before closing the door.

'Jan, I've something to tell you.' Ruth's voice was high with excitement, her face slightly flushed, the tips of her fingers templed in her lap. Janthina swung her feet down to the floor to sit alert, waiting, guessing. 'Benjamin proposed to me last night and I accepted.'

The younger girl sat open-mouthed for several seconds, speechless. It was wonderful, thrilling news. No wonder her dearest Ruth looked so radiant. 'Oh! How terribly exciting! But . . .' she hesitated, frowning. 'But Ruth, you cannot! I mean . . . well, surely he must ask Papa?'

'Certainly not! I told Ben that whilst we are in Scotland our grandparents are our guardians and that he must speak with Grandpapa. But not Papa. Never,' Ruth replied vehemently.

Janthina waited until Ruth had regained her composure, then asked, 'When will Ben speak with him?'

'Today, I hope.'

'Have you thought about when you would like to marry?'

'We have talked of it. Some time this year, if possible.'

Janthina was silent again, digesting this information.

'I'd like to get married right here in the village church,' Ruth went on. 'In April or May, perhaps. Would you mind very much? I mean, you will still have Elinor here and the two of you are very good friends.'

This was an aspect Janthina had not yet had time to consider. Did this mean Ruth would be going away from Glenfalk? But of course she would; how stupid to imagine otherwise. She would have to go wherever Benjamin went. The full implication gradually dawned on her and she swallowed hard and gave her sister a wide happy smile. 'Mind? Of course not, darling Ruth. I am so happy for you. But you will let me be a bridesmaid, won't you?'

Ruth gave a sigh of relief. 'I was about to ask you. I want you to be my chief attendant. Dearest Jan. . . .' She crossed to sit with Janthina on the chaise longue, taking her hand. 'I was so worried you might be upset – feel I was abandoning you in the middle of our visit here.'

'Silly goose! I shall be just fine with all the family. But . . .' she hesitated. 'What about returning to Canada? And Mama?'

'I'm hoping that Mama will be able to come over for the wedding. As for Canada, I don't know when we'll be able to visit there. You see, Ben expects to be posted to India by the autumn if he is not sent to South Africa, and naturally I will be going with him.'

Janthina nodded, slowly. 'Yes, I see.' The happy smile remained on her face, masking the fact that she was seeing far more than she wanted. There was suddenly a lead weight in her stomach as it occurred to her that their childhood, their sorority, their seventeen years of affectionate companionship, had come to an abrupt end. She gave Ruth's hand a convulsive squeeze. 'Dearest, darling Ruthie, I am so happy for you both. Now, why don't you go on downstairs, the family must be wondering if we've survived last night's festivities. I have to go back to my room for a moment; I've forgotten something. I'll be down in a few minutes.' And she hugged and kissed her sister before hurrying away to weep in the privacy of her bedroom.

She hated herself for giving way to selfish tears . . . but the thought of returning to Canada without Ruth was too awful! Drear pictures appeared in her mind, unbidden, of sitting in the parlour, skimming the cream pans in the dairy, baking batches of cakes and biscuits for hay picnics . . . all without Ruth. And what would happen when Papa got angry? She would go up to her bedroom alone, no patient sister to talk to, to calm her miseries. Was this why she had felt so shattered when they had left home? Had some sixth sense warned her that they would never return together?


The subtleties and obscurities of the previous night's Treasure Hunt clues were under heated discussion when Janthina joined the family group.

'What did you think of them, my dear?' Grandpapa asked as she sat affectionately on the arm of his chair. She had bathed her face and held a cool, wet towel over her eyes until the swollen lids had returned to normal.

'I managed to get most of the Shakespearean clues, but was quite lost when it came to Robert Burns.'

'Who was your partner? Was he any use to you?'

'Oh, yes, marvellous. He seemed to know nearly all Burns by heart. Mr Mears and I were runners-up, remember?'

'*Mr* Mears! You mean Viscount, surely. Isn't he the eldest son of the Earl of Frey?' He paused a moment, frowning. 'Yes, that's right. I remember handing you your prizes.'

'Viscount!' Janthina's fingers pressed her lips to smother a gasp. 'Oh, dear! I'm afraid I made a terrible blunder. He introduced himself simply as Anthony Mears, and I called him Mister!'

Grandpapa laughed. 'Don't let that worry you. Young men who are too impatient to wait until they are properly presented must expect such mistakes. Mears is just their family name.'

'Where do they live?' his granddaughter asked, very casually.

'They have an estate not far from here, down by the coast, but they only come north for Christmas and Hogmanay. Like your grandmother, the Countess is an Englishwoman and likes to celebrate Christmas in a big way, much more than is normal up here in Scotland. They bring parties up for the grouse shooting, too, but apart from that their time is divided between their house in Grosvenor Square, London, and their country seat in Hampshire, in the south of England.'

She felt an immediate ache of disappointment. Did this mean Anthony would soon leave Scotland? Oh, surely not. She had liked him so much and he had said he hoped they would soon meet again. She realised she was not concentrating on what Grandpapa was saying. ' . . . at the Castle Conweir on Thursday. We will have to leave early and hope that there is no more snow. . . .'

'Castle Conweir? But. . . .'

'Yes, yes, child, were you not listening? I was just saying that when we go to the Earl and Countess of Frey's party we must leave here early to be sure to arrive in good time.'

Janthina tried to hide her excitement. So they were to meet again, and soon. 'Yes. Yes, indeed we must leave in good time,' she agreed, getting to her feet so that Grandpapa would not hear the thumping under her blouse. Her sadness over Ruth's plans to marry was forgotten. Presumably, as his parents were still in Scotland, Anthony would have remained, too. Was it possible that he felt the same as she did? Did he have the same urge to be with her, touch her, look at her across a room – run his tongue softly over his lips, remembering their New Year kiss? She had the same strange sensation low in her stomach, now, as she had had last night at midnight. Her mouth was moist and she was suddenly aware that subconsciously the tip of her own tongue had curled over her lips.

Four days later two carriages conveyed the family from Glenfalk to the party at Castle Conweir. Janthina was extremely excited at the prospect of seeing Anthony again. Always providing he was still there. She gnawed a thread on the finger of her glove anxiously. If he was there, might his attentions not be on another girl tonight? Her heart sank at the thought.

He was standing at the door of the ballroom with his parents and sister greeting their guests. His welcome was formal and proper, seemingly no different from that accorded to everyone else. But at least he was there and she prayed the pounding of her heart was not audible to everyone around.

Once again the Canadian girls met lots of new faces and answered the inevitable polite questions about Canada and their opinion of Scotland – the latter difficult to answer as they had seen little of the country as yet, due to the cold and the conditions of the roads. They sipped a fruity punch, nibbled canapés, and compared notes on the activities at Hogmanay with those who were not at Glenfalk that night.

Apparently this was to be an evening of dancing, with a buffet supper laid out in the dining hall to be taken as and when anyone desired. The ballroom was far larger than that at Glenfalk, the ceiling twice as high, with the orchestra seated in a gallery above the dancers.

Young men clustered around the girls eager to gain their attention, fill their programmes. Ruth was happy to see Ben among the guests and allowed no more entries on her card than etiquette demanded, reserving as much as possible for her beau, but Janthina was confused. Should she reserve some dances for Anthony, or. . . . She felt a hand on her waist and turned to meet those deep blue eyes.

'Be sure not to make any promises I will not allow you to keep,' he murmured in her ear. 'As your host, I demand as much of your time as possible. All the waltzes and polkas and your company at supper.' She was about to tell him, laughingly, that he was presumptuous, when he added, 'Please!' and the gentleness of his look and touch melted her will and her knees. She allowed him a half smile under lowered lashes . . . and resolutely complied with his wishes despite the groans from his competitors.

Grandpapa led her into the 'Sir Roger de Coverley'. She knew he loved the dance and had brazenly asked him to partner her, much to his delight. Benjamin squired her into an 'Eightsome', and among others Roderick took his place on her card.

Anthony appeared at her side as soon as his duties were dispensed. 'That was a memorable Hogmanay,' was his opening remark. 'I hope you enjoyed it?'

'Yes, thank you,' she replied modestly.

'Hallo! You're very restrained this evening!'

'Perhaps I was too unrestrained on New Year's Eve,' she suggested, but a lively smile betrayed her.

She was swept away into a polka, Anthony's strong arm sending shivers of happiness through her body. They danced discreetly apart, only catching each other's eyes fleetingly, but none the less aware of the magnetism between them. When the orchestra had led them to a whirling finale and they left the floor he asked if she was interested in rare plants. She was not, and guessed that he had little interest in that direction either, but said recklessly, 'Oh yes! Do you have some?' so that he could lead her away to a quiet conservatory.

There he hesitated only a moment before taking her in his arms. 'I was so afraid it might snow and you wouldn't come,' he whispered in her hair. 'I have dreamed of you every night since the New Year.' His lips caressed her ears, neck, cheek before touching her mouth, toying with her lips, continuing up to each eyelid before she herself sought his mouth and they clung together, tongues circling, bodies pressed close. Her excitement soared. She saw in his eyes deep pools of liquid adoration and knew she conveyed the same in return. Oh, dearest, dearest Anthony, now I know for certain that we were born for each other.

'Have you been invited to the house party at Farthingales?' he asked over supper.

Having spent a while upstairs straightening her hair and smoothing her crushed dress, Janthina had recovered some of her composure. 'On the tenth? Yes, we have. Have you?'

His answering smile nearly demoralised her again. 'Yes,' he said softly. 'Yes, I'll be there.'

They parted with great effort and went their separate ways to seek other promised partners. They danced at opposite ends of the floor – but all the time they were aware of exactly where the other was, while trying not to hold each other's gaze, to look like lovers.


There was great excitement in the air at Glenfalk when Grandpapa announced he had written to Hamish and Adeline recommending Benjamin as a prospective son-in-law.

Ruth was ecstatic. Janthina had never seen her look so happy or so lovely and felt elated for her, pushing to the back of her mind all thoughts of their coming separation. She no longer sought to confide to her sister her feelings for Anthony; she knew it would be unfair to distract Ruth from the plans she and Ben were making in anticipation of their parents' approval.

'I have to say,' Grandpapa was standing in front of the fireplace, 'that I find this all very sudden. Benjamin' – he turned a fierce scowl on the Highlander – 'you have moved with almost indecent haste, considering my granddaughters have been here less than three months.'

'You're a fine one to talk, Donald MacDougall,' Grandmama laughed.

'Have you forgotten how long it took you to tear me from the bosom of my family?'

'That has nought to do with it. . . .'

'Tell us, Grandmama,' Elinor begged.

'It is not relevant,' Donald persisted.

His wife looked him squarely in the eye as she replied, 'Two weeks after he first had sight of me he was knocking on my father's study door, and within three months we were married.'

'This is the everlasting problem of falling in love with such extraordinarily beautiful women,' Benjamin remarked. 'You have to act fast before they are snatched away from under your nose.'

'True,' the laird agreed. 'Or you could say that if you canna act when your interest is raised, when will you?'

Alexandra clicked her tongue in feigned irritation, but the love she had felt for the huge MacDougall nearly fifty years before still shone in her eyes as she returned his gaze.


It seemed unlikely that all the cases and band-boxes could possibly be accommodated on the staff carriage. Malcolm and two groomsmen wrestled with the problem while the maids supervised, becoming quite angry when a carefully packed trunk of gowns, all neatly arranged with tissue-paper between each fold, was turned on its side so that it might better fit the space available. When the last item was secured the maids and Roderick's valet climbed aboard. John returned to the house to inform the young people that their carriages were ready, and soon their happy chatter preceded them to the front steps.

Ruth's coat was pale blue, richly trimmed with grey fur, and with it she wore a matching, fur-trimmed hat. Janthina's coat was jade green, like her hat, both trimmed with bands of deep golden fur. Elinor's brown coat was edged with braid and her hat had cream and brown material ruched around the brim. But Roderick outshone them all. His coat and trousers were pale grey worn with a red waistcoat which matched the lining of his pale grey cloak, and his pale grey hat had the tall crown and curling brim currently favoured by the King. The older members of the party had declined the invitation, excepting the fun-loving Aunt Laura, who was delighted to accept the role of chaperone to the Glenfalk ladies attending the house party at Farthingales. She was assisted into the carriage, nearly losing her elaborate hat bedecked with tall pheasant-feathers and wings, and arranged her pink coat with its several layers of capes to avoid unnecessary crushing.

73

Unlike Glenfalk, Farthingales bore no resemblance to a castle. Built as a country seat years before, it had been enlarged and embellished to present an imposing picture among ancient trees and formally laid gardens. The drive from the public road was over a mile long, winding through a valley, around a lake, and climbing to the mansion on its low hilltop.

The visitors from Glenfalk were assisted from their carriage by a liveried major domo and footmen, while the staff carriages were sent to the rear of the building where the luggage and staff could be conveyed to their places via the servants' stairs. Wide, shallow steps led up under the huge, pillared portico into an immense marble foyer.

Their hosts were an English family named Monkford whom the Canadian girls had met on New Year's Eve and who now swept Aunt Laura, Elinor and Roderick into enthusiastic embraces before turning their attention to Ruth and Janthina. The Honourable John Monkford and his wife were both short, round, jolly people like their son Geoffrey, who, with his much taller wife, Helen, joined in the welcome.

'Elinor!' a voice shrieked, and Maisie Monkford bounced down the marble staircase to hug her best friend. 'I am so glad it didn't snow again. I was so afraid you might be unable to cross the moors.' Politely the plump girl greeted the other new arrivals then turned back to her friend. 'I've had another bed put in my room for you so we may share. It will be such fun, there is so much to talk about. Shall we go up?'

Roderick was led away by Geoffrey, and Helen took charge of Aunt Laura and the girls. 'We have three single bedrooms for you, two are adjacent in the west wing, and the other is in the east, rather a long way apart, I'm afraid.'

Knowing that Benjamin was amongst the guests, Aunt Laura decided to take the room next to Ruth, lest young love encourage indiscretion, leaving Janthina, with her unattached heart, to be led away to the east wing. The room was very small in comparison with those at Glenfalk. Having removed her hat and coat and freshened her face and hair, Janthina left Mary unpacking her boxes and wandered along to find Ruth, whose room was even smaller than her own.

'I suppose they prefer to have lots of little rooms to accommodate more people at their house parties,' Ruth suggested.

'Never mind, I doubt we will spend much time in them other than asleep,' Janthina replied, but judging by the tongue-clicking and heavy sighs Polly did not agree.

'It's too early to change yet, so I'll just fix my hair and we can go along to the upstairs sitting room and see who has arrived. Helen Monkford said tea would be served there.'

'What you really mean is that you cannot wait another minute to see your Benjamin!'

'Oh! You are a tease. Just wait until you have a beau, then it will be my turn to rib you.'

So Ruth had no idea about her growing affection for Anthony. Was this because her sister was totally blind to everything save her world with Benjamin, or due to her own discretion, Janthina wondered.

At a table laid with sandwiches, hot scones, cakes and a silver tea service, Mrs Monkford was pouring tea. 'Do help yourselves to anything you wish, my dears, then Helen will introduce you to the others.'

Ruth and Janthina were both several inches taller than Helen, but the fact didn't seem to bother her as, hand under an elbow of each, she steered them from group to group, making introductions wherever necessary. There was no sign of either Benjamin or Anthony; in fact, young men were conspicuously absent.

'Sorry I can't present the young blades to you at the moment,' Helen explained. 'They're all in the billiards room drinking beer. Afraid you'll have to wait till later.' And though the girls were disappointed at the extended wait they both sighed with relief to know that at least their beaux had probably arrived.


'So you've been avoiding me, have you?' Ruth chided two hours later, when, changed and re-coiffed, the girls came downstairs and were joined by Benjamin. 'I understand beer was available in the billiards room.'

Benjamin looked at her anxiously, detected the teasing laughter in her eyes, and relaxed. 'I do apologise, but as nearly all the men seemed to be gathered there while the ladies were upstairs, I was reluctant to invade the feminine precincts alone. Am I forgiven?'

Ruth slid her hand under his arm and squeezed. 'Only if you promise to be good from now on.'

Janthina stood by, feeling totally excluded from the tight circle of their love, until Maisie Monkford bounced up, followed by Elinor.

'Your cousin tells me you are an enthusiastic horsewoman. Would you like to join us tomorrow morning? We plan to ride down through the valley and on up to Ben Torrie. I could arrange a very nice mount for you.'

'Er . . . yes. Thank you. Lovely. You're so kind,' she murmured, hardly conscious of her words, her eyes darting from doors to staircase, watching, waiting. . . .

Elinor stared at her for a moment, then shrugged. 'Maisie, have you seen anything of the Boltons this season?' And the friends drifted away to chat with mutual acquaintances.

Then she saw him. His eyes lit on her for a moment, then turned away, even as he moved casually towards her. 'Hallo!' he said at last in mock surprise. 'Fancy seeing you here!'

He was teasing her. Their eyes sparkled with pleasure as he took two glasses from the tray of a passing footman and they drank a silent toast to each other.

Janthina danced with several young men before Anthony claimed her for supper. They sat with Ruth and Ben but conversation was rather stilted as the two men had little to say to one another.

'Don't you like Ben?' Janthina asked when they returned to the ballroom.

'Very nice fellow, I'm sure,' he murmured. 'But I can't say I find these Army people easy conversationally. They always seem so stiff and pompous. Kirkpatrick is a lucky chap, your sister is very beautiful. Not my type, though,' he added hastily, 'and not nearly as beautiful as her sister.' His arm tightened round her waist as he spun her round to the rhythm of a waltz. 'What are you doing tomorrow?'

'Maisie and Elinor have asked me to ride with them in the morning. What are you doing?' She rather regretted her commitment, wishing she had waited till she saw him before making any plans.

'Nothing. I shall lie in bed dreaming of you until luncheon. However, I shall expect an hour of your time during the afternoon. Hm?'

Janthina laughed as they whirled faster and faster until the orchestra finished with a grand crescendo.

That night she lay in the darkness hugging her pillow, enjoying the warmth pressed against her nightgown.


After luncheon next day they agreed to go out walking and, in hats, coats, gloves and scarves, Anthony led her through lovely walks bordered by huge, moss-covered rocks and clumps of fern to a steep track. Here the heels of her boots caught in the loose stones and she panted for breath against her tight corset, but Anthony continued to tow her along by the hand until they emerged onto a rocky spur with the countryside laid out before them in a vast panorama.

'Oh, isn't it beautiful,' she gasped, sinking on to a stone slab. 'This is the best picture I have yet had of Scotland. Look, you can see whole villages down there, clustered about their churches; herds of cattle; flocks of sheep.'

'Rather like playing God, being up here, isn't it? One almost feels one could direct all those lives down there.'

She looked at him. 'I suppose you will have that sort of power, one day, down in Hampshire, or at Conweir, once you are an earl.'

He paused before replying. 'Hmmm. Never thought of it like that before. An awful responsibility.'

'Do you think so?'

'Yes. I rather dread it. It's bad enough now, just being heir.'

'In what way?'

'Can't do this; have to do that. All the decisions about my life are made around what is right for the earldom, the estate and the image. Father takes it all very seriously, quite rightly, no doubt. Reaction, I suppose. My old grandfather rather let things go to pot. He was a bit of a lad, known for his slow horses and fast women.' He sighed, then suddenly turned and smiled. 'Never mind about all that, let's only talk about us. I know so little about you. Tell me – everything.' He sat beside her and held her hand.

'Where do I begin? What do you want to know?' She felt the warmth of his fingers through her gloves, and the view was forgotten.

They talked, comparing notes on their homes, countries, parents, friends and interests.

'You say you love to sketch and paint,' he exclaimed with excitement. 'So do I.'

'Oh, I'd love to see some of your pictures.'

'I'd be embarrassed. I'm not very good.'

'Nor am I.' She swayed towards him, laughing, and all at once was in his arms.

'Janthina,' he whispered. 'Dearest Janthina. I miss you so terribly when we're apart, dream of you all the time. Do you ever think of me?'

'Constantly,' she admitted, spellbound by the adoration in his eyes.

'Janthina, darling, I'm afraid I have fallen terribly in love with you.'

She continued to gaze at him for a few moments, nodding dumbly, then closed her eyes as his kisses sent shivers of excitement right down her legs to her toes.

He pulled away. 'I'm a selfish brute. You're shivering, frozen. Come, we must get back before you take a chill.'


She had to tell Ruth. Bursting with excitement she raced along the corridor of the west wing to Ruth's room, but only Polly was there, laying out her mistress's clothes for the evening.

'No, miss, I'm sorry, I haven't seen Miss Ruth since luncheon,' the girl told her.

Never mind. She must be in one of the salons, she thought, and hurried to her room where Mary was waiting to help her out of her coat and boots.

'Will you have your bath now, miss?' the girl asked.

'No. Just fix my hair a little, I want to speak to my sister,' and she hummed a lively reel, hardly able to sit still while the stray wisps were brushed back and pinned into place. Love, love, love. So what did this mean? Would they, too, get married this year?

But that would mean not returning to Canada. Well, as long as she was with Anthony she supposed it wouldn't matter where she was. . . .

'Thank you, Mary, that's fine.' She jumped up from the dressing stool and skipped to the door. 'I won't be long,' she called over her shoulder.

Ruth was wedged on a sofa between Benjamin and Aunt Laura, surrounded by chattering friends sipping tea and nibbling tiny iced cakes. It was impossible to get near her, let alone speak privately. Janthina accepted a cup and a cake, perching herself on a stool to await her opportunity. But it never came. Several times she tried to catch Ruth's eye to signal her to break away, but someone always got in the way or claimed her sister's attention, and in the end she gave up trying, knowing she had to get changed in time to meet Anthony again.


'We obviously make a magic team,' Anthony gloated as they walked off with yet another prize for a party quiz game.

'We'll have to handicap you two if you go on like this,' Maisie laughed. 'Afraid we weren't expecting eggheads and blue stockings when we compiled the questions.'

'Come on, Maisie, we're not even trying yet,' Anthony teased back. He turned to his partner and said quietly, 'Shall we give the others a chance? Let's wander off and find a corner for ourselves.'

Janthina tucked her pencil into her reticule. 'Good idea. Where shall we go?'

He held her elbow to steer her across the foyer into another salon where a footman approached them with a tray of glasses and a bottle of champagne. They accepted a glass each.

'To us!' Anthony toasted, clinking his glass against hers.

'To us,' she smiled.

He looked around the salon. 'Let's sit over there,' and led her to a pair of satin brocade Louis Quinze chairs in a corner. 'It's so difficult to find anywhere to talk privately. I just don't want to share you with anyone.'

They discussed horses and the characteristics in different breeds; the difficulties involved in painting wild birds and animals; oils versus water colours.

'Ah! There you are! I thought I'd lost you. Are you enjoying yourselves?' Aunt Laura approached arm in arm with Mrs Monkford.

'Anthony, dear,' gushed the latter. 'I see you are looking after Janthina. How sweet of you.' She turned to her friend. 'So many of the young men drift off to the billiards room or the card tables leaving the girls alone to amuse themselves. Most unfair. Have fun,' she ordered. 'We'll see you later.' And the two women moved away to talk to a group on the other side of the room.

'Whew! For a moment I thought they were going to join us,' Janthina gasped.

'No, thank heavens. But tell me, why is your aunt here? Rather older than the average guest, isn't she?'

'Yes, she is. Actually, she came to chaperone us three girls, and of course the Monkfords are old friends of hers.'

'Chaperone? I didn't think you had one. Not been much in evidence, has she?'

'I don't think she takes the responsibility very seriously. She knows we can all look after ourselves without her help.'

'At last!' Strains of a polka reached them and Anthony jumped to his feet. 'Now we can dance. Come on, Janthina.' He took her hand to assist her but she was already on her feet. They bounced around the ballroom with gusto, there being so few other dancers that they had vast areas of floor to themselves.

'I can't imagine how we will ever get a chance to be alone together,' Anthony complained. 'The weather is far too cold to stay out of doors long and there doesn't seem to be any privacy indoors, anywhere.'

'I know. The only time I've been alone since arriving has been in my bedroom, and then only when I've dismissed my maid,' Janthina panted, unthinkingly.

Anthony stared at her. 'I'm not even sure of that much privacy. My room is next to Fothergill's, and he keeps bounding in through our adjoining door to borrow things.'

She was returning his stare. Obviously they had both had the same thought, and both knew it. Oh, how badly she wanted to ask him to her room so that they could have a little while alone, but it was far too improper to suggest. Their eyes remained locked a moment longer, then she dropped her gaze and flushed.

79

When the dance finished they deliberately separated, sought other partners. Janthina ate with Elinor and Maisie, half-heartedly listening to hunting stories and the comparative successes of various meets. Once, later, she was obliged to dance with a veritable popinjay. His head scarcely reached her shoulder and she was afraid he would leave his macassar oil on her dress as he clutched her close, eyes riveted on her low-cut bodice. He danced extremely well, however, and but for his pushiness and hair oil she might have enjoyed being so expertly whirled about, skirt and train flying. Strange, she thought, how some people matched so perfectly, like Anthony and herself, whilst others did not. She could not imagine herself ever wanting to be kissed by a man like this. She turned her head away, quickly, as he gazed up at her, fearing he might read her mind and not wishing to offend him.

She didn't see Anthony again to wish him goodnight before going up to bed. Mary was waiting as usual to help her out of her gown and corset. She watched in the long mirror, pleased that despite all the rich food she had eaten in the past three months, the only weight she had gained was in her bosom, and if anything, her corset could be laced tighter now than when she had arrived in Scotland. Funny to think that before then she had never worn one. She wondered if Mama did. But then Mama was so thin. . . . Poor Mama. How was she managing without them? How would she manage if both her daughters married in Scotland and never returned to live at home?

Lying in the darkness, listening to the last of the revellers pass her door to their respective rooms, she thought about Anthony and his declared love for her.

And hers for him. She wished she had had a chance to ask Ruth how long it had been from the moment Ben avowed his love for her before he actually proposed. Days? Weeks? How long would she have to wait for Anthony's proposal? Dear, darling Anthony. Soon those wonderful, loving eyes, the wide soft mouth with the beautiful white, even teeth, those gentle hands, would be exclusively hers. She presumed they were now, but still dreamed of being married and having him to herself every day. She hugged herself with excitement. And added to this she would be a countess! That would surely show Papa she was not so worthless as he had always made out. He would no longer be able to criticise her, even if he had the voice to do it. She could see him at the church door, the congregation clustered round him asking after his daughter, the Countess of Frey. My, how grand it sounded. Poor Papa! He might never be able to reply. Memories of the scenes leading up to his stroke clouded her mind, briefly, but she pushed them away.

Perhaps, she speculated, returning to happier thoughts, she and Ruth might even have a double wedding – no, no, that would detract from the great day for both of them. No, she and Anthony would wait until Ruth and Ben returned from their honeymoon for their ceremony, then Ruth could be her matron-of-honour. She hugged herself again and giggled into her pillow. After all, he hadn't even proposed yet.

The exciting thoughts chasing through her mind kept her awake for ages and the house was very still and quiet, but for the flurries of rain on her windows, before she began to slip into smiling dreams. They were riding together, she and Anthony, along the river near the farm in Canada; her hair was loose, streaming behind her as Pickle cantered ahead along the grass bank. Anthony chased after her; she could hear him call her name, heard his horse's hooves pounding up behind . . . but the hoofbeats were irregular, started and stopped, started and stopped.

She sat up in bed with a jolt . . . and heard it again. But it wasn't hoofbeats at all, there was someone knocking on her door. Who on earth . . .? The unfinished conversation she had had with Anthony while they were dancing the polka came back to her. Was it him? Her heart pounded with the thought, then pounded even harder with fear that it might not be. It could be a burglar! No, that was ridiculous: a burglar surely wouldn't knock. The soft tapping came again. Mouth dry, she slid her feet to the floor and felt her way through the darkness to the door.

'Who is it?' she asked in a loud whisper.

'Me, my love, can I come in?' Definitely Anthony's voice.

She gasped with relief and turned the handle. 'Heavens, you frightened me. I thought you might be a burglar.'

He closed the door quietly and took her in his arms. 'Silly goose. After we had both discussed the lack of privacy in this house and you said . . . well, that your room was the only place, I rather thought you might be expecting me.'

'I did think it might be you . . . oh,' she shivered. 'Let's get away from the door; the draught coming underneath from the corridor is icy.'

'Hop back into bed and keep warm.'

'What about you? Aren't you cold? Why don't you lie under the quilt.'

'Can't we have some light?'

'Better not. Mary might see it and think I'm ill.' She snuggled down between the sheets and felt him climb onto the bed beside her, on top of the blankets, drawing the quilt over himself. Then they turned

81

towards each other, both heads on her pillow. Their noses touched and then he was kissing her again. His arm slid under her neck and he drew her against him, his other hand caressing her face, ears, neck.

'My darling,' he whispered. 'How I wish I could see you. You are the most beautiful creature I have ever known in my whole life,' and his moist lips returned to their task.

The sensations she had felt when he had kissed her on the three previous occasions were nothing compared to the fire which raced through her now. She clung to him, ran her fingers through the golden curls on the back of his neck, pressed herself against him so that she could feel his body, from top to toe, through the blankets. And when his hand slipped through the neck of her nightdress to cup her breast she gasped at the delicious reaction she felt between her legs and pressed even closer to him.

'Oh, Jan, my darling Jan. My sweet, dearest love. I don't think I can stop,' he panted between kisses.

Stop? Why stop? Why shouldn't he kiss her passionately, even touch her breast? After all, she was his as he was hers. They were in love and would marry.

'My dearest Anthony, I love you so much,' she whispered and sought his mouth again. Nor did she resist as, without breaking their kiss, he pulled down the blankets and top sheet and worked his feet over the top to slide down beside her. Now she could really feel him against her, thrilled again as she rolled onto her back and felt the weight of his chest crush down on hers.

'Jan, sweetheart, I shouldn't . . . I mustn't . . . but I cannot stop myself,' he moaned, his hand straying down over her leg, drawing up her nightdress.

'I don't think I could, either, even if I wanted to,' she answered. Her body was burning, frantic for . . . more kisses? Then she felt his fingers probe through her hair, down there, and blushed in the darkness. What was he doing? He shouldn't. . . .

His hand withdrew. 'Jan, have you any idea what is happening?' His voice was thick as though his tongue was swollen.

'Of course, my darling. We are loving, kissing. You are touching me . . . ahh!' She gasped as his fingers returned, stroking up and down, causing her back to arch involuntarily as a million sensations rippled through her body, making her feel quite faint.

Gently he pushed her legs apart and moved over her. 'Jan,' he paused, gulping, 'I'm so afraid of hurting you.'

'Darling, it doesn't matter. Just don't stop,' and she clasped her arms across his back, drawing him down. 'Oooh!' she gasped as something large and hard forced its way through the hair in her groin.

'Jan, I'm sorry, but I can't stop. . . .'

She lifted her body to meet his, gasped again at the pain, yet pressed up again, up and up, as unable to stop as he. He was inside her, stretching her, moving back and forth. Painful but glorious. Their bodies thumped rhythmically, faster and faster; sore, so sore, but . . . the soreness eased as a warm flood filled her, soothing, comforting. The hard tightness inside her softened and they lay panting until he rolled away, leaving his head nestled between her breasts.

She cradled him gently, nuzzling into his blond curls, floating on waves of happy contentment. And for the first time in her life she was aware of the full meaning of the term 'making love'. Nagging little doubts scratched away at the edges of her mind, but she pushed them aside.

Anthony sat up.

She knew he was tense, withdrawing. 'What's the matter?' she murmured sleepily.

'I should never have come to your room.' He was rocking to and fro, hugging his knees.

'Why not?'

'Because I love you too much. I couldn't stop myself.'

'I didn't want you to stop.'

'But you were a virgin. Did you know what was going to happen?'

'Well . . . no. I mean. . . .' She felt herself blushing again in the darkness, hating her ignorance. 'I did grow up on a farm, so I couldn't help but know . . . well . . . what cattle and pigs do. . . .'

'But you didn't know that that was what we might do, would do, if I came in your bed,' he moaned.

'No. But don't be upset, dearest Anthony.' She reached out to touch him. 'I love you so and I wanted you to go on and on.' She sighed. 'It was so wonderful; just a pity it has to hurt so much.'

'It won't, again.'

'Why? Aren't we going to do it again?'

'Oh, Jan! Don't you know what being a virgin means?'

'No,' she admitted.

'Er . . . well, you'll have to ask your sister. But for heaven's sake don't tell her what we've done.'

'I doubt if she knows what it means, either. We've always talked about . . . everything. She would've told me if she'd known. You tell me.'

He rocked in silence for a few minutes, then said, 'You were born with something across there, a sort of skin. When you make love for the first time it is broken. That's what hurts.'

'Oh! And doesn't it heal up again?'

Suddenly he caught her in his arms again. 'Janthina! My dearest, sweet, innocent darling. No, it never heals back as it was. Once it is gone it is gone forever. Oh, I do love you.' He wriggled back down the bed again.

Later he sat up. 'Jan, promise you won't tell Ruth or anyone about us. Please.'

'Not that we have done . . . made love, no. But will you mind if Ruth knows that we love each other?'

'Yes. I think it better to keep it a secret.'

She was disappointed. 'For how long?'

'I don't know. We'll see.' He slid out of bed. 'I must get back to my room, now.' He leaned over the bed, reaching for a last kiss. 'Goodnight, sweetheart. Sleep well.'

'Goodnight, darling Anthony,' she whispered back.

# 4

THE FAMILY were in the Great Hall, entertaining the Reverend
Cameron and his son James, when the party returned from Farthingales.

'Did you enjoy yourself, my dear?' asked Grandmama as Janthina
bent to kiss her. 'My goodness, your face and hands are frozen. Come
and sit by the fire and tell me all about it.'

'Good afternoon, Miss McKenzie, welcome home.' James Cameron
crossed the room to shake her hand. 'I've not had the opportunity yet,
to offer you my good wishes for the New Year. I hope it will be a very
happy one for you.'

Janthina allowed her arm to be pumped up and down. 'Thank you,
Mr Cameron. I am quite sure it will be,' she replied, trying to disengage
her hand.

But he clung on. 'I hear you've been over at Farthingales for a few
days. Magnificent place they have there, I'm told.'

'Yes, yes, huge.' At last she was able to pull away from his clasp
and turned back to her grandmother. 'The Honourable John and Mrs
Monkford were most insistent that we remember to give you their
regards and good wishes.'

Alexandra MacDougall smiled. 'And I hope you remembered to give
them ours when you arrived. Tell me, was the weather good while
you were there?'

'I doubt you had a drop of rain,' James Cameron cut in again. 'It
really is quite mild for the time of year.'

'Did you go out riding at all?' Grandmama was now pointedly ignoring
him.

'Yes, Maisie Monkford took Elinor and me through the valley up to
Ben Torrie. . . .'

'Grand view from up there I should imagine, though you really canna
beat the view from. . . .'

'Come, James, we must not take up any more of these good people's
time,' the minister said, moments before his hostess lost her patience
with his son. Instead she quickly tugged the bell rope to summon John
to show the visitors out.

'Well, really!' she exploded when the door eventually closed after long and over-polite farewells. 'That young man is dreadfully forward. And that's the second time he has called in two weeks.'

'I think he has taken a shine to Janthina,' Elinor remarked.

'Nonsense,' growled her grandfather. 'He's just trying to be friendly.'

'Too friendly, Donald. He persistently interrupted our conversation.' Sitting in her straight-backed chair, head high and long earrings swinging, Grandmama could look very autocratic.

'Hmm. Well, I doubt we'll be seeing much more of him. He hopes to be taking up a position in some store in Edinburgh, soon. Determined to make something of himself, you know, and I think he'll succeed. I hope so; I admire his drive. Now, supposing we all go up and get ourselves changed for dinner, then we can hear about Farthingales over a wee dram before we eat.'

Ruth waited for Janthina to catch her up on the stairs. 'It seems ages since we had a chance to talk alone, Jan. Will you come to my room as soon as you're dressed, and if I'm ready first I'll come to you?'

'Er, yes, lovely. See you soon.' Janthina hoped her sister didn't notice her hesitation; the fact was she no longer wanted to exchange confidences.

Mary had the bath filled and waiting. Lying back, soaking, Janthina couldn't stop smiling to herself, remembering every little detail of the love-making. Rain had persisted throughout the Sunday at Farthingales, proving that James Cameron didn't know what he was talking about. Dutifully, she had listened to Roderick's poetry before luncheon, joined with other guests in the darkened music room for a lantern slide show in the afternoon, dressed for dinner and taken part in the evening activities, impatient for the end of the day, hoping he would return to her room that night. Anthony had pointedly avoided her most of the day, so that although they had exchanged secret glances, she had no way of knowing if he would come . . . until, long after midnight, she heard a faint tapping at her door.

They had made love and it was even more beautiful than the first time. She had asked Mary to leave her a tiny wax nightlight and by its glow they had shyly removed their clothes then lain side by side on the bed glorying in each other's bodies. He stayed most of the night, sleeping while she watched him, loving him so. When he awoke they made love again, and he crept away just before dawn.

They had spent last night together as well, and as they would not be seeing each other again for two or three weeks she had hoped he would propose. Again and again he repeated his love for her, made love to her till they were both so exhausted they fell asleep just before light. Maids could be heard scurrying about downstairs when they finally woke up, and he had hurried away in alarm; which was possibly why he forgot and never mentioned marriage.

'That water must be getting cold, miss,' Mary called from the other side of the screen.

It was – and her fingers and toes were all white and wrinkled.

Mary was still pinning her hair when Ruth came in, so the sisters only talked about hairstyles and clothes until Janthina's toilette was completed.

'That will be all for the present, thank you, Mary. You may leave the bath water until I go down.'

'Yes, miss.' The maid bobbed and left the room.

'Oh, Jan, I'm so happy!' Ruth squealed and hugged her sister for joy. 'It was so wonderful to be under the same roof with Ben for days on end.'

Janthina eyed her quizzically. 'What was so special about it?'

'Why, the opportunity to spend all day, every day, together of course.'

'Of course. It must have been wonderful to see so much of each other, talk together . . . kiss a lot.'

Ruth grinned. 'Yes, a lot.'

'When did you get the chance, though, with so many people around? I mean, I never saw you kissing.'

'We went for several walks, and then occasionally we found ourselves alone in a room.'

'I would have thought the only place you would have found any privacy was in your bedroom,' Janthina observed, carefully arranging the lace ruffles on her bodice.

'Heavens! Nothing would persuade him in there.'

'Why?'

'Oh, Benjamin is terribly proper, much more so than I would be, I think.'

'Do you mean he only kisses you occasionally?'

'Yes.'

'And that's all?'

'Well, we embrace a little, but as soon as we start to warm up he breaks off and says, "That's enough of that until after we are married." '

'I wonder why?'

'As a matter of fact I asked him once. Rather bold of me, I'm afraid. He said he didn't want to go on till it became too difficult not to go all the way. I asked him what that meant, and he blushed and changed the subject.'

87

'Oh! Well, do you think it might be anything to do with what the cows and bulls and the sows and hogs used to do on the farm?'

Ruth looked at her younger sister very seriously for a moment then burst into fits of giggles. 'Jan! You are a scream. I suppose it may be something like that in a way, though not too similar, I hope. I can't honestly imagine how it could be managed, can you?'

Janthina was bent over, busily rearranging a perfectly tidy drawer of hairbrushes, when she replied, 'No, I've no idea,' in an off-hand tone of voice. She was more positive now than ever, that Ruth must not find out that she and Anthony had known one another intimately.

'What I really wanted to talk to you about is Ben's family and all the arrangements we'll have to make for the wedding. The trouble is that being so proper, Ben refuses to discuss details until Grandpapa receives a letter of approval of our engagement from Mama and Papa.' She sighed. 'It's so difficult not to think about things like a wedding dress and the cake and who should be invited and I'm just bursting to talk with somebody about it all.'

'Naturally you are,' Janthina sympathised, and willingly allowed herself to be drawn into the safer topic.


The letter, penned in Mama's stiff hand with long, even loops on the ells, gees, and effs, arrived with heavy snow in mid-February. It was the last postbag that Malcolm was able to collect before hedge-high drifts made the roads impassable, bringing all social events to a temporary halt. Not that either of the Canadian girls was much bothered by the latter; Benjamin had returned to Aldershot with his regiment, and Anthony to London with his family. The long-awaited reply giving absolute approval not only of the betrothal but also of the plans to have the wedding in May, gave rise to such a degree of revitalised activity, discussion and excitement as to relieve any chance of boredom whilst they were snowbound.

Much to Grandmama's delight, Mama had given her carte blanche to proceed with whatever wedding arrangements she wished and with which she herself would assist as soon as she arrived in late April. She had already spoken with Mrs Callaghan, who had agreed to cook and care for Papa and Joseph in her absence. So the ladies of the household threw themselves wholeheartedly into the planning and listing of wedding guests, trousseau, presents, tasks to be tackled and deciding who should make the gowns for the bride and her attendants. Ruth's going-away outfit had to be chosen, and accommodation provided for those whose homes were too far distant to allow them to return on the same day from the reception. Thus the men of Glenfalk were left very much to their own devices.

When the snow thawed sufficiently to allow post through again, a letter arrived for Janthina from Anthony. Heart pounding, she hurried away with it to her room.

'I miss you so terribly,' he wrote, 'and have convinced my father that I should supervise some work at Castle Conweir chiefly that we might be able to meet. Could you find an excuse to visit Perth, unaccompanied, during the second week of March? I would meet you there. Address your reply to me at Castle Conweir, if possible giving a date and time. Every minute we are apart I die a little. I long to hold you in my arms again. All my love for ever, Anthony.'

It was not until she had read it three times that she realised he was referring to next week! She must make some plans, quickly . . . but how? What excuses? Her sleep was short and restless that night, the problem looming larger and more impossible, until she finally appeared at breakfast with deep shadows under her eyes.

'Are you sure you are feeling quite well, miss?' Mary had asked as she tied the laces on her corset.

'Yes, yes, don't fuss,' she had snapped back, quite out of sorts and out of character.

'You don't look very bright this morning, dear,' Aunt Meg observed from the breakfast table.

'I didn't sleep very well, that's all,' Janthina mumbled.

It was Aunt Laura who saved the day. 'Have you thought about your present to Ruth and Benjamin yet, dear?' she asked.

The golden opportunity. 'Yes,' Janthina nodded, her eye on the door lest Ruth appear and overhear. 'I have two or three ideas. What I would really like is a day to myself in Perth to follow them up.'

'Why not? You can get Malcolm to take you down as soon as the snow has thawed sufficiently for the carriage to pass safely.'

'It seems a shame to keep Malcolm waiting around all day for me.' It wouldn't serve her purpose at all having him waiting about, observing, and possibly reporting back on, her every move.

'Don't worry about that, dear girl. After being out of communication for so long we will all have lists of errands for him and Cook tells me she has a list of purchases required to re-stock the larder.'

'Splendid. And how long do you think it will be before the road is usable?'

Uncle Andrew looked up from his fried sausages. 'By the weekend, I should say. You'll certainly get down by Monday or Tuesday.'

Ruth hurried in at that moment. 'Oh, dear, I am late this morning.

It was ages before my brain would stop making unnecessary lists last night, and consequently once I did get to sleep I couldn't wake up.' She helped herself to porridge from the sideboard and sat next to her sister, giving her a happy, loving, intimate smile. 'Good morning, Jan.'

'Good morning, Ruthie.' Janthina smiled back . . . and wondered why she suddenly felt so guilty. She hated to have a secret from Ruth; hated not being able to tell her what had happened; hated not being able to confide her plans for going to Perth to meet Anthony. She felt miserable inside, when she should have felt so happy . . . and this made her angry. She tried to swallow another spoonful of porridge; it was thick and lumpy. 'Ugh! I'm afraid I'm not very hungry this morning. I think I'll go back to my room for a while. I want to write a letter to Mama before Malcolm goes down for the post.'

Ruth was busily chatting to her aunts as Janthina left the room.

'My darling Anthony, your letter arrived yesterday. Unless there is more snow I should be at the Perth Family Emporium by eleven o'clock on Tuesday morning. I am so longing to see you again and miss you dreadfully. All my love dearest, Janthina.' The note was tucked into the envelope and set aside while she tackled her letter to Mama.

Days dragged by, and the weekend seemed a million years away. Riding was impossible without risking a snapped leg on the ice. She read a little, did some sketching, listened to reams of poetry from Roderick and had Mary try a number of different styles with her hair. Because of her guilty feelings she avoided Ruth's company and therefore was not involved in the current wedding discussions.

Fortunately, Uncle Andrew's forecast was correct. Tuesday was a bright, sunny day, the roads wet with the remnants of thawing slush, snow only evident in the remains of drifts against hedges and walls. Excited anticipation had pushed all feelings of guilt aside as she sat in her most charming outfit, bowling down the country lanes, trying, desperately, to concentrate on what she could possibly bring home as a present for Ruth. Glass and china would surely be smashed in her travels with Ben. Bulky things would have to be left in storage in England, possible for years. Jewellery? Excellent if she could only afford something nice for each of them, but with her sadly depleted pin money. . . .

Malcolm drew up beside the Family Emporium at ten minutes past eleven.

'What is the latest time we can leave for home?' Janthina asked as he handed her from the carriage.

'Not too late, miss. Even if we leave at three thirty it is going to be dark before we're at Glenfalk.'

'Oh, dear! That doesn't give me much time.' She sighed and looked about her. There was no sign of Anthony. 'Well, can we say three thirty?'

For a moment Malcolm looked as though he wanted to argue for an earlier time, then he shrugged. 'Very well, miss,' and climbed back into his seat while Janthina hurried into the store.

Anthony was casting a critical eye over some riding boots, and turned in feigned surprise. 'Why, Miss McKenzie! What brings you to Perth?' he asked, for the benefit of the assistant.

'Shopping, my lord,' she replied. 'My sister is soon to be married, and I wish to purchase a gift for the happy couple. Perhaps you could assist me with some suggestions.'

'Indeed.' He left the boots and took her arm. 'There is only one gift, in my opinion, which is always acceptable and which people can take with them wherever they go.' He opened the door and held it for her to step onto the pavement. 'I'll show you.' Fifty yards down the street he paused in front of a small shop window. Displayed inside were a grandfather clock, wall clocks, mantel clocks, brass, wood and marble clocks, plain and fancy. 'Look.' He pointed at a small brass carriage clock. 'Isn't that perfect?'

It was. Standing no more than six inches high, the glass panels at front and sides were set in a rectangular box frame of brass with brass ball feet and a handle on the brass top. The face was white enamel with neat black Roman numerals. Behind it stood the red, velvet-lined case into which it obviously fitted.

'Anthony, it looks lovely! I'd love to buy it for them, but it may be far too expensive.'

'Never mind. If it is, I'll contribute towards it and it will be from both of us. Though you mustn't tell her yet.'

The clock was far more expensive than she had imagined, but Anthony swept aside her protests and paid for it. 'Please ensure that the movement is in first-class order and the timing well tested before we collect it,' he instructed the elderly shopkeeper. And in no time they were hurrying along the pavement again.

'I'll be expected to bring home my purchases,' Janthina puffed, trying to keep up with him. 'What can I say when I arrive home empty-handed?'

'That you're delighted with the result of your day's shopping and will have to return to Perth to collect Ruth's present at the beginning of April. That's when I'll be back here and we can meet again.' He turned down a side street and stopped in front of a glass panelled door. 'Here we are.'

A small brass plate on an inner door declared, 'Brown's Hotel'.

Upstairs, Anthony drew a key from his pocket and opened Number 32 for Janthina to walk into the small bedroom.

'I hope you don't mind, darling. There seemed little point in spending hours dashing out to Conweir and back. I thought it better to take this room so we can be alone together for as long as possible,' he explained.

'Yes . . . I suppose you're right,' she agreed in some surprise, then she was in his arms and everything but the closeness of him went out of her mind.

Undressing was rather embarrassing; the curtains did little to keep out the light and Anthony had to help her with the laces of her corset. They made love, urgently, then lay side by side, caressing, whispering.

Some time later there was a knock on the door and Janthina shot up in bed, clutching the sheet across her chest. Anthony wrapped a large towel round his waist and opened the door to admit a waiter bearing a loaded tray. The man looked slyly at Janthina, a half grin on his face, accepted Anthony's tip without comment, and withdrew.

Janthina slipped into a petticoat and chemise to sit at the low table for luncheon. She was really too excited and happy to eat, chattering away with all the little bits of news about the wedding . . . yet waiting and wondering when Anthony was going to propose.

When they had finished all they wanted of the soup and sandwiches, they automatically drifted back to the bed and soon slow caresses quickened and they made love again.

'Anthony, Anthony.' She shook him awake. 'What is the time?'

'Uh?' he grunted. 'Time?' He reached for his pocket watch on the bedside table. 'A quarter past three. Quite early yet.'

'It isn't! Oh, dear. Quick, help me, I promised to meet Malcolm at the Family Emporium at three thirty.' She leapt off the bed and stepped into her petticoat while her lover turned over under the blankets, yawning. 'Please, darling. Help lace me up again into my corset.'

The buttons on her boots fought back, her hair would not obey her frantic fingers, and she knew her corset was far looser than when Mary had tied it that morning. Anthony was still wrapped only in a towel when she kissed him a hasty farewell and hurried out into the street where she ran as fast as her flapping skirts would allow until she saw Malcolm pacing the pavement. She slowed to a sedate walk and as she approached him her face was smiling and composed.

'I hope I'm not too late, Malcolm,' she said sweetly. 'I've had such a successful day. Took a long time choosing, but I finally bought my sister a most beautiful clock for a wedding present; from that dear little shop down there.' She pointed. 'I'll have to return next month to collect it when it has been thoroughly overhauled and tested. Now mind, don't tell a soul. If Polly gets to hear she may disclose my secret to my sister.'

'Don't worry, miss, I won't breathe a word. Now let's just tuck that rug well round you and we'll haste away.'


'I'm afraid you're not as slim as you were when you first came here, miss,' Mary panted as she tugged at the laces of Janthina's corset. 'And if I canna do better than this you'll not fit into your pale green tonight.'

'Then I'll just have to wear something else till the dress is let out or I lose some weight,' her mistress told her, irritably. 'But I cannot stand the corset any tighter. I have felt quite ill and short of breath these past few evenings, and I'm sure it's because you've done me up too tight.'

Mary looked at her in the mirror, opened her mouth as if to speak, and then closed it again. She tied the laces as they were and returned to the wardrobe, leaving Janthina to sink onto her dressing stool, eyes closed.

'Are you sure you're feeling all right, miss? You're very pale.' Mary studied her in some concern.

'I'm sure it's just the corset.' She eyed the wine velvet gown on Mary's arm. 'That should fit easily, it's quite loose.'

The fit wasn't as easy as she'd hoped, but at least the buttons did up without pulling the material too much.

Downstairs she was amazed to find James Cameron had called again. He greeted her enthusiastically then returned to his discourse, delivered to the assembled family, on the advantages of living in the great Scottish metropolis.

Ruth entered, paused at the sight of her sister's ill-disguised boredom while James Cameron held the floor, and tried to mask her amusement. Janthina looked up, caught her eye, and hastily looked away again, choking on the sudden laughter that bubbled into her throat.

'. . . in the best stores . . . Oh, I say, Miss McKenzie, are you all right?'

'Yes, I think so,' she nodded, still coughing. 'But if you will excuse me I'll run up to my room a moment.'

93

'I'll come with you.' Ruth took her cue and the two girls quickly left the room before fresh giggles overcame them.

At the top of the stairs Janthina said, 'Oops,' swayed, and slumped onto the ottoman.

'Whatever's the matter?' Ruth demanded.

'I don't know. I feel quite out of breath. I'm sure it's because Mary ties my corset too tightly. She tries to make me look as slim as you and I never was and never will be.' All at once she wanted to cry. She was desperately depressed, perhaps because of not seeing Anthony for weeks on end and also, perhaps, because he still had not proposed. It had been wonderful to see him in Perth, but an unpleasant feeling lurked in the back of her mind that there must be something wrong for them to be meeting only in secret now. Why couldn't he come to call at Glenfalk like Ben did? Why did he insist that no one should know?

Ruth was sitting beside her, a comforting arm round her shoulders. 'Darling Janty. Would you like to go and lie down for a little while? Just until adoring James leaves?'

'I think maybe I will.' Janthina nodded and leaned heavily on Ruth until she reached her door. 'You'd better go down and say I am just spraying my throat and will be down soon.'

'Very well. But if you decide you don't feel like coming down again I'll see something is brought up to you on a tray.' Ruth helped her on to the bed and pulled up the quilt.

'Just let me know when James Cameron leaves, will you? Then I'll come down again,' Janthina told her, her eyes closed.

Ruth tiptoed out of the room, but the younger girl was not asleep. She still wanted to cry, but still without knowing just why. It was such a pity that Anthony hadn't proposed yet. They too could be getting on with wedding plans. All those wonderful pictures of wedding gowns, from which Ruth had made her choice, had sent her into raptures. She knew exactly the style she wanted, in stiff, heavy white satin with a long train and fastened with a long line of satin buttons right up the back. The front of the skirt would be cut short to reveal a froth of lace underskirts. Ruth was going to wear Grandmama's veil so presumably she would be allowed to borrow it, too. She had seen it, an exquisite creation in hand-made lace, now turning to a slightly ivory tone with age. Ruth and Elinor would attend her, of course, but it would be nice to have one or two more. Perhaps it might be possible to have her cousins over from Kingston. They would love it, and be so pleased to attend Lady Janthina Mears, the future Countess of Frey.

94

She felt much better by the time Ruth returned, and was able to face dinner with the family quite happily.

However, twice during the following week she had dizzy spells, both times in her bedroom while Mary was with her. In fact, she had noticed Mary looking at her in an oddly anxious way several times lately and now, as she swayed against the bedpost, the maid caught her round the waist and helped her onto the bed.

'I don't know what is the matter with me,' Janthina frowned. 'I think I must have eaten something that disagreed with me. I feel quite nauseous.'

Mary stood looking down at her, face flushed and serious. 'Excuse me asking, miss, but aren't you very late with your . . . well, you know, your monthly?'

'Yes, very. Do you think this is something to do with it? Perhaps I'm slightly anaemic.'

Mary frowned. 'You didn't come on at all last month, did you?'

'No, I didn't. The excitement of all the parties, I expect.' She opened her eyes to smile up at Mary, then quickly sat up. 'Why, Mary,' she exlaimed, 'you're crying!'

'Oh, miss, I've been so worried about you, ever since we stayed at Farthingales,' the maid sobbed, pulling a hanky out from under her pinny and turning away to blow her nose.

'What is it, Mary? Tell me!' Janthina was off the bed and standing in front of the weeping girl, whose head didn't reach her shoulder.

'Oh, miss! Did you really not know what you were doing at Farthingales, with that Lord Mears?'

Janthina's turn to flush. 'What do you mean?'

'I was so worried when I came to make the bed and saw what you'd done, for fear of the consequences. And Polly knew I had something on my mind 'cause she kept badgering me to tell her. But I didn't. I've never said a word, I swear.'

'For God's sake, Mary, will you tell me what you mean!' She shook the maid's arm.

'I've suspected for some time that the worst had happened, and now I know I was right. Oh, miss. . . .' The girl grasped her young mistress's hand and looked up, her face streaming with tears. 'You're pregnant, miss. You're going to have a baby.'


She lay awake in the darkness, thinking, for ages. Pregnant. Mary seemed quite positive. There was the dizziness and the nausea, particularly when she smelt certain things like Grandpapa's cigar smoke, which she had so liked at first, as well as the fact that she had now missed two monthlies. And already her bosom had grown bigger and even her waistline, too. So she was actually carrying Anthony's child inside her; a little boy, perhaps, who would one day be the Earl of Frey! She couldn't see why Mary was so upset. Why, if anything, it was wonderful news. The only pity was that she wouldn't see Anthony again for another ten days, for the sooner he was told the better. They really would have to hurry up with their wedding plans.

All the family, except Roderick, noticed how much better she began to look and how much happier. She joined in all Ruth's wedding preparations with cheerful gusto, only wishing she could reveal the thrilling secret, but of course the baby's father would have to be told first. She still had bouts of nausea, usually in the evening though occasionally in the mornings, too, and Mary had advised against any strenuous riding. There was no way she could suddenly start riding a decorous side-saddle without Elinor raising comments and questions, so she simply feigned disinterest.

At last the day planned for their April meeting arrived, and once again Malcolm drove her down to Perth, to collect the carriage clock. Fortunately he had a number of errands in town and as the days were getting a little longer, he agreed to collect her a little later than last time for the return journey.

With the beautifully gift-wrapped clock safely in her tapestry bag, she strode down the street and took the turning to Brown's Hotel. Anthony was in the foyer.

It was a different room this time, somewhat smaller and on a higher floor.

'Three whole weeks! It seems like a lifetime,' he said, drawing her into his arms.

'Yes. And there is much to talk about,' she murmured, before his mouth covered hers.

'Did you fetch the clock?' he asked a few minutes later.

'Yes. It's in my bag.'

'Have you missed me?'

'Dreadfully. Brrr,' she shivered. 'It is cold in here.'

'Then the sooner we're in bed the better,' he whispered, and the deep blue eyes, smiling into hers, nearly melted her knees. 'Hallo! No corset today,' he commented, as they began to undress. 'Is that wise? Won't your maid notice?'

'It doesn't matter. She knows about us anyway.' She stepped out of her petticoats and let them lie in a heap on the floor.

'She what?' Anthony snapped. 'You promised that you wouldn't tell a soul.'

She saw his anger and she tilted her chin. 'I didn't,' she replied hotly. 'She has apparently known from the start, at Farthingales.'

'You mean she guessed and now you've admitted the fact, discussed it with her,' he accused.

She slipped between the sheets and sat up, pouting. 'Anthony! Don't, please. Come to bed and I'll tell you all about it in a minute.'

But within a minute they were making love and it was nearly half an hour later that he murmured, 'Well, tell me about your maid now,' from the cushion of her breasts.

She had rehearsed this moment over and over for ten days, yet suddenly she was lost for words.

'Must be serious,' he commented. 'Your heart is thumping like a steam engine.'

'Well, it's really very exciting, darling Anthony.' She paused to take a deep breath. 'You see, you are going to be a father.'

She felt his body become rigid, knew he was holding his breath. 'Aren't you pleased?'

'Pleased!' He sat up and stared at her. 'Pleased! You can't be serious.'

'Anthony?' she gasped. 'What's the matter? It only means that we will have to get married earlier than we had meant to. Is that so terrible?' A nasty, nameless fear brought beads of perspiration out on her face and her scalp was tingling.

'Oh, my God! Oh, my God!' He buried his face in his hands.

'Anthony, what is it?' she whispered. 'Don't you want to marry me?' Surges of fear gripped her throat. This wasn't at all the way she had imagined he would react.

'Jan! My darling Jan, of course I want to marry you, but . . . oh, don't you see, it's not as easy as that. In fact, it's going to be damned difficult.' He lay down again to wrap her in his arms, smother her face with kisses. And to her horror his face was wet. He was weeping!

Waves of nausea returned. She felt dizzy and her mouth filled with saliva. 'Oh!' she wailed. 'I think I'm going to be sick!' She tore open the bedside cabinet and grabbed the flowered china chamber-pot just in time. Her shivers shook the bed but she didn't dare lie down again, just sat there with her legs dangling over the side of the bed, holding the pot with its foul-smelling contents on her knee, while tears spilled down her face.

'Oh, God!' Anthony said again. 'Here, you'd better have this round you,' and he draped the quilt over her shoulders.

They both jumped in fright when someone knocked on the door, then realised it was the waiter with lunch.

'Tell him to leave the tray on the floor outside, Anthony,' Janthina begged. 'You can fetch it when he's gone.' She returned the chamber-pot to its cabinet, and closed the door. 'I couldn't eat anything, anyway. I think I'll get dressed.'

They wrapped blankets over their shoulders before sitting down.

'Now, Anthony, please explain the problem. I'm afraid I don't understand why you are so upset.' She tried to keep her voice calm.

'Oh, Jan, my darling, I don't know where to begin.' He sat back in his chair, a deep frown between his closed lids. 'It's all to do with what I was telling you about a few weeks ago. Responsibility. You see, ages ago my father and the Duke of Conway decided that I should marry the Duke's second daughter, Marianne. I don't want to; I'm not the slightest bit in love with her, or she with me, I imagine.'

'Well, why should you? I mean, they can't force you, can they?'

'I don't know. Not exactly, I suppose. All I do know is that if I don't marry her my father will be absolutely furious.'

'But surely you must have known this before we . . . made love?'

'Yes. But I never said anything about marriage, did I? I never let you think I would be able to. . . .'

'You told me you loved me! When Benjamin Kirkpatrick told Ruth he loved her he proposed within a few days. I've been. . . .' She tried to stifle her sobs. 'I've been waiting for weeks and weeks, wondering why you didn't propose, but I never doubted that you would.' She grabbed at her reticule and pulled it open, searching for a handkerchief.

'Didn't you realise that the earldom isn't just a created title, it's a royal one? The Earls of Frey have royal blood, are descended from King Charles II. We are expected to marry with nobility, not commoners. Not that I mean you're common,' he added hastily, seeing her flush, 'but you are not of blue blood.'

She was staring into space, not yet fully comprehending.

'However, no matter what happens, I will look after you. I do love you, my darling, and I desperately don't want to lose you. I will buy you a house somewhere in London. You could have your maid with you, two if you like, and I'll visit you there quite often, certainly every week.'

'But not marry me?'

He swallowed. 'No.'

'You mean you're asking me to be your mistress? Your kept woman? And our son would never know you were his father?'

He swallowed again and shook his head.

She gasped, gulped, opened her mouth to speak but no words came. Her heart was thumping so hard she could see the material of her blouse quivering with each beat; but it wasn't that delicious, excited thumping she had had when Anthony kissed her, pressed his body against her, but more like the pounding she used to feel when Papa was angry with her, and approached her with his riding crop. She had loved Papa, too, could never believe that he would abuse that love, betray it with the weakness in his character that caused him to lose control of his temper. But he had. And now Anthony. . . . No. No, surely he would not. . . .

'Darling Anthony, are you sure your father won't relent when he knows how much we are in love and that he is going to be a grandfather?' she begged.

He threw himself on his knees beside her, put his arms round her waist and buried his face in her lap. 'My dearest darling, I can only pray he will. But if he will not you will let me buy you a house. . . .'

'No! Our son must have a proper home, a father, family. It wouldn't be fair.'

'Yes, my darling, of course I understand. I'll return to London tomorrow and explain everything to him. I'm sure, between us, Mama and I will convince him that you are the perfect wife for me.'


Janthina felt quite ill every time she recalled that day. And during the next two weeks she recalled it frequently. She and Anthony hadn't even bothered to fetch the lunch tray in from the corridor; neither could have swallowed a morsel. Malcolm had looked at her with one eyebrow slightly raised as he handed her into the carriage, but said nothing, and the moment they stopped before the great, studded door of Glenfalk she had fled up the stairs and straight to her room. Mary's immediate reaction to her distraught appearance had been to undress her and tuck her into bed with an earthenware bottle of hot water, wrapped in a towel at her feet. Ruth was notified through Polly that she was unwell and had hurried along to see her before reporting to Grandmama. All the ladies of the household had apparently agreed that the poor thing had taken a bad chill.

Mary entered into the conspiracy to maintain her secret until she heard from Anthony again. As the days passed she grew more confident that the earl would give them his blessing. She scarcely even bothered to check the postbag each morning, convinced that this time he would come up to Glenfalk so that they could explain everything to her grandparents and Ruth. Of course she was perfectly aware that they

99

would not approve of what had happened. She and Anthony would doubtless be severely scolded, but the family would certainly be delighted that she was to make such a good marriage.

*If* Anthony managed to sway his father. But he would, she knew, because he loved her and wanted her.

Fortunately the awful feeling of nausea was almost gone; just as Mary had prophesied it would after three months. Three months! That meant that the baby would arrive in October. Oh, what was keeping Anthony? Why didn't he come? If he didn't hurry up she would be unable to get into a wedding gown.

They were all sitting in the Great Hall. Because an easterly wind persisted in sending icy blasts across the North Sea and the coastal lowlands, up through the valleys and into the hills, the April evenings were still cold and a big log fire blazed in the iron cradle on the hearth. Ruth and Aunts Laura and Meg were sitting at a table, lists scattered in front of them. Uncle Andrew and Elinor were discussing a problem which had arisen in the stables and Roderick was reading poetry to Grandmama, who seemed to be concentrating more on her embroidery than the verse. Janthina's book lay open on her lap, and Grandpapa was in his huge chair, all but the top of his head and knees and feet hidden behind *The Times*.

Grandmama looked up as the door opened. 'Ah, here's John. Is dinner ready, John?'

The butler inclined his head. 'Yes, madam. Will you prefer to wait a few minutes, or should I have it served immediately?'

She glanced at the laird, who was still noisily turning his pages. 'We'll be along in just a few moments, John,' she told him.

Janthina set her book aside and stood up, not without noticing the slight additional effort required.

Ruth noticed, too. 'Little sister, you are eating so much that you are soon going to be my very big sister,' she said quietly, as they moved towards the dining hall together. 'But I am very glad to see you looking so much better. You appeared quite poorly for a while.'

'I am feeling very well, now,' the younger girl replied in all honesty. Then quickly, to change the subject, she picked up a porcelain figurine from a sideboard in the dining hall, remarking, 'I do love this set of crinolined ladies Grandmama has collected. Just look at the detail.'

Ruth moved towards her usual place at the dining table as the others drifted slowly into the room, Grandpapa bringing up the rear. As he stopped to draw out her chair he remarked, 'I see today's *Times* has the announcement of the engagement of the Earl of Frey's son,

Anthony, Viscount Mears, to one of the daughters of the Duke of Conway. Good match, that. Frey will be pleased. . . .'

There was a crash of breaking china behind him. Janthina had collapsed on the floor, blood oozing from her hand where a shard of pink frilled porcelain had cut her flesh.

# PART THREE

## *INTERLUDE*

## 1902 – 1903

'O put not your trust in princes, nor in any child of man; for there is no help in them.'

*The Book of Common Prayer, Psalms,* cxlvi, 2

# 1

OH, THE excitement!

The weeks of preparation, and planning, of ordering and arranging, choosing and fitting were over; now was the climax. And this beautiful May day was to surpass all their hopes; the sun shining from the moment it lifted its face over the distant plains, until it dipped in a blaze of glory behind the western hills.

The castle had been transformed. Miraculously, Aunt Meg had obtained hundreds of rhododendrons and azaleas in full bloom and stacked them on either side of the great studded front door, filled every corner in the reception rooms and formed a bower of blossoms with narcissi, irises, gladioli, hyacinths and armfuls of roses around the raised dais in the ballroom where the three-tiered wedding cake stood awaiting its great moment.

In the stableyard, grooms and lads tried to cope with the congestion of coaches and carriages, while in the kitchen and pantries Malcolm and Cook nodded proudly to each other, satisfied that all the last-minute problems had been solved, late orders finally delivered, and every detail of the wedding banquet was ready for a signal from the laird.

'They'll not eat better at Balmoral or even at Buckingham Palace, Mr McKenny,' Cook gloated.

'Aye, you're right there, this'll be the finest feast ever,' Malcolm agreed. He knew, too, that every item of silver was polished, that the crystal goblets shone, and that all the chandeliers had been carefully washed so that every facet of every pendant and droplet flashed, reflecting beams of light from the candles.

Upstairs, maids fussed over their ladies and scurried from room to room begging and borrowing extra pins and ribbons. Valets eased their masters' feet into highly polished boots, and resident guests rifled through their vanity cases searching for items mislaid.

Sitting quietly on the dressing stool before her mirror, smiling encouragement to Polly as the girl's anxious fingers pinned coils of black hair into place, Ruth, the radiant bride-to-be, was the coolest and calmest person on the whole of the Glenfalk estate. The accommodating of guests and quartering of their servants had not concerned

105

her; Cook's capabilities, she knew, verged on genius, and the aunts had made the castle look utterly beautiful. No, her concern had centred on her wedding gown, going-away outfit, and trousseau – and they were all perfect. She tried to picture Benjamin at this moment, nervously preparing himself, assisted by his batman and groomsmen, the latters' sole use being to supply steadying brandy to their friend – and some lively repartee.

Janthina was already dressed and waiting.

Knowing how well the colour suited her sister, Ruth had chosen the palest green satin for her bridesmaids' gowns, trimmed with slightly deeper green velvet ribbons and deep gathers of ivory lace. A small lace cap, trimmed with tiny apricot buds, held her curls in place, and a beribboned nosegay of matching roses waited on her dressing table. She was as beautiful as ever, poised and graceful in her movements, but although as tall as her sister, she appeared somewhat thicker at the waist, and her bodice encased a full, thrusting bosom.

She was not smiling.

In fact, anyone examining her closely could see that the pretty flush on her cheeks came from a rouge-pot, and the soft twinkle of merriment had left her eyes, as though a grey veil had been drawn across them to hide her secret. A secret now shared with several people – but not with Ruth. It had been agreed that Ruth should not be told until after she and Ben returned from their honeymoon.

After Mary, her maid, Grandmama and Aunt Laura had been the first to know. They had come to her room after dinner on that fateful evening on which Grandpapa had read the announcement of Anthony's engagement in *The Times*, and sat beside her bed, talking of sending for a doctor to examine her.

'Your health has not been normal for the past few months,' Grandmama observed. 'You've looked odd at times and only pecked at your food. Yet,' she frowned, 'you seem to be putting on weight. Anyone would think you were anticipating a happy event,' she added with a smile.

Janthina had not known where to look, or how to prevent the deep flush from creeping up from the neck of her nightgown to flood her face.

The two women watched in amazement, eyes and lips agape.

'You're not, are you?' Aunt Laura squeaked, and her amazement turned to horror as her niece burst into tears.

They had waited impatiently for her to recover.

Why hold back? she had asked herself miserably. They'll have to know sooner or later. But what about Mama and Papa? And Ruth?

106

Oh, no, not Ruth! She will worry about it and it will spoil the wedding for her. She looked up at the anxious women. 'Yes,' she whispered. 'I am.'

'Oh, great heavens! I don't believe it! You're only joking.'

'Tell me it's not true!' Grandmama demanded; for once her poise was shaken. 'You cannot be serious!'

'Who is the father?'

'When did it happen?'

'Where?'

'How?'

The questions were shot at her in quick succession.

She hesitated. Should she tell or not? Would it be fair? He would be furious if she did, but . . . he hadn't been fair to her. She still couldn't quite believe this was happening: that Anthony would not suddenly arrive to claim her as his bride. Yet that engagement announcement in *The Times* had to be true. He had known all along that he was not going to marry her. He had only wanted. . . .

'Anthony Mears,' she said dully. 'I thought we were going to be married. I thought we would have a double wedding with Ruth and Ben, but. . . .' She broke into sobs again.

'Lord Anthony? The Earl of Frey's son? But didn't Father read of his engagement. . . .' Aunt Laura clapped a hand over her mouth. 'Oh, no! Did he tell you . . . oh, you poor child!' And she took her niece in her arms and rocked her, ignoring the growing tear stains on her gown.

'Please don't tell Ruthie, please! I don't want to upset her just before the wedding. She can be told after their honeymoon,' Janthina pleaded, gasping the words through her tears.

'Of course not, my love. We won't tell a soul.' Her aunt was almost in tears, too.

Grandmama pursed her lips; she had taken a more practical view. 'Some people will have to be told, immediately, I'm afraid. Your grandfather, for instance. But first of all I think you had better tell us all about it from the beginning so that we can decide what should be done.'

Slowly the story unfolded, punctuated by efforts to control the unwanted tears, and when it was finished Grandmama had left the room for a few minutes and returned with a powder to help her sleep. Not until the next morning did Janthina remember that, despite Grandmama's severe expression, neither she nor Aunt Laura had uttered one reproachful word. It might have been easier if they had.

Grandfather had left for London in a towering rage the day after

107

hearing the news, vowing to 'sort something out with Frey and that scoundrel son of his', and the scowl he shot in his granddaughter's direction as he left did not encourage her to feel he thought any better of herself.

'Janty, did you see Grandpapa before he went off to London?' Ruth had asked later, in the privacy of her bedroom. 'He looked angry enough to burst! Have you any idea what might have upset him?'

'I can't imagine,' the younger girl lied. 'Most unusual for him.'

'Yes. Do you know, for a moment I almost thought he was angry with you.'

Janthina had forced a smile and promptly asked her sister if she had decided on which colour gloves to wear with her going-away outfit.

Mama's reaction had hurt.

On the morning after her arrival, Aunt Laura had been detailed to lure Ruth out of the way whilst Janthina herself confessed all to her mother, in front of her grandparents.

'Oh, no!' Mama had cried. 'No, no, no!' Tears coursed down her cheeks. 'Oh, Janthina! You wicked, wicked girl. Oh, Mama! Papa! I am so ashamed.'

'So you should be, Adeline,' Grandmama had agreed. 'Seems the little girl had no idea of what was happening. No one . . .' she looked pointedly at her daughter, 'had seen fit to explain those things to her, or their consequences.'

'Mother! That is nonsense! No decent young lady would dream of allowing a young man into her bedroom – let alone into her bed,' Adeline had protested.

'Quite. But you must admit that she would be even less inclined to do so had she known it could result in pregnancy and dishonour,' the laird commented.

'I dread to think how Hamish will react when I get her home,' Mama moaned.

Even now, more than two weeks later, Janthina cringed as she had then, at the thought of facing Papa.

'She doesn't have to go home, you know,' Grandmama said, quietly.

'What do you mean? Of course she must. I will have to take her back with me after the wedding.' Adeline buried her face in her hands and gave a long, shuddering gasp.

Grandpapa had been standing, gazing out of the window. Now he turned. 'It is entirely up to you, of course. She's your daughter, and between you, it's your problem. But naturally we have discussed the matter at some length before you arrived and it seems there is an alternative to taking the silly child back to Canada. In fact, I think it would be far better for you not to. For one thing, you have your hands full coping with that husband of yours, and for another, I see little chance of the girl ever making anything of her life, stuck out there on your farm with a bairn. No. . . .' He held up his hand as Mama made to interrupt. 'Let me finish. Your sister Laura apparently feels that this . . .' he gestured towards Janthina's stomach, 'has happened partly because of her failure as a chaperone. I cannot say I agree with her, but however that may be, she has come up with a suggested solution you should consider. You may recall that Laura's late husband had a sister, Anne, who married a Frenchman, Henri Lorcet. Anne and Laura have remained good friends over the years, and your sister believes that Anne and Henri would agree to take Janthina back to their home in the Dordogne region of France when they complete their holiday over here after the wedding. She could stay with them until after the birth, when the bairn would be put up for adoption, leaving her free to return to Canada if you wish, or come back here . . . providing she doesn't get up to the same tricks again.'

Janthina had felt like an unwanted piece of furniture. Shall we put it in the attic or out in the old barn? They didn't discuss it with her or even appear to notice she was there, other than as the object of their conversation.

'I went to see the Earl of Frey as soon as I was told of this catastrophe,' Grandpapa continued. 'He was furious with his boy, and sent for him immediately, really lambasted him in front of me. The youngster must have previously told his father about Janthina, and said he wanted to marry her, but had not dared mention anything about the babe. Anyway, Frey would not hear of breaking the engagement to the Duke of Conway's daughter. Instead he offered to settle five thousand pounds on Janthina for the baby – which I accepted. I saw no point in trying to blackmail him into changing his mind by a threat of publicly denouncing his son. It could only lead to an even more unhappy situation for all concerned. At least she'll not be penniless.'

There was a stunned silence as Janthina and Mama sat, assimilating this information, but before anyone could speak, footsteps were heard approaching.

'Think about it,' Grandpapa ordered, a moment before Ruth came in.

'My!' exclaimed the bride-to-be. 'How serious you all look. Is anything wrong?'

'Yes. Cook has dropped the wedding cake on the kitchen floor and is hastily trying to bind it together again with string; the dressmaker accidentally poured soup on the bridesmaids' dresses but hopes to make another set in time, and . . .'

'Oh, Grandpapa! You are a tease!' Ruth scolded, rushing forward to kiss his cheek.

So Grandpapa had really decided for them. Mama had agreed with him, with some relief; Grandmama thought it was an excellent idea and nobody considered discussing the matter with the mother-to-be. She wasn't expected to have an opinion on the subject and even if she expressed one, no one would have thought it relevant. So it was fortunate that she did share the same opinion on the subject as the others. Soon after the Lorcets' arrival, yesterday, Aunt Laura had sought an opportunity to broach the subject with them.

'All her expenses would be paid, and she would have a maid of her own so she would not be an extra burden to you,' her aunt had coaxed. 'Would you be able to engage a good doctor and nurse for her?'

'Yes. This is possible,' Anne Lorcet agreed, hesitantly. 'What do you think, Henri?'

Her husband shrugged and spread his hands. 'There are good nurses in the district and I'm sure our local doctor is competent. You are the mistress of Berenac, *chérie*. You do as you wish. I have no objection.'

So it was decided that she would be removed to France with the Lorcets, when they returned home just one week after Ruth and Benjamin were due back from their honeymoon, to have Anthony's child in secret shame. . . . Once again her throat tightened and her eyes began to sting. No, I mustn't. I must not let Ruth know, she told herself, examining her face in the mirror for tell-tale signs. Then she stood up, smoothed her gown, squared her shoulders and, picking up her bridesmaid's posy, set off to Ruth's room to offer her assistance.

Through the open front door and up the stairway came the sound of carriage wheels scrunching on the driveway as guests left to take their places in church; Malcolm's voice could be heard summoning the coachmen and grooms.

'Ruthie! You look absolutely beautiful!' Janthina exclaimed. 'Is there anything I can do to help?'

Polly was carefully pinning a small diamond tiara, lent by Grandmama, over the veil.

'Janty, dear. No, I don't think there is, not until I actually step into my gown, and I'm waiting till the very last minute for that. That colour looks marvellous on you. You should wear it more often. You look lovely.'

'Do you feel nervous?'

'No, not at all. But I'll wager Ben does. I'm glad we had a rehearsal in church; it makes it much easier to perform one's part in the ceremony correctly.'

'Does that feel firm enough, miss?' Polly asked.

'I think so.' Ruth shook her head to test the security. 'Mm. Perhaps just one more pin this side. I don't want to lose it halfway down the aisle.'

There was a knock on the door.

'Come in!' Ruth called.

Adeline stepped into the room.

'Mama!' her daughters exclaimed together. 'You look wonderful!' They were so accustomed to seeing her in drab grey, that this tall, slender vision in cream lace, with a wide-brimmed matching hat sheltering a cluster of roses against her dark head, quite took their breath away.

'Thank you, my dears. I'm so glad you approve. Your grandmother had a hand in selecting my outfit, need I say.' She stepped forward to regard herself in the long mirror.

'You should wear lighter colours at home, Mama,' Janthina commented. 'I'm sure it would make you feel much brighter.'

'Possibly. But you know your father would not approve.'

'Oh . . .' the younger girl began, but was stopped by a glance from her sister. 'Er, you'll be the most beautiful woman there today, apart from Ruth, of course.'

'I doubt that!' Adeline laughed. 'Now, what can I do to help?'

The wedding gown was truly perfect. When the last of the thirty tiny, satin-covered buttons had been fastened at the back, the bride stood in front of the mirror while her mother, her sister, and her maid fussed with the petticoats, adjusted the train and arranged folds of heavy, ivory satin carefully across the ivory lace underskirt. Narrow lace peeped from the ends of her tight sleeves and above the high collar.

Adeline opened her reticule and drew out a double row of pearls. 'I want you to have these as a wedding present, Ruth. They were given to me by Grandmother MacDougall for my wedding.'

'Ooooh, Mama! They are so magnificent! But are you sure you should be giving them to me, now? You may want to wear them. . . .'

'Of course I'm sure and you know I never wear them in Canada. Here, let me fasten them . . .' and she passed one end round Ruth's throat, under the veil and slipped the gold tongue into the sapphire

111

and diamond clasp. The pearls fell in two neat loops, one lying inside the other, over the close-fitting satin bodice.

Ruth was speechless for a moment, her eyes filled with tears. Both girls could guess the dreams evoked by those pearls on her mother's wedding day – and knew that none of those dreams had ever materialised.

'Dearest Mama!' The bride disregarded her finery to hug her mother close. 'I love them. And I shall wear them and wear them. They will be seen at all the military balls, soirées given by the general's lady, tea-parties in the colonel's house and all the other smart occasions.'

'I'm glad, my dearest, so glad.' Adeline smiled proudly at her eldest daughter. 'Now, I think Janthina and I should be going. Will you come down so that we may help you into your carriage before we leave?'

Polly bobbed in front of the mirror to put on her own hat, they all satisfied themselves that they had their gloves, reticules and bouquets, and then assisted Ruth down the wide stairway, Polly carrying the train.

The laird and his lady were waiting in the hall, the former resplendent in his MacDougall tartan kilt ready to fulfil his role, in loco parentis, of giving the bride in holy matrimony.

Janthina wondered who would have given her away had this been a double wedding; might the two sisters have walked down the aisle, one on either arm of their grandfather? She swallowed hard, and forced her shoulders back, prepared to be a bridesmaid – only.

She and Mama rode to the church with Grandmama, Elinor, the other bridesmaid, and Cousin Ian's young daughter Anne, who was flower-girl. Mary and Polly rode beside the coachman, to be on hand with finishing touches to the gowns of bride and bridesmaids at the church door.

Roderick ushered Grandmama and Mama to their front pew; the organist played Bach and Handel; and the minister led his silent choir to the back of the church, while Major Benjamin Kirkpatrick tried very hard not to cast frequent, anxious glances over the heads of the waiting congregation towards the open church door.

Heads turned as carriage wheels approached. There was a rustling near the door, the choir straightened their ranks, the minister signalled to the organist, and, to the strains of Wagner's 'Wedding March', the bridal procession followed the choir and minister up the aisle.

Janthina was aware of heads turning as wedding guests watched their progress. She allowed her eyes to stray, briefly, over the flowers massed on the windowsills and in every corner. Huge arrangements stood either side of the altar and beside the chancel steps and pretty circlets of rosebuds and alyssum were hung from the end of every pew. It was so beautiful. . . . Quickly she looked back at her sister's train and the broad back of her grandfather. It was hard not to think, not to let her mind wander. . . . This ceremony, or one like it, should have been hers, too. Anthony should have been up there at the chancel steps, waiting for her, love glowing in his eyes, like Benjamin's were for Ruth. Anthony, dear, gentle, beautiful Anthony. What a tragedy his life was so dominated by his father. Or was it? Wasn't he just weak, to allow his life to be so ruled? She couldn't imagine anyone ordering Ben's life for him. . . .

Ruth was holding out her bouquet.

Janthina took it, and looked down at the huge spray of lilies as she laid them on her arm. She swallowed hard, but the lump wouldn't leave her throat and her eyes were stinging.

Suddenly she was jolted by a bump on her stomach . . . as though someone had knocked into her. But no one was near enough. And there it was again, inside her stomach! The baby! Mary had said it would start moving soon. Ooh! She gasped and pressed Ruth's bouquet against her gown. There was another ripple of movement across her abdomen . . . then nothing.

'I do,' Ruth's response reached back down the aisle.

Oh, Ruth, Ruth! What am I going to do without you? You who have always helped me out of trouble. You're married now and soon you will be gone, out of reach, caring only for Benjamin. She closed her eyes. Anthony, Anthony, how could you?

Blindly she followed the newlyweds into the vestry to sign the register, smiled broadly as she hugged her sister and pecked her brother-in-law's cheek, helped straighten the veil and train and laid the bouquet on Ruth's arm. Mendelssohn's 'Wedding March' summoned them out amongst the congregation again and they all winced in the brilliant light as the sun blazed down on them from a cloudless sky as they emerged from the church.

All day the unhappy bridesmaid smiled. She waved to the assembled villagers as the carriages bore them back to the castle, clapped at the speeches and cheered as Ruth and Ben stood on the dais amidst the banks of rhododendrons and azaleas to cut the wedding cake with Ben's regimental sword.

And when the wedding breakfast was finished, she went upstairs to assist Ruth out of her gown and into her blue and white striped going-away suit and matching blue hat with white ostrich plumes.

She stood in the doorway throwing confetti and rice over the

113

departing couple . . . and was startled when a voice spoke softly behind her.

'Well done, Janthina dear. I can guess how difficult this day has been for you,' and Mama's arm slid round her waist.

Their eyes met. She tried to smile but the gentle sympathy in her mother's dear, loving face was too much. Clutching the bridal bouquet she had caught from her sister a few moments before, Janthina gathered up her skirts and fled, across the gravel, up the steps and through the open door; upstairs, along the corridor past the unspoken criticism of her ancestors whose dignified and moral images gazed down at her from their gilded frames, and reached her room with tears streaming down her face. The door slammed behind her as she flung herself face down across the bed – then moved uncomfortably as the babe protested at such violent treatment.

Adeline crept in nearly an hour later. 'I'm sorry I couldn't come up before; I had to stay to say goodbye to all the non-resident guests. Are you all right?' She picked up the bouquet of lilies from the bed and laid them gently on the dressing table.

Janthina sat up and stared at them, vaguely. 'They're very bruised, I'm afraid. They don't last long, do they?' Her breath came in short, irregular gasps, her eyes were red and swollen, the bridesmaid's gown sadly crushed.

'They looked lovely during the ceremony and reception.'

'So did Ruth. More beautiful than I have ever seen her.'

'Yes.'

'I felt the baby for the first time while they were taking their vows. I wonder if it will be a boy or a girl.'

'It doesn't really matter. The Lorcets have promised to contact an adoption society and proceed with all the necessary arrangements before the birth. They can find you a wet nurse, too. Then you need never see the child.'

Janthina stared into space, said nothing.

'Then you can return to Canada for Christmas, and start afresh.'

'If it is a boy, he will be Anthony's son and heir.'

'No, he won't. He will not have Anthony's name.'

'I know. I'm just dreaming – or perhaps having a nightmare.'

Mama looked at her pensively. 'After the first time, when you knew what he was going to do if he got in your bed, why did you let him into your room?'

'Because I so desperately wanted him to do it again.'

'Do you mean you liked it?' Mama's eyes widened.

Janthina smiled, briefly. 'It was the most glorious thing that had ever happened to me.' She noticed her mother's frown. 'Didn't you think so? I mean, you and Papa must have done it or we children couldn't have been born.'

Adeline flushed. 'I hated it,' she whispered.

'I don't understand. Why? I even loved it the first time when it hurt so dreadfully. Anthony was so gentle and kind. . . . So loving.' She closed her eyes as a tremor shook her body.

'You were very lucky, then,' her mother murmured, walking over to the window.

Janthina watched her, frowning, but said nothing.

'Well, I suppose it's time to get changed and ready for tonight's dinner party,' Adeline said after a few minutes' silence.

Her daughter sighed.

'Come, dear, make the effort. It will be better for you than sitting up here moping, alone.'

Mary helped with her toilette, poured her bath and re-dressed her hair, held her gown and fastened it and touched her cheeks with rouge.

'Would you put the flowers in water, Mary? They may last a day or two longer.'

'Yes, miss, I will. Now, you look fine. You go and enjoy yourself and forget your troubles for a bit.'

Her mistress gave a sickly grin into the mirror, took a deep breath, and picked up her reticule.

She sat at dinner between two attentive young men whose names she couldn't remember, contributing only monosyllables to the conversation.

Several people joked that having caught the bridal bouquet, she would be the next bride.

She danced . . . and when midnight struck she found she was able to slip away unseen, up the back staircase.

The awful, beautiful, dreaded day was over.


There were times, during the following week, when Mama was loving and sympathetic – and others when she was less so. Sometimes Janthina would glance up to see her mother gazing at her, sadly shaking her head, or she would click her tongue impatiently and frown, lips pursed.

Over and over Adeline had apologised to her mother and father for the shame and burden of this problem; Aunt Laura apologised for ineffectual chaperoning. Elinor and Roderick looked embarrassed – obviously they knew – and their parents, Andrew and Meg, were very

115

jolly and pretended that nothing was amiss. With Ruth's departure, Janthina's downfall had become an open topic.

The skies opened on the morning Adeline was to leave, rain battering on the windows and flooding the driveway. Janthina dragged herself out of bed, forced herself to wash and dress, reluctant to face the day. She had dreaded the thought of her mother leaving, far more than she had dreaded her arrival and having to confess her misdeeds. Loving or scolding, Mama was very dear; so important, the most important person in her life, now that she had lost both Ruth and Anthony.

The door opened and Adeline came in, hat already pinned in place. 'I thought I would come and say goodbye in private, my dear.' She kissed the top of her daughter's head as the girl sat at her dressing table applying rouge again.

'Will that be all, miss?' Mary asked. 'If you wish I'll leave you alone with your mother.'

'Yes. Thank you, Mary.'

'Thank you for looking after my daughter so well,' Mama added.

'Not well enough, I'm afraid, ma'am. I am sorry.' In the dark blue uniform, her curls hidden under the matching mob-cap, she was a tiny, woebegone figure. 'Goodbye, ma'am. I hope you have a good journey.'

'Goodbye, Mary.'

When the door closed, Adeline sat on the little armchair which matched Janthina's curtains. 'Such a pretty room,' she remarked. 'Don't you love it?'

'Yes. Wasn't it kind of Grandmama to have these rooms redecorated for us so beautifully? Oh, Mama!' she gasped. 'I feel so dreadful for letting them down. And you. Will you ever forgive me?'

'As to that, I suppose your grandmother is right; it is all partly my fault. I should have explained these things to you, told you about love . . . and intimacy . . . and conception.'

'Why didn't you?'

Her mother sighed and studied the carpet. 'Because it is a subject which has only brought me horror and humiliation.'

Janthina swung round on her stool. 'Mama! How do you mean? Why?'

Adeline spread her hands and drew a breath. 'Your father was never really able to control himself in these matters, I'm afraid. It was like a . . . a sort of sickness with him. He became very violent when he needed to do it.' She stroked her forehead with the tips of her fingers, eyes closed. 'It became worse over the years. So painful; so

116

humiliating.' She looked up and smiled. 'You are the first person I have ever told. It's a poor excuse, I suppose, for a mother's failure to prepare her daughter.'

Janthina dropped to her knees to slide her arms round her mother's waist, burying her face in her lap. 'Oh, Mama! How awful! Awful!'

'I really shouldn't complain; I have been very lucky in other respects, for which I should be grateful. Apart from this one failing, your father is a splendid man. He has been very successful with the farm; we've had four wonderful children and a lovely home.'

Janthina was no longer listening. Her brain was reeling, picturing Papa's violent scenes of the past. Were they all part of Mama's dread of 'the subject'? She opened her lips to form the question – then closed them again. It would only distress her mother to talk about it any more. No; she would ask Ruth when she came home.

'I must go, the carriage is waiting.'

Both women stood up.

'I'll come down with you.'

'Are you sure?'

Janthina nodded. She wanted to hold on to her mother until the very last moment. There was a lead ball in the pit of her stomach; her throat was tight and dry, her knees felt weak.

Standing beside the carriage, mother and daughter clung together.

Adeline could feel the girl's distress, and said, 'Don't take on so, my love. You will be home for Christmas.'

'Yes. Yes, of course. Have a good journey and enjoy the haymaking,' Janthina smiled. 'Remember me to Luke and give my love to Joseph and Papa.'

'Try to enjoy France. I'm told the Dordogne is one of the most beautiful regions in the country.' Adeline spoke with brittle cheerfulness from the carriage window. 'Goodbye.'

'Goodbye.' The word was hardly more than a whisper.

As the carriage rolled away down the drive, Alexandra could see that her granddaughter was trembling. 'Come, my dear,' she said. 'Christmas is not so very far away. Anyone would think you were never going to see your mother again, the way you take on.'

Janthina gasped, turned, and fled to her room.


Although everyone went out of their way to be nice to her, Janthina was aware of a change in the atmosphere amongst the family. Whether at the dinner table or sitting in the Great Hall in the evenings,

117

conversation was seldom directed towards herself; Roderick no longer asked if he might read her his poetry, and when visitors came to call there was no longer a ring of pride in Grandmama's voice when she was introduced.

The excitement of the wedding over, and no more planning and organising to keep everyone busy, the household fell into its old, quiet routine – to which, Janthina realised, she did not belong. In fact, despite everyone's attempts at kindness, she was beginning to feel like a pariah. An unwanted embarrassment.

The only person who was unaffected by the situation, obviously because he didn't know, was James Cameron, who came to call ten days after Mama's departure. Having been informed, in answer to his enquiry, that Miss McKenzie was out walking by the burn, he had come out to find her and asked permission to accompany her. Apart from Aunt Laura, who had an oversized sense of responsibility for the situation, Mr Cameron was the first person to seek her company for some time, and despite her dislike of him she actually found herself grateful for his attention.

'I would have expected to find you mounted, Miss McKenzie,' the young man remarked. 'I'm told you are a fine horsewoman.'

'I rode a great deal in Canada but spring is so beautiful here in Scotland I find I can enjoy the smaller details, the tiny buds and creatures, better on foot.'

'Er . . . yes, I'm sure you're right.' He had apparently never noticed them himself.

'Are you enjoying business in Edinburgh, Mr Cameron?' An attempt to lead the conversation away from herself.

'Indeed. I believe I am learning fast and making good progress. I am determined, one day, to have my own business.'

'Splendid. I don't doubt you will. I am sure your determination will bring you success.' She paused to admire a clump of buttercups.

'What of yourself, now that your sister is married? Do you have plans to wed?'

'Er . . . no, I can't say I have.' She turned away to look up at the hills beyond the burn, hoping he didn't notice the sudden colour fill her cheeks. 'Are you married?'

'Good gracious, no.'

'Why not?'

'I do not intend to marry until I have a business well established. It will take two years at least.'

'Will you remain in Edinburgh?'

'Aye, for now. But who knows where the pursuit of business may

118

take one?' He smiled at her, boldly. 'I'll wager, though, it won't be long before a beautiful young lady like yourself ties the knot. How long do you intend to stay in Scotland?'

'I am actually planning to visit France soon.' She stopped to catch her breath. The day was hot and the incline sufficient to tire her. 'Do you mind if we turn back, now? The sun is quite fierce.'

'Whatever you wish, Miss McKenzie. But tell me, you will be returning, won't you?'

She looked at the stockily built young man, his slicked-down hair, a row of pens and pencils clipped to the breast pocket of his ill-fitting suit. It was not surprising, she thought, that he is still single; it was hard to imagine any girl falling in love with him. . . . Oh dear, she was probably being very unfair; he might be quite nice when one got to know him.

'You will come back here, won't you?' he repeated.

Would she? Probably, if only briefly. 'I expect so.'

'Good. I hope to have the opportunity to walk with you again some time.'

Well, that was no good reason to return! But it was strange how vague the future seemed. The family, Grandmama and Aunt Laura, were all quite definite about what she should do, where she should go and when. They had the next year so neatly planned for her – so why was she so uncertain?

They halted at the front door. 'Goodbye, Mr Cameron,' she said rather pointedly, having no intention of inviting him in for refreshment.

'Er . . . goodbye, Miss McKenzie.' He took her hand and held it firmly. 'Until we meet again.'


Ruth and Benjamin arrived back from their honeymoon on the Riviera bursting with health and happiness. They had arranged to stay at Glenfalk for a few days in order to pack up their wedding presents and Ruth's clothes, ready for dispatch to the house they were to rent close to Ben's regimental station.

'Ruthie. Can you spare a short while, some time, to come to my room? I must speak with you,' Janthina asked, the day after their return. She could no longer delay the evil hour.

'Of course, I'll come right away,' her sister replied, looking faintly puzzled, taking her arm as they went up the stairs together.

'Now,' she said, as she sat on Janthina's dressing stool. 'What's on your mind?'

Janthina took a deep breath . . . then exhaled again. She had

119

rehearsed this moment, over and over . . . but she couldn't remember the words.

Ruth cocked her head on one side, frowning. 'What is it, Jan? What's the matter?'

'Rather a lot, I'm afraid.'

'Go on.'

'It's hard to know where to begin.' Janthina hung her head, apologetically.

'Come on, I'm still your sister, remember, even if I am married. Tell me, have you fallen in love, or something?'

'Yes. I did. And . . . oh Ruthie, I've been so stupid. I . . . I'm going to have a baby.'

Ruth just sat and stared, open-mouthed, while her sister leaned back in her chair, biting the edge of her forefinger, squeezing her lids together to hold back the tears.

'Janty, darling!' Ruth's voice was barely above a whisper. 'Who? When? Aren't you going to marry?'

'No. It's Lord Anthony and he's going to marry someone else; the daughter of a duke.'

'What? You're not serious! Why, the absolute cad!'

Gradually the whole story was told, and gradually Ruth's ebullient mood became sombre.

'Oh, Jan,' she said at last, when Janthina had finished. 'Jan, what have I done to you?'

'You?' Janthina looked up with a start. 'What do you mean?'

'I remember, now, how you wanted to talk to me, sought to be alone with me. I thought you were just a little jealous of Ben . . . and all the time you were needing to confide in me. Oh God!' She put her face in her hands.

'I wish people would stop trying to take the blame for me. Very kind, of course, but it's not really Aunt Laura's fault for not chaperoning me more strictly, nor yours for not listening to my lovesick tale, nor Mama's for not telling me about married love and how babies are conceived. It's nobody's fault but mine – and Anthony's. I was the one stupid enough to imagine that if you were in love with someone and he with you, marriage would automatically follow. I believed – I suppose because I wanted to believe – that what we did together was just part of the natural development of a loving relationship – of complete trust. I know I've been stupid, idiotic, but . . .' she sighed. 'I'm afraid I still cannot bring myself to regret it. Does that shock you?'

Ruth stared at her, deep brown eyes burning into green for a few

moments. 'No, I'm certainly not shocked, but maybe a little surprised.'
She paused a moment before continuing. 'You say you will let the baby
be adopted? Is that . . . is that what you want to do?'

It was Janthina's turn to stare at her sister; her dear, dear sister
who understood so well. 'No,' she admitted for the first time, even to
herself. 'No, I don't think that it is. I don't know. I don't know how
I'll feel after it's born.'

'You mustn't do anything you may regret . . . I mean regarding the
baby. I wish I could help. I wonder if. . . .'

'No. It is enough that I seem to have wrecked my own life; I will
not allow you and Ben to become involved too. I will go off to France
next week as arranged with the Lorcets. I will enjoy seeing France,
enjoy whatever each day brings. I will write to you, often, and I'll let
you know what I decide to do.' She smiled. 'I think I am beginning to
grow up at last; I'll try not to be so stupid in the future. Strange how
a girl can make such silly mistakes. Seems Mama made a big one,
marrying Papa.'

'What do you mean?'

The younger girl hesitated. 'Ruth, do you like . . . well, married
life? Do you enjoy what you and Ben do together or do you do it
because it's your duty and you love him?'

It was Ruth's turn to look embarrassed. 'Well . . . to be honest, I
thought it was awful at first. But Ben is so kind and understanding –
and gentle, I am getting quite to like it.' She smiled. 'So much so, in
fact, that I sometimes want him to do it even when he hasn't thought
of it.' Her sister gave a sigh of relief. 'But what's that got to do with
Mama and Papa?'

'Before she left, Mama told me that when Papa wants to do it he
gets very violent. She says it's horrible.'

Ruth nodded. 'I know. We've all seen her bruises.'

Janthina's mouth fell open. 'Is that how she got them?'

Ruth nodded again.

'And do you think it had anything to do with the way he used to beat
me?'

'Oh, yes. It was always the night after those beatings that he hurt
her. . . .'

'Honestly? I was always puzzled by what happened at home, but
now it is all fitting into a picture. Poor Mama! How awful, never to
have enjoyed it.'

'Do you? So much?'

'Oh, yes, yes. It was wonderful. Even though it hurt the first time,
it was still wonderful.' She stared dreamily into space. 'Come on, Mrs

Kirkpatrick.' She stood up. 'Your husband will wonder where on earth you are. I'll just freshen up my face and we'll go and find him.'


Ruth confided, later, how furious she and Ben felt towards Anthony. 'He is either a rogue or a weak-minded little fool,' she said, vehemently. 'I can't help but feel it is just as well you are not going to marry him; I doubt he'd be faithful for long. Your life would probably be miserable even with a title and all that money.'

Janthina had to admit that her sister could be right.

It was marvellous to have Ruth and Ben there. They were loving and attentive, included her in all their conversation, in everything they did, and made her feel quite human again. Ruth was especially happy since the news that the Boer War had ended had reached them in Nice; she had always dreaded that Ben might be shipped out to South Africa.

The days flew by all too quickly and soon they were ready to leave for Aldershot.

'I will try to visit you in France if I possibly can, Janty,' Ruth promised as they bade their farewells. 'And I will write to you, often. I have your Dordogne address with me. Look after yourself.'

'And you look after yourself . . . and Ben. Be happy.' The sisters hugged.

'You must be happy too,' Ruth added.

'I'll try. I vow I'll try.'

Ben gave his sister-in-law a hug and kissed the top of her head before joining his wife in the carriage.

Janthina waved them out of sight, squared her shoulders, and went upstairs to pack.

# 2

THERE WAS no question about the beauty of the Dordogne.

Sitting at her window immediately above the river itself, Janthina smiled instinctively as the waters swirled and eddied along the opposite bank, bubbling over the smooth stones. Her fingers itched to sketch the views of every direction, capture each scene on paper so that she might carry it with her wherever she went for the rest of her life.

It was so peaceful. She was so peaceful; it was as though all the pain and unhappiness of the past few months had happened in another time, another life totally unrelated to here and now.

Henri and Anne were considerate – but distant. Having had a tearful farewell with Mary, a large, fat, jolly woman called Thérèse had replaced the Scottish girl, assuming her duties in attending Janthina's needs at Château de Berenac. After a few days they had both decided they liked each other, although communication was difficult. Thérèse spoke not one word of English and Janthina, having given the language classes a minimum of attention during her one year at Kingston Ladies' College, was little better in French. But she was determined to learn.

The story told locally, for the sake of decorum, was that Janthina's husband was at sea with the Royal Navy. It was a necessary token of respectability, even here, tucked away in the heart of the French countryside.

Letters had arrived from Ruth and Mama; they seemed very far away, in time as well as geographically, and it was difficult to picture Mama's welcome home from Joseph and Papa, or her sister's social life as a British Army officer's wife.

She had never felt so alone, so totally removed from family, from anyone who cared. Yet there was this. . . . She put her hands on her stomach and smiled as the baby's movements rippled under her dress. He was a lively little fellow. She would name him Charles, Anthony's second name – Charles Mears. . . . No, no, not Mears, he could not ever bear his father's name. He would be Charles McKenzie, because he would be born a bastard. For a moment she wanted to weep; to shut her eyes against the silver birch trees dipping over the river, and the birds drifting lazily against the sky, then swinging low over the water catching insects. Beautiful scenery, like beautiful poetry and music, evoked such painful memories . . . thoughts of what might have been. She wished she could feel anger and resentment against Anthony, then the hurt might go away. But she knew that if he walked into her room right now she would throw herself into his arms, wanting him as much as ever. Stupid? Idiotic! Oh, she was angry enough that Charles was disinherited, not only of the titles and wealth but even of his name; but not for herself, not for what he had done to her, for what they had shared.

Henri and Anne Lorcet spent a great deal of time away in their Paris apartment and in their villa in the south, so that Janthina was often alone. Days dragged out into weeks and months. Her birthday passed almost unnoticed but for the letters which arrived from Mama and Ruth – the first ever spent without family around to help her celebrate. She was not too unhappy. She tried to fill her time with sketching, and stitching tiny garments for Charles; then there was French to learn, aided by Thérèse whose accent was far from Parisian, but she was the only person who could spare the time.

There were some outings. She was invited to accompany the Lorcets on a visit to friends of theirs at Belcastel. This was a lovely château perched dramatically at the top of a limestone cliff, perfectly mirrored in the river below. This almost impregnable eyrie commanded a breathtaking view up and down the valley and must surely have provided a safe fortress for its builders. Anne also arranged for them to make the long drive to Rocamador, a little town built into a cliff face. The façades of the buildings were constructed of limestone blocks, or rough stone for the humbler dwellings, behind which the rooms were of simple caves tunnelled into the rock. On the outer side of the narrow streets pillars of wood and stone supported the rooms and terraces which overhung the valley far below. Anne explained that a sanctuary built there high in the cliff face, by St Amador, had become a place of pilgrimage in the Middle Ages since when it had been enlarged and now included a Romanesque Basilica as well as the twelfth-century crypt of St Amador.

Before they visited the town the coachman, Gaston, was instructed to take them to the village of Hospitalet, where a hospital had been built centuries ago to accommodate the chronically sick pilgrims. Here they left the carriage, briefly, to stand on the high vantage point and gaze along the steep-sided valley of the River Alzou for Janthina's first sight of Rocamador.

'The pilgrims must have been quite overwhelmed to see this. It looks enchanted.' Janthina gazed, stupefied by the magic scene of

124

precarious limestone walls washed pink by the sun, standing in sharp silhouette against the dark shadows of the valley beyond.

'One can understand them believing that their ills might be miraculously healed,' Anne agreed.

Unfortunately these excursions were rare, and although she had been encouraged to ask Gaston to take her wherever she wished, she was hesitant to trouble him, taking brief walks alone or occasionally accompanied by Thérèse. Sometimes she would take a little folding stool, walk along the river bank until she was tired, then sit and rest awhile, sketching or just dreaming. And thinking – pondering her future, wondering.

Her chief companion, all of every day, was within her, growing, kicking, keeping her aware of his presence. When they were alone she would talk to him aloud, even read to him the more interesting passages of the book she was currently reading.

Sometimes her anger would rise, that her son should be denied all the privileges that should have been his. She would recall her excitement when Mary had told her she was pregnant, her impatience to tell Anthony the joyful news – and the look of horror on his face when she did.

Would it have been better to remain in Canada? Never to have met Anthony and conceived this child who must be given away, as though unloved and unwanted by his mother? What effect might that have on him when he learned the truth? What would his adoptive parents be like, could they possibly love him as much as she already did? But staying in Canada could only have meant more beatings for herself and Mama; even though Papa could no longer speak he was still able to move quite normally, quite capable of dealing out more humiliation to his women. Strange how the events of a woman's life can be so governed by a man. If only Papa had not beaten her so for his own peculiar reasons; if only Roland had written; if only Anthony had stood up to his father and insisted on marrying her . . . but what might life have been with Anthony? And what might have happened if Roland had come to see her at Glenfalk?

All questions which seemed imponderable . . . except for the last, to which she had an answer quite suddenly.

It came by post, enclosed in a letter from Grandmama in which was written all the family news.

'. . . Elinor has acquired a gentleman admirer whom she takes great pleasure in avoiding whenever possible. . . . We hope August will be dry and warm, the burn is now merely a trickle. . . . Everyone sends their regards' (not love, Janthina noted) 'and the enclosed letter arrived

125

for you last week. . . . Your affectionate grandmother, Alexandra MacDougall.'

She pictured the old lady sitting straight-backed at her bureau, lips slightly pursed, long earrings swaying to the movement of her pen. She was a loving, spirited woman, but try as she might she had been unable to conceal her sorrow at her granddaughter's downfall.

Janthina moved in her chair, trying to adjust the growing bulge into a more comfortable position, before slitting the enclosed envelope. There was something rather odd about the handwriting, and the London address at the letterhead was quite strange.

'My dear Janthina,' she read – who on earth could this be from? She turned to the bottom of the next page and gasped, quickly turned back and read on. 'I was worried on my return from South Africa that you had not replied to my letter and wonder if it ever reached you. You may have thought me rude not to have written, but I am afraid mail from the Cape is very uncertain. I only wish there had been time to write to you before my hasty embarkation. Knowing that the war could not last much longer, I asked you to reply to me in Gloucester – if you wished to reply at all. I wonder? I shall wait anxiously, hoping you will reply to this. If so, I wish that we may soon meet again. Would it be possible for me to visit you in Scotland? I will pray each day that you are still there and that we will have an opportunity to renew the friendship I so treasured. Yours in great hope, Roland.'

She looked out across the river – and sighed. Another time, another place, another if . . . another maybe. If only his first letter had arrived. . . .

So she had been too impatient to wait until he wrote again – but would she have waited seven months? Of course not, that wasn't reasonable. And even if she had, who was to say he would not have proved to be another Anthony – or Papa? Except she found that hard to imagine. Yet who could have guessed that Anthony would be so . . . there was no point in going over all that again. Instead, she should try to think how to word her reply to Roland. Dear Roland, what bad luck your first letter was lost. In waiting I was seduced by an English nobleman and have now been sent into exile to produce his bastard son – how about that? No, she was obviously in the wrong frame of mind to reply now.

Janthina pushed herself clumsily out of her chair, opened a drawer in her bureau, and dropped the letter inside.

Tomorrow, she thought. I'll write to him tomorrow.

\*   \*   \*

In fact it was more than a week before Janthina could force herself to tackle the unhappy task, and even then it was difficult. She longed to see him again, remembered the hugeness of him, his gentleness, frequently looking at the sepia photograph he had given her. Dear Roland. Had he sensed that she was still too young for him to touch her – too innocent and naïve? Should she suggest that they meet when she returned to Scotland? There might be a few days before she left for Canada.

Looking down into the waters of the Dordogne, picturing that meeting, the things they would say to each other, and remembering the open honesty of their friendship, she knew she could not face it. How could she admit to him all that had happened and watch that sweet, gentle expression turn to horror? And she would have to tell him; if that basic honesty was not maintained their friendship would become meaningless.

She went to the bureau and sat down, drew out a sheet of paper and began to write.

'Dear Roland, I would have enjoyed meeting you again very much but as you see from the above address I am staying with relatives in France where I will remain until late autumn. Unfortunately it is not possible to make an arrangement to meet when I leave here as the date is uncertain and I will be in Scotland only a day or two before sailing back to Canada.'

She decided to write on about her impressions of Scotland, noting the difference between the Highlands and Canada. Then she hesitated before concluding: 'I really am very disappointed that we have been unable to meet but it was nobody's fault except the beastly Boers. I will often think of you.

'Yours very sincerely, Janthina.'

Two days after posting her letter to Roland, Janthina received one from Ruth. It contained the news she dreaded – they were leaving for India at the end of September – within the next week, too late for her to write a farewell.

Thick fog, swirling against her windows, only added to her gloom. She sat holding the letter, reading and re-reading it as though to hold on to her sister for as long as possible. India seemed so far away, the other side of the world. Letters would take months instead of weeks, and weeks had been bad enough.

The Lorcets were in Paris. Apart from Thérèse she was alone – with Charles. She placed her hands over him. His movements were no longer ripples under her gown, they had become violent kicks. Soon he would be ready to make his début – within the next month.

She had been brooding on the approaching event, thinking, picturing it, longing to hold her baby in her arms.

As though in a dream she left her little sitting room, walked down the wide corridor and opened the door of the room designated as temporary nursery. The crib stood waiting, tiny baby clothes folded in a neat pile on the quilt. He would be whisked away from her as soon as the cord was cut, washed, put into one of these little gowns and tucked into this crib . . . to await his wet nurse.

They had said she mustn't see him, hold him; it would only make it more difficult for her to part with him, activate her maternal instincts. As though she didn't have those instincts already.

A leaden ball settled in her stomach, adding to her discomfort.

She heard the door handle turn behind her and she was joined by Thérèse, who peered into her face, questioning, *'C'est très difficile, n'est-ce pas?'*

Janthina stared back and knew the woman understood. She sighed, *'Oui, très,'* and sank on to the little antique nursing chair.

*'Je comprends le problème.'* Thérèse re-tidied the baby napkins which were already stacked in perfect order. *'Vous ne voulez pas perdre votre bébé, n'est-ce pas?'*

Janthina looked up, saw the big woman's sympathy, sighed again, and said, *'Non.'*

Her legs felt heavy as she walked back to her room; heavy as her mind, and the weight in her stomach. She knew she could not keep the child; there was no way she could take him back to Canada, to the farm and Papa. Though speechless, Papa would still make life hell for her and for Mama, even for the child, always supposing he didn't throw them out. And she had assured Mama that she would be home, alone, for Christmas.

Two days after the Lorcets returned from Paris, a woman from the adoption society Anne had contacted came to interview Janthina.

Anne asked Janthina down to her private sitting room where she was introduced to a small, thin faced woman dressed in slate grey with a small, crushed-looking hat pinned precariously to her thin hair.

'Good afternoon, madame.' The woman grasped the girl's hand in a bony claw. 'I have brought all the papers for you to sign today so that when the baby is born all the formalities will have been completed.'

'Oh!' Janthina was surprised. 'I had understood that I didn't have to sign anything until afterwards.'

The woman's eyes narrowed and she glanced at Anne.

'Madame Bouget thought it would be a good idea to finalise everything now, Janthina. Er . . . won't you both sit down.'

Madame Bouget opened a big, black leather bag and drew out a cardboard folder, laying it on the sofa beside her. 'I must have a few details from you regarding your age, nationality, and so on,' she began, addressing Janthina in rapid French. Anne, seeing that Janthina had not understood, translated, continuing to act as the interpreter until the visitor had laboriously written down all the girl's answers.

'Now Madame Bouget only requires your signature,' Anne told her, as the woman stood up to take the papers to Janthina.

The girl looked from one to the other. 'But . . . I would prefer not to . . . I mean . . . I had been told it would be done after he was born. . . .'

'I believe that was suggested earlier but as Madame Bouget has had to come all the way from Paris, you had better sign it now. We really cannot ask her to return again in a month's time just for the want of a signature.' Anne smiled encouragingly.

Madame Bouget placed the papers on the coffee table at Janthina's knee, holding out the pen.

Hairs on the back of Janthina's neck prickled. She opened and shut her mouth, looking from one to the other, feeling trapped. They had cornered her – were forcing her to this final, awful decision. Of course they thought the decision had been made months ago – it had been, by everyone else – but no one had ever asked her what she wanted to do, if she really wanted to give her son away. Instinctively her hands moved over the huge swelling. Charles. Not so little now. What would be best for him? If she refused to let him go would he be any better off than going to a good home and family, being brought up as a legitimate son of an established household? What had she to offer him except the name of – bastard? No home. Not another soul in the world to love him. And how could she ever face telling him that he should one day have been a viscount, and an earl; that his father had rejected him?

She took the pen and wrote.

Two tears slid silently down her cheeks. She pulled herself awkwardly to her feet and, without looking at the women, walked to the door with as much dignity as her bulk would allow. She turned to speak but no sound would come – except for a sob.

Thérèse was waiting in her sitting room, took one look at her and wrapped her in her huge arms, gently rocking.


The next four weeks dragged endlessly. Janthina found she could no longer carry her load very far and anyway, heavy rains had made the riverside paths too muddy for safety and comfort. Thérèse often accompanied her around the flower beds, the occupants now drooping their heads as the colours faded and died. Despite Janthina's still limited command of the French language, the two had developed an understanding which went deeper than words. They enjoyed being together, often crocheting or sewing in silence, or Thérèse would watch in awe as Janthina's pen recreated yet another angle of the château or simply a bird or a flower.

There was no word from Ruth, of course; she was undoubtedly still at sea, and Mama's note was surprisingly brief. The one exciting thing that happened was the arrival of another letter from Roland.

Janthina whisked it away to read in the privacy of her room where she sat savouring every line, reading it through again and again.

It was a long letter, full of details of the South African war, the Boers, the natives and the food. And of the wound he had received in his right arm rendering it almost useless and forcing him to write with his left, hence the odd handwriting of this and the previous letter. This was very irksome in his law work, he said, but he was becoming used to it. He hoped his letter would arrive before she left France.

'October 30th, 1902. Dear Roland,' she began, then nibbled the end of her pen. 'I was so glad your letter arrived while I was still here in the Dordogne. My cousins very kindly invited me to remain a while longer. . . .' What to tell him? There was virtually no news. '. . . Am enjoying my sketching and have also experimented with oils. . . . The weather has been very wet. . . . So sorry about your arm but in the circumstances I find your hand very legible. . . .' She told him about her visits to Belcastel and Rocamador and said she was hoping to make the excursion to Laroque Gageac before returning to Canada.

Finishing the letter left her with a strange, empty feeling. She was restless, tried to concentrate on her crochet – and couldn't. She attempted a letter to Mama, but there seemed nothing to say. She rang for Thérèse and together they walked out into the garden, shawls held close against the chill air. The maid followed obediently as Janthina's steps led slowly out of the huge, wrought-iron gates and down the hill to the river. The rain had stopped and birds glided swiftly, only inches above the water, to snap up the flies.

Janthina leaned heavily against a low bough, sending a cascade of yellow and rust-coloured leaves on to the water to swirl away downstream.

'Ugh!' she grunted suddenly.

'Qu'est-ce que c'est?' Thérèse asked in alarm. 'Qu'est-ce que vous avez?'

'Nothing. Nothing at all, Thérèse. My tummy is just uncomfortable. Can you blame it? But I am quite tired, so let's go back home.' Funny how she thought of the château as home, now. Canada and Scotland seemed so remote.

A local farmer passed them on his way home from fields downstream, his donkey laden with produce. He and Thérèse were apparently acquainted and after a brief *'m'dame'* to Janthina and her brief *'m'sieur'* in reply, the two held an unintelligibly fast exchange for several minutes while Janthina dawdled up to the gates – where Thérèse found her a few minutes later, doubled up with pain.

It felt as though she had eaten something bad . . . brought her out in a sweat. She swayed, nauseated, as though on a ship. The pains in her stomach were as though she had taken a large dose of castor oil.

When at last the spasm was over she looked at Thérèse and saw that she was smiling. *'C'est le bébé, madame. Il arrive. Maintenant, venez dans votre chambre prendre une tasse de thé à la framboise.'*

'Raspberry tea? Whatever for?' the girl exclaimed.

*'C'est bon, parce que ça facilite la naissance.'*

'Helps the birth?' Janthina laughed, then shrugged. 'Oh, well, if you think it's so good. . . .'

*'Oui, Oui, très bon,'* Thérèse nodded confidently.

Janthina sat drinking her raspberry tea, reading and talking to Thérèse while cramps came and went. Soon after the midwife's arrival she was undressed, bathed, and assisted into her nightgown.


Day turned to night.

Anne came in to see her before retiring. Thérèse dozed in a chair. Tiny, damp curls stuck to Janthina's head and neck.

The doctor arrived at three in the morning.

'I am so sorry you have been disturbed at such an inconvenient time,' Janthina apologised.

A round, fat, jolly man with a shiny bald pate, he laughed. 'Babies do it to me, always. Never do they arrive at the daytime.' His English was atrocious.

Now that the tedious hours of first-stage labour were over, she was happy to concentrate on heaving a son into the world, though after another hour she began to think he had no intention of leaving her. Until, just when she felt too weary to make another effort, the doctor shouted excitedly.

*'C'est bien, madame, c'est bien! Encore, encore. Hmmm. Hmmm,'* he imitated her grunts of endeavour, encouraging her to try again.

131

She took a deep breath, pushed down with all her might and felt the baby slide out in a warm rush.

Moments later there was a wail.

'*Voilà, madame! Vous avez une belle petite fille!*' The doctor reverted to his native tongue as he made the announcement, proudly, as though he had achieved the entire miracle single-handed.

'*Une fille? A girl!*' Janthina was dazed, confused. 'No,' she shook her head. 'You've made a mistake. It's a boy. His name is Charles.'

'*Madame! Monsieur le docteur ne se trompe pas. C'est une fille.*' The midwife, a sour, thin-faced woman with a thick moustache, corrected severely. '*Regardez!*' She held up the tiny, red mite as high as the umbilical would allow.

There was no denying the fact.

Janthina shook her head wearily, and, too tired to think, she fell asleep.


Screams of agony awoke her. They were her own . . . and the torture in her stomach was unbearable. The midwife was pummelling her middle, a look of grim determination on her face.

'*Non, non, non!*' The doctor commanded, glaring at the starched cap. '*Ce n'est pas nécessaire!*'

'What is the matter? What are you doing?' Janthina gasped.

'*Aucun problème.* The . . . er . . . 'ow you say . . . afterbirth, you still 'ave it inside. It must come. *Quand vous avez une* . . . a little pain. You push, *oui?*'

The nurse walked away from the bed with an impatient, 'Huh!', while the little man patted his patient's head before settling himself in the only armchair and taking a pipe and tobacco pouch from his pocket.

Thérèse opened the door and raised her eyebrows enquiringly at the doctor.

'*Non,*' he shook his head.

The maid frowned. '*Pas bien!*' she said, and clicked her tongue. '*Mais si vous donnez le bébé à madame, le . . .*'

'*Madame Lorcet a dit "Non".*'

Thérèse backed out of the room, saying, '*Je parlerai à Madame Lorcet.*'

A few minutes later she was back, carrying the tiny bundle to the bedside to place it gently into its mother's eager arms.

'Oh, my little doll. My darling little girl. I am so glad I was wrong,' Janthina crooned, nuzzling the fair down on the baby's head. Immediately the infant turned to nuzzle her in turn.

'She wants to feed already!' Thérèse said.

Instinctively the young mother moved the bundle down onto her chest and immediately the nuzzling became more imperative. Tears shone in Janthina's eyes as the communication with her daughter developed, the nightdress buttons were released and the tiny mouth found its target. The result was immediate. Her knees came up with a jerk in response to the pains. 'Aah!' she gasped, convulsed with the urge to bear down again, and in doing so, felt she had produced another baby.

When the afterbirth had been removed, the midwife grasped the baby.

'No!' Janthina said, determinedly. 'She will stay with me.'

The moustache bristled over the thin lips as the woman tugged, scowling, and it was Thérèse who intervened, starting a violent quarrel between the two, which Janthina could interpret more from the gesticulations than the words. The tugging ceased.

She dozed contentedly until she was aware of Anne Lorcet standing by the bed.

'Isn't it wonderful?' Janthina whispered. 'It's not a boy after all. We needn't have worried. She's a beautiful little girl with blue eyes and fair hair, just like her father, and I shall call her Caroline. Aren't I lucky? If it had been a boy I would have had to give him up, I know that. But because it's a girl I won't have to. I can keep her with me, can't I?' It wasn't a question but a statement. Janthina sighed, a relaxed smile on her face. 'I am so pleased,' she murmured.

Anne Lorcet opened her mouth to argue but lacked the will to break the enchanted scene. She gave a weak smile and muttered something about discussing the problem later, at a more opportune moment.


The period of euphoria lasted another week before Janthina finally dared to face the problems she had heaped on herself by keeping the child. Firstly there would have to be a confrontation with the adoption people, probably the awful Bouget woman; then she was going to have to face the fact that, with the baby, she would be welcome in neither Canada nor Scotland. So what? she thought. I would rather be with Caroline than anyone else in the world, even Anthony. Anthony . . . I must write and tell him about Caroline's birth, how beautiful she is and how much she resembles her father. Would he reply? Would he want to see his daughter and . . . herself? Perhaps. She would write immediately, and to Mama as well, saying she would not be in Canada for Christmas after all. Dear Mama. Would she understand? And what about Ruth? Oh, she would understand; she had known from the beginning how hard it would be to give up the baby – better than she had known herself. And Grandmama? Whether or not she understood, she'd never forgive. Never.

The next problem was going to be deciding where she could go. Perhaps she might continue to use part of the château, paying rent to the Lorcets so she might remain here in the Dordogne, where she and Caroline and Thérèse might live happily, quietly together.

Before she had time to suggest this, Madame Bouget arrived. The Lorcets were out and a maid came upstairs to announce that a lady was waiting in the main hall to speak with her. Janthina was puzzled, and hurriedly placed her daughter in the crib, removed her pinafore, straightened her hair, and ran down the stairs – quite heavily, as she was still rather overweight.

'Good afternoon, madame,' Madame Bouget smiled thinly. 'I see you have recovered from your delivery very quickly. I won't detain you. I have come to fetch the baby.'

'Come for the . . . didn't Madame Lorcet contact you? Tell you not to come? I asked her to explain that my daughter is not for adoption. . . .'

'Oh, yes, yes. I'm afraid all young, unmarried mothers want to change their minds. I am quite accustomed to it.' She prattled on in broken English and fast French, neither of which Janthina understood fully. All she did know was that this woman was determined to take her little girl away to a waiting, childless couple, and she, Janthina, was equally determined not to allow Caroline to leave the château.

The little woman was wearing the same slate-grey clothes and silly, bobbing hat as on her previous visit and Janthina wondered vaguely if she ever took them off, even at night. She was gesticulating vigorously, her voice rising an octave as she saw the look of vague incomprehension on the young woman's face – which was partly assumed. Janthina had gathered enough of the gist of the woman's rhetoric, the demands and threats she was making in her effort to gain possession of the child, but rather than attempt to argue she simply shrugged her shoulders and said in her worst possible accent, *'Pardonnez-moi, madame. Je ne comprends pas,'* until the woman gave up and with a look of fury tugged on the bell rope until the maid came in. She was of little help as an interpreter, and eventually excused herself and returned a few minutes later with Thérèse.

There was no question about whose side Thérèse was on. She squared her shoulders, glared down at the grey, bird-like creature and said, *'Non. La petite reste ici,'* in reply to every spate of fury fired at her. Eventually even her patience was tried to the limit, and politely but firmly she took a bony little elbow in her hand and escorted the unfortunate representative of the Paris Adoption Society to her carriage, even giving the waiting horse a hearty smack on the rump to encourage him on his way.

Janthina was waiting in the hall, threw her arms round Thérèse's neck, and the two laughed until the tears ran down their cheeks.


It was no longer possible to put off the dreaded moment; she had to discuss her future with Anne, raising the idea of renting rooms from them.

'I am afraid not,' Anne said. 'It won't be possible as we are in the process of selling this place, and remaining in our Paris apartment permanently. Of course it may take some months, and you are welcome to stay as long as possible.'

So she stayed on, trying not to think of the future, just living each day, enjoying her little girl.

She drew several sketches of Caroline and sent one to Ruth and another to Mama. Mama had told Papa that their younger daughter had accepted an invitation to remain in France over Christmas and into the New Year, in the hopes of seeing her sister again before returning home. But in her letter she had added that she hoped Janthina would have changed her mind about the adoption before too long. . . .

However, there was no sign of Ruth coming back from India for some time, because, in a letter received shortly before Christmas, Ruth had confided news of their own anticipated 'happy event' in April, and went on to discuss having her confinement in Darjeeling: 'Delhi is always so hot; it will be far more pleasant in the mountains even though I will see less of Ben.'

It was a very strange Christmas indeed. Anne explained that she and Henri would be celebrating it in Paris with their family. 'It will be lonely for you, I'm afraid.'

'Don't give it a thought. I will be perfectly content to spend it here in your beautiful Berenac with my little doll and Thérèse,' Janthina assured her.

The weather was mild, the sun streaming across the river and through her window. She left Caroline with Thérèse, very briefly, to drive into Souillac with Gaston to do her Christmas shopping, returning with soft, furry toys for the baby and a beautiful piece of Limoges china for Thérèse. Otherwise her days drifted by peacefully, much of the time spent nursing the baby, feeding her, crooning to her, brushing the blonde wisps of hair into curls and rocking her to sleep in the crib. She had never been very good with her needle, but under Thérèse's tuition she learned to smock and soon enjoyed creating the pretty, colourful patterns on the fronts of the tiny baby dresses.

She had sent off letters of seasonal greetings to Ruth, her parents, and the family at Glenfalk, and was delighted to receive a large post in response. After several abortive efforts she had finally composed a letter to Anthony and, heart pounding unreasonably, posted it off.

Unwilling to eat alone, she invited Thérèse to discard her domestic uniform and join her for Christmas dinner. But it was a strange and sombre meal, in the absence of the noise and bustle of a big family.


Anthony's letter arrived the day the Lorcets returned from Paris. The coat-of-arms on the envelope revealed its origin, but Janthina delayed opening it for some time for she was afraid he would refuse to see Caroline. The hope was still there, that perhaps once he saw his own, beautiful little girl, who so resembled himself. . . .

A smile played round the corners of her mouth as she bore the letter upstairs.

# PART FOUR

## *CAM*

### 1903 – 1920

'It is not in the storm nor in the strife,
We feel benumb'd, and wish to be no more,
But in the after-silence on the shore,
When all is lost, except a little life.'

'On Hearing Lady Byron Was Ill', Lord Byron

# 1

'DEAR JANTHINA,' she read. 'My wife and I have recently returned. . . .'
Wife! '. . . from our honeymoon, spent touring Europe. . . .' Oh! '. . .
which is why I have not replied earlier to your letter. I am sure you must
realise that it is quite out of the question for me to see the child, or
yourself, in these circumstances; it could only cause pain and embarrassment to us all. Thank you for notifying me of the birth, but I would
appreciate you not communicating with me again; I am sure you will
understand. Yours, etc, Mears.'

He didn't even sign it Anthony. She screwed her eyelids up tightly,
as though to obliterate the fearful picture of him honeymooning with
another woman. She wondered how long they had been married? A
pity no one had thought to write and tell her; she would never have
written to him if she'd known. Picking up the letter she crossed to the
hearth and dropped it into the flames, watching it flare up, as their
love had done, and dwindle away into nothing. Nothing.

The finality hurt painfully, but she had no urge to weep; no lump in
the throat, no stinging tears. All she knew was a great void, stretching
ahead into infinity.


Days, weeks, months drifted by and although the feeling persisted
that she was living in a vacuum she was not unhappy. Caroline
progressed rapidly, nurtured by the adoration of her mother and
Thérèse, though Anne and Henri were fairly remote.

Only one thing disturbed Janthina's mind particularly, and she mentioned the subject to Anne one day.

'Is there no church within reasonable distance where Caroline might
be baptised in the Anglican or Presbyterian faith?' she asked.

'Not that I know of.' Anne shook her elegant head. 'Solid Roman
Catholicism everywhere in France, so far as I know. I could be wrong,
though. Would you like me to make some enquiries?'

'I suppose it doesn't matter just now. There's no hurry, but I must
have her christened eventually.'

\*　　\*　　\*

139

When finally the blow fell and the sale of Château de Berenac was completed, Thérèse told Janthina that she could move into the cottage she shared with her sister in Pinsac, just across the river. 'Just for a leetle while until you leave France.'

Leave France! For what? Where could she go? How could she return to either Scotland or Canada? And yet . . . maybe once the family at Glenfalk saw Caroline they would love her and . . . what? She couldn't ask to live at Glenfalk with them, but maybe a cottage could be found. . . . She would write to them.


June. The air was hot and still, birds dozed on well shaded branches while fat bees bowed the heads of flowers as they harvested the pollen. Thérèse brought a letter back from the village to where Janthina was sitting under a walnut tree, smocking. 'This one's for you, from India.'

'Oooh, at last. It will have the news from Ruth of the birth.' She tore open the envelope, scanning the pages rapidly. 'Yes! They have a son! Wonderful! She is still up in Darjeeling, and says she doesn't intend returning to the plains till the autumn. They have christened the baby Giles, after Benjamin's father! And a friend of theirs stood proxy for *me* as his godmother. Well! So I have become an aunt and a godmother all at the same time!'

Thérèse's expression was very serious as she watched Janthina finish reading. She was concerned about the young woman and, as the summer progressed, and Janthina's nineteenth birthday passed and Caroline's first birthday approached, she broached the topic one day.

'I'm worried about you,' she started, hesitantly.

A blustery wind was exciting piles of autumn leaves out of their hiding places under the bushes, pulling wisps of hair out of their restricting pins and tangling their skirts round their ankles as they walked the pram towards the river.

'You're young and beautiful, and you ought to be finding yourself a husband, making a life for yourself and Caroline – you'll never do it here.'

Janthina was silent as they negotiated a difficult stretch of path until they reached a favourite part of the river bank, where a clump of silver birch trees swayed and rustled over a grassy hump which dipped to a beach of small pebbles. Here the river made a sharp turn to the right, diverted by the tall, rocky cliff on the opposite side, rearing dark and gloomy, shaded from the afternoon sun. She took a rug from the foot

140

of the pram, spread it on the dry grass, and sat Caroline in the middle while she and Thérèse made themselves comfortable beside her in the sun.

'I know I am very fortunate to have such a good friend as you have been, Thérèse.' She also knew that Thérèse's sister Ninette did not like or approve of her, and guessed that her presence strained the sisters' relationship. Impulsively she reached out and took Thérèse's hand, holding it to her cheek. 'Thank you for being so good to me. I will soon go, I promise.'


A promise not easy to keep.

She wrote to both Aunt Laura and her mother – several times – and tore up the letters. Days became weeks before she finally summoned up the courage to commit her efforts to the mail and weeks stretched into months before a reply finally arrived.

It was from Aunt Laura, suggesting that she might visit the family in Scotland – leaving the little one with Thérèse, of course.

Caroline was twenty-one months old, walking steadily and able to say a few words through her tiny milk teeth when Janthina finally, and with some reluctance, waved goodbye to her and started her journey to Scotland and Glenfalk. It was a journey which seemed to go on forever, but tired as she became, her nervousness kept her alert. Aunt Laura's letter had been warm and welcoming, but she had had no direct word from Grandmama, had no idea how she would be received, and dreaded the thought of a possible icy reception.

Her clothes had been chosen with great care, made by a local dressmaker in a plain, slim, modest style, with a bustled light tan skirt and short, matching cape with high, stiff collar. Under the cape she wore a cream blouse, high-necked and with full leg-of-mutton sleeves. A straw hat trimmed with cream and tan silk, tan shoes and handbag and a cream, frilled umbrella with a long ferrule and handle, completed her attire. She knew that with the advantage of her height and good figure she looked quite elegant, and held her head high as she stepped down from the carriage and smiled happily to the family who were waiting beside the open door to greet her.

There was a moment's hesitation as they stared at her. Despite her nervousness at meeting them all again and of Grandmama in particular, she followed her impulsive instinct and rushed, girlishly, into the elderly woman's arms. Perhaps her grandmother was taken aback, Janthina couldn't be sure, but she was quickly aware of an affectionate, even if slightly reserved, response. And of course the rest of the family followed the matriarchal lead. There were hugs and kisses all round before she was led upstairs by Aunt Laura – to her old room.

'Janthina, my dear!' her aunt exclaimed, leaning heavily against the bedroom door as it closed behind her. 'You look splendid. So grown up! What has happened to you?'

'Motherhood, I suppose.' Janthina sat on her dressing stool to remove her hat.

'I have thought about you so much in the past couple of years. But tell me, my dear, why did you change your mind about the baby? What made you keep her?'

'I never wanted to part with my baby, whether it was a boy or a girl, but because I had fixed in my head that it was definitely a boy I felt it would be wrong to keep him, saddle him for life with his illegitimacy. He had lost so much by Anthony's refusal to give him a name. I had braced myself against the pain of parting with him for months before the birth, but when I realised that in fact I had a little girl, well, the problem no longer seemed that important . . . and oh, Aunt Laura, you would love her; she is absolutely beautiful. Once I had seen her, held her in my arms, there was no longer any question of parting with her. I have done lots of sketches and paintings of her. I will show them to you tomorrow when my trunk is unpacked.' She failed to notice the smile fade from Aunt Laura's face.

During the first few days after her arrival the family gradually adjusted to this new, older, Janthina. The atmosphere of reserve relaxed. Elinor invited her out riding and Roderick took great pleasure in presenting her with a copy of the book of poems he had just published.

Once her confidence had returned, she introduced the subject of a christening service for Caroline and was immediately aghast at her grandparents' reactions.

'Not here! Not in this locality, thank you!' Grandmama said severely. 'That unpleasant episode in our lives is forgotten, I hope, and we don't want any reminders. You were a silly girl to keep the child, but it was your choice, and now you will have to live with the consequences.'

She was alone in the Great Hall with her grandparents and Aunt Laura, and turned to the latter in alarm. But her aunt stared down at her tapestry, offering no support.

'And what do you intend to do with yourself, now, young lady?' Grandpapa glared at her over *The Times*. 'Where do you plan to live? Are you going back to Canada? Can't imagine Hamish giving you much of a welcome if you've a fatherless bairn with you.'

'It would be best if Janthina could meet up with a nice young man and get married,' Laura remarked.

'Married? Who's going to marry her with a child in tow?' the laird demanded.

'Janthina.' Grandmama laid her embroidery on her lap and stared hard into the girl's face. 'Won't you reconsider? It's not too late, you know. If the baby is as beautiful as you say she is, it should be very easy to find her an excellent. . . .'

'No, Grandmama,' Janthina interrupted, quietly. 'Never. I will never part with Caroline. I love her dearly, she is the most important person in my life, and if it is a matter of choosing between her and a husband, I'll keep my daughter and remain single.'

Alexandra MacDougall picked up her needle again. 'Well, in all fairness I must say I admire both your spirit and your sentiments, but I do hope you realise the difficulties you are piling up for yourself – and the child.'


Next day was Sunday.

Janthina knelt in church and prayed fervently for a solution. Dear God, You would not have wanted me to give my little girl away, would You? You gave her to me and she is so precious. Please show me a way to resolve this problem.

After the service they shook hands with the minister and his family.

'How very nice to see you again, Miss McKenzie. Will you be with us long?' Mrs Cameron was wearing the same hat with the bobbing feather as she had worn two Christmases ago to sing carols at Glenfalk.

'It is very nice to be back, Mrs Cameron, but I'm afraid my visit will be much shorter this time. Oh, Mr Cameron, I didn't see you in church.'

The minister's son shook her hand enthusiastically. 'Ah! But I saw you. What a great stroke of good fortune that I should be visiting my parents this weekend. Perhaps you would do me the honour of allowing me to call on you?'

He looked different, what was it? Oh, of course, the beard: he had grown a neat little goatee. And his suit was new and smart, a definite improvement. 'Er . . . oh, yes, if you wish, Mr Cameron, that would be very nice. Tomorrow, perhaps?'

'I'm afraid I must away to Edinburgh tonight. Must be at business early in the morning, you know. I was hoping that I might come out to Glenfalk this afternoon.'

Janthina glanced at her grandfather, who nodded briskly. 'Yes, yes. Why not?'

They drove back to Glenfalk in the carriage as Alexandra found the walk rather too far for her nowadays. There was silence for most of the way and Janthina was aware of some significant glances between her grandparents which she could not fathom. She looked from one to the other but nothing was said before Malcolm drew rein at the door and they all hurried upstairs to prepare for lunch.

James Cameron arrived at two thirty and suggested he might escort Miss McKenzie on a walk up the valley to the burn. Janthina agreed and they set off together in the warm, breezy sunshine.

They talked trivialities – the weather, problems of travelling abroad – and then Janthina said, 'Tell me, Mr Cameron, are you still working in a store in Edinburgh?'

'Yes, Miss McKenzie, and I have been appointed departmental manager.'

'Oh, splendid! Congratulations.'

He smiled broadly. 'Thank you very much, you are most kind. I wish I might show you the place if ever you are in Edinburgh. I think I have up-graded my department considerably, and I am very pleased with it. However, I must tell you that it is not my ambition to remain there. I am saving and planning all the while to open my own store, eventually.'

'Really! Where? In Edinburgh?'

'No, no. I want to move south. I believe there should be a very good trade on the south coast of England in one of the popular resorts.'

'What a splendid idea! What a great deal of ability and determination you must have, Mr Cameron. I wish you every success in your venture.'

'You really are very kind.' His smile broadened even further and he gave her a long, searching look, appeared to want to ask her something . . . but said nothing.

Grandfather was in the garden when they returned. 'Are you coming in to take tea with us, Mr Cameron?' he invited.

James Cameron looked surprised, but pleased. 'Yes, sir! Thank you very much.'

Janthina was surprised, too, and even more so when, tea finished and the tray removed, Grandpapa asked the young man if he would care to step into his study for a few minutes. She watched them leave the room together and turned to her grandmother who just smiled and picked up her embroidery. *She knows what is going on between those* two, the young woman decided, and she won't tell me. What are they up to?

She was to learn soon enough.

James Cameron returned to the Great Hall only long enough to politely take his leave of the ladies and the moment he had gone Donald MacDougall told them of his conversation with the young man.

'I guessed he had taken a fancy to you, so I asked him into my study to enquire about his intentions. Well, young lady, it looks as though you are in luck. With a little encouragement from me, because normally you would be quite beyond his reach, he asked my permission, in the absence of your father, you understand, to court you with a view to marriage.' Janthina's eyes grew wide and her mouth fell open. 'Now there was no point in beating about the bush, so I told him straight about the bairn and asked if he was still interested.'

'You did what?' Janthina was horrified.

The laird ignored her interruption. 'He looked somewhat astonished, not to say disappointed, but eventually said yes, he was. . . .'

'James Cameron? Disappointed?' she exclaimed. That . . . that ordinary little store clerk had the nerve to ask if he might court her . . . and then was disappointed. . . .

'So you see you are very lucky. He may not be a viscount, but his family is very respectable and he is a very go-ahead young man.'

Grandmama sighed. 'He is not the man we would have selected for you, but in all the circumstances you can see there is no choice – no choice at all.'

'But I don't even. . . .'

'I hope you are not going to start creating difficulties,' the laird interrupted her. 'As I see it you have no option, no choice in the matter at all. Either you accept or you hand the bairn over for adoption; there can be no question of you bringing embarrassment to this household.'

Janthina's mind reeled from anger to misery, rebellion to horror. She opened her mouth to argue – but found herself unable to form the words. There was no argument.

'You realise that it would be most unfair to the bairn to refuse this offer, don't you? You will be committing her to the stigma of illegitimacy probably for the rest of her life. Frey's money cannot buy you out of that.'

Although the whole idea struck her as utterly preposterous at first, seen from Caroline's point of view she had to agree it could probably not be bettered. Apparently James had assured her grandfather that if she would agree to wed him, he would automatically adopt the child as his own. Caroline Cameron – it didn't sound right. Too much of a mouthful. But had she the right to turn him down? To reject the opportunity to make her daughter legitimate – and keep her? So he had made a very bad first impression with his gauche manners and over-opinionated ideas of his own importance. But he did appear to have improved somewhat in the past two years.

Was James Cameron God's answer to her prayers?

He arrived the following Saturday evening, having been invited to join the family for dinner. Somehow he managed to please Elinor with a discussion on horse-doctoring; he had read Roderick's book of poems and even memorised some of them. He brought a rare potted orchid for Grandmama's conservatory, and conveyed the compliments of some of Edinburgh's leading businessmen on Grandpapa's herd of cattle. In fact, by the time he had bidden them all goodnight, it was generally felt that James Cameron was a quite acceptable young man.

Janthina was forced to agree; her only reservation was one she could not discuss with anyone. . . . The thought of sharing a bedroom with him, a bed, of making love with him as she had with Anthony, was quite abhorrent.

They went walking again the following afternoon and that evening she was invited to the minister's house for dinner where she was made most welcome. James collected her in his father's gig and delivered her home quite early.

And the next weekend he proposed.

Although she had known it was his ultimate intention it still came as a shock. She hadn't expected it quite so soon. She wasn't ready yet – couldn't answer.

They had climbed on to a hilltop overlooking the Glenfalk valley, both panting and red-faced from the exertion. Suddenly he took her hand and said, 'Miss McKenzie, Janthina, you must be aware that I have spoken to the laird, so it will not come as a surprise to you when I tell you I would like you to accept my proposal of marriage.'

All so formal, and he had not so much as attempted to kiss her cheek yet.

'Oh, Mr Cameron. . . .'

'Please call me James.'

'James . . . I. . . . Yes, my grandfather did tell me of his conversation with you. Please excuse me for sounding so unsure, but you do understand that we know so little of each other and. . . .'

'I do understand, Janthina, very well. It is so difficult for us to meet more often; Glenfalk is a long way from Edinburgh – and France is even further.'

She looked at him as he spoke. An aggressive and determined young man, no more than her own height, dark hair blown into disorder by the summer breeze despite the liberal use of macassar oil. His eyes were dark and deepset under heavy brows, his nose bony, and when he was not smiling his mouth was quite lost behind his whiskers. And as she looked she wondered why there was no surge of interest, no spark of response in her to his nearness, his masculinity. There was no draw as there had been towards Anthony . . . and even to Roland.

She recalled the first time she saw Anthony waiting in the crowded hall as she walked down the stairs for the Hogmanay party, and even now there were flutterings in her stomach as, briefly, she relived that moment. Oh, yes, how she had been drawn to him – an animal attraction for a beautiful creature of the opposite sex – but could that be called 'love'? Shouldn't love and respect go hand in hand? But how could you respect someone of whom you knew nothing? Her social life in Scotland had probably given her some exalted ideas on prospective suitors, especially after meeting Anthony, so perhaps she was being somewhat over-critical of James. Wasn't he just the sort of young man of whom Mama and Papa would have approved had he made such a polite and proper approach in Canada? And as her grandparents and Aunt Laura had so forcefully pointed out – she was very lucky to get such an offer. . . .

James was staring at her, waiting.

'Well, Mr Cam . . . I mean James, you are so kind and I would like to consider your offer. You understand I have to bear in mind the welfare of my little girl.'

'Of course. I have no wish to hurry you or appear pushing in any way. Just let me assure you that as soon as we are married – that is, if you will consent to be my wife,' he interjected hastily, 'we will move to the south of England, and you will be able to send for the child.' He saw her face fall and went on. 'She would not be made welcome here at Glenfalk, I believe, so it would be far better if we introduce ourselves as a complete family in Brighton, or wherever.'

'Ye . . . es. I see your point. But then you would be prepared to adopt her?'

'Naturally. No question about it. It will only be a matter of arranging the legalities at our convenience.'

She was looking down at her boots, unseeing, trying to assemble all the thoughts and feelings, facts and anxieties into one single, logical answer.

For which he waited in silence. What was he thinking of her long-delayed reply – her request for time to consider? She glanced up, suddenly, and for the first time saw the ardent desire in his eyes. He quickly resumed his polite mask of reserve and smiled gently, encouragingly.

Well? What had she to lose? Nothing. And she would gain a husband, respectability – and a father for Caroline. The choice must be obvious; there was no point in delaying her answer.

'Yes, James,' she smiled and nodded. 'I will marry you. I am sure we will be very well suited and I am very happy that Caroline will have a name, too.'

'Dear Janthina, you have made me very happy.' He beamed, and took possession of her arm to lead her back down the hillside.


James estimated it would take him some months to find a home for them in the south and a suitable business in which he could further his ambitions. So Janthina returned to France to wait until he sent word that all was ready.

The older generation at Glenfalk were obviously relieved that the whole dreadful affair should have reached such a satisfactory conclusion, though Elinor and Roderick were conspicuously silent on the subject.

Alexandra wrote immediately to her daughter in Canada recommending the match, knowing full well that Adeline would warmly welcome the news. Janthina wrote too, pleased at last to be conveying such acceptable plans for her future, though she wondered how long it would be before she would be able to see Canada again. For, despite her love of Scotland and France, and no matter how remote it seemed at the moment, in her mind Canada would always remain her only real home.


Soon after her return to France, Janthina had stopped trying to anticipate the future. Her decision to marry James was made – she would not change it. She was determined to think only positively about what would happen, and not to dwell on what might have been.

James wrote to her only occasionally, notes so brief as to seem almost curtly abrupt, starting 'Dear Janthina' and ending 'Yours truly, James Cameron', almost as though theirs was a business association. Which perhaps it was, in a way. He didn't know that her birthday was in August, so no post arrived from him, but Mama, Papa and Joseph had sent her some pretty table linen for her trousseau, and Ruth and Ben a beautifully embossed Indian silver rose bowl. From Scotland she received a letter of description of the suite of cut glass and the dinner service which awaited her return to Britain, there being little point in dispatching such breakables across the Channel only to be returned in so short a time.

A letter from James arrived in mid October asking Janthina to pack up and leave for Scotland immediately.

'Oh, no,' she exclaimed to Thérèse. 'He doesn't realise it's Caroline's birthday in two weeks. I can't go before then.'

Thérèse agreed. 'Of course not. After waiting all this time two more weeks can hardly matter. I'm sure he won't mind. You can be all packed up and ready to leave the day after, though, so there will be no more delay than necessary.'

James was waiting for her at Dover.

She was tired by the long journey through France and a rough Channel crossing, and still feeling sad after the farewells to Caroline and Thérèse, so she was not cheered at all by James's cool reception.

'I've had to cancel the ceremony that was already arranged, you know,' he grumbled. 'The child's birthday was surely not the only reason you delayed, was it?'

She stared at him in amazement; she had never known him to be so churlish. She remained silent, fearing that if she attempted a reply she would either explode or weep – she wasn't sure which.

They drove directly to a small hotel where, before she had time to remove her hat, James asked her to select only the few essential garments she might need in Scotland for the ceremony, so that the remaining trunks might be dispatched directly to their new home in Whitehaven, just beyond Brighton.

Their first meal alone together was a little disappointing. Although James's mind and Janthina's stomach had regained their equilibrium, the chipped paintwork and peeling wallpaper in the hotel dining room correctly forewarned them to expect the worst – watery soup, tough meat, over-stewed vegetables, and stodgy pudding. They chewed in silence, and not until the plates had been removed did James begin to tell her, over cups of undrinkable coffee, about the business and home he had acquired for them. It was a corner grocery shop just inland from the coast road in an area made popular as a holiday resort by its lovely wooded valley dipping down to a picturesque sandy beach.

'It is gaining a good reputation for hotels, too, and the shop is ideally situated within easy reach of several of the smaller hotels and boarding houses and a number of smart private houses which are rented out throughout the summer.'

'What happens to our trade in the winter, when there are no visitors and the hotels are empty?' Janthina asked.

'The local people will have to eat as well. We'll have to build up a good trade with them.'

'And what about the house? Is that near the shop?'

'Couldn't be nearer. We'll live in the rooms over the shop.' He tried to drink the coffee but gave up in disgust, setting the cup noisily back in its saucer.

Rooms over the shop! It didn't sound very exciting. 'How many rooms? And is there a garden?'

'Two on the first floor and two on the second. No, there's no garden, just a paved yard at the back. Can't expect to start with anything too lavish; but don't you worry, we'll soon build up and improve,' he tried to assure her, unsuccessfully.

Over and over, that night in her single, musty bedroom, she endeavoured to convince herself that the sinking feeling in the pit of her stomach was purely nervousness of the unknown, an illogical fear of marriage, of going to live hundreds of miles from any friends or relatives with this chunky, determined Scot whom she hardly knew.

She fell asleep frowning, and woke with a headache.


November 4th, 1904 was a bleak day, rain driven in from the North Sea by Arctic winds. The brief ceremony was performed by the Reverend William Cameron, and attended only by a small, close group of relatives and some friends of the groom's family. Aunt Laura had placed vases in the church, filled mostly with leaves and a few flowers, plus some potted plants borrowed from the Glenfalk conservatory, and Cook produced a quite lavish wedding breakfast, served in the dining room, without need to add more than two leaves to the great table.

All the MacDougall clan, and Janthina herself, were tall, stately figures, dwarfing the Camerons completely, and although James matched her in height, his bride, elegantly attired in a cream grosgrain gown and matching jacket, again made in Souillac by Anne Lorcet's dressmaker, and worn with a cream and beige fur hat, towered over his parents and their guests, overaweing them, knotting their tongues.

She circulated amongst them, trying to make conversation, but failing miserably and only comforted by the fact that none of the MacDougalls appeared to be having any better success. Looking at her new in-laws, simply if not dowdily dressed, she realised that her outfit was probably far too splendid . . . and James was frowning again. All a very far cry from the magnificent, joyous occasion of Ruth and Ben's marriage.

The speeches were short and uncomfortable and in a way it was a relief to climb into the carriage amidst a dusting of confetti and drive off on the first leg of their journey south.

James had reserved a tiny, two-berth compartment in a second-class carriage on the Edinburgh to London overnight express. Fortunately their few boxes were stowed in a luggage van as there certainly would not have been room to turn round otherwise. They ate a dinner of cold chicken legs, rolls and cheese washed down with home-made ginger ale which had been packed into a carrier for them by James's mother, over paper napkins spread on their knees. Afterwards, as they rolled up the remains, Janthina rubbed anxiously with her handkerchief at a greasy mark left on her skirt.

'You chose a rather impractical outfit for travelling, didn't you?' James remarked, unhelpfully.

'I'm afraid I hadn't expected to eat from my lap in such cramped circumstances,' she replied irritably.

'Well, you are going to have to get used to second-class travel for a while. And no more ladies' maids to look after you, either. Now, why don't you go along to the bathroom while I arrange the top bunk and then I'll go down the corridor while you get to bed.'

The thought struck her that at least they wouldn't be able to make love tonight, and hoped her sigh of relief wasn't audible. She was tired and miserable; the wedding had been a most disappointing and depressing affair, and her despondency at the idea of being tied to James for the rest of her life was increasing by the minute.

And she was even more disappointed when, fifteen minutes later, as she lay in the lower bunk facing the wall, James gave her a nudge and said, 'Come on, wife, move over and make room for your husband.' She turned to face the unromantic vision of 'her man' snugly encased from neck to wrist and ankle in a pair of long, woolly combinations.

Obediently she squeezed up against the wall as he lifted the blanket to wriggle down beside her. Immediately his left hand clutched her right breast, not gently and caressingly, but rather as though he was attempting to tear it right off. Then he fumbled for a few moments with the buttons at her neck before abandoning that idea and transferring his attentions to lower down the bed.

151

'Er . . . don't you think we should wait till we are in a proper bed?' she suggested, backing away as far as the narrow space permitted.

'No, why? It should be fun to do it travelling at over sixty miles an hour,' he laughed, and continued probing. His fingers found their target, dug and prodded, fingernails carelessly scratching. 'I've waited a long time for this moment, my love, and I've no intention of delaying any longer.' His free hand released the appropriate buttons on his combinations and immediately he pushed a leg over her, parting her thighs. She felt him pressing and fumbling before he finally forced an entry, dry and abrasive, thrusting, grunting, and, within seconds, exhaling in a long, low hiss to collapse heavily on her chest.

It was unquestionably the most unpleasant and degrading single experience of her life – worse, even, than being bullied and beaten by Papa.

'Mmm,' James murmured as he left her to climb up into his bunk. 'That was very good, wasn't it? I've been wanting to do that with you ever since the very first time I saw you.' And within minutes he was snoring.

Janthina lay in the darkness, swaying with the motion of the train, throbbing with the regular thump of the wheels. Not even a kiss! He had never attempted to kiss her at all. Sleep was a million miles away. Dared she put on the light? She twisted uncomfortably, wondering if she could put some clothes on and go to the bathroom to wash away the stickiness without disturbing him.

James didn't stir as she edged out of bed and stepped into her skirt. And he was still snoring contentedly when she returned from the bathroom ten minutes later.

152

# 2

JANTHINA WAS immediately impressed with the nice locality surrounding the shop – mostly small but smart-looking hotels and houses. The shop itself looked run-down, but as James pointed out, it really only needed a coat of paint to smarten it up. Inside, the shelves were dirty and bare, floorboards showed through holes in the tattered linoleum and the whole place smelt of the dirty yellow oilcloth which still clung in patches to the shop counter.

'I can see we could do wonders with this place. It's a good size, isn't it?' She stood amidst their trunks and boxes, looking about her.

'Yes, I'm very pleased to have found it. And there's a big double storeroom behind, with room for an office.' James's good humour had returned, much to his wife's relief.

She could picture it all clean and spruce, walls painted a soft green, perhaps, and white-painted shelves well stocked with cans, bottles and packets. 'I'd love to help you straighten it out and repaint it,' she went on enthusiastically. 'Will you let me?'

'Indeed, your help is essential. There is so much to be done and we cannot afford to employ anyone. Now, let's get these boxes upstairs, though for the life of me I cannot think where we are going to put it all.'

The rooms which were to be their living quarters were equally scruffy. Wallpaper was peeling and the paintwork so badly chipped that several layers of different colours, chosen over the years by various occupants, were revealed. Stuffing showed through a hole in the sofa, an armchair wobbled on its three remaining castors, and the dining table was ring-stained and pitted. In the larger of the two small attic bedrooms the wardrobe door hung askew off a broken hinge, the mirror on the chest of drawers was cracked and spotted, and when James sat on the bed it sagged and groaned.

Janthina's spirits sagged too. 'Oh, dear! But I suppose we can smarten this up as well. A scrubbing brush and a coat of paint will make a world of difference,' she said, more in hope than in conviction.

'Yes. Easy. I'm so glad you see the possibilities as I do. But you realise we are going to have to fix the shop up first. Got to start getting some money in as soon as we can.'

'Yes, I realise that,' she nodded, trying not to look as gloomy as she felt.


A church clock chimed three.

Janthina shifted her hip slightly to avoid a particularly bad lump in the mattress, but remained close enough to James to gain a little warmth. The wardrobe door creaked on its one good hinge, moving in the draught which whistled in under the door from the stairway. She pictured the lovely clothes hanging in there – quite useless for the task of cleaning up and daubing paint in this dilapidated place; she had not a garment in which she could kneel in soapsuds, scrubbing. And anyway, most of her gowns would have to remain in their trunks in the storeroom; there was no room for them up here and she couldn't imagine having the need for any of them in the near future.

It had been a strange evening. While she unpacked sheets and pillowcases and blankets to make up their bed, James had lit a fire in the living room – then went out to buy fish and chipped potatoes ready cooked. The fire had a grid across where a pot or two might stand to boil, and beside it were set two small ovens, one above the other, the whole fireplace surround being set with green, patterned tiles. They sat at the table eating their supper from cracked china – awful, thick, yellow plates printed with white flowers and green leaves. She thought of her beautiful white dinner service with its delicate festoons of flowers, and wondered where she could possibly keep it. The cupboards were quite inadequate for the skeletal pieces already here, and there was no space to add another cabinet.

James snorted, turned over, and grabbed a handful of breast. Having repeated his performance of the night before on the train, he was in a deeply contented sleep.

Janthina was not.

She found it hard to believe that two men could be quite so different as Anthony and James . . . but she must put Anthony out of her mind, stop comparing the two and learn to accept James as he was. After all, he had married her, was hard-working and industrious, honest and straightforward, even if he was unable to rouse a spark of response in her with his love-making; if it could be called that.

Grateful for his body warmth, she eventually fell into a shallow, restless sleep.

Next morning, while James was out purchasing paints, brushes, soap and pails, she found a little general store where she bought a chequered gingham dress and two cotton pinafores.

'What did you go and waste money on those for?' James demanded as she unwrapped her shopping. 'Jumping Jehosaphat! You've got a trunk full of clothes already – enough for a flipping queen.'

His wife laughed. 'Oh, James, of course I haven't. And I certainly have nothing suitable for working around her. I can't ruin good, expensive gowns on these floors.'

James pursed his lips, clicked his tongue, and walked out of the room.

It was too much, she supposed, to expect a man to understand these things.

Together they started on the shop, tearing up the old linoleum, removing the offensive oilcloth, and scraping off years of grease and dirt with kitchen knives, while pots of water were heating before the scrubbing could commence. Janthina hadn't worked so hard since leaving Canada, and even there she had never been required to tackle anything quite so filthy and malodorous. But in a way it was fun. It was a challenge, attempting to transform this appalling mess into a place which, hopefully, might attract customers. It was actually enjoyable to be working with James as a team. They flicked soapsuds at one another, 'borrowed' each other's cloths and brushes, teased, joked and laughed. James could be very good company, his wife discovered, keeping her amused as they worked with stories of his experiences in the Boer War, well embellished, she had no doubt, for the sake of the yarn.

They had begun with the ceiling, then worked on the walls and shelves, but when they paused at lunchtime little progress could be seen. The comparatively clean areas looked far too small in ratio to the energy expended, and by mid afternoon every muscle in Janthina's body was burning.

'I'm sorry, James, but I don't think I could face another pail of dirty water today. Do you mind if I go upstairs and change and sit down for a few minutes before cooking the supper?'

'If you must. I suppose I'll have to carry on alone.' There was no word of praise or thanks for the hours of scrubbing she had done on the first day of her honeymoon, which hurt.

Two days later they opened the first tins of paint and by the end of the week had started stocking the shelves.

Janthina drew on a sheet of paper her ideas for corner shelf units for window displays. James was very pleased with her drawings, bought wood and nails and made up four units for each window, and also extra stands for the base. She hemmed narrow, green and white check curtains and matching shelf-cloths and arranged on them neat little stacks of tins and packets each clearly labelled and priced on small pieces of stiff board. When it was done the two stood together outside on the pavement and James admired her handiwork.

'That really looks good, my love. Very artistic.'

He came in on Thursday lunchtime with a newspaper, to show her his advertisement proclaiming the 'GRAND OPENING OF CAMERON AND CO., GROCERS AND PROVISIONERS'.

Together they stretched bunting across the shop-front early on Friday morning, and pinned up paper Christmas decorations inside.

'A bit early in the season, perhaps, but it all helps to attract people,' James said confidently, testing the weighing machine yet again. For the umpteenth time he consulted his pocket watch, adjusted the sacks of dried lentils, split peas and beans, sniffed the cured hams hanging from the ceiling and turned the bottles on the shelves so that the labels were facing exactly forward. And when the chimes of the church clock coincided with his watch at eight o'clock sharp, he unlocked the shop door, and waited.

Two minutes later the doorbell rang. 'Me Mam says are ye open for business?' a cheeky youngster asked, head just high enough for him to peer over the counter.

'Indeed we are, sonny,' James smiled benevolently. 'You run home and tell your mother we look forward to seeing her.'

'Do yer give tick?' the boy called from the door.

James's face clouded as he summed up the ragged trousers and tired boots. 'No, definitely not,' he called back.

'What's tick?' Janthina asked as the boy ran off.

'Credit.'

'Oh. But surely we cannot expect hoteliers to pay cash down. Won't they want weekly or monthly accounts?'

'Of course, and so they shall. But we will know darn well they've got the money to pay with at the end of the month; at least, we'll hope they have. That kid's mother probably hasn't got two farthings. We'll not give tick to the likes of her. You'll have to learn to judge the difference.'

Trade was slow to start and Janthina went upstairs to boil more water to make a start with the cleaning of their upstairs rooms.

'What are you doing?' James had come up to fetch a file of bills, relying on the shop bell to summon him if necessary.

'Making a start on the mess up here,' she told him, rolling up her sleeves.

'Wait a bit! The storeroom's got to be done next. We can't stock up properly till that's cleaned up.'

Her heart sank. Her whole body still ached from her efforts in the shop, while every time she walked into their living room and bedroom she recoiled from the squalor. 'Oh, James! Can't that wait just one more day – this is so awful.'

'There'll be no money for paper and paint till we start to make some; and if we can't replace what we sell with stock from our storeroom, but have to wait for the wholesalers to deliver, we might as well give up now. We'll lose the customers as fast as we get them.'

She sighed. 'I suppose you're right. Well, here's your pail and brush. I'll heat some more water for myself and bring it down in a few minutes.'

'Don't bother.' He shook his head. 'I can't be getting myself messed up in the back there. I've got to stay smart for the customers. You'll have to get on with it by yourself.' The shop bell rang and he ran eagerly down the stairs.

Two weeks passed before Janthina was able to finish with the storeroom and cleaning the upstairs room, but there was no money for decorating and repairs.

'How long will it be?' she asked, close to tears.

'Maybe next month.'

'Next month! Oh, James, no! Well, look, why don't I buy what we need? I have some money. I do want to get the place straight as soon as possible so that Caroline can join us.'

'I didn't know you had any money. You'll have to give it to me to handle. It would be better spent on good stock than primping this place up unnecessarily. Where is it?' he demanded.

'No, James, it is my money, for Caroline and me. Definitely not for the business. I'll work as hard as I can to help you but I won't hand over the money.' She spoke quietly but resolutely.

James was furious. 'Who the hell do you think you're talking to, you silly bitch? I'm your husband, or have you forgotten that already? What's yours became mine automatically when we married. It's your duty to hand it over.'

She seethed with anger, but managed to control her voice. 'You are wrong, James. That money is a trust and may in no circumstances, marriage or otherwise, be used other than as I see fit. I don't intend to squander it, but I do mean to try and turn this mess . . .' she swept a hand round the room '. . . into something reasonable for ourselves and Caroline, until we can afford a maid.'

'A maid? Not bloody likely. That I absolutely forbid. . . .'

'But she'll keep the flat clean and look after Caroline while I help you in the shop.'

'No, I said! No! I won't need you except when I have to go out; then the kid can come downstairs with you. Now you just listen to me, my girl.' He wagged his forefinger under her nose. 'Your fancy gentleman didn't marry you – he found something better. I've married you, and agreed to give his kid a home, but I don't have his thousands. I have to work damned hard for my money and you, my girl, are going to have to forget your fancy ideas about maids. Maids! And you're going to have to climb down a peg or two as well. You're too darned hoity-toity, the way you dress up in all your fancy finery and look down your nose at people. Very embarrassing it was, at the wedding, the way you made my relatives feel so uncomfortable.'

She was too dumbfounded to reply; to think of anything to say. He was so boorish, uncouth! She wanted to tell him so, tell him how coarse and crude she found him – but that could only make matters worse. Instead, she lifted her head high, looked down her nose at him, and walked quietly up the stairs to their bedroom. She heard him slam the living-room door and stamp down the stairs to the shop.

By suppertime her anger had cooled. She fried him some fish, mashed potatoes with butter the way he liked them, and boiled some carrots and beans. Mama always used to say that the way to a man's heart was through his stomach.

James cleaned his plate and followed it with two helpings of steamed syrup pudding. When he had finished and was sitting by the fire with his cup of tea he actually smiled – into the flames.

Encouraged, Janthina said sweetly, 'Dear James. I'm so sorry if I appeared hoity-toity at the wedding. It wasn't intentional, but my height does give that impression sometimes. I'm really a very warm person, truly.'

'Warm!' He turned to face her, his beard failing to mask the sneer on his face. 'You think you're warm? Why, you're the coldest female I ever met!'

'James! Why do you say that?'

'Why! Because night after night you lie there in that bed, under me, never so much as twitching a muscle. I'd get more joy out of a dead fish.'

She covered her face with her hands. He was right. She felt no response to him, so gave none. It was her own fault.

Later, while James banked down the fire and turned down the gas mantles, she went upstairs and put on her prettiest nightdress, too thin a material for such cold weather but it did look more attractive than the woollen ones. She brushed out her hair and dabbed perfume on her skin, climbed into bed and waited. When he joined her, before he had time to make his customary grab, she took his face between her hands and kissed him, opening her lips to seek his tongue with hers. He stared up at her, eyebrows raised. She ran her hands over his body, caressing what she could feel of it through his nightshift, then drew up the coarse material so that she might take hold of what was underneath – something she had never seen, unlike those parts of Anthony's body she had so loved.

'Dear James,' she whispered. 'I'm so sorry I made you think I was cold.'

He didn't reply. Frantically he pulled up her nightgown and threw himself on top of her, thrusting inside . . . just in time before exploding.

He rolled off her on to his back. 'Ahh! That's better. That's more like a warm and loving wife.' And in two minutes he was asleep.

Janthina crept out of bed and by the light of the streetlamp washed herself and creamed away the soreness. Back in bed she closed her eyes and tried to think of Caroline, of happy times, anything to blot out the fear that she might never again experience the ecstasy she had known with Anthony.


James was in an excellent mood next day and that evening even took up a paintbrush to help her decorate the flat.

Maybe I misunderstood Mama's advice about the way to a man's heart, his wife thought; perhaps I was tackling his stomach from the wrong end! She painted all the ceiling herself, glad for once that the rooms were so small, and when all the paintwork was completed, James even helped her hang the wallpaper, laughing with her as bits of sticky paper glued to their clothes.

At a second-hand furniture store, Janthina picked an eager salesman's brain on how to restore stained and chipped furniture, unperturbed by his expression when she walked away empty-handed. She stripped the dining table down to bare wood, as the poor man had instructed, and restained and polished it; replaced the missing castor on the armchair, and patched the hole in the sofa before covering it with a tartan rug.

The flooring was horrible and James would not hear of purchasing new linoleum, so she simply tore up the old, and scrubbed the bare boards, sanded them, and applied stain and polish. A great improvement on any lino, she decided. She did purchase a cheap hearthrug and two small bedside mats; possibly James didn't notice, for he said nothing about extravagance, only praised her efforts. 'I must say, my love, you are a born home maker . . . and good in bed, too.' She was managing to maintain her efforts in bed each night.

She hung a painting of Château Berenac over the mantelshelf, one of the river fitted nicely over the sideboard, and her favourite of Caroline, holding a bunch of wild flowers, went up in their bedroom. All were unframed, but nonetheless gave added life to the freshened rooms.

Now that the heavy work was finished, Janthina was able to take advantage of the unseasonably dry days to explore Whitehaven. The older part of the town nestled against the steep hillside east of the valley where the stream – it could hardly be called a river – emptied into the sea. It had scooped, over the centuries, a basin deep enough to give shallow-draught fishing vessels safe anchorage, protected by a stone pier extending west from the chalky headland which gave the town its name. During the previous century, wealthy Londoners, anxious to leave the stifling summer heat of the city, had discovered its peaceful beauty and built splendid holiday houses to the west, overlooking the sands. Others had followed, bringing merchants in their wake. Hotels sprang up or were converted from the homes vacated by their original owners, appalled by the new influx.

Today, a modest promenade held back the spring tides pushed up by southerly gales; it reached from the bridge east of the little harbour, across the mouth of the valley in front of the large hotels, more modest hostelries and boarding houses, past the terraced homes overlooking the west end of the beach, and ending at the far cliffs. A new town centre had grown up behind the seaside buildings where the old and new town converged, and meandering lanes led east and west from the main north road to serve homes sprawling up the hillsides where newcomers reached for a glimpse of the sun.

Cameron and Company was only one block away from the promenade, a few streets west of the town centre. A good position, she thought, for summer excursions to the beach with Caroline.

'How does one go about adopting a child?' Janthina asked one evening after supper. 'Have you made any enquiries yet?'

'It has to be done through a lawyer,' he replied, then laying down his newspaper, went on, 'I've been meaning to talk to you about that. These things do take time, I'm afraid, and as you wanted to get her over here so soon, before all the papers are ready, we'll have to invent a surname for her; we don't want folks round here knowing the truth. We can say she's your sister's child, if you like, and we're taking her on because her parents have died or something.'

Janthina frowned. 'Do you really think that's necessary?'

'Definitely. She can call you "auntie" until the legalities are completed.'

'How long will that be?'

'I don't know. I haven't spoken to a lawyer yet. Lawyers cost money. I'll do it as soon as business picks up.'

'It might not be easy to train Caroline to call me "auntie" – she knows me as Mama.'

'She'll learn.'

'And what happens if Ruth and Ben come back to live in England?'

'We'll invent a third sister, who married a man called . . . let's see . . . how about Morton? Yes, that'll do. Caroline Morton.' And he picked up his newspaper again, closing the subject.

Caroline Morton! Auntie! How awful. This wasn't what she had expected at all. She wanted to argue, to insist that she use her own money to pay the lawyer; but things had been so much better between them in the past few weeks, ever since she had been putting up such a pretence in bed, that she was reluctant to disturb the peace. She just hoped it would only be for a month or two, and thanked heavens the child was too young to be upset or confused by the situation.


Christmas was really quite fun, despite the lack of any but the most inexpensive presents, and even those limited to the purely practical.

James had been right; Caroline adapted quite quickly to calling her mother 'auntie', overjoyed as she was to be with her again. The child loved her tiny room and obviously found the forced intimacy of her new home a vast improvement over the huge rooms and long corridors of Berenac. She took a fancy to James immediately, flattering him with her attentions, coquettish smile and the way she would climb onto his knee, uninvited, to hug him and stroke his beard. Living in such close proximity to a man was a new delight.

They were both thrilled and excited at how quickly trade picked up. Janthina spent much of each day serving in the shop, Caroline playing around her, trying to be helpful, while James carried boxes of provisions to the customers on the third-hand delivery bicycle he had bought. Cooks from the few hotels that were open for Christmas strolled in to cast a critical eye over the shelves – and stayed to purchase; the prices were too competitive to be missed. The cleanliness and freshness of the shop and its contents pleased the local housewives, and the friendliness of the obliging young couple attracted people to return.

Even when trade slackened after the New Year there was still a

161

steady stream of regulars whose names and faces were becoming familiar. James contracted with a local baker to stock bread, cakes and pies, freshly baked each morning, on a sale or return basis; the canny Scot had no intention of being left with stale food on his hands, and this additional line proved more lucrative than they had dared to hope.

During February, Janthina brought up the subjects of Caroline's adoption and christening again.

'Let's just wait until the summer starts,' James suggested. 'Then the money will be rolling in and the lawyer's fee won't be such a strain. We really do need all the cash we have at the moment to stock up for the Easter trade.'

A little of the profits from Easter were used to buy a second-hand desk for James's 'office' in the corner he used in the storeroom. The bicycle too was replaced with a large tricycle which had a huge carrier on the back, and sometimes, when they were very busy, he would give sixpence to a young lad to make the deliveries for him.

Several of Janthina's trunks and boxes remained unopened – there was simply no room for all the china and cut crystal, nor for many of her clothes; anyway, all these things seemed too refined for their present surroundings. She didn't always agree with James's priorities; there were many things she felt they needed and had to do without, but she tried not to argue with his decisions. For one thing she hated his angry reactions, and she also knew that they would all benefit in the end if every possible penny of profit was ploughed back into the business.

'I reckon that at the rate we're going we'll be able to pay off this building in a few years,' James told her as he peered over his ledgers on the dining table, one evening.

'Do we really want to?' she queried.

'Too true we do! I had an option to buy written into the lease, fortunately, because after what we've done to this place the price will rocket. Once it's ours we can sell it at any time for a damn good profit. Then we might get two shops and double our income.'

'But that would mean employing someone to run one of them, wouldn't it? Won't that cost too much?'

'No, silly girl! We'll live over one of them, like here, and I'll run both the shops and leave you to serve in the one while I'm at the other. You've got the hang of how to take orders, serve, and re-stock. You'll be fine,' he added, seeing her doubtful expression. He didn't realise that it wasn't the shopwork that was bothering her, but rather the thought of all the washing, ironing, cleaning and mending she would have to do, as well as looking after Caroline.

162

Her heart sank . . . but he was in such a cheerful frame of mind at the moment it would be silly to say anything; he would only get angry, and anyway, that idea was at least two years hence. 'Yes, dear, I'm sure I'll manage,' she said, stretching another holey sock over her darning mushroom.

James was delighted, two months later, when she told him she was expecting a baby. He suggested she should start looking after herself more, and put up her feet whenever possible, a reaction which pleased her at the time, but somehow opportunities for his solicitous ideas to be implemented seldom occurred. Caroline's playground continued to be the shop or storeroom floor, with Sunday visits to the beach when weather permitted, and Janthina's mind drifted back to the long, lazy walks beside the Dordogne River, the rides along the lakes and streams in Canada, sitting on grassy banks tossing pebbles idly into the waters, dozing in the sun. How she longed for an opportunity to pick up a sketch pad or set up her easel; she hadn't held a crayon or brush since leaving France. However, she sighed, I must not look back, only forward to the future when the business is prosperous and we can afford a nice home for our family – and perhaps even a maid.

Letters she wrote to the family all contained cheerful news about the business, how happy Caroline was in her new home and descriptions of the town of Whitehaven, its lovely beach and surrounding countryside. She received replies conveying everyone's delight that Janthina was so happy – and so lucky. She was glad that Grandmama and Ruth could not see her calloused hands and broken fingernails, the once beautifully dressed hair now drawn tightly back in a knot, all she had time or energy to do, nor how much weight she had lost despite her pregnancy.

It was Grandmama who first queried the fact that in none of her letters had she mentioned the christening and adoption of Caroline, though they imagined it must all have happened some time ago. It was difficult to think how to reply to the veiled question. She thought about it for several days and eventually summoned up the courage to broach the subject again with James. They had enjoyed a lucrative day; the till was full and, during the brief spell when there were no customers in the shop, he had joked with her and playfully slapped her rump when she teased him; this should be a good moment, she hoped.

'I do wish you'd stop nagging me about this! I've told you before, lawyers cost money and we need every penny we make, right now, for building up the business.' He was sitting at his desk in the store-room, not looking up from his ledger as he spoke.

She winced. Why? Why did he become so aggressive? It wasn't fair. He had promised. 'But the business is doing so well,' she persisted. 'You say so yourself, and heaven knows, apart from the rent, we scarcely spend a penny on ourselves. Our food is mainly unsold perishables that would otherwise be thrown away, and the cheapest cuts of meat and fish. Why, I had no idea it was possible to live on so little.'

James slammed his pen down on the desk and looked up. 'What the hell are you whining about? You're not hungry, are you?'

'No, I didn't say I was. But we've been married for nine months now, and you still haven't made any attempt to start the adoption proceedings. You did promise.'

'Yes, I did,' he shouted. 'And in your marriage vows you promised to serve, love, honour and obey me. Yet here I am, working like hell every day and night to make something of our lives, constantly worn out and tired, struggling to put aside two or three hundred pounds over the next few years so we can buy this ruddy grocery shop, while you're sitting on a bloody fortune.' He stood up and came towards her. 'Grocery shop, indeed! Do you think that's all I want to be – a grocer? Well, if so, you're wrong. I want to get into the hotel business. That's where the big money is. There's a hotel on the market right now, a little beauty on the outskirts of town and overlooking the beach. Christ Almighty, if I had that five thousand pounds, I could. . . .'

'How do you know it's five thousand? I never told you,' Janthina flared.

'Never mind how. I made it my business to find out,' he roared. 'And so if and when you ever decide to keep your marriage vows and love and honour me sufficiently to share everything with me, I might decide to keep my promise, but until then. . . .'

'But it's not just mine to hand over. It was given to me to bring up Caroline,' she shouted back.

'I know! By that fancy lord of yours. What's the matter with you, woman?' He sighed, and sat down again. 'Why can't you be reasonable? You're expecting me to adopt his brat, feed, house and clothe her, yet you hoard that money all to yourself when we would all benefit from it, so much. Do you want us always to be little grocers? Do you like seeing your husband pedalling his tricycle around in the rain delivering orders to people who are no better than us, just richer? Wouldn't you rather we drove somewhere in our own carriage to visit our friends

164

while someone else was delivering our groceries? Wouldn't you like to invite nice people to dine with us in our lovely home and send Caroline to a good school where she could learn to be a lady?' He turned away from her, closed his ledger, switched off the bare bulb over the desk, and went upstairs.

Janthina felt numb; hurt but not wanting to cry; angry yet at the same time thinking that maybe she was being unreasonable. Perhaps James was right. Perhaps, through her stubborn resistance to his request for her to hand over her money, she was preventing them from becoming hoteliers, property owners, committing them, instead, to remaining humble grocers; saying 'Yes, madam,' 'No, sir,' 'Of course we'll delay our supper time till we're too tired to eat so that we can make up and deliver the order you forgot to give us this morning.'

James had already proved he was a good businessman. There was no doubt he would use the money to make far higher profits than the miserable interest it produced where it lay. And the money was not entailed. She could withdraw it with the stroke of a pen. Furthermore, if she wanted James to be Caroline's legal father, he should be entitled to handle the money as he saw fit. It was only fair, she supposed.

She lay awake most of the night, thinking, worrying, weighing the problem again and again as the scales dipped first one way and then the other. But by morning she had made up her mind.


She had never seen James so excited.

'Oh, my love, my love, that's wonderful!' He hugged and kissed her, picked up Caroline and danced them round. 'Now our lives will take a big swing upwards,' and he swung the child up to the ceiling.

Caroline squealed with delight and pulled his beard. Janthina grinned happily, increasingly confident that she had made the right decision.

'Let's see what time it is.' James consulted his silver pocket watch. 'Why, only a quarter to seven. I know, we'll have a treat! The three of us will go out to supper.'

It was already past Caroline's bedtime, but Janthina was not going to argue. It was good to see her husband in such an ebullient mood. 'Oh, how lovely, James, we'd adore that, wouldn't we, Caroline?' She looked down at her soiled, gingham dress. 'May I have five minutes in which to change?'

Actually, the five minutes stretched to ten, but James remained patient, admiring the elegant gown his wife had chosen and the little girl's pretty dress. In the street he hailed a passing cab and directed the driver to a genteel hotel on the seafront where a uniformed boy held the horse's head, while the top-hatted doorman handed them down and they were shown to a window table by the head waiter.

The menu was in French, and Janthina interpreted for James in such a way that the waiter might not suspect his ignorance. She wanted her husband to appear as sophisticated as any other gentleman diner, and he winked his appreciation, also taking her whispered advice before ordering the wine. He was proud of his wife, whose beauty outshone that of any other woman in the room, and watched carefully how she handled her cutlery and addressed the waiters, diligently following her lead.

'Why, Mr Cameron, isn't it? Good evening to you.' A tall, middle-aged man, with a plump little woman on his arm, paused at their table.

'Mr Barnes, Mrs Barnes.' James sprang to his feet. 'May I present my wife and our niece, Caroline. Mr Barnes and I met at Creighton's a few days ago, my dear,' he added as hands were shaken.

Pleasantries were exchanged before the couple moved on to their table.

'Creighton's?' Janthina queried when they were alone.

'Er . . . yes. It's another hotel further along the esplanade. Business-men meet there around midday. A bit like a club; very useful place at which to become known. That's where I heard about the Dolphin Hotel.'

Janthina could not fail to notice the sudden affectation of an Oxford accent, smiled, and said casually, 'Really? I don't remember you mentioning it to me before. No, sweetheart.' She leaned over to assist Caroline. 'Not with your fingers.'

The evening was a great success. James sat back smoking a large cigar while they drank their coffee and Janthina was relieved that despite her sleepiness, Caroline behaved perfectly. The only jarring note of the evening had been hearing the child introduced as their niece – but never mind, it wouldn't be for much longer now.

'This is the life for us, my love,' James smiled as he placed a hand over hers. 'I want us to live the good life. You'll see, in just a few years we'll have it all.'

She observed his efforts to play the gentleman with interest and had no doubt that with a little practice he would develop the art very well. He was happy and relaxed, in excellent humour and she felt herself responding to his mood. Obviously the money from the earl had been the cause of much tension between them – understandably so, she thought on reflection. But the decision was made and things were going to improve from now on. The only pity was that she hadn't offered the money to him earlier. In fact, she couldn't help wondering what reason she had had for holding back for so long.

Janthina and Caroline were left alone in the shop a great deal while James hurried in and out of lawyers' offices. It was difficult to follow all the negotiations and legal intricacies of the contracts and anyway she was too busy and tired in the evenings, after the shop closed, to question James about the deal. Also, he had decided that, for the convenience of their customers, the shop would remain open until seven o'clock on weekdays and ten on Saturdays, at which times he was usually able to answer the shop bell himself. She was experiencing a great deal of backache with this pregnancy – something she'd not had with Caroline – and though thinner in herself, the bulge protruded much more, as though her stomach muscles couldn't support the weight.

Mrs Harris, the cook up at the Carisbrook Hotel, with whom Janthina had become quite friendly, made some maternal comments one day. 'I don't think you are looking after yourself enough, my dear, you worry me. Usually, when one is expecting, one is plumper and healthier than normal, but you're not, and I know why. The trouble is you're overworking; you haven't got a good colour and you always look tired, even early in the morning. I hope you don't mind me mentioning it, but I do think you should see your doctor and ask him for a tonic.'

Janthina smiled and gave a little sigh. 'It's sweet of you to be so concerned; I appreciate it. It is difficult when one is starting up a new business in a new place where one doesn't know anyone. We have to work very hard but things should start to ease up soon.'

'I hope so, for your sake.'

'I'll take your advice and see a doctor. Is there one near here you could recommend?'

'You mean you haven't seen one yet? I know! Don't tell me! You've been too busy.'

They laughed together.

'Got a pencil? Here, I'll write down Dr Martin's address. His surgery is not far from here.'

Soon after Mrs Harris left, the postman arrived and dumped a heap of envelopes and packets on the counter, mostly business letters and accounts addressed to James, but there was a large envelope for herself from France. It contained a laborious letter from Thérèse . . . and a sealed envelope addressed to 'Miss McKenzie' in Roland's handwriting. She felt herself flush and looked up instinctively to see if James was approaching across the street. Of course he wasn't, he

167

wouldn't be back for at least another hour. She slit the envelope and withdrew the close-written sheets. Foolish of her not to have told Roland about her marriage – she must do so. It would not be proper to continue their correspondence any longer.

Roland told her about the new line of studies he was about to follow in the London branch for two years before returning to Gloucester. He was sorry not to have heard from her for so long, hoped she was still well and that this letter would find her still in France. If so, was there any chance of her coming to England, and might they meet?

She had to reply – but how?

A customer came in and before she had completed her purchases another was waiting. Janthina was kept busy throughout the remainder of the morning, Roland's letter burning a hole in the pocket of her dress . . . and James was with her for the afternoon and throughout the next day. So it was not until Friday evening, when James said he was going out for a while after supper, that she was able to take the letter from its hiding place and reply.

Precious time was wasted and ink dried on her pen, as she tried to think what to say. She had told him nothing of Caroline, nor could she face admitting that she had returned to England without seeing him, had suddenly married a grocer and was now working as a shop assistant. Yet how could she spin a string of lies about being in the Dordogne, enjoying summer by the river?

In the end she decided to say that she would be leaving for Canada very soon and that she regretted that they would be unable to meet again. To explain away the English stamp and postmark she told him that a visiting English friend would post it on her return home, to save time. The remainder of the letter she filled with news of Ruth and Ben and their son Giles, and Ruth's description of life in India, and with news from Scotland.

So that was that. A final goodbye to her first love. She closed her eyes, trying to blot out the visions of the past, before sealing the envelope and secreting it behind the torn lining of her handbag, where it would remain until she had an opportunity to post it.

Roland occupied her thoughts frequently during the next few days. She could still picture him quite clearly, even without taking the photograph from its hiding place – huge, handsome, gentle and caring. He had always treated her like a kitten, as though she was fragile and precious . . . the only person who had ever done that, perhaps because he was one of the few people in her life taller than herself.

\*     \*     \*

The Camerons moved into the Dolphin Hotel in September. James had hired a young, married man to work in the shop, retaining a sizable proportion of his salary in lieu of rent for the upstairs rooms. The Dolphin had five floors starting with kitchens, pantries and sculleries in the basement, public rooms on the ground floor, guest bedrooms on the next two floors, and, tucked away under the roof, storerooms and maids' rooms. Two of the latter were knocked into one, by the simple process of removing the thin wooden partition between them, to make what Janthina considered a dreadfully small living room. Next door to it a double bed was wedged into a room even smaller than the one they had just left, and beyond that a room for Caroline, to be shared with the new baby in due course.

Janthina found it hard to conceal her disappointment. She had expected the move to be an improvement, but it was far from that. The rooms over the shop had been in so bad a state as to need complete redecoration. Here, the nailholes from the removed partition were filled with putty and a strip of ill-matched wallpaper pasted over the marks. Furniture too dilapidated to remain in the residents' lounge was brought up for their use. The unopened trunks of clothes, china and glass, which had been lying in the shop storeroom for nearly a year, were transferred to an attic storeroom, and she could see no possibility of their contents ever seeing the light of day in the near future.

The hotel did not possess a lift and there were no kitchen facilities upstairs, and although James assured her that this matter would be put right as soon as possible, the four flights up and down proved a tremendous strain, especially in her condition.

'For God's sake!' he exploded one evening. 'Aren't you ever going to stop nagging? I've told you over and over again, it's going to be a far better arrangement for you, once the hotel re-opens. You won't even have to cook any more; it'll all be done for you. Just be patient for a few more weeks. We can't take staff on before we're ready to open.'

'It's not so much the cooking,' she argued, 'as the stairs, and carrying the meals up four flights. Dr Martin says I'm underweight and must rest more than. . . .'

'Doctor who? You didn't tell me you'd been to a doctor.'

'I told you last night that I had an appointment for today. You couldn't have been listening.'

'What did you go to a doctor for? Is there something the matter with you or did you just want a good moan?' He peered at her, unsmiling. 'You look all right to me.'

'I've been getting a lot of backache, and. . . .'

'Backache? Is that all? My God, if you had a back like mine you'd really have something to complain about.'

'Mine is undoubtedly more serious,' she retorted.

'Rubbish! Mine is all to do with my leg wound. Yours is perfectly normal and natural with childbearing. Now come on, are we going to eat or not? I suppose we'll all have to come down and eat in the kitchen since you're making such a fuss. You go ahead with the kid. I'll be down in a minute.'

She thought of Ruth's last letter. It had contained so much happiness on every page; anecdotes about her beloved Benjamin, the most adoring and attentive of husbands, and about baby Giles. Surrounded by servants and an *ayah* for the baby, she never had to lift a finger in the house, spending her days enjoying her son, attending tea parties and being escorted by Ben to regimental dinners and balls. Ruth – whose heart had been thawed by the love of a good man. Oh, lucky Ruth.

By careful scheming, Janthina managed to avoid climbing the stairs more than three times a day. Even so, just carrying the slop-pail down from the attic each morning, to empty it in one of the bathrooms on the second floor, pulled her back and shoulder muscles painfully, and when Dr Martin saw her again a few weeks later he shook his head angrily.

'You have not been obeying my instructions, have you, young lady?' he growled.

'Well, it's very difficult. . . .'

'And so it's going to be a very difficult birth, if you're not careful. I don't like the position the baby is in at all. The head should be well down by now – and it's not. Where were you planning to have the baby?'

'In our rooms at the hotel, I suppose.' She really couldn't imagine anywhere else.

The doctor was emphatic. 'No. Definitely not. I want you to book into the Cottage Hospital in Whitehaven. I have no wish to alarm you, but I want you where there is everything at hand should there be any complications.'

'I'll have to ask my husband,' she murmured.

'Oh, no you won't, you'll tell him. And if there is any doubt in his mind, you can send him along to see me. Understand?'

Surprisingly, James accepted the doctor's ruling without more than

170

a shrug of his shoulders – which was fortunate because, on a bleak day at the end of November 1905, after thirty hours of labouring with a breech position, Angus Cameron was eventually delivered with forceps.

Dr Martin confronted James in the hospital corridor. 'Your wife has had a very hard time, Mr Cameron, and I must tell you that if she had not been in here I doubt we'd have saved either of them. It is apparent that she has strained herself badly during pregnancy.'

'Really?' James exclaimed in astonishment. 'I cannot think how.'

Dr Martin's eyes narrowed as he went on. 'She's been badly torn, inside and out, and lost a great deal of blood. I've stitched her up, and think, and hope, she'll recover all right, but I must warn you, here and now, that there must be no more babies. If she were to have another it could kill her.'

James opened his mouth to reply – but closed it again.

'Your wife must remain in the hospital for at least two more weeks, then I'll decide if she is well enough to go home.'

Janthina recovered quickly. The bed rest was a wonderful tonic and she was thrilled to feel so well again. Unwisely, she assured James, in answer to his enquiries, that she was feeling marvellous and couldn't wait to get home, adding to James's conviction that Dr Martin was a fussing old hen. An opinion which grew, aggressively, when the doctor visited his patient at the hotel, three weeks later, and expressed horror at their domestic arrangements, telling James flatly that they should move two floors down immediately.

'Why the devil did you just sit there saying nothing?' James exploded after the doctor had gone. 'You deliberately left him to think you agreed with him. All you had to do was say how well you are and that his fussing is unnecessary.'

'I do agree with him. I felt very well when I arrived home, but already I feel dreadful again. Oh, James, those stairs. . . .'

'Oh, James, those stairs.' His cruel, high-pitched mimicry made her wince. 'I'm too tiny and frail to walk upstairs. Why don't I buy you some smelling salts in case you get the vapours?'

But he did make a temporary compromise, and they moved down to a living room on the first floor and bedrooms on the second until the rooms were needed for Easter residents. Janthina had agreed with him that there was no point in taking guests before then, as they wouldn't get sufficient bookings to cover staff wages; but money could be made in the dining room, billiards room, and lounge bar.

'There's always money to be made selling food and liquor,' he

171

said. 'Especially liquor – providing the surroundings and company are congenial. So those rooms must be our first priority.'

Caroline adored her baby brother from the first moment she saw him. Her mother was noticeably distressed that he should be introduced to her as her 'little cousin' – the whole situation wrung her heart. Every time the child called her 'auntie', it was as though the little voice was driving daggers into her soul. She felt wretched.

James was very busy and preoccupied over the next two months, but as the hotel began to take shape she dared to raise the dreaded subject with him again, relating it to the need to arrange a joint christening.

James finished his last mouthful of supper and stood up. 'No hurry.' His voice was casual. 'No time to talk about it now, anyway. Got to get back to the bar.'

The bar had opened before Christmas and was an immediate success. So Sundays were now the only evenings they shared, James playing 'mine host' throughout the week. He was obviously very popular and had an ever-widening circle of friends and acquaintances, all of whom now referred to him as Cam.

When the hotel opened to residents, James planned to act as manager, and Janthina agreed to take on the responsibility of the upstairs housekeeping, supervising the chambermaids, the maintenance of linen and bedding, hotel and guest laundry and fresh flowers in the rooms, daily. It sounded a not-too-onerous task which might be fitted into her routine with the children, besides which she was happy to play her role in the operation.

But by July she was exhausted.

'James, the situation is impossible. If we don't pay the chambermaids a reasonable wage we cannot hope to keep them.'

'Rubbish. They're not even worth what they get.'

'Possibly. But that's the trouble. We offer so little that we only get the worst available, and even they won't stay if they can find someone to offer them more.'

'I don't agree with you, and we are definitely not going to offer more. The only trouble is lack of supervision. You're just not chasing them up enough.'

'I most certainly am, but the fact is that the girls simply cannot get through all the rooms in a day and I'm having to clean some of them myself.' She felt she should stand her ground.

James thought otherwise. 'The problem is entirely yours. It's your department and you have the staff. If you can't get the work out of them you will have to go on doing it yourself. You just don't seem able to grasp the basic rules of business, do you? The only way to make a decent profit is by keeping the overheads down and the takings up. Aye, and there's another thing, remember. We haven't finished paying off all the redecorating and furnishing, either. When that's done and the place grows in popularity, then we can ease up a bit.'

'Huh!' she snorted. 'I've heard that one before.'

'Now you look here. . . .'

'Oh, no. No more lectures tonight, thank you. I've had all I can take. I'm going to bed.' And she strode out of the room with all the dignity her weary muscles could muster.


Angus was a beautiful baby. Dark haired, like his father, and with his father's eyes and brows, yet he had the length of body to suggest he would grow tall. It was unfortunate that he cried so much, day and night, greatly adding to his mother's problems.

Janthina spent every spare moment with her children and was delighted to see how proud James was of his son, only wishing that he would occasionally get out of bed at night to take a turn at comforting the boy. Caroline was very helpful, though not yet four years old, loving to nurse and cuddle the baby and amuse him with toys and chatter. When, as happened too often, their mother was obliged to turn out a guest room, the children were with her, so, although she would have much preferred, in easier circumstances, to do her own family cooking, she was thankful that throughout the busy season she had no need to think about food, nor do their personal laundry – both being arguments held against her by James if she dared complain of tiredness. She longed for the end of September and the close of the hotel season, even looking forward to being sufficiently rested to join the men for an occasional evening in the bar.

In the meantime, it was with sinking heart that throughout August she prayed every night for evidence that she was not pregnant again . . . prayers that were not answered. She worried about Dr Martin's warning, and despaired of ever being able to cope with her work with three children round her heels. Well, James would just have to see sense.

James, however, seemingly quite unperturbed by the doctor's words, brushed her worries aside with some vague comment about waiting to see how things worked out when they opened next season.

\*  \*  \*

Towards the end of March 1907, there was an unusually fine spell of weather, only a few benign clouds drifting across the almost windless sky. A fine Sunday was a rare treat and the Camerons took the opportunity to walk along the promenade, with Angus in his pram and Caroline trotting beside them. They seldom spent any time all together as James was working every day and in the bar every evening, and even on Sundays, if the weather was not fair enough to venture out, he simply fell asleep in his chair. His only regular contribution to parenthood was sitting with the little ones on Sunday mornings while Janthina went to church, attending evening service alone in preference to coping with embarrassing wails from his son in front of the congregation. Not that James was devoutly religious . . . but he did believe it good business to impress the local congregation with one's piety.

Janthina's height and loose cloak helped to mask the fact that another child was expected, though the bulge was heavy and she had to walk leaning backwards to keep her balance. She hadn't raised the subject of Caroline's adoption for several months, hoping to give James time to say something about it himself. But he never did, and time was passing. Caroline was going to be five this year, she would soon be starting school, her name registered for ever more as 'Morton'. Was she being weak, letting year after year pass without forcing the issue? Or was she worrying unnecessarily, antagonising James into resisting the idea? Somehow she knew she must speak up again today, there was so seldom an opportunity nowadays.

'James,' she started tentatively. 'I do feel that we have waited long enough to proceed with the adoption, don't you? There is no longer a dire shortage of money for lawyers. And as soon as it is all done we can arrange with Reverend Cooney to have the three children christened at the same time.' She paused beside a slipway which led down to the beach. 'Let's go down here. It's quite warm enough for Caroline and Angus to play on the sand while we talk.'

James followed her in silence, watched as his son was lifted down from the pram to toddle off with Caroline to collect shells.

'Well?' Janthina prompted. 'Which lawyer do you think we should have?'

'I don't know. I've been thinking about the matter recently, and I'll tell you straight, I don't like it. I've been in two minds about it for some time.'

Her heart had jumped as he started to speak. Now she wasn't sure. 'What do you mean? About what?'

'Whether or not I want to plant an elder sister on my son.'

Janthina swayed, held on to the old wooden breakwater for support,

174

and tried to get her breathing back under control. 'James! You're not serious, are you?' she whispered. 'You're only teasing me, aren't you? Answer me!' she cried. 'Tell me you're only playing.'

James looked around the beach in concern. 'For God's sake keep your voice down, woman. There's no need to make a public spectacle of yourself. No. I'm perfectly serious. Caroline is not my daughter and I don't see why she should be made senior to my son.' His eyes were hard and angry and she recognised the stubborn jut of his beard that she had learned to dread.

She closed her eyes, face lifted to feel the warmth of the sun on her lids. She shook her head. 'No, James. You cannot do this to me. You have promised over and over. You promised before I agreed to marry you . . . and again when I drew out the money for the hotel. . . .'

'That's not true. Think back. What I did say was that I might consider it, remember?'

'No, I don't. And even if you had, it's still cheating. I would never have agreed to marry you if you hadn't promised. . . . I trusted you, and again over the money. I still cannot believe you would really let me down. Angus!' She called. 'No, you mustn't put shells in your mouth, you might swallow one.' She hurried across the sand to poke a finger into the child's mouth and hook out the offending object. 'Caroline, darling, please don't let him have the little ones.' She returned to James, who had lit a cigarette and was leaning against the breakwater, a bland smile on his face. She smiled back, hopefully. 'James. You do really mean to adopt Caroline, don't you?'

He tilted his hat back on his head and blew a smoke ring into the still air. 'No. I have now finally made up my mind. Caroline is perfectly happy; she has a good home and I know I can be a perfectly good father to her without going through all the legalities. No. . . .' He held up his hand. 'There is absolutely no point in trying to argue with me. My mind is made up, so let's drop the subject once and for all.'

'No,' she shouted, stamping her foot ineffectually on the soft sand. 'I will not drop the subject, ever. You are a damned liar, a cheat and a thief. . . .'

'Shut up, woman,' he hissed at her. 'You are making a confounded exhibition of us.'

'On the contrary, you are. I may be doing the shouting, but you are the liar and cheat. It's your fault, you hateful little runt. You wait. . . .' Never, in her whole life, had anger raged in her so completely out of control. She wanted to hit him, kick him, wipe that silly smirk off his face.

He walked away, picked up Angus, and carried him to the pram.

'I'm taking the children home. You may care to follow when you have recovered some of your sanity. Come along, Caroline.'

Tears streamed down her face.

People a little distance away were watching her, whispering together. She didn't care. My God, if they knew . . . if those precious cronies of James's ever learned what a stinking little bastard he was. . . . It was amazing how much foul language she had learned from him! She hurried after them. There was still plenty to be said and she was determined to continue the battle. He'd just have to face facts. If he failed to keep his promise he'd lose everything . . . she'd see to that!

'James!' She stormed into their sitting room. 'You will have to understand that if you fail to keep your part of our bargain I will leave you. The hotel will have to be sold so that I can have my money back and I will take the children. . . .'

'Only Caroline. Angus is mine,' he said coolly, sitting cross-legged in his armchair. 'Oh, and by the way, I won't allow the hotel to be sold.'

'You won't have an option. It belongs to us, jointly. If either of us wishes to sell at any time or buy out the other, we can. That was what we agreed. It was written into the contract.'

'It was not.'

'It was! That was a condition in our agreement and you told me yourself that it had been done.'

'The Dolphin is in my name, only.'

'Wha-a-at?' His words exploded in her mind. 'You swore . . . why, don't tell me you were planning to cheat me from the beginning. . . .'

'So if you leave me it will be without money and with only Caroline, and I will claim the baby you are carrying, too. The choice is yours.' He picked up his newspaper and left the room.

# 3

FLORA CAMERON, named after her paternal grandmother, was born the following day. She was a very small baby, being a month premature, and she arrived quite quickly, causing her mother little discomfort after the hasty dash to the Cottage Hospital, and confounding Dr Martin's gloomy warnings.

A year later she was presented with a baby sister, Alexandra, named after her maternal great-grandmother, who had died only two months earlier, and the many friends and acquaintances of the proud parents called at their charming new house overlooking the bay, to offer gifts and congratulations.

Reverend Cooney, from St Mary's Anglican Church, was delighted to officiate at the baptism of all three children and attended the christening party afterwards to raise a glass in toast to 'this delightful family, such a shining example to all young people contemplating matrimony'. He went on to compliment the Camerons on their hard work and devotion to each other, 'without which no one can hope for a happy and successful life' and for 'the generosity with which they have opened their hearts and their home to their niece, this beautiful child so tragically orphaned. Anyone can see,' he continued, gazing at Caroline, 'that her mother must have been an outstanding beauty . . .' adding, 'er, just like her aunt.'

The party over and the guests departed, Janthina began clearing the mess, while James returned to the hotel.

The house had belonged to an hotelier who, through illness, had fallen on hard times. Unable to pay his outstanding account with Cameron and Co., he had assured James that all would be settled in the new season, if James were prepared to wait. James had offered a smiling verbal agreement – providing the man could offer some security, like, for instance, a bond on his house, as his hotel was already mortgaged. Unwisely, and without taking legal advice, the man agreed: and when the hotel was newly stocked at the start of the summer, increasing his debt considerably, James foreclosed and took possession.

Knowing nothing of this, Janthina was greatly relieved to move into a real home where the children had room to grow and a small garden at the rear in which to play; where she could, at last, unpack the trunks full of clothing, some quite gawkishly out of date, and boxes of wedding presents.

There had been little time for letter-writing since her marriage, only occasional brief pages to Canada, Scotland, France and India, depicting a happiness and contentment she did not feel. She was glad of the opportunity to convey some genuinely good news to Ruth who, as ever, understood far more than was said or written, and whose letters contained so much love and concern. The house couldn't compare with the Kirkpatricks' residence in Calcutta – a comparative palace with tiled fountains and extensive verandahs offering shade on every side, all kept spotlessly clean by a team of servants – but, after the privations and inconveniences of the past few years, Janthina was more than content. James had finally got his priorities right, putting a home before the further expansion of the business she knew he wanted, though at the same time well aware that his motives were entirely selfish; he was far more interested in acquiring a status symbol for himself than in providing a home for his wife and family.

James was already a well-respected businessman, no mean achievement at the age of thirty-four, in an era when businesses were normally built by succeeding generations expanding or failing, when new ideas and enthusiasms were introduced as sons inherited control from their fathers. He had obtained the lease of what had been a millinery shop in the town centre and filled it with bric-à-brac and objets d'art, items which delighted the summer visitors particularly. The disused storerooms above were now being converted into tea and coffee rooms where he intended that smart ladies and gentlemen might meet to exchange gossip and consume appetising but expensive cakes and pastries. Better still, he was negotiating the purchase of the Excelsior, a very smart and luxurious hotel at the eastern end of the promenade, and Janthina, familiar with the workings of her husband's mind, knew very well that he intended to expand still further. He had already voiced an interest in the wholesale trade, so that he might reap a profit from his competitors while provisioning his hotels at cost.

*His* hotels! Bought with money extracted from her with his false promises. Money belonging to her and Caroline, with which they could have had a comfortable house and an income large enough to keep a maid. . . . Oh, what a fool she had been! Imagine believing in a man who was so grossly dishonest. At first she had meant to expose him – go down into the bar and denounce him for a thief and a liar to his cronies – but who would have believed her word against that of their great pal, Cam? Cam, the straight, honest businessman, the great raconteur, the pious churchgoer? They would say her confinement had turned her brain or that she must have milk fever.

She had longed to talk to someone, confide her distress – but there was no one. There hadn't been time, since coming to Whitehaven, to make any really intimate friends, and as for the family. . . . What point was there in revealing to Grandpapa the result of his meddling in her life? Anyway he, poor old thing, was quite grief-stricken by Grandmama's death, according to Aunt Laura's letters. She couldn't mention her problems to Mama because Papa had never been aware of the 'arrangement' with James, and telling Ruth, who could do nothing to help even if she were in England, would only distress her. . . .

She carried a trayload of dirty dishes into the scullery, setting it on the table to unload her precious china carefully into the sink, pausing to gaze, unseeing, into the little garden. Of course, if she hadn't married James she would never have had her darlings, Angus, Flora and Alexandra. She could hear Caroline playing with them now, their excited squeals echoing round the house as they hid from each other and waited, breathless with anticipation, to be discovered and pounced upon. She loved them all, including poor little Alex, who had been conceived in hatred rather than love.

The moment of conception was still quite clear in her memory. James had come up to their bedroom very late that night – and drunk. The light had woken her and she watched in disgust as he fumbled about the room and fell as he tried to step out of his trousers. Since the scene on the beach, the day before Flora was born, she had hated him to touch her, turning away from his advances, had lain on her back, face averted, while he did what he must. But this night had been different; never before had he been so inebriated. He came at her, naked, snatching the bedclothes right off the bed. She had tried to grab them back, only succeeding in tearing the sheet, and when she jumped away from him he grasped her wrist, yanking her towards him.

'No!' she had hissed at him, fearing the guests in neighbouring rooms might hear. 'Leave me alone. I won't have you touch me when you are drunk.'

'Drunk? Who's drunk, you icy little bitch?' he roared.

She shoved him away with her free hand – and he fell off the bed. Escape was her only hope, but before she could reach the door he had hurled himself at her, face distorted with fury, hitting her again and again about the head and shoulders. She fought back, kicked and struggled, gouged his face with her nails. But he was too strong for

179

her, threw her across the bed and held her down. The fight had only served to sober and excite him; he forced himself into her and, as always, was finished in seconds, rolling off sideways to snore on his pillow. In anger and humiliation she crawled away to her edge of the bed, where, under a tangle of blankets, she lay sleepless until dawn.

When he had come up from the bar the following night the door was locked and there was no way he could get in without bringing all the residents from their rooms to investigate the noise. So he slept in the living room and stole the bedroom key next day. . . . She smiled at the memory. Having anticipated this she had bought a padlock and plates in town, screwed the plates on to the door and door post herself and, when, having been frustrated a second night, James removed the plates while she was out, she replaced them with another set; since when he had occupied another room. Too late – she was pregnant again.

Alexandra was the loveliest baby, good, quiet and contented, by far the easiest of James's three, and Janthina had every hope that she would develop the sweet nature of Caroline. She loved them all dearly and was never happier than when she was with them, despite the hard work, the endless washing, ironing, mending, cooking and nursing, not to mention the cleaning, scrubbing and polishing, and laying on splendid dinner parties for their friends, acting the charming hostess and loving wife. Oh God, how she hated him! How she would love to have her revenge.

Washing and drying the dishes, carefully stacking them away in their cupboard, she continued to brood, angrily. Men! She loathed them: they had caused all the misery in her life. She had trusted them, over and over, and been betrayed. She had loved Papa – and been beaten and abused by him. Anthony! Could any man have been more adored? She sighed: what a weak-minded little worm he had proved. Even Grandpapa, a fine, upstanding figure, loved and respected by all who knew him, was hidebound by his attitudes on morality, refusing ever to see his great-granddaughter, and to ease his own shame at his granddaughter's downfall, arranging a marriage for her with this – this lying, cheating, avaricious, lecherous beast with whom she was now saddled for the rest of her life. Oh, and there had been Roland, of course, the only one who had never betrayed her . . . perhaps because he had never had the opportunity. No. That wasn't fair. He had remained consistent throughout the years. Each Christmas a greeting card arrived via Thérèse, signed 'affectionately, R.' And each Christmas she sent one back the same way signed, 'Affectionately, J.'

\* \* \*

180

The cold sea mists cleared a few days later, the sun shone, and Janthina dressed the three younger children and wheeled the pram across to the beach. Caroline was at a little kindergarten run by two elderly spinsters and would have to be collected at three thirty, but in the meantime, Angus could play on the sand. It was pleasant to be in the sun, though not restful, as the little boy wanted to be amused, have sandcastles built for him to destroy in violent attacks from his lead soldiers – several of whom inevitably disappeared in each assault.

The telegram was waiting on the floor, just inside the front door, when she returned with the four children. They waited for their coats to be removed while she read it . . . and re-read it. Stunned, she laid it on the hall stand while she mechanically undid buttons and Flora's pram harness, fetched milk and biscuits and pushed the pram into the living room. She breathed in short gasps, mind reeling, and sat on the sofa to read it again. Her eyes closed and she allowed the flimsy paper to fall in her lap.

'MAJOR KIRKPATRICK KILLED IN RIOTS STOP MRS KIRK-PATRICK AND CHILD EN ROUTE TO BOMBAY FOR SHIP TO ENGLAND STOP WILL CABLE ARRIVAL DATE STOP COLONEL BENTLEY.'

Ruth!
After only six years of marriage she had lost her beloved Benjamin.
'Auntie! Why are you crying?' Caroline was standing beside her, stroking her head.
Janthina put an arm round the child to draw her closer, letting her tears fall into the fair curls. 'I am very sad for my sister, your Auntie Ruth. She is very unhappy.'
'Why?'
'Because her husband has died.'
'Why?'
'Some wicked men killed him, darling.'
'Why?'
'I don't know why. Perhaps because he was such a very good man.'
'And he tried to stop them being wicked?'
How wise little children can be. 'Yes. I expect so.'
'Was he Giles's papa?'
'Yes.'
'Poor Giles. But he's still luckier'n me. I haven't ever had a papa that I can remember.'

181

'You've got Uncle Cam; he's like a papa to you.' She looked into Anthony's beautiful blue eyes, trying to fight down the pain and bitterness which tightened in her throat, sickening her for the millionth time. Why was fate so unfair? Why did it have to be Ben? Why? When they loved each other so dearly, were such a perfect, happy pair. Better if it had been James, ending this miserable partnership, this sham marriage. Then she flushed at the wickedness of her thoughts.

Caroline watched her, shaking her head. 'I do love you, Auntie, but I'd rather have my own Mama and Papa, like the other children in my school. They all have mothers and fathers.'


The SS *Rangoon* docked at Southampton on the morning of the fourth of June, and Janthina and Caroline were there to meet it.

James had agreed to have the three younger children at the Dolphin for two days, looked after by a temporary nursemaid, while Caroline made the journey with her mother to be a companion for Giles on the return to Whitehaven.

Ruth was easily identifiable at the ship's rail, a tall, solitary figure in black, firmly holding on to the little boy at her side, and returning a wave as she found her sister in the waiting crowd.

The two children eyed each other in silence as the sisters embraced, weeping, neither woman able to speak.

Though six months younger, Giles towered over his cousin. Caroline gazed up into his dark brown eyes and he smiled down into hers of deep, violet blue, and there began, immediately, a devoted friendship which was to last all their lives.

While the children watched the countryside speed by the train windows, Giles exclaiming at how green everything was and how funny the cattle were after those in India, Ruth began to tell Janthina the terrible story.

There was always unrest somewhere in India, and earlier in the year it was particularly bad at Muzaffarpur, north of Patna, culminating on April 30th when a bomb was thrown by insurgents killing the wives of two Army officers. Colonel Bentley had immediately ordered Benjamin to take a company up from Calcutta, to seek out the ringleaders, imprison them and keep order in the area until the disturbances ceased.

Most of the troublemakers had been caught – but not all. The couple of dozen who escaped had secretly rallied a force of over a hundred supporters who stormed the officers' quarters one night. The soldiers on guard duty must have been asleep, for everyone was taken by surprise. Ben's room was one of the first entered and though he fought back fiercely, he was overcome by numbers and murdered. A young subaltern had alerted the men in their barracks in time for them to defend themselves, turn back the attack and, eventually, convey the dreadful news to Calcutta.

Ruth didn't weep, just sat immobile, her beautiful features white and frozen.

'What do you plan to do now?' Janthina asked after a while.

Her sister shrugged. 'I don't know. I have little idea of my financial situation yet, except that it won't be very good.'

'Might you go to Scotland?'

She shook her head. 'I don't think I could bear the reminders.'

'No. Of course not, silly of me. Have you considered returning to Canada?'

'Never! I'll never go back there.'

Her sister's words made Janthina aware of a certain void in her life, a strange yearning for . . . she knew not what. It was hard to understand Ruth's attitude, her lack of interest in Canada. Personally she found the very name brought back the scent of new-mown hay, fresh-baked bread, and soap suds in the washhouse – making her blood tingle. How wonderful it would be to mount up and ride – away, alone. Canter, with the wind streaming through her hair, along the river banks, through the forests; or even to stroll along the lanes of the Dordogne to . . . anywhere. Anywhere to find peace and tranquillity to refresh one's soul. The over-populated beach at Whitehaven was her limit, now. But how selfish to be thinking such thoughts when poor Ruth was without husband or home.

'Well, you can certainly live with us. Why don't you? The house is quite large enough and Giles could have the companionship of his cousins,' she suggested. 'He is my godson, remember.'

'Ooh, Auntie! Can Giles stay with us, always?'

'I don't know . . .' Ruth began.

'No, I mean Auntie Janty. If she says he can it will be all right. You will, won't you, Auntie?'

Ruth stared in amazement.

'Yes, wouldn't it be lovely, darling,' Janthina replied. 'We'll have to wait and see.'

'Auntie?' Ruth asked quietly when Caroline returned her attention to the window. 'I don't understand.'

Janthina flushed. She had never mentioned the subject to anyone else, always hoping . . . but there was no way of avoiding it now. 'The

183

adoption never . . . well, James hasn't done anything about it. . . .'
Where to begin? How much should she tell?

'Being a bit slow about it, isn't he? Janty!' Ruth studied her sister's face more closely, noted the grey circles under her eyes, the prominent bones, the look of weariness, defeat. 'Janty, what is it?'

Janthina tried to smile brightly. 'We were very short of cash at first and lawyers are so expensive . . .' but their eyes met and she could no longer act the lie. The brightness ebbed away and she sank backwards in her seat. 'I don't want to burden you with all the details now. You have far too many troubles of your own. I'll tell you all about it some time.'

'He didn't keep his promise?' Ruth persisted.

'No.' Ruth was the first person ever to know the truth – and it hurt.

'Couldn't you insist?'

'How? Don't imagine I haven't tried.'

'There's still time, I suppose.'

'No. He has flatly refused. Now that he has children of his own it is too late.'

'Are you very upset about it?'

'Upset?' Janthina's gaunt face twisted into a bitter smile. 'Never being allowed to acknowledge my own daughter? Hearing her call me auntie? Having her tell me she wishes she had parents like her friends at school?' She turned her face away, swallowed hard, then swung back to gaze into her sister's eyes. 'I hate him, Ruth. With all my heart, I hate him.'


This was certainly a much changed Janthina! Ruth could swear she had never heard her sister vow she hated anything or anyone, before now. She recalled the look of horror on Janty's face when she, Ruth, had told her, years ago in Canada, that she hated Papa . . . Papa, whom the girl had had every reason to hate. Nor had she failed to notice her sister's red hands and chipped nails, and the hair hastily pinned back in an unfashionable knot. However, it did not take long after their arrival at the Cameron house to understand the cause. The house was not large by the standards set by British residents in India, but to be obliged to manage it, and four small children, without the help of so much as one maid Ruth found appalling.

Built in a continuous terrace of identical houses, the Camerons' house appeared deceptively small and narrow, but it was deep and tall, containing six bedrooms upstairs plus a maid's room beyond the kitchen, as yet unoccupied. There was a large living room, a dining room, a huge kitchen, scullery, pantry and wash-house in the back garden, all with high sash windows opening, in the main rooms, to the sea.

Ruth was fascinated by the paintings, demanding to see everything her sister had done in France. 'These are superb, Jan. But you must have painted lots more since these. Where are they?'

'I never seem to have had time, even for sketching, let alone painting.'

'That's dreadful. You really should keep it up,' Ruth scolded, but seeing Janty's tired smile decided to say no more.

Janthina had begged her to be charming and friendly towards James. 'It will be better for us all if we can keep him in a good mood. I try not to reveal my feelings as far as possible.'

So James received a warm greeting from his sister-in-law that evening, welcomed her into his home with all the charm for which he was famous, offering his condolences on her tragic bereavement with such an appearance of sincerity that Ruth found it hard to believe that this was the same man of whom her sister had spoken on the train.

It was a great joy for the sisters to be together again. They shared household tasks, confidences and sorrows, seeming to take strength from each other. Janthina felt more relaxed, more content in herself, having Ruth with her, even being able to laugh, secretly, at her husband, who, knowing she must surely have told Ruth all his short-comings, did his utmost to disprove any slur cast on his character by being utterly charming and sweet, not only to his sister-in-law but also to the children and herself. Ruth gave him every encouragement to believe she was fooled . . . but she wasn't; the two women had to take care, sometimes, not to catch each other's eye for fear laughter would betray them.

'It is a great relief having you here,' Janthina remarked one day when they were alone. 'James is behaving so nicely with you in the house. Sad as I am for the reasons you are in England, I have to admit I haven't been so happy, in myself, in years.'

'I often wished you could have been with me in India, we would have had so much fun together.' Ruth sighed.

'I would have felt a dreadful gooseberry. It's so different with James and me.'

'No matter how close and happy a marriage, I think it's always good for a woman to have a close female confidante; I never did strike up any intimate friendships over there. The other wives all seemed to be much older, or dreadfully blasé, or they were having enormous fun running affairs with each other's husbands. I couldn't make up my mind if they were all abnormal or only me.'

'I can't imagine a mother with young children finding time for affairs,' Janthina remarked.

'Out there, with servants to do everything and *ayahs* for the children, the women have far too much time on their hands. There appeared to be a constant competition going on to be the best dressed, give the best dinners, land the most lovers, and score off one's nearest rivals with cutting witticisms. Oh, there were some very nice couples but they tended to be quieter types and by the time we met them and started to make friends we were moved on again to a new station. We were never in one place for more than two years. And now, I suppose, I will have to be thinking of another move.'

'Why?'

'Well, we can't stay here indefinitely.'

They were interrupted at that moment by the children and it was not until suppertime that the subject was raised again.

'Ruth thinks she should be moving on,' Janthina told James. 'But she really has nowhere particular to go. What do you think she should do?'

'Move on! Why, for heaven's sake?' He reacted as she had hoped.

'I cannot inflict us on you, forever. You've been so kind and hospitable and I am truly grateful, but. . . .'

'Nonsense! We won't hear of you leaving. This is your home, now, for as long as you want to remain. Isn't that so, Janty my love?'

'Janty my love' was delighted. She had hoped he would suggest they stayed . . . but knew the idea would have to appear to be his. She must remember to thank him tonight – let him have the use of her body without protest, even show a little enthusiasm, perhaps, as a reward.


One hot, sultry evening in July, James came home from the Dolphin in a towering rage. 'Slap, bang in the middle of the season, when we couldn't be busier, and my confounded clerk walks out. Heaven knows she was a feather-brained little idiot anyway, but she was better than nothing. Now what the hell am I going to do? It will take at least a week, or more, to replace her.'

'Perhaps I could help,' Ruth suggested. 'I have no idea of clerical work but I do have a neat handwriting and would be happy to learn. You have both been so generous to give Giles and me a home; I would welcome the opportunity to contribute in some way in repayment.'

James looked as though he would refuse, had begun to shake his head . . . then paused, looking at her. 'Mmm,' he smiled. 'I daresay you could do the job very well, once you've been taught.'

'Do you think so?'

'Well, shall we give it a trial period? See if you like the work.'

'See if I can do it, you mean,' Ruth laughed. 'I'm sure I will enjoy it. But,' she added most sweetly, 'I could not possibly consider leaving Janty to do all the extra housework and catering for us. Not unless you could find a maid to help her in my place.'

Janty held her breath, watching James open and shut his mouth like a fish, weighing the cost of a clerk against that of a maid. Dear Ruth! She had manoeuvred this quite beautifully.

'Yes, very well, I'll see what I can do. When can you start?' he asked brusquely.

'As soon as the maid arrives to take over,' was Ruth's bright response, denying him any hope of delaying his search.

So began a trial period that was to last twelve years.


To all four of his cousins Giles was a hero, a leader; they loved him. To Caroline he was a knight in shining armour, a confidant, a playmate, and she worshipped him. Angus listened in awe to his tales of battles in the mountain passes between India and Afghanistan, and the two would lie together on the floor arranging dozens of lead soldiers – many inevitably headless but this handicap was disregarded – around books and cushions. Janthina had made a drawing of a fort and James took it to a man he knew in the town who modelled a copy in wood, presentation of which earned James enthusiastic hugs and great popularity.


Janty, as she was now known to everyone, watched Ruth's slow recovery with some anxiety. Until her shattering bereavement, life had treated her sister well; her figure was as trim as ever, far better than her own, her features fine, unlined and beautiful, but even when the colour returned to her face and the shine to her thick hair, Janty knew she was far from being her old self, beginning to doubt that she could ever be the same again. Her laughter lacked the bubbling quality of the old Ruth, her eyes lacked the sparkle, her crispness of repartee and movement was gone.

Ruth was very impressed by James's business ability; he had the knack of turning everything he touched into profit. She soon realised he was as mean as a church mouse, grossly underpaying his staff, criticising them constantly, yet, with intermittent bursts of praise, charming the maximum effort and loyalty from them.

He paid her a salary, a fraction of that received by her predecessor she eventually discovered, but, together with her small army pension, she had sufficient to dress herself and Giles and to put a little aside with which to fulfil Benjamin's original intention that the boy should go to his old school in Edinburgh and, if he wished, on to Sandhurst.

James was always charming to her, which, together with the way she sometimes caught him staring at her, faintly disturbed her, but she enjoyed the work once she grasped the basics, and he proved to be a very good instructor.

The arrival of the Kirkpatricks into the Cameron household brought nothing but happiness. Janty, having suddenly acquired a dear confidante, plus a maid, Susan, to do the heavy chores, soon felt remarkably relaxed. The fact that James, anxious to impress his sister-in-law, was almost constantly on his best behaviour, limited the bickering and nagging between them to the brief periods when they were alone in their bedroom – and even these bouts were few and far between. Janty was not unaware of James's interest in her sister; there was frank admiration, not to say desire, in his occasionally unguarded glances, but she wasn't in the least bit worried; she knew he would receive no encouragement from Ruth.

As the atmosphere between them eased, Janty found herself responding more to his approach during their intimate moments. Not that she loved him in the least, or hated him any the less, but she was human, felt the natural desires of any normal, healthy young woman – but no matter how tired he might be, James's relief always came within seconds, leaving her feeling tense, like an overstretched rubber band, wanting more, needing more . . . unfulfilled.

One evening she put on her best nightgown and when he joined her in their bedroom she helped him undress.

'What's all this then?' he asked in surprise.

'I just wondered if we couldn't put a little more into our love-making, a little more romance. There's no great hurry; let's make it last a bit longer.'

'I've had the impression in the past few years that you'd gone off the whole idea, that you wanted to get it over as quickly as possible.'

She ignored the remark. 'As long as we do continue to make love we might as well get the maximum pleasure from it. Don't you agree?'

He raised his eyebrows. 'Of course. What have you in mind?'

'You could kiss me, for a start, and caress me.'

188

He lay on the bed beside her. 'You mean, stroke your breasts, like this?'

'Yes. And down there, too.' She guided his hand.

'What for?'

'I would like to get pleasure from it, as you do,' she whispered gently.

'Don't be daft! Women don't have it like men. Come on, you've got me all worked up. I can't wait any longer. Quick, quick!' And she was left more wrought up than ever.

How could she tell him that with Anthony it had been so different – so beautiful and complete?

From time to time she tried again, but always with the same results.


Ian was born in the July of 1911, with a great deal of difficulty and discomfort. It was as if his mother's body was tired of the whole birth process, straining hard to carry out its natural functions. Janty had not wanted another child but James was delighted to have a second son, even lashing out into the extravagance of a gold fob watch for his exhausted wife.

'Thank you, James, what a lovely surprise!' She kissed him on the cheek.

'We must look after you more carefully, next time,' he told her. 'You have been doing too much for the children, they have exhausted you.'

Surreptitiously she caught Ruth's eye; they both knew that she had no intention of ever becoming pregnant again . . . an intention she contrived to achieve. At the age of twenty-seven her family was complete. Five children were enough – one more than Mama had had. Dear Mama. How much more she must have suffered from Papa's treatment than she had from James's. How she longed to see that dear face again. In her last letter, Mama wrote that she had not been well but was on the mend. She didn't say what the problem had been but said that maybe, when she was quite better, she might be able to arrange a visit to her daughters, a prospect that excited both sisters who immediately began discussing plans. They decided to ask her to come next spring, and eagerly awaited a reply to their joint letter.

The reply came from Joseph, saying that Mama was gravely ill in Kingston Hospital.

'We must telephone,' Janty said in horror. 'We must know what is happening.'

'How will you know where to find Joseph?' Ruth asked.

'He'll be with the cousins in Kingston, I should think.'

She sat in the office at the Excelsior throughout the following day, becoming increasingly frustrated by the delays and excuses, crackles and hisses and officious remarks from the operators. And the day after that, Simon arrived.

The excitement the two women felt at seeing their brother again after so many years was quite overshadowed, from the beginning, by the expression on his face. They knew, before he spoke.

'Mama died later the same day that Joseph sent the letter, and the funeral was two days later.'

'But how did you manage to get here so quickly?' Ruth queried.

'I've come up in the world. I'm now assistant purser on the *Lusitania*. She sailed for England the following day.' He hugged both of them together. 'I am so sad to bring such awful news.'

He explained that Mama had had a malignant growth in her stomach. The doctors did not tell her, and Papa was not in stable enough health to be told either. So Joseph had been the one contacted. There had been a period of remission when they had held their breath and hoped. . . . It was then Mama had written to the two girls, two days before being rushed back to Kingston. Simon was grateful that fate had decreed he should be on leave at that time and had shared the vigil with Joseph until the end. 'She died smiling, though in great pain, as we talked about the old days when we were all at home, working in the hayfields and you helping her with the baking, remember?'

'What will happen to Papa, now?'

'I don't know. He insists on remaining at the farm but life is very difficult for Joseph. His heart isn't in farming. He is studying to go into the church, you know.'

'Is he? Well, it will probably suit him admirably, but what will happen to the farm? Will the Callaghans run it?'

'I suppose so. Papa certainly wouldn't hear of selling it.'

It was an unhappy visit. Simon could only stay four days before rejoining the liner, though he promised to return again soon. 'You may see me quite often in the future, now I am with Cunard. My next visit should be a little less sad.'


Ruth thought a normal man would have been satisfied owning the splendid Excelsior Hotel at the east end of the promenade as well as the Dolphin, high on the cliffs to the west, two grocery shops, a fancy goods shop and coffee rooms in the town centre as well as what was fast becoming the leading wholesale suppliers in the county. In ten years James Cameron had risen from small-time grocer to head the largest business combine in Whitehaven, fast approaching millionaire status – at least on paper. His esteem within the local community was high. A sidesman at St Mary's, a Rotarian and Freemason, he was noted for his generous donations to charity. The office he had created for himself behind the shop in the town centre was visited daily by his cronies and admirers, and the mayor had asked him more than once if he would take part in local politics. He already sat on a number of committees but was 'reluctant to waste any more time on unprofitable affairs as yet', he confided to his sister-in-law.

But James was not a normal man. There was always another goal, something further to reach forward and grasp. Now, in 1913, he wanted the Grand Hotel.

The largest purpose-built hotel in Whitehaven, having seventy bedrooms, numerous reception rooms and an immense ballroom, the Grand had regrettably lost some of its grandeur in recent years, possibly due to the effects of absentee ownership, and could nowadays be justly described as shabby genteel. It was occupied mainly by elderly residents who had come to regard it as home, and it was unfortunate that many of the rooms were taken on long-term leases, allowing the owner only a minimal profit margin – unfortunate because no ambitious hotelier would therefore be remotely interested in purchasing it.

Except for James. In a roundabout way he let it be known that, almost as a charitable gesture to the town, he might consider taking it over, if the owner weren't asking too high a figure, if only to smarten it up a little: it was shameful to see the depressing effect the peeling paintwork of its façade had on that section of the promenade. He made his position perfectly plain – and his offer – ensuring that the vendor was left in no doubt as to just how grateful he should be for such a generous gesture.

Ruth knew only too well how over-capitalised James would become on completion of the transaction. Working capital became a constant problem, bringing permanent lines between his heavy brows, causing him to twist the bedclothes into a shocking tangle at night, disturbing him and worrying his wife.

'What do you think can be the matter with James?' Janty asked her sister one Sunday as they sat together on the beach watching the children playing. 'There must be some burden on his mind. Have you any idea what it might be?'

'None at all,' Ruth lied. 'Though I have noticed it myself. Probably to do with one of his committees; he has taken on an awful lot of responsibilities.' She had no intention of confiding her knowledge of the financial situation. There was nothing Janty could do about it except worry, and James would be sure to guess who had told her – and that would never do. She didn't want to endanger her job or her place in the Cameron household. Janty had repeated over and over again, how sweet and peaceful these past five years had been, attributing the fact to Ruth's presence, and one would have to be blind not to notice how healthy and relaxed she was now. She had put on some much-needed weight, filling out her figure admirably; her hands were white and smooth, nails well manicured, and she spent the time necessary each morning to dress her hair fashionably, swept up from the nape of the neck and piled in a mass of curls on the top of her head in a style made popular by Queen Alexandra. The tired lines and grey circles round her eyes were gone, and even her bitter anger against James over the broken promise seemed to have abated.

The only disturbing factor in their lives, apart from the business, was another which Ruth was unable to discuss with her sister, though Janty had to be aware of the situation in some degree. It was, of course, James's interest in herself. She had known, from the moment she had set foot in their house, that James admired her and liked to engage her in lively conversation, but that was harmless enough providing he behaved quite properly towards her; which he had not for nearly a year now. He had begun an increasing familiarity – unnecessary touching, over-enthusiastic demonstrations of affection at Christmas and New Year and on birthdays – until he finally started the habit of standing behind her chair in the office and, on the pretext of reading over her shoulder, allowing his hands to rest on the tops of her arms, slipping them slowly, caressingly, down, brushing against her breasts, while holding his face close to hers in pretended concentration.

She had pondered on the best way to deal with the situation for nearly a week, dreading to create a scene or perhaps even a rift in their relationship, finally resolving to wait until the next incident and, in as light and flippant a way as possible, warn him off.

'Hey! Brother-in-law!' she laughed one day, ducking away. 'Do you know what you are doing to me? You are giving me the urge to rush out and find myself another husband.' As though he could possibly arouse her in the least, or that she could ever dream of replacing Benjamin.

'Now that would be a pity, wouldn't it?' he replied, archly, advancing again. 'I'm convinced we could come to a better arrangement than that.'

She had stood up on the excuse of fetching another ledger. 'I can't

192

think how,' she smiled. 'Unless I borrow someone else's, and that, James dear, I'll never do, not even my sister's.' She spoke jokingly, but firmly enough to leave no doubt in his mind of her meaning. 'Now come on, let me get back to these accounts or they'll not be finished today. Then I'll be in trouble with the boss, won't I?'

The incident had coincided with the appearance of a very attractive young assistant housekeeper at the Excelsior, so Ruth was never quite sure whether her ploy or the amiable young lady was responsible for his cooled ardour.

The sun was warm on the beach, and both women had removed their shoes and stockings so that they might wade with the children in the shallows. The children were now playing in their bathing costumes while their mothers' feet dried in the sand.

Ian was a placid child. Though very steady on his feet and able to master a number of words, he was content to sit quietly beside his aunt and mother, watching Giles building an intricate sandcastle, all moats, tunnels and turrets, which he patiently repaired after Angus's haphazard attempts to help.

Flora and Alexandra were having a dolls' tea party, using cockle shells for cups and plates, chattering together, though Flora, as always, was insisting that the game be played her way, her straight, dark hair, thin frame, narrow features and unsmiling expression contrasting vividly with her little sister's light brown curls, chubbiness, and cheerful grin.

Caroline had a cold and had not been allowed to take off her dress. At eleven years old she was tall and utterly beautiful – a fair, almost transparent beauty, blonde curls framing her exquisite features: features which looked very sore today, matching her aching head. She walked listlessly over the beach, kicking at small pebbles, occasionally stooping to pick one up and toss it out to sea, and then returned to lean against Janty. At that moment there was a squeal from Flora. She had trodden on a sharp piece of broken shell, drawing a pin-prick of blood on her big toe.

'Ooh, Mama!' she wailed. 'I'm hurt.' And ran for the comfort of her mother's lap. Before Caroline could step aside she was shoved violently by the smaller girl.

'Now, now,' Janty chided. 'There's no need to be nasty.'

'She was in the way,' Flora complained.

'No, she wasn't, and even if she had been . . .'

'She was. She's got no business to be with you all the time. You're my mama, not hers. Go away, Caroline,' and she gave her step-sister an extra push.

The sand was soft, and Caroline stepped back, into a hole just dug by Ian, and fell. Only her dignity was hurt, but once again she was the outsider and withdrew into her shell.

Janty and Ruth were furious, the latter controlling her reaction to a mere exclamation, but her sister grabbed Flora, threw her across her knee, and smacked her soundly on the behind.

The child screamed, briefly, then revolved on Janty's lap to wind her arms around her mother's neck. 'I'm sorry, Mama,' she whimpered.

'Good. I'm glad, because that really was very unkind.' How she longed to tell them all the truth, let Flora know that Caroline was her sister, her elder sister, and allow Caroline the comfort of having at least a mother. She was tempted, repeatedly, but now, as always, resisted. Instead, she compromised. 'Now I want you to go and say "sorry" to Caroline. Give her a kiss and make her feel better.'

Flora obediently walked over to the breakwater where Caroline bent to receive the proffered kiss. 'I'm sorry,' the smaller girl said in a loud voice, adding in a whisper, 'I hate you and wish you'd stop hanging on to my mother all the time.' She then returned to Janthina for comfort to the damaged toe.

No one had heard but the two girls. Not even Janty guessed how badly Caroline's feelings were hurt for the girl put on a brave face, not really seeming to care. Only Giles came to understand, over the years, how much misery Angus and Flora, particularly Flora, caused their 'cousin'; it was always done slyly and secretly so that their mother could not guess, knowing that if Caroline accused them they could easily deny it, staunchly supported by their father. So Giles became Caroline's protector, spending more time with her than with her tormentors, adding to their jealousy but creating her only solace.

On the day contracts for the Grand Hotel were signed, a letter arrived from Joseph telling his sisters that Papa was in hospital following a severe stroke. Three doctors had examined him thoroughly, as well as Uncle Robert, and all agreed he had suffered extensive brain damage. He had lost control of all save the fingers of one hand and could recognise nobody. Joseph said he was in a quandary. Papa could never return to the farm, and he himself no longer wished to remain there. Would the girls agree that it should be sold? He had written to Simon, too, asking his opinion.

'He can do as he likes, as far as I'm concerned,' Ruth said. 'There seems little point in keeping it unless one of us wants to return there to live.'

194

Janty walked across her drawing room to gaze out across the bay, seeing only the dearly loved home of her childhood – the home she had left so reluctantly on the assurance that it would only be for one year. And already twelve years had passed. There was a leaden ball in her stomach; her chest ached; she felt exactly as she remembered feeling as she had waved goodbye to Bear Foot . . . for the last time. Had she somehow known, then? Had an inexplicable sixth sense been warning her that if she left, it would be never to return? 'Yes,' she sighed. 'I suppose you are right. It will have to go. I wonder what will happen to Pickle? He must be seventeen years old now.'

The prospect of disposing of the farm didn't have nearly so depressing an effect on Ruth as did the acquiring of the Grand, full, as it was, of all those sweet, elderly residents. She had dared to express her worries to Cam two or three times, but he had only teased her, saying everything would be resolved in due course. He never explained how.

Working mostly at the office in town and occasionally at the Excelsior, she put the Grand out of her mind and concentrated on juggling with accounts, stalling creditors and, as far as possible, keeping the ledgers up to date. Giles had long been enrolled for Edinburgh Academy and in September she would travel north to see him installed and arrange for him to spend some weekends with Benjamin's parents.

Cam had enrolled Angus at Brighton College, but the boy would have to wait another two years before he became a weekly boarder there. In the meantime, the boy walked with Caroline, each day, to Whitehaven Grammar School where he was still in the junior department. It was a small school and the teaching standards unimpressive.

'I don't think anyone at the Grammar School is qualified to teach children over the age of ten,' Janty complained to Cam one evening. 'Caroline would do far better at a good girls' school like St Margaret's in Brighton. I'd like to contact the headmistress there to see if they could take her in September.'

'Rubbish. A total waste of money. The standard of education here in Whitehaven is more than adequate for girls. All they need to know is how to write legibly, count their housekeeping money, and cook.' He didn't bother to glance up from his newspaper as he spoke.

'Oh, Cam, that's not true. There are so many. . . .'

'There is no reason whatever, other than snobbery, for sending Caroline to St Margaret's.'

'Then why are you sending Angus to Brighton College?'

'That's different. A boy has to be prepared for all the responsibility he must carry when he is a man. I want Angus in the business with me. He will have to take over when I retire.'

'But I. . . .'

He stood up and knocked out his pipe. 'I'm going out. Don't wait up, I may be late.'

'Cam! I'm talking to you. Haven't you. . . .'

'There is nothing more to be said. I have told you my answer. No!' And he walked out, leaving her seething with anger.


'Cam, I don't know if you are aware of it, but five of your old residents at the Grand have not paid up this month.' Ruth was frowning as she went over the hotel ledger.

'Oh, don't worry about that, they've left. I forgot to mention it.'

'Left! But some of them have years yet to run on their leases.'

'They decided to move. I think there are some others going too, thank goodness.'

'Good gracious!' Ruth exclaimed. 'I wonder why?'

'I can't imagine. Though I have heard a rumour that the previous owner of the Grand has offered them better terms at a place he owns in Brighton.' Cam had his back to her as he spoke.

'How very fortunate for us . . . well, for you, I mean.'

'Yes. It means we can get the decorators in soon, to make sure the place is ready to open in plenty of time for next season.'

What an enormous stroke of luck, his sister-in-law thought . . . and then forgot all about it.


Donald MacDougall had a bad attack of influenza, early the following year and, despite devoted nursing, developed pneumonia.

Ruth and Janty hurried north to see him, receiving a great welcome from everyone including the sick man. His sudden rapid improvement was accredited to their arrival, and the two women felt quite girlish again, sleeping in their old bedrooms, the décor somewhat faded now, but otherwise the same.

'Tell me, Ruth,' the old man whispered hoarsely one day when they were alone. 'I never did hear about the adoption of Janthina's first child. We asked her in letters but she never gave a direct answer. It did go ahead as Cameron promised, didn't it?'

She wanted to spare him from the unpalatable truth, but before she could frame the lie her heightened colour betrayed her.

Grandpapa was watching her closely. 'It didn't!' he exclaimed. 'Tell me what happened.' It was an order.

'Er . . . well, I'm afraid Cam, James that is, changed his mind.'

'Changed his . . . but he gave me his word.'

'Yes. He promised Janty, too. But in the end he decided he didn't want Caroline to be senior to his own children and refused to go ahead with the plan.'

Grandpapa's colour rose and his jaws gnashed furiously. There were so many things he wanted to say, to do, but he lacked the strength; he just lay back against his pillows, slowly shaking his head.

Elinor came for a weekend visit and she and Janty were soon mounted and galloping up the glen. Janty was elated. It was wonderful to feel a horse under her again after so many years, though she had no doubt that her muscles would suffer next day. She pulled the pins from her hair, letting the wind blow it wild, streaming across her shoulders.

Aunt Meg, Uncle Andrew and Aunt Laura looked older, but seemed otherwise unchanged and Malcolm had been at Perth Station to meet them and drive them up to Glenfalk. It was as though they had never left.

They departed almost reluctantly, leaving Grandpapa looking far better than when they had arrived, and with fervent invitations to return.

'Will you go back?' Ruth asked as their train pulled away from the platform at Edinburgh.

'Perhaps, when Grandpapa has gone, if I feel the others might welcome Caroline. I can't really keep up friendly associations with relatives who won't acknowledge my daughter.'

Ruth was tempted to tell her about the conversation she had had with Grandpapa . . . but, as was her nature, decided to keep quiet.


The Grand Hotel, Whitehaven, re-opened during Easter week, 1914, with a fabulous reception.

Cam had lashed out a great deal of money he didn't have on refurbishing, assuring his many creditors it was money well spent and would be repaid with interest before the end of the first season. And who, knowing his successful business record, would doubt his word?

The huge ballroom, hung with three massive chandeliers, gilded mirrors and long, fringed velvet curtains, had a vast table down the centre from end to end. On the white cloths were piled a fabulous array of glazed turkeys and hams, whole salmons and lobsters dressed

197

and decorated by the hotel's team of chefs working under Antoine of Paris. There were fancy pastries and creamy desserts and dainty finger morsels, and waiters passed among the invited crowd with trays of champagne.

The Camerons and Kirkpatricks circulated among the guests, all save Ian who, still only three years old, remained at home with Susan. The town councillors and their wives attended en bloc, and the mayor mounted the orchestra stage, quietening the players, in order to make the opening speech. He was eloquent in his admiration of the redecorating and furnishing of the hotel and informed his audience that they and all Whitehaven should be grateful for the presence of James Cameron in their community, a man, he said, who was responsible for so much of the development and progress of the town as well as being a most gracious public benefactor. Glasses were raised in James's honour and again to his charming wife and family, before the mayor declared himself delighted to announce that the Grand Hotel was now open.

Cam and Janty stood together smiling for the newspaper cameramen, the children grouped around them, Janty having adroitly manoeuvred Caroline into the picture, much to Flora's disgust. Tall for her age, Caroline was wearing her first long dress, white organza scalloped at hem and neck and beribboned in deep violet blue to match her eyes. The blonde curls had been tied in rags overnight and now hung in graceful ringlets, and round her throat was a necklet of seed pearls – a present, years before, from Ruth and Ben.

Giles Kirkpatrick stood beside her as soon as the cameramen had finished, swaggering slightly to swing his Kirkpatrick tartan kilt and small sporran. 'When do you think we can start eating?' he asked, drooling at the sight of the loaded table.

'We'll have to wait until Uncle Cam has fed the mayor, I suppose. What are you going to start with?'

'Lobster,' he told her decisively.

'Mmmm. Me too. Then some of those tiny sausages.'

'And just look at that chocolate mousse!'

Janty had bought herself a dress in Brighton, at Cam's instigation; a rare event prompted only by his desire to show her off to advantage. It was pale green lace over a matching satin lining, with short sleeves and a low neckline. A seven-row choker of imitation pearls rode high up her neck, a matching bracelet clasped her wrist and long pearl earrings swung from her ears. Janthina had always been a handsome woman, but Cam's friends and associates had never seen her looking quite so regal and she was amused at the way they turned from the jocular banter round her husband to bow, and address her in tones of deep respect.

Ruth had made her own dress, simply cut in blue, a darker shade of piping trimming the seams and hem. Having met most of the men present in Cam's office, she was able to make introductions, assisting Janty in her duties as hostess.

Everyone expressed profound admiration for the restored hotel, several of the town's leading businessmen nodding sagely over its obvious profitability, so that Ruth dared to hope that her fears were unfounded. After all, the British economy had been improving for the past seven years and, although there was much head-shaking over the crisis in Ireland where many people anticipated the outbreak of civil war at any minute, they were all quite confident of England's financial stability.

How could they have guessed that within four months their country would be swept dramatically into Europe's horrifying holocaust?

# 4

WAR!

But nothing seemed to be very different – except for Cam's limp which, until August 4th, 1914, he had always been at pains to camouflage, but which suddenly became quite pronounced, particularly after a recruiting office opened in Whitehaven. Not that he need have worried; his Boer War wound had been duly noted by the authorities, and he would never be required to take up arms in defence of his country – but it was necessary to reassure one's friends and acquaintances that one wasn't a coward.

The Grand Hotel was almost full in August after a rather slow start in the earlier months, and for a few weeks Ruth breathed more freely as she carefully wrote up the diminishing debts. Even Cam was smiling a little more, grumbling a little less, though he was still obviously very anxious, snatching away ledgers on which she was working, pacing the office, book on arm, and sometimes summoning Antoine or Mrs Panton, the housekeeper, to complain of wastage. But the good weeks soon gave way to an abrupt end to the season and by the middle of September the English were no longer in holiday mood.

'Damn this war!' Cam exploded. 'Damn, damn, damn!' He was sitting at his desk in the town office, Mr Chartwell, a market gardener and Cam's chief source of fruit and vegetables, opposite him.

The visitor was smiling cheerfully, glass in hand. 'Ah, don't take on so, Cam old fellow. It's not going to last long. It'll all be over by Christmas. The Frogs'll make short work of these Bosch, you mark my words.'

'I doubt there is a soul will disagree with you, John, but nevertheless I hate holding up payment of your account. I feel very badly about it.'

'You've been a good friend and customer for too long for me to worry. I know my money's safe. Let's just drink to a bumper season in 1915 and forget the subject until then.'

Ruth heard the glasses clink from her desk in the outer office . . .

and sighed with relief. John Chartwell had come in half an hour ago in a very belligerent mood, determined to collect on his overdue account; he had even spoken roughly to her when she had tried to intercept his charge towards the 'boss', leaving her breathless as to the outcome . . . wondering was this the creditor who would push them over the top? Sue? Start the spiral down into bankruptcy? She allowed herself a slightly cynical smile, knowing she need not have worried. The famous Cameron charm had worked again.

The telephone jangled on the wall behind her, and she got up to lift the earpiece off its hook.

'Ruth? It's Janty here. I've just had a telephone call from Aunt Laura. It's Grandpapa. He died last night in his sleep.'

'That was sudden!' Ruth shouted into the mouthpiece; she still couldn't get used to the idea that anyone could hear her from so far away unless she shouted.

'A massive heart attack, Aunt Laura said. I wondered if you thought we should go up for the funeral?'

They were busy in the office at the moment, and she doubted if Cam would want her to go. 'Why don't you go, Janty? Susan will look after Ian during the day, and I'll see to them all in the evenings. I don't think I should leave the office for that long, just now.'

Janty stood in front of the full-length mirror on her wardrobe door, examining herself in detail. She was now thirty, and thanks to Ruth's coming to live with them, she no longer looked drab and old for her years. Her hair was still the same light brown, almost sand-coloured, curling without assistance, and now that she had put on a little weight, she had lost that gaunt look, there was hardly a sign of a wrinkle on her face and her eyes were bright and lively – especially now, at the prospect of a few days away from Cam. Not that Grandpapa's funeral would be a very jolly occasion, but although she was dressed entirely in black – which suited her very well, she decided, turning to admire the narrow crêpe skirt and matching coat which hung from the nipped waist in three soft tiers almost to her knees – and she and Ruth were both sad at the passing of an era, she could not weep for him. It was not as though he had been cut off in his prime – why, he must have been well into his eighties. He had had a good innings, and a full life, but the past few years had been lonely without Grandmama and he had railed against the infirmities of old age. Not that he hadn't deserved his bit of misery before he went, after pushing her into marriage with James Cameron. She tossed her head in a flash of anger, but it was

201

soon over, and she smiled at her reflection. It would be nice to see Elinor and Roderick and the aunts and uncles again.

Selecting a pair of pearl-topped pins from the glass tray on her dressing table, she fixed the veiled black hat firmly into place and then hurried downstairs to the cab, waiting to take her to the station.


Her father-in-law conducted the funeral service, his hair now as white as his surplice and a distinct droop to his shoulders. The church was packed and the overflow of people out in the churchyard divided to allow the pall-bearers through with their immense burden.

After the interment, friends and relatives made the sombre walk up the hill to Glenfalk where cakes and sandwiches were passed round and the ladies drank tea while their menfolk took something a little stronger.

'Janthina, dear, will you come into the library, please?' Aunt Laura whispered. 'Mr Alcott, Grandpapa's advocate, is about to read the will.'

Janty followed as bidden. The thought of a will hadn't crossed her mind and she couldn't imagine it had anything to do with her; it was a matter of all the family being present, she supposed.

The bequests were much as might be expected. Family retainers were remembered and impoverished cousins assisted. Aunt Laura would be well provided for for the rest of her life.

' ". . . and five hundred pounds to each and all of my grand-children. . . ." ' Janty's eyes lit up, but only for a second, ' ". . . excepting Janthina Cameron." '

Oh, no! Surely Grandpapa hadn't carried his puritan antagonism to the grave.

Mr Alcott coughed before continuing. ' "As a token of apology for an old man's mistake, I leave her five thousand pounds. She will understand why and, I hope, forgive." '

Everyone present, including the lawyer, turned to smile at Janty, acknowledging their pleasure at her good fortune. But she didn't notice. Her face was buried in her hands and she was weeping, appalled at the bitterness she had nurtured for the past ten years.


St Mary's Anglican Church boasted a strong membership in the Ladies' Circle, matrons who met at least once a week to sew, knit, exchange recipes – and a little gossip – and make collections for charity, under the eager eye of the rector's wife. And from time to time, when the mayor and his councillors deemed it politic, a lady from the group, invariably named by Mrs Cooney as a suitable choice, was invited to stand for election to a local committee. There were ladies on the Nursing Committee, the Books for the Enlightenment of the Poor Committee, for Relief of Impoverished Gentlewomen and also on the Education Committee. The lady who had held a seat on the latter for some years had been obliged to resign due to ill-health and Janty, a long-standing member of the Circle, thanks to Mrs Cooney's forceful powers of persuasion, had been approached by the lady mayoress and asked to stand in her stead. She had never been on a committee, had no idea what it entailed, but decided that if some of the women she knew could handle the responsibility, then she had no right to fear her own inadequacy. And it was a subject which interested her, particularly in respect of the education of young girls.

It was in regard to the latter that she was required to attend a joint meeting of County Education Committee representatives and head teachers of girls' schools, held in Brighton. Among those present, not unnaturally, was Miss Entwhistle, headmistress of St Margaret's, who, at the end of the meeting when tea and biscuits were being served, came to sit beside Janty and introduced herself.

Janty held out her hand and reciprocated.

'No need to tell me who you are, Mrs Cameron. As soon as I saw your name on the agenda I guessed you must be Flora's mother.' Mrs Entwhistle's head bobbed up and down on its long neck as she spoke.

'Flora?' There might be a number of reasons for her name to be noised abroad, but she had never visualised being Flora's mother as one of them.

'Yes. It is always so encouraging when a member of the Education Committee enrols their daughter at one's school. When will the dear child be joining us?'

Janty's mind raced. Cam! Cam must have enrolled her, the two-faced. . . . Damn him! After refusing to allow Caroline to go to St Margaret's. 'I . . . er . . . I'm not sure. Whenever you consider she is ready, I imagine.' How dare he! If only she had known. . . .

'We usually take girls as near to their eleventh birthday as possible, occasionally earlier if they are exceptionally bright. But sometimes a little older, too.'

'How old?' Caroline was almost twelve. Would that be considered too late?

'In special circumstances, up to almost any age, providing we have a place.'

'Really? I had no idea. Otherwise I would have asked you to consider

203

taking my eld . . . my niece, Caroline.' The adrenalin was working now. 'Such a sweet girl,' she added. 'So sadly orphaned as a baby.'

'Oh! How dreadful, the poor child.'

'She has been part of our family ever since,' Janty pressed on. 'Grown up almost as Flora's sister. It would have been so nice for the two girls to have been at the same school.' Cam could scarcely refuse to pay the fees now that he had enrolled his own daughter, but if he did refuse she would pay them herself out of Grandpapa's money, though she hadn't wanted to let him know about that. It was securely invested in a Brighton bank, for in case. . . .

'But of course, I couldn't agree with you more. I am sure something can be arranged.'

'I suppose it is already too late for this year, as we are well into October.'

'What age did you say she is?'

'Almost twelve.' She held her breath.

'Excellent! I happen to know we have a vacancy in Miss Bater's form. When could you bring her to see me?'

Presumably it was bad business for a headmistress to have vacancies. 'Early next week?'

'Would Monday suit you?'

'Beautifully! About eleven o'clock?'

At last! At last she had won something for Caroline. The girl could at least have a decent education, even if she couldn't have parents.


'Where is Caroline?' Cam asked.

'At school.'

'School! It's seven o'clock! What's she doing there at this hour?'

They were gathered in the drawing room around the fire, Janty busy with her darning needle, Ruth knitting, Angus and Flora frowning over school homework and Alexandra playing with Ian on the hearthrug. Cam was drinking, a favourite pastime of his, nowadays.

'She won't be home until Friday night. She started today as a weekly boarder at St Margaret's.'

'What?' There was a crash of breaking glass as his arm knocked the whisky tumbler off the coffee table beside him, into the grate.

Ruth jumped up from her knitting. 'I'll get a dustpan and brush,' she said quietly, and left the room.

'How dare you? I told you. . . .'

'Flora, will you ask Susan to see Alexandra and Ian to bed, please?

204

Then you and Angus can go up and finish your homework in your bedrooms. I'll be up in a few minutes.'

Cam had sat glaring for a few moments before going to the chiffonier to pour another drink, standing with his back to her until she finished speaking and the children had left the room.

'Now.' He swung round as the door closed. 'What have you been doing behind my back?'

'Exactly the same as you have been doing behind mine. I enrolled my daughter at St Margaret's . . .' she was speaking quietly, her needlework on her lap.

'I. . . .'

'The only difference between the enrolment of Caroline and Flora is that Caroline's should have been done two years ago. She should have been able to start at the beginning of term, instead of having to try to catch up with the other girls. Flora will be more fortunate.'

'Flora is not at St Margaret's yet; I don't even know if she will go there. I may not be able to afford it. Anyway, that has nothing to do with it. I told you that Caroline could not go. . . .'

'You cannot possibly justify sending Angus and Flora to good schools, and deny Caroline. . . .' She was trying to keep hold of her temper.

'I'm hoping that by the time the younger ones are ready there will be sufficient money for fees. . . .'

'. . . from the business you started with money stolen from Caroline and me. . . .'

'Stolen!' he shouted. For a moment she thought he was going to strike her as he crossed the hearth and stood over her chair, face contorted with fury.

'Obtained from me under false pretences. Call it what you will, you had no right to it. . . .' She knew she was pushing him to the limit of his temper, already shortened by whisky, but was determined to make her point, come what may.

'I had every right to it. I married you, didn't I? I. . . .'

'You didn't have to. I didn't ask you. . . .'

'Your grandfather did.'

Yes. And lived to regret it. 'That's beside the point. You persuaded me to hand over the money and failed to keep your part of the bargain. So the money, and all the money it has produced over the past ten years, rightfully belongs to Caroline and me.'

'Rubbish!' He bent over to snarl in her face. 'Absolute rot! I. . . .' He tapped himself on the chest. 'I have built our business empire. And you and your bastard are having a damned good living out of it, aren't you?' He paused, then demanded, 'Answer me, damn you! Answer!

205

Aren't you having a bloody sight better living out of it than if you were trying to live off the measly interest on five thousand pounds?'

Janty laid her darning aside and stood up, heart pounding with anger. 'An above average sized house hardly compensates for the stigma of being a bastard and being deceived into the belief that both one's parents are dead. It doesn't compensate me for hearing my daughter call me auntie.' She walked to the door. 'I'm going to say goodnight to the children.'

'You come back here, you confounded bitch!' He lunged at the door, which suddenly opened and he was confronted by the tall, cool figure of his sister-in-law, dustpan in hand. He gave her one furious look, pushed her aside, and headed for the front door, grabbing his hat from the hall stand and slamming the door after him so hard the stained glass rattled and nearly broke.


If, in only ten years, Cam could turn five thousand pounds into a business empire with three shops, a restaurant, and the biggest grocery and liquor wholesalers in the district, then why couldn't the five thousand that Grandpapa had left her do the same? Couldn't she invest it in some business? But what business could thrive as long as there was a war on? A munitions factory, Janty supposed, or a clothes factory making uniforms . . . yes. She would take a trip to Brighton to see Caroline, soon, and pay her bank manager a visit at the same time.


Christmas was much quieter that year, mainly because they were short of money. Cam had paid Caroline's school fees without further comment but had cut back on the housekeeping and warned Janty not to waste money on presents.

Giles came home from his first term at Edinburgh Academy seeming to have matured amazingly in the three months and eager to tell his family all about Scotland. Especially Caroline. The two spent most of the holidays together comparing their new experiences, obviously feeling too grown-up to spend much time with the four young Camerons, other than condescendingly to amuse them.

In fact, Janty had twinges of jealousy. She had looked forward to Caroline's return for the holiday, and now, finding herself audience to the natural rapport between the cousins, something she had wanted with her daughter for so long and yet had never achieved, she longed to step in and make opportunities which otherwise never presented themselves. Unfortunately, she and Caroline always felt slightly uncomfortable in each other's company, the lie between them forming a tragic barrier; a barrier which Janty feared was increasing steadily. So, when it was time for Caroline to return to school after the festivities she was, in a sense, relieved to see her go, relieved of the constant hurt, and prayed that the next period of separation might heal the rift. Perhaps at Easter they might get a little closer. The weekend visits were too brief, she told herself, to expect any improvement before then . . . a subconscious defence against more hurt?

The winter season didn't prove to be as financially disastrous as Cam and Ruth had feared, despite the dashing of everyone's hope of the war ending by Christmas.

Caroline and Giles came home for the Easter holidays to find everything bustling with preparations for the opening of the new season, but before they could begin another period of pairing off together, boredom was relieved by the arrival of their two uncles, Simon the sailor and Joseph the 'Sky Pilot', as Cam called him irreverently behind his back.

The Canadian church, deciding that the lack of army padres was more serious than Joseph's lack of experience, had declared his qualifications adequate and he was duly commissioned. Certainly, with baldness adding to his thirty-seven years, plus his ever serious demeanour, no one could dispute that he looked the part.

Simon had had the sense to forestall any embarrassing situation regarding Caroline by explaining to Joseph, on their journey to Whitehaven, what had actually happened to their younger sister. So that on their arrival, dog-collar firmly buttoned on the nape of his neck, the padre smiled benevolently on the presumed repentant, cast an eye of judgement over her husband, and laid fingers of benediction on the fair curls of 'the problem'. He was sincerely delighted to meet all his nephews and nieces, though in his awkward way he was as shy of them as they were of him.

Simon, on the other hand, treated the world like a playground. He loved his job on the *Lusitania* and told innumerable incredible tales of his adventures to his appreciative young audience.

It was the first time the four brothers and sisters had been together since the girls left Canada, a time for gaiety and celebration, so the sisters decided to give a buffet supper party. Cam, bolstered by his high hopes for the coming season, was prepared to be indulgent, offering the services of Antoine and his staff from the Grand, much to Janty's delight.

It was not a big party, only twenty-four people invited, selected from the friends and acquaintances, met mainly through business, whom Ruth and Janty liked most. Two town councillors and their wives came, two hoteliers and a wine and spirit merchant and their wives, friendly rivals of Cam's, and various of his customers – though none of his creditors.

The four older children had been allowed to stay up late and, the boys dressed in Eton suits and Caroline and Flora in pretty dresses, they handed round trays of canapés, speaking politely to everyone, and introducing their uncles to their guests.

Reverend and Mrs Cooney were delighted to meet Joseph and monopolised him in profound discussion on the part played by the church in Canada, as opposed to England. Simon found himself quickly drawn into lively and humorous conversation with Janty and Freddie Gordon, a tall, slim man in his late forties, who, whilst holding his drink in his right hand, gestured without embarrassment with the gloved model of a hand attached to his left arm, all that remained after a Boer bullet and a field surgeon had done their work.

Janty had noticed Arthur Cranston, one of the hoteliers, standing alone, and left Simon and Freddie to join him. 'What do you think our prospects are for the coming season?' she asked.

They discussed the hotel business for a few minutes, then Arthur said, 'Changing the subject, I have been wanting to tell you how much Alice and I admire your niece. Your other sister must have been a very beautiful woman. What did you say her name was?'

'Morton.'

'I knew some Mortons once. Where did your brother-in-law come from?'

'Er . . . the north of England.' Hopefully that was sufficiently distant.

But it wasn't. 'Yes! That's right. Oswald was his name, I remember. What was your brother-in-law's Christian name?'

Oh, God! How she hated these lies. 'Charles.'

'Charles.' He frowned. 'No, I don't recall that name. Where exactly did they live?'

'I couldn't say for sure. They lived abroad except for occasional visits.' She was watching Caroline and didn't notice Flora standing at her elbow offering a dainty selection of vol-au-vents, minute sausage rolls, and other savoury pastries.

'Where did she get those gorgeous eyes?' Arthur persisted. 'Are they from your side of the family?'

Janty's expression softened. Even from across the room, it was obvious that those were Anthony's eyes under the long, dark lashes – his fair skin and blond hair. 'No, Caroline takes after her father,' she said softly.

Arthur Cranston could not help but notice his hostess's expression – an extraordinary blend of tenderness, love and . . . sadness, particularly strange in an aunt.

Flora saw it too. Her little mouth tightened and she moved away towards Angus.

'Arthur, you really must come and meet my brother, Joseph.' Janty took his arm and led him to the trio by the window. She made the introductions and turned away, saw Simon leave Freddie and Ruth together and come towards her.

'What an awfully nice chap that Freddie is,' Simon remarked. 'Is his wife here?'

'No, no. She died of appendicitis about two years ago. Terribly sad, she was such a nice person. The doctors decided to operate too late.'

'Really?' Simon looked back at the man with his sister. 'That's interesting. Any chance of him pairing up with Ruth, do you think?'

'You mean for supper?'

'No, you goose! For keeps. Marriage. Ruth is far too young and beautiful to remain a widow for the rest of her life.'

Janty laughed. 'You incorrigible match-maker! We-ell, I suppose anything is possible.'

'With a little bit of help I reckon the possible could be turned into the positive.' He wagged a finger at her nose. 'You work on it, little sister. Next time I visit you I will expect to see some progress.'

'Simon! You're the limit,' his little sister admonished. 'Where do you get such ideas?'

'Passenger liners. We're doing it all the time. It's amazing the number of people who take cruises because they're lonely: they need to meet and make friends – and more. Every cruise has its crop of shipboard romances.'

Suddenly there was a tremendous crash.

Janty and Simon hurried through the throng of guests towards the source of the noise and found Caroline sprawled on the floor near the fireplace, a mess of mangled canapés scattered over the tiles and carpet and the silver salver lying amongst the firetongs.

'You stupid, clumsy girl,' Cam was complaining irritably. 'Come on, get to your feet and clean up this mess.' He gave her arm a tug, not noticing that he was standing on her dress and Caroline gave a whimper of horror as a seam ripped apart.

Janty bent over her. 'Darling! Whatever happened? Come, let's go upstairs and quickly find you another dress. Cam, find Susan, will you, and get her to clean this up. We won't be long, and as soon as we're down we'll start supper.'

Cam glowered, but didn't argue as his wife and 'niece' left the room.

Only Joseph noticed Angus and Flora giggling together in a corner, obviously highly delighted by the episode. He raised one black eyebrow . . . and wondered.


'When do you intend telling her the truth?'

Janty looked at Joseph's serious expression. 'I don't think it should be before she grows up.'

'Too late.' Joseph shook his head.

'But she will have to keep it a secret, even from her step-brothers and sisters; won't that be too much of a strain for her?'

Joseph hunched his shoulders and sighed. 'I don't know. Would it be any more of a strain than she already has?'

There was a loud knock on the front door.

'That will be the cabby. What a pity you must go so soon, I wish we had more time to discuss this. When are you coming back?'

'Just as soon as I can, I promise. But I cannot say when that will be.'

'We'll talk about it again. I suppose there is no great hurry.'

'I don't know about that. I wouldn't leave it too long.'

Simon bounded down the stairs, a canvas bag on his back.

Luggage was handed to the waiting men and Janty stood on the doorstep with her two brothers.

'Au revoir, little sister.' Simon put his arm round her shoulders. 'Remember what I told you about Ruth and Freddie. I'll expect to see progress by next time I come.'

'A good thing she can't hear you, Simon,' Janty remarked; Ruth had said her farewells earlier, before leaving for the office.

'What's all this, then?' Joseph asked.

'Your little brother has decided Ruth should marry again, and wants me to arrange it.'

'Fine one he is to talk! He hasn't made it to the altar once, yet.'

'Nor have you,' Simon answered back.

'True. But then I was never the type. But you, why, I bet you have a girl in every port. It's high time you settled down to a respectable union.' Joseph spoke severely but couldn't suppress the laughter in his eyes.

210

'I'm working on it, padre, I assure you. Now, Janty, thanks again for a lovely holiday and a super party. It's been marvellous.'

Janty felt a lump rise in her throat. She hated goodbyes at the best of times, but now . . . in time of war. Not that Simon was likely to go to the front line, but Joseph almost certainly would. She kissed them both and stood waving until the cab disappeared from sight. She hadn't felt so dejected by a farewell since leaving Canada.

Less than a month later, on May 8th, 1915, the *Lusitania* was sunk by a German U-boat. Simon McKenzie was not amongst the survivors.


No one could have guessed the war would continue quite so long. The effect on the hotel industry was disastrous, especially for people like Cam who were burdened with overdrafts and debts, and by the end of the practically non-existent summer of 1917 Ruth knew that, to all intents and purposes, Cam was bankrupt.

Of course no one would have believed it, seeing him strutting importantly across the town square to his office; to his friends, acquaintances and creditors he exuded confidence and bonhomie. Few, if any, suspected what Ruth and Janty knew, that all Cam's confidence was acquired from a whisky bottle; only they could guess, when he stood at a gathering, thumb hooked in the armhole of his waistcoat, head thrown back as he pontificated on the ineptitudes of the government and the generals, on the shortsightedness of bankers and business investors, just how low the level of the latest bottle must have dipped. Because only his womenfolk and one or two of his closest cronies ever saw him drunk.

Ruth had felt it only fair to explain the financial situation to Janty, let her understand how precarious their livelihood was; she would have felt very guilty if, when the axe fell, her sister had not been forewarned.


The children were growing up fast. Caroline at fifteen was no longer a child at all. As tall as her mother and aunt, she had learned much, at St Margaret's, about deportment, poise and the social graces. Perhaps because of the inadequacies of her earlier education she did not shine academically, but was enormously popular amongst her group of friends and excelled at tennis and swimming.

At home she nearly broke her mother's heart. Smiling coolly, she adroitly avoided Janty's efforts to close the gulf between them, making it abundantly clear that she considered a girl might only be truly open and relaxed with her mother, if she was lucky enough to have one – never with her aunt. Joseph was still in France. He had returned to Whitehaven only briefly to share his sisters' grief over Simon's death, before embarking for the Continent. So he and Janty had never resumed their discussion of Caroline's problem. Several times, as school holidays approached, Janty vowed that 'this time' Caroline must be told the truth. Over and over she had tried to manoeuvre them both into an opportune situation – and over and over she had been thwarted. Perhaps if she had been more determined, more convinced she was doing the right thing, if Joseph had been there to advise and encourage her. . . .

Ruth was sweet and loving, caring as ever when she wasn't exhausted after working all day at the office, but she could give no advice on the matter, expressed no opinion either way. So Janty's efforts were seldom more than half-hearted, knowing as she did how furious Cam would be with her if he found out that Caroline knew – and the atmosphere between mother and daughter cooled further. Caroline was always polite, friendly, charming to her 'aunt', never more.

Giles Kirkpatrick was already a giant at fifteen. A star at both rugby and cricket, an academic prize-winner and universally popular, he breezed into the house at the beginning of each holiday revitalising all the family. Ruth was so proud of him and glowed as, towering over her despite her own considerable height, he enveloped her in a bear-hug, lifting her off the floor and swinging her feet, endangering furniture and ornaments.

He was kind enough to Angus and Flora, who worshipped him, and especially sweet with Alexandra, now a petite nine years old, and to Ian, aged six. These two he would perch on his shoulders in turn, to race along the beach, or sit them on his chest as he swam out to sea on his back. He played ball games with them, teaching them to catch and throw, brushing off Cam's cutting remarks with a smile. No one, it seemed, could dislodge his good humour.

Angus was twelve. Spectacles made him look studious, which he was, but while on the one hand he hero-worshipped his huge cousin, he resented being so dwarfed, hated being dislodged as senior child in the household . . . senior because of course Caroline didn't count, according to Flora, and he was perfectly willing to agree. It was always safest to agree with Flora: she could make life deucedly uncomfortable if one didn't.

Actually, Flora held a considerable sway over everyone in the house – excepting Giles. The thin-featured ten-year-old could be so sweet, attentive and loving when it suited her, or, when it didn't, could pack so much acidity into her verbal punches that, consciously or subconsciously, everyone tried not to cross her. Even the adults attempted to avoid her unpredictable outbursts, allowing her to manipulate them from time to time. Angus was her favourite person, perhaps because he made most effort to please and agree with her; Cam she fawned over, bending him to her will with coquettish glances, arms twined round his neck and loving gestures he assumed to be genuine – and Caroline she hated. Much of her hold over Angus was directed into united efforts to increase Caroline's misery – as, for example, their success in tripping their 'cousin' and causing her to fall at the party for the uncles, two and a half years ago.

Flora avoided Ruth, rightly sensing her aunt's mistrust. For Ruth had voiced suspicions to Janty on more than one occasion; but Janty, wanting to believe all her children were loving friends, tried not to listen. Though ever-watchful in the protection of her illegitimate daughter, she had no idea of the extent of Flora's jealousy, nor of her power to hurt the older girl.

Despite Flora's loving attentions, it was little Alexandra who was Cam's favourite. There was no question about the sincerity of her devotion to her parents, and only she had the power to charm Cam out of his depressions and make him laugh. She was like a little elf, dainty but well proportioned, light brown curls bobbing and hazel eyes dancing as she bounced on her father's knee, on those evenings he was at home, telling him about her day at school. At nine years old she was top of her class and promised to be the brightest of his brood.

Unlike Ian. At six he was a little old man. Asked a question he would sit and cogitate until long after the questioner had lost interest in the answer. Slow, heavy and ponderous described him best, though no one could doubt that he was totally kind, thoughtful, and outgoing.

It was September, and Giles, Caroline and Angus were preparing to depart to their respective schools. A cloud of disappointment had settled over Janty as she helped Caroline to fold dresses neatly into her trunk. She had had such high hopes for this summer, of making friends with the girl, close enough to allow an approach to 'the dreaded subject'. But her hopes had been downed from the outset. The telephone had been in constant use summoning repeated gatherings of young friends to the beach or to each other's houses. Caroline and Giles were always in demand, and when they came in alone it was always '. . . How sweet of you, Auntie, but will you excuse me if I don't try your fudge right now, I simply must wash my hair before tonight . . .' or '. . . What a lovely idea, Auntie. Yes, I'd love to take a drive with you over to Seaforth for tea some time, but not today,

I'm afraid. I've already promised to go with Giles and Sarah to Elizabeth's for tennis. We simply must organise it for one day next week.'
But for one reason or another it never happened.

She stood up to pin a stray curl back into place, taking a surreptitious glance at her daughter. Caroline looked up, caught the glance, and smiled.

Janty smiled back, warmed and encouraged. 'Dear Caroline, we have so little time alone together and there are so many things we should talk about.' She reached out and touched the girl's hand. 'You are so very, very dear to me.'

Caroline's cool hand turned to squeeze her mother's fingers.

Janty's heart lurched and she hurried on. 'Do you understand that I love you just as much as . . . as my own children? Or more?'

Caroline's hand withdrew. 'Oh, no, Auntie. You mustn't say that. It would be most unfair if it were true. The others would be so hurt if they thought you preferred a mere niece to your own sons and daughters.'

'But Caroline, dear, that's the point I've been wanting to explain to you for so long. You see. . . .' She took a deep breath. 'You see, you are. . . .'

'Caro! Caro! You're wanted on the telephone,' Giles's voice came up the stairs.

'Excuse me a moment, Auntie. I'll soon be back.' The beautiful, elusive girl hurried out of the room.

Janty sank on to the bed, trying not to allow her frustrations to spill over. However short the phone call might be, she knew the moment had passed.

Alexandra was very fond of her Aunt Ruth and from the time that Giles went to Edinburgh Academy the child went out of her way to keep her company, convinced she must feel lonely without her son. Which was true. Ruth enjoyed Alexandra's visits to her room, to her office, and the sweet invitations to go for a walk or take tea together. Throughout the summer term Alexandra's mop of curls would appear round the office door, two or three times a week, and she would creep in to do her homework in a corner, waiting to accompany Ruth home. The town office was on the route between school and home and if Ruth was not there the child would go on to seek her at the Excelsior Hotel. Even during the holidays Alexandra would sometimes walk into town so that they could come back together. However, now that Ian was six, he had left the kindergarten and moved up to the junior school with Alexandra; thus she had the responsibility of accompanying him home each day, breaking her old routine.

'As business is so slack I've decided to keep only the public rooms at the Dolphin and the Grand open for the winter and close up the Excelsior completely,' Cam told Ruth one bleak day late in September. 'If we should be lucky enough to get anyone wanting rooms we can always open up one or two. Otherwise we'll have to rely on some business in the billiards room and bars. I've dismissed all the Excelsior staff and a number from the other two.'

'That's a sudden decision; you hadn't mentioned you were thinking of it. But it's just as well. As it is I think some of the creditors are being very generous and patient. One only wonders how much longer they'll wait.'

Cam was silent.

'I seem to be up to date with everything today; I came in early, you remember. So would you mind if I leave now? I've some urgent shopping to do.'

'Er . . . oh . . . no, that's all right, you go ahead.' His mind was obviously engaged elsewhere.

So she pinned on her hat and went out through the little shop to cross the town square, towards the department store on the other side. Arthur Cranston's wife, Alice, was sitting looking through fashion magazines. 'I'm so glad you're here!' Ruth exclaimed. 'I need your advice about the material for my new dress.'

'I'll only give it if you'll sit here with me a minute and help me choose the style for a winter outfit.'

An hour later Ruth climbed into a cab with her friend, having accepted an invitation to tea, and it was late and dark before she arrived home.

'There you are, I wondered where on earth you were.' Janthina met her in the hallway. 'But where is Alexandra?'

'Alexandra? I haven't see her,' Ruth frowned.

'Oh!' Janthina put her hand over her mouth. 'But I was sure she must be with you.'

'She doesn't come to call for me any more, now that she has to bring Ian home.'

'But Ian is in bed with a cold. He didn't go to school today, and as she was free, I assumed . . .'

'Then where on earth is she?' Ruth exclaimed in consternation.

'She must be with Cam.' Her sister spoke more in hope than conviction.

'I doubt it.' Flora had come out of the drawing room to investigate. 'Papa is in the bath.'

'Bath? I didn't know he'd come in. I didn't see him.'

'I saw him. He was all dirty, and he went straight upstairs and then I heard the water running.' The child looked pleased with herself.

'And you haven't seen your sister?' Ruth asked.

'No.'

'Are there any school friends she might be with?' Janty wondered aloud.

At that moment the telephone bell jangled on the wall beside them.

'Thank heavens! That'll be a parent to say where she is.' Janty reached for the earpiece. 'Hello? Yes, speaking.' She frowned. 'Oh, heavens, no! My husband's in the bath, but I'll tell him to get there immediately. Yes, yes. Goodbye.'

'What is it?' Ruth demanded.

'The Excelsior! That was the police to say it's on fire.'

'Fire! Oh, my God!'

'Can we go and watch?' Flora was jumping up and down with excitement.

Janty ignored her to dash upstairs. 'Cam, Cam, get dressed quickly. The Excelsior's on fire.'

'Wha-at!' His voice roared through the bathroom door. 'How do you know?'

'The police just called. They want the keys for the firemen.'

'Tell them I'm coming. I'll be there in five minutes.'

Downstairs, Ruth stood holding Janty's hat and coat. 'You go with him. Better to be there seeing what's happening than sitting at home, waiting. I'll stay here and wait for Alexandra. I expect she'll soon be here.'

'Can I come with you, Mama?' Flora had already put on her outdoor things.

'No, sweetheart, you stay and keep Auntie Ruth company.'

'No! I want to see the fire.'

Janty turned to her. 'Flora! I said no! Go and take those things off.'

Cam ran down the stairs buttoning his jacket.

'Papa! Can I come with you to see the fire, please?' Flora grabbed his hand and looked up at him with adoring, pleading eyes.

He smiled down. 'Of course, my sweet, why not? Come on, we must hurry,' and he opened the front door, ushering her out before him.

'But Cam, I have already told her. . . .'

'You coming too? Good, I may need you. It'll be quicker on foot than waiting for a cab. Come on.'

Janty pursed her lips and followed.

\*    \*    \*

216

A large crowd had gathered to watch the gigantic flames leaping into a starless sky.

'It all seems to be at the back of the hotel,' Janty commented.

'Fires normally start in a kitchen, don't they?' said a woman beside her. 'But at the rate it's burning, it's soon going to be through to the front.'

'Surely not if the firemen hurry.' She could see them laboriously tugging their hoses from the reels.

'Huh! What a hope. With all our able-bodied men in the trenches there's only old men and cripples left to man the engines.'

Suddenly, one of the dark windows overlooking the promenade smashed, glass falling three storeys to shatter on the paving stones.

'Look, Mama, it's Alexandra!' Flora was tugging at her coat.

Janty peered . . . and screamed. 'Alexandra-a-a!'

The little girl was waving frantically. 'Papa! Mama! I can't open the door,' she cried.

Cam was with the firemen nearer the building. He looked up as someone pointed, and staggered. 'Alexandra!' he shouted. 'I'm coming, my love. I'm coming.' He ran towards the front entrance.

At that moment there was a deep, rumbling explosion from inside and an ominous glow appeared behind some of the windows.

Janty had abandoned Flora, dashing forward to Cam's side as he opened one of the big double doors . . . and was nearly knocked off her feet by the rush of hot air escaping.

'You can't go in there!' one of the firemen shouted. 'You'll be a cinder in ten seconds.'

Cam ignored him and ran inside.

Janty tried to follow but someone held her back, as a fireman plunged after Cam . . . and reappeared a few moments later supporting the choking man, brushing out the flames on his jacket.

Tears streamed down James Cameron's face. He turned to rush back in again . . . and stopped, his features contorted at the sight of a solid wall of flame across the stairway.

Janty rushed back into the crowd to call up at the trapped child . . . but Alexandra had disappeared, and smoke billowed from the broken window.

'DEATH BY misadventure,' was the coroner's verdict, and he went on to offer his sympathy to the parents, a prayer of thanks that the hotel was closed, thus preventing greater loss of life, and a homily on the insecurity of empty buildings.

Ruth, normally so cool and controlled, broke down three times while giving evidence of Alexandra's habit of coming to visit her after school, either in the town office or at the hotel. 'When she found I wasn't in the hotel reception office she must have gone upstairs to the housekeeper's room. She knew I checked the books up there regularly,' she murmured through her veil, shoulders heaving.

In the charred remains of that room firemen had eventually found the child's body.

'If only . . .' Ruth had said it over and over, especially to herself. 'If only I hadn't left the office so early that day. If only I had known Ian wasn't at school. I would have known if only I hadn't left home so early that morning.'

How the little girl had managed to get inside the empty hotel remained a mystery. She usually entered through a side door approach in the back yard to save walking all the way round to enter from the promenade, but this area of the building had been totally destroyed, making it impossible to tell if it had been left unlocked.

All the children were terribly distressed, wandering the house red-eyed and restless, picking up and discarding one distraction after another. Caroline, Giles and Angus were luckier than the other two, being able to return to their respective schools, away from home and all its painful reminders. Left behind, Flora and Ian missed the sister who had bridged the gap between their ages. Though nearer Flora in years, Alexandra had been Ian's constant playmate, preferring his sweet gentleness to Flora's sharp tongue. Now he was 'little boy lost' and Janty worried for him, through her own grief, when she repeatedly found him sitting alone in the window seat the two had so often shared, gazing expressionless, unseeing, at the damp days beyond.

Janty herself could still hardly believe it had happened. If the child had been ill, and they had watched her declining on her eventual deathbed, she thought she might have been prepared, better able to accept. For Ian and Flora's sake she tried to hide her misery, but even weeks later, just when she thought she had at last brought her emotions under control, some little incident or the distant soprano piping of Ian's voice, so like Alexandra's, would trigger a subconscious reaction, cause her to watch the door almost expecting the beloved brown curls and smiling eyes to appear . . . as though the whole tragedy had only been a nightmare. And within seconds reality would bring a resurgence of misery – anger at Fate and God.

James Cameron tried, daily, to blot out memory with alcohol; of them all, his was the worst distress. He would disappear for long hours at a time, no one knew where, and if he reappeared for a meal, it was only to toy with the food on his plate until, with a sigh, he would push back his chair and stumble out of the room, shaking his head. Janty and Ruth seldom saw him in the evenings as he found his own fireside too painful; and when he eventually arrived home, as often as not the cabby would have to assist him up the steps and ring the doorbell. Then Janty would go down in her dressing gown to thank and pay the cabby and help her husband to bed; but sometimes it was impossible to get him up the stairs and she had to leave him in an armchair with a rug wrapped round him and the fireguard securely in place, and all the time she was tending him he fought and cursed her. He never seemed to have a hangover, only appalling fits of renewed depression each morning, necessitating an early start on the next bottle, restarting the miserable cycle of inebriation.

Friends were kind. Gifts of flowers, out-of-season fruit, notes of love and sympathy were delivered to the house, and Reverend Cooney frequently dropped in, sensible enough to restrain himself from homilies like 'the Lord giveth and the Lord taketh away' knowing that otherwise he was likely to be refused admittance next time he rang the bell.

Janty noticed that Freddie Gordon established the habit of escorting Ruth from the office at least once a week – and was pleased. She encouraged Ruth to invite him in and enjoyed his easy, natural conversation. But he never stayed long, perhaps fearing to stretch the hospitality of the sad household.

As expected, Christmas that year was a gloomy affair. Assembled round the fire or the festive table, no one could free their minds from the picture of a lonely little stone in the cemetery on the rainswept hillside behind St Mary's.

Nor were their emotions helped by the news of poor Arthur Cranston's death in France. He was only one of so many they knew, and as the age limits of the enlisted stretched to older men and younger boys, Ruth feared that if the war lasted much longer, Giles too would have to go.

This was only one of her many worries. She had sympathised with Cam's distraught inattention to business after the tragedy, but when, months later, the initial pain eased for Janty and herself and the children, and the household began to return to normal, Cam's continued absence from the office for long periods made her job increasingly difficult.

The fire insurance company had paid up handsomely, more than enough to solve all the financial problems with which she had been juggling for so long; all it needed was Cam's signature on the cheques to pay off all the creditors, leaving ample balance as a future cash flow. She realised that although the money was intended primarily for rebuilding the Excelsior, it would be pointless to do so at a time when there seemed no hope of an improvement in the hotel industry for the foreseeable future, and in fact, but for the injection of that money, she couldn't see how Cam's empire could survive. She had never had access to all his books and papers – there were stacks of them in a safe in his office, but the keys never left the chain attached to his pocket. He had deliberately avoided taking her fully into his confidence, limiting her authority to make any but the most trifling decisions.

So she waited, the insurance cheque not even banked yet, as he refused to discuss into which account it should be paid.

Papa died early in the New Year. The news came as no surprise, and there was no question of either sister going to the funeral. His estate was divided equally between his three surviving children – an amount that staggered his daughters.

'I have no intention of allowing Cam to know of this money, any more than he knows of Grandfather's bequest,' Janty told her sister. 'There would be far too much risk of his trying to badger it out of me. He won't notice a few new clothes for myself and the children, from time to time, nor if the kitchen is redecorated; he never goes in there.'

'Good for you.' Ruth nodded approvingly. 'I do like to see your occasional flashes of independence. You've always put up with far too much nonsense from the men in your life.'

Janty looked at her and gave a wry smile. 'Weak-minded is the term you're looking for.'

'No, just too trusting.'

'Didn't you trust Ben?'

Ruth's head came up with a jerk. 'Of course. Absolutely. But that was different, we loved each other. Lived for each other.'

Janty sighed. 'Yes, I know. You were very lucky.'

'Was I?' For a moment Ruth's eyes reflected the old sadness. 'You think, "better to have loved and lost. . . ." '

'I don't know. Would I be any happier now if I had done just that? I did think I was in love, once, but my god had feet of clay.'

They heard the front door slam and Cam's irregular footsteps in the hall. They looked at each other and Janty closed her eyes for a moment – before heading for the kitchen to get supper. Susan had left over a year ago to work in a munitions factory, so once again she was on her own doing the cooking and housework.


Early in February John Chartwell decided that Cam had had long enough to settle his debts and would have to be told so in no uncertain terms. He had been to Cam's office with that intention before, and found himself out on the pavement an hour later with his stomach full of whisky and a fat cigar clenched in his teeth – and still no settlement. This time was going to be different.

Wisely, he arrived early and by ten thirty he was being shown into Cam's office by the tall, dark, sister-in-law.

'No thanks, old chap, I won't sit down. I don't mean to stay longer than is necessary.'

'You'll have a drink!' Cam picked up a decanter.

The market gardener could see a glass of whisky on the desk. 'No thanks. Far too early to start drinking. A man can't do business with his brain fogged up.'

Cam looked at him coldly, topped up his own glass and replaced the stopper before returning the decanter to its tray. 'Well, John old chap, what can I do for you?' As though he didn't know.

'Pay me.'

'Oh, don't worry, you'll get your money.'

'I've heard that one before. I've been very patient, Cam, very patient indeed. I know the war has hit you hard, same as it has for a lot of folks, but you've had a great big windfall. Very lucky for you, the Excelsior burning down like that, very convenient indeed, what with it being so well insured. Oh, yes, you can't keep anything secret in a small town like ours.' He smiled confidently, watching Cam come out from behind his desk towards him. 'So now I've come to collect before you drink the lot away. . . .'

He saw the blow coming too late, a look of amazement spreading over his face as the bunched knuckles slammed into his mouth. He reeled backwards, his foot striking a chair, and crashed against the open door before hitting the floor.

Ruth had heard everything. She strode in, ignoring Chartwell, grabbed the decanter and smashed it into the grate. 'Damn you, James Cameron, for a drunken fool!'

'I'll have you in court for this, Cameron,' Chartwell mumbled through broken teeth as he pulled himself up.

'And damn you, John Chartwell, for a sober one,' Ruth went on. 'Damn you for coming here to dun a man who's still beside himself with grief. Get out of here. I'll see you get your cheque, but I warn you, if you start getting the police involved you'll get neither cheque nor sympathy, not when I testify to the foul suggestions you've just made. Now go on, get out. Out.' She picked up his hat and walking stick and shoved them at him, took his elbow and guided him forcefully through the outer office and empty shop, leaving him on the pavement.

The market gardener stood stock still, mouth hanging open, eyes dazed. Slowly he put his hat on his head, back to front but he didn't notice, pulled a handkerchief from his pocket to mop blood from his split and swelling lips, and walked off along the pavement in the wrong direction.

When it arrived, the cheque had to wait to be banked until his dentist had made necessary repairs and his face regained its normal shape. He didn't want any embarrassing questions asked.


Ruth was shocked by her own daring . . . but Cam was amazed. Shaken into temporary sobriety by the whole incident, he hovered between gratitude for her intervention and annoyance at her effrontery.

The most important result as far as Ruth was concerned was that Cam agreed to bank the insurance money, talk, work, and instruct her each morning, take over the responsibilities, and, most important, revitalise what business there was. He absolutely agreed that the Excelsior should not be rebuilt at this stage, and instead signed cheques for all the outstanding debts so that, at last, Ruth's ledgers were straight.

But Cam had changed. For a while his daytime drinking was controlled, he started to laugh again and entertain in his office – men who, like himself, were exempted from army service by old war wounds or because their jobs were 'essential to the war effort'. They were not people Ruth liked so much as the pre-war friends; they were not as well mannered or educated, not the upright citizens Cam had previously sought to emulate. With these men Cam was in a better position to pontificate, show off as a leader of business and society – and he seldom missed an opportunity.

As a holiday season, the summer of 1918 was non-existent, certainly as far as the hotel trade in Whitehaven was concerned. Not that the hotels would have operated anyway – there were no staff. The men were in the front line and the women were in the factories. Nor were the shops doing much better, now that food was rationed, but together with the limited meals served in the hotel dining rooms, cooked and served by the few elderly women Cam had recruited locally, and trade during the restricted wartime licensing hours in the hotel bars, business kept going – just. Certainly Cameron and Company were much luckier than some, though Ruth wondered how much longer they could survive as yet another winter approached.

Then suddenly it was all over.

They were in the town centre, singing, dancing, laughing, everyone kissing everyone, including total strangers. The children were allowed home from boarding schools to join their parents in celebrations. Janty and Cam hugged each other – and so did Freddie and Ruth.

No more war. It had been the war to end all wars.


It was a time for new beginnings.

After much soul-searching, Ruth told Janty and Cam that she had accepted Freddie's proposal of marriage, not unexpected by her sister, the only surprise being that as Freddie had been offered an excellent business opportunity in Brighton they would be unable to live in Whitehaven, and Freddie had already sold his house. Cam was to lose his now very competent secretary and Janty her sister's treasured companionship.

The wedding, held at Easter 1919, in St Mary's, Whitehaven, was a small family occasion. Elinor and Roderick brought the aging Aunt Laura down from Scotland and only a few close friends were invited. Reverend Cooney conducted the ceremony, Giles gave his mother away, Caroline and Flora were bridal attendants, and Cam remained moderately sober while carrying out his duties as best man.

Where Ruth had been described as beautiful at her first wedding, this time she was magnificent. Her long, slender figure was ideally suited to current fashion, and her pale lilac gown, its full skirt reaching barely to her ankles, made her skin appear transparent and her eyes glow. Freddie looked even more radiantly happy than his bride, and at their reception in a private room at the Grand his speech was full of joy and humour.

Janty was happy for her sister, but sad for herself: she was going to miss Ruth terribly, and it was hard to hold back the tears as they drove away.


As soon as Ruth announced that she was leaving, Janty volunteered to replace her at the office. 'Ian is at school all day and now that Susan has come back she can keep an eye on him till I get home in the evenings. What do you think?' she asked Cam.

'Fine. It'll save another salary,' had been his only reaction, and though she didn't relish the thought of too much more of his companionship, judging by Ruth's comments he spent very little time in the office anyway.

So Ruth had undertaken to show her the books and the system she had developed, and explain all she could in the time.

Janty was horrified at first, doubting she could ever cope, but she had always enjoyed maths and figure work and soon the mists cleared.

Demobilisation and the easing of restrictions soon revitalised business; staff returned to the hotels and even holiday visitors filtered back to the seaside. Wholesale orders rolled in, the grocery shops were re-stocking fast and even the little boutique in front of the office was re-opened, while upstairs the tea and coffee shop was serving a steady stream of customers.

Janthina imagined that Cam would be delighted. She remembered his enthusiasm in the days when they still lived above the first grocery shop, and watched and waited for a similar reaction. But his heavy drinking continued. Publicly he was the life and soul of every party gathering: 'dear old Cam' was invited to every reunion and coming-home party, with his lady of course, and somehow it always happened that they were the last to leave. But in private he was morose, aggressive, and inattentive to business.

'Do you have any plans for rebuilding the Excelsior?' she asked him one day.

'No.'

She waited for him to continue, but he remained silent, so she said, 'We do own the site still, don't we?'

'Yes.'

'Cam! Why don't you talk to me? We are supposed to be working together yet you seldom utter a word.' It really was exasperating.

'Right. What do you want to talk about?'

'Business, family, our home, anything – everything.'

'What about them? Something wrong?'

'No, of course not. All I'm meaning is that there seems to be so little communication between us.'

'I guessed you were working up to some criticism or other. You never stop, do you?'

She frowned. 'Stop what?'

'Criticising.'

'Me! Criticise you? That's a laugh. Why, apparently I have done nothing right since I've been here. "Why can't you write more neatly – like Ruth?" "Ruth could tot up figures at twice that speed." "No, not those envelopes for accounts, don't you know anything?" ' she mimicked. 'But I'd be very interested to hear when I've criticised you.'

'You're always criticising my drinking, for a start.'

'Only when I have to put you to bed, or you wet it. That's justified, isn't it?'

'Every man gets tight and wets the bed from time to time.'

'Rubbish!'

He got up and walked to the door. 'Anything you say, dear,' he smirked, and walked out.

He was very late that night. She didn't get out of bed to go down and open the door for him, just let him fumble about with his key. He never made it up the stairs and next morning she found his armchair saturated.

As the months went by and the summer passed she noticed that a number of his older friends no longer called in at the office, and some afternoons Cam would lead in a bunch of new cronies, all artificially jovial, to ply them with drink and lectures on politics and business. She could see that none were interested in his monologues, and who could blame them, but they stayed – as long as the drinks kept coming.


During the spring of 1920, Janty became seriously worried. The phone rang incessantly with complaints of undelivered orders – which had been given directly to Cam; unpaid bills – he had never had her name put on the mandate, supposedly paying all the accounts himself. No one had come yet to unblock the lavatories by the bar at the Dolphin – Mr Cameron had promised to send a plumber. Why hadn't the new chef at the Grand been given the Rotary Dinner order for tonight? Cam was a member and had taken the details at their last meeting.

Cam was usually out in his car. He had bought a Ford Trojan of which he was enormously proud, plus all the gear to go with it. Tweed jacket and breeches, soft cap with a button on top and leather gloves – he had to look the part – and he would drive off into Brighton on 'business' from which he returned to the house swaying, very tight. Janty could never understand how he drove all that way in that condition without killing at least himself.

'Are you suggesting I'm drunk?' he snarled at her one evening when she remonstrated with him.

'No, just telling you. You are going to kill someone one of these days if you carry on like this.'

'Shut up!' he shouted, then sagged into a chair.

She looked down at him in part disgust, part pity. He was a pathetic, pitiable sight. His weight had suddenly increased dramatically, straining at the few waistcoat buttons he could still do up, while a fat bulge of long johns spilled over the top of his trousers where his shirt had pulled open. Watery red eyes peered at her from the bloated purple face; his beard was straggled and his thin hair stood up from his scalp in sweaty points.

There was no doubt in her mind that he was a sick man. But what could she do? What could anyone do to help him? Cam, the dynamic businessman, so proud of the empire he had built, so respected, so popular throughout Whitehaven. Oh, Cam! What has happened to you?

Feeling almost guilty of disloyalty, she discussed the problem with Freddie and Ruth.

'Can't you get him to see the doctor?' her brother-in-law suggested. 'Surely he would listen to him.'

'I've suggested it several times; I've even spoken to the doctor myself. But he says that unless Cam is willing to see him, he can do nothing.'

'What about Reverend Cooney?'

Janty caught Ruth's eye and they both grinned. 'That'll be the day,' Ruth said. 'And I doubt poor old Cooney would survive the meeting.'

'I dread what is happening to the business. Money seems to be disappearing like water but I cannot imagine what on. He never lets me see a balance sheet.'

'It looks as though we can only wait for him to pull himself together, I'm afraid,' Freddie said.

'Or kill himself,' Janty added.


Neither happened before Cam's drinking came to an abrupt halt.

Janty was summoned by phone to the Dolphin one evening: the barman said Cam was ill. She arrived to find him laid out on a couch in the bar, an over-dressed, buxom woman with dyed hair holding his head possessively and a strange doctor in attendance.

'I'm Mrs Cameron,' she introduced herself.

The woman flushed and retreated while the doctor held out his hand. 'Moultrie's the name. I've sent for an ambulance to take him to hospital. Mrs Cameron, I have to tell you that I believe your husband is seriously ill.'


Dr Moultrie had been right. Cam lay in a coma for over a week, at the end of which he was unable to focus or to speak. His liver and kidneys were damaged, amongst other organs, leaving his skin bright orange, and he ran an intermittent fever.

The diagnosis was indefinite and the prognosis poor.

'But how long is he likely to remain in this state?' Janthina asked anxiously. 'The business. . . .'

'. . . Will have to do without him for a long time, Mrs Cameron,' one of the doctors present told her. 'And I can assure you that he will have nothing of value to offer the business for some months, at least.'

What was going to happen in the meantime, she wondered? She only knew half the operating of it, if that, and there were people telephoning all the time, asking for instructions, or payment of outstanding accounts. There were urgent matters to be dealt with.

She hurried to the office. Perhaps she could stall, explain to people that Cam was seriously ill. They would surely sympathise and give her time.

His desk was a mess, letters, invoices, accounts, final demands and meeting agendas all muddled together and circled with bottle stains. When she had them neatly sorted and stacked she opened the drawers and faced similar confusion. And in the top right hand drawer a photograph of Alexandra lay on top of the heap, dog-eared and obviously much handled. Poor Cam, she thought, his whole life went wrong from the moment the child died.

And what of her own life? When had anything gone right? She was thirty-five years old and what had she achieved? What joy had she to look back on? Well, there were the children, of course, but anyone could produce a family – in fact, the difficulty for some of us is not to, she thought bitterly. There was poor Caroline, never able to claim a parent, growing up feeling like an outsider, becoming more and more remote each year. She would be leaving school in July, three months before her eighteenth birthday. How and when can I ever tell her? If only Joseph had stayed in England instead of returning to Canada to complete his theological studies, interrupted by the war, he would have been a tower of strength.

Angus was no happier. Cam insisted that he should come into the business when he left school, but the boy wanted desperately to go on to university and read law. He was so keen, worked so hard, had pleaded for his father's permission – but so far Cam had flatly refused to consider it. Well, the boy was only fifteen: there was still time.

Flora was a strange girl in a rather disturbing way. She tried to appear open and friendly, yet one could catch an oddly cold expression on her face in unguarded moments. She was a secretive creature.

Ian was happy enough. He was only nine, still at school in White-haven, and always had a retinue of friends in attendance. He was quite loving and affectionate in an offhand way, but seldom gave the impression of needing her.

Ruth was miles away in Brighton, and now Cam. . . .

What a mess her life had been. She had always tried to please the people around her, yet only managed to pile one dreadful mistake on to another. Grandmama had died without ever forgiving her; Anthony . . . ? She sighed. Her dearest Alexandra had died horribly, and now Cam, bold, aggressive, businesslike Cam, unloving and un-loved except for the daughter he had lost, now lying in that awful hospital bed fighting for his life – a life which had dissipated into drunkenness, the business of which he had been so proud in chaos.

Oh, she was sorry for him, sorry for them all, but most of all she was sorry for herself.

Dear God, what have I done to deserve this? Have I been so very bad?

Bitter salt trickled into her mouth.


She took the safe key out of her handbag next morning and turned the lock. Miraculously, she had slept reasonably well, waking refreshed and determined to get the business sorted out and decide what she could do without assistance.

The heavy door swung open. Another jumbled mess. There was little point in bending double to sort it where it was; better to pile everything on the desk and work on it there. Papers on clips, bundled with string or rubber bands, shoved into big manila envelopes; card-board files, a box file, its tape wound round and round its cardboard button, deeds tied up with narrow green ribbons, ledgers, all came out to be heaped on the desk – and underneath it all was her little

228

leather jewel case. Cam had offered to keep it here when they decided to get a maid, years ago, and it had lain here ever since, though Susan had proved totally trustworthy. Not that there was anything of great value in it. It wasn't locked and she clicked open the spring – to allow her memory to drift back for a moment. Cam's cufflinks and dress studs; a pair of pendant amethyst earrings on fine silver chains, with their matching pendant necklet – a gift from Aunt Laura; a silver filigree brooch and an antique gold one set with a large oval chalcedony were brought out of concealment and laid on the desk. There were several other items, and underneath them the velvet pad lay lop-sided because of something bulky below . . . it was the necklet of janthina shells given her by Uncle William thirty-five years ago. She smiled as she touched the delicate purple spirals. They had lain there forgotten since long before going into Cam's safe. There was a small mirror in the outer office, installed ages ago by Ruth, and she stood in front of it to clasp the shells round her throat.

Janthina: sea shells shaped like snails. Slow, always late, Papa had said. She found herself thinking of Bear Foot and remembered showing them to him in the farmyard; remembered him explaining the clever-ness of the little sea creature, how it developed its shell from that tiny pin-point in the middle, changing its shape to suit its environment so that it might survive the great ocean waves. He had told her that she, too, must adapt. She watched her fingers in the mirror as they traced the spirals; a good theory, but hardly correct, for hadn't she tried to be adaptable? Hadn't she been willing to change, to try to please? She had tried to be all that Papa had demanded – when she was at home – but that hadn't been enough. To prove her love for Anthony she had set aside all preconceived reserve – and been discarded like an old coat. Hadn't she been adaptable to Grandpapa's wishes, abandoning the tranquillity of the Dordogne to marry James Cameron? Where had it all got her? Had it made her strong, and given her a happy life, as Bear Foot had said it would?

She pursed her lips and turned back to the desk, she was wasting time. Scooping the jewellery back into the case she snapped the lid closed and picked up the first bundle of papers.

An hour later the worst was tidied into neat piles and she was able to open the first of the books, one about the size of a large cashbook. She studied it for some time, trying to fathom its purpose, until a small number of copy receipts fell out of the back. They were signed, 'pp the Management, Grand Hotel.' They were rent receipts, the figures corresponding with entries in the book. Residents' names were listed with the amount of their monthly rents, a tick appearing under each consecutive twenty-fifth day of a month. She turned the pages. Against one of the names was a note in Cam's writing, 'Notice received – 25.11.13.', and against another, and another, all within a month of the purchase of the hotel. The rents were totalled, and then deductions made for various amounts to 'Harper', 'Kennels', 'Harper and Brown'. She shrugged, and set the book aside, replacing it with a ledger.

Inside the stiff, marbled cover was written, 'Cameron & Co., Grocers,' and underneath, 'Cameron Wholesale Ltd.,' and below that, 'Cameron Wine and Spirits', 'Cameron Fancy Goods', 'Cameron Tea & Coffee Shoppe', 'The Dolphin Hotel', 'The Excelsior Hotel', and finally, 'The Grand Hotel'.

By comparing the figures entered on its pages with the ledgers for each individual business, she ascertained that this book contained only quarterly totals, giving an overall picture of general progress – or otherwise – through the years. A very clear picture! One did not have to be an experienced book-keeper to see how well Cam had done in the early years – nor what a delicate situation had been created by the purchase of the Grand, which might have been very successful but for the evident disastrous effect of the war. These were dreadful figures, all written in red in Cam's writing; and, worst of all, the awful total of debts in September, 1917. It was the final entry – apart from a note in pencil underneath, which was very faint so she held it to the light: 'Insurance on Excelsior. . . .' The figure alongside showed only a few hundreds more than the red ones above – and there was a question mark after it. Strange that there were no further entries in the book, she thought, and looked back again at the last date: 'September 25th, 1917' – only two days before Alexandra died. Two days before that tragic fire. . . .

Goosepimples rose on her arms and legs, and she shivered. The fire. The insurance! Oh, no, surely not! Her heart pounded and she gasped for breath. Cam! You didn't do it! You didn't set fire to the hotel deliberately? And kill our little girl?

She remembered Ruth coming home that night without Alexandra, and Flora saying that Papa had come in dirty and gone straight upstairs to bathe. That poor, dear, terrified little face at the window of the blazing building . . . and Cam's maniacal attempts to save her.

They had all been stricken with grief, but Cam . . . his had been more than that. Guilt? She was shaking violently, choking on the lump in her throat, tears streaming down her face. No! Oh, God, no! Please tell me it isn't true, she whispered aloud.

But Janthina knew her plea was in vain. She lay her head on the desk and sobbed, knowing that she had at last discovered the truth.


She stood on the cliffs beyond the point, overlooking the sea. Wind whipped her skirts around her ankles and drove icy shafts through her clothes, through her skin and into her bones. She had known it would be cold up here but could think of nowhere else to go. She could not have remained in the office another minute and to go home would have meant facing Susan. She couldn't face anyone right now; all she wanted was to walk, run, get away from . . . from the knowledge of how and why Alexandra had died. Away from the horror, anger, bitterness and more anger; from the hatred and fury at the monster who had fathered four of her children, who had lit the funeral pyre under their beautiful, lively, loving and adored daughter. Just as soon as she could stop weeping, could get herself under control, she would go back to the house and telephone the police. He would pay, would James Cameron, for the arson and murder he had committed.

The sky was overcast, staining the sea a bleak grey. She watched as far-out waves formed a succession of menacing humps, growing, building higher and higher, until they hurled themselves in passionate fury on the rocks below. Spray, even flecks of foam, swirled up on the wind to moisten her face and she closed her eyes, momentarily, inviting the stinging salt to mingle with her tears – to cleanse away the turmoil in her mind.

She drank in great gulps of air, heard the gulls, and lifted her swollen lids to watch their effortless ballet on the invisible streams of air. A sense of timelessness enveloped her, an awareness that the sea, the sky, the cliffs, had been, and would be forever, natural phenomena of eternity. So where did she, Janthina the Shell, fit into the pattern of things? She touched the necklet, still clasped round her neck. She hadn't really adapted at all, hadn't grown strong. She was only a piece of flotsam, battered by the storms and finally flung up on the beach . . . with her murderous husband. She shuddered again. How could he have stooped so low? No wonder he kept that ledger locked away in his safe.

Thinking back to the hidden heap of books and papers, she suddenly remembered the little 'rent' book from the Grand Hotel, and the way the residents had so abruptly terminated their leases after Cam became owner. She recalled Ruth saying at the time that the place was worthless as an hotel, the long leases of those residents making it non-viable. Yet *they* left, *they* gave notice. And what were those odd

231

payments about, to 'Harper', 'Harper and Brown', and 'Kennels'? Kennels? Dogs? Dogs! Might Cam have used dogs, and Harper and Brown, whoever they were, to worry those elderly folk? To frighten them into leaving voluntarily? The more she thought about it the more possible it seemed . . . yet she had no proof. But she could make enquiries. For what reason? What would she do if she had proof? Report it as yet another crime when she went to the police? He must be punished for all his crimes. . . .

Turning away from the sea she looked down at Whitehaven, at the half circle of sand crowning the bay being vigorously washed by breakers, and the sea wall which protected the promenade from high tides and winter storms. There was the Grand, Cam's ultimate and proudest acquisition, and, a few hundred yards nearer her, wooden boards which masked the blackened ruins of the Excelsior from passers-by – the site of Cam's desperate, criminal effort to recoup enough money to pay off the debts incurred by war. The site he could not bear to think about, source of his guilt, shame, dejection and misery. Misery which had driven him to virtually suicidal drinking for the past three years.

Further up the valley behind the town was the Cottage Hospital, where he now lay, dangerously ill, a pathetic, bloated wreck of a man . . . and now she understood why: because of the horror and guilt at having caused the terrible death of the one person in the whole world he had most loved. How he must have suffered. How many times must he have relived those horrifying minutes when, desperate to reach his darling child, he had tried to force his way through the flames? Would he ever cease to hear Alexandra's voice screaming, 'Papa! I can't open the door!'

Could society inflict any greater punishment?

Anger dissolved into pity. Almost she could have wept for him – almost, but not quite.

The wind had dried the tears on her face. She took a deep breath and squared her shoulders. No, she would not go to the police; she would never reveal to a living soul, save Cam himself, the ghastly secret she had discovered. Nor would she ever forgive him.

Gravel and stones crunched under her feet as she strode down the path back to the town.


A week later, following consultations with Cam's doctors and bank manager, Janthina realised that someone would have to take over control of the business, and decided that person should be herself.

The bank manager had explained that she must obtain power of attorney, as all the companies were in Cam's name only, and the first thing she should do was to contact her husband's lawyers for their help and advice.

From the time of purchasing their first property in Whitehaven, Cam had insisted on using a firm of London solicitors, paranoically convinced that to consult a local firm would be to broadcast all his affairs amongst his friends and rivals.

Janthina found letters on headed notepaper from 'Williamson, Williamson and Finey', and telephoned to explain her problem to one of the Williamsons.

'I am so sorry to hear of your husband's illness, Mrs Cameron. Please accept my sincere wishes for his early recovery,' the elderly voice droned. 'Now, it seems to me that you are going to need some business as well as legal advice, and we have here the very person you need, an excellent man who has been with our firm for several years.'

Was she going to be fobbed off with an assistant, just because she was a mere woman? 'Oh!' she said, in exaggerated surprise. 'I had hoped you would be able to come down yourself, Mr Williamson.'

'I would be delighted to, Mrs Cameron, but I must confess that whilst I am more than confident of my ability in legal matters, I have absolutely no training whatever in commerce. Whereas. . . .'

'I see.' It did seem to make sense; she could only hope that the assistant would be reasonably competent. 'Very well, I'll expect your colleague to come instead.'


The office looked quite different after her hard work of the past few days. The windows behind her were now clean and hung with fresh curtains. The drinks cabinet had been scrubbed out, polished, and re-stocked with glasses and decanters as well as beverages both alcoholic and soft. The old rug between desk and door had been committed to the refuse cart and replaced. The grate had responded well to a good cleaning and re-blacking, and a coal fire warmed the room in place of the old gas one. She had even bought a potted plant for the top of the filing cabinet.

There was not one book or paper on the brightly polished desk, the drawers were re-stocked with notepaper, pens and pencils, and the blotting pad on which her hands now rested was spotless.

Janthina flicked open her little gold fob-watch to check the time – two minutes to three. She glanced around the room, satisfied that Mr

233

Williamson's colleague would not suspect the state it had been in while Cam was around forbidding her to clean it.

The bell on the shop door tinkled and a moment later the visitor was shown in by the shop assistant, who immediately retired, closing the door behind him.

He was not what she had been expecting. Far from being small, thin and bespectacled, the man in front of her was tall, strikingly handsome, with dark, slightly wavy hair, combed back from his forehead, dark grey eyes, a long straight nose and powerful chin.

She stood up and held out her hand. 'Good afternoon. You must be the gentleman from Williamson, Williamson and Finey. Welcome to Whitehaven. I'm Janthina Cameron.'

She saw the slight frown form between his brows and watched as his eyes widened into an incredulous stare and his formal smile broadened to a grin. She raised an eyebrow. 'Is something wrong, Mr . . .?'

His fingers tightened on her hand, and he shook his head slowly and said, 'Janthina! Janthina Cameron, née McKenzie, I presume?'

She nodded.

'So we meet again at last. I'm Roland Burrows. Remember me?'

# PART FIVE

## *JANTHINA*

### 1920 –

'The secret sympathy,
The silver link, the silken tie,
Which heart to heart and mind to mind,
In body and soul can bind.'

'The Lay of the Last Minstrel', Sir Walter Scott

# 1

'ROLAND?' JANTHINA drew her hand away to grasp the chairback for support – then wished she had not. 'It's beyond belief! Too much of a coincidence, after all these years.' She sat heavily on the corner of the desk, gazing at him. He had changed, of course – the threads of grey in his hair, mature lines at the corners of his mouth. . . . She realised she was staring, rudely. 'Forgive me. . . .'

'Janthina,' he whispered softly, then straightened, adjusting a professional mask over his face. 'Well, fact is stranger than fiction, is it not?'

'Yes. Yes, it is,' she agreed, hurriedly removing herself from her perch and returning to her chair behind the desk. 'Would you like to hang up your coat? There's a hook behind the door.' While his back was turned to her, she studied his movements. 'Yes, it is quite amazing . . . and to think that you've been handling my husband's affairs for years.'

'That's not quite true. Mr Williamson was your husband's solicitor. I was very junior in the firm when Mr Cameron first consulted us.'

'I see. Well, why don't you come and sit down and I'll explain my problem.'

It was difficult to concentrate, and only by studiously avoiding looking at him was she able to keep her story coherent. She told him of her husband's serious condition, without referring to the cause, adding that he had not been well for some time and business had suffered. 'I won't ask you to examine all the books today, but I have here a list of the various separate companies my husband owns and the current balance sheets for each, as nearly accurate as I can make them with the information I have managed to gather. I'm afraid my husband's health has prevented him from maintaining his ledgers as well as he used to.' She took a sheaf of papers from the desk drawer and passed them to him.

Janthina watched him as he studied the figures. It was impossible not to think of what might have been if. . . . Looking at the wide shoulders, bent slightly over the opposite side of the desk, the top of his dark head, the long, strong fingers with neatly clipped nails, and

237

thinking of the big white teeth he occasionally exposed with his easy smile, she trembled slightly. He was making notes in the margin with his left hand, keeping the pencil between his fingers when he picked up his cup, and she recalled the letter in which he had told her of his wounded arm. He had developed the use of his left hand very well; no one would notice anything wrong with the right without close scrutiny.

'I see your problem,' he nodded. 'Perhaps I shouldn't make any specific comments regarding viability until I have examined the individual accounts in detail, which I will do tomorrow. First of all I think we should apply to the court for you to have power of attorney; there would appear to be some urgency in this regard.'

'Yes. Cam's bank manager said the same. Also, I'm afraid the accounts are badly out of date. You see, Cam was . . . well, rather nervous of people learning the details of his business. He wanted to keep everything private, which is why he didn't use local solicitors.'

'That's understandable.'

'Yes, excepting that he wouldn't even allow me access to all the papers and ledgers although I was working here as his secretary. I did what I could with the books I had, but even those. . . .' She flushed. 'Well, I don't know if they are correct. You see, Cam was seldom in the office. . . .'

'I'm sure you don't have to worry about that, Mrs Cameron. I'll sort it out; that's my job.'

'Thank you,' she smiled, and realised that his hair still grew away from his temples and curled back in front of his ears, as it did in the photograph she had kept all these years.

Roland stayed at the Grand and each morning they met in the office promptly at nine o'clock. Twice they lunched together, once at the Grand and once upstairs in the café, but the atmosphere was never relaxed between them, though they did agree to use each other's Christian names in private.

The court had no hesitation, on the evidence of Cam's doctors and bank manager, in granting Janthina power of attorney. Returning to the office from the courtroom, she quickly stoked up the fire into flames.

'Brrr, it's cold,' she said, rubbing her hands together. 'I know it's only eleven, but I'm going to have a sherry. Will you have something?'

'Thank you, the same.' He busied himself setting papers out on the desk while she poured. 'Now we are going to have to get down to some serious discussion. If something isn't done quickly, I'm afraid your creditors are going to foreclose and you will be bankrupt. Sorry to be so brutal,' he added, seeing the expression on her face as she passed him his glass. 'But we really mustn't lose any time. Once one person sues, everyone will follow.'

'I've realised that for a long time. My problem was simply being unable to do anything about it. Now that has changed, perhaps you will advise me on what *you* think should be done.' Her tone left him in no doubt that whatever he might say, she intended that hers would be the last word.

They sat facing each other across the desk and he pulled a notebook in front of him. 'Firstly, as you know, there is no cash at all, even your weekly housekeeping is increasing your overdraft. It is obvious that large sums have been paid out to 'Cash' and disappeared without trace; are you sure you have found all the ledgers, cashbooks and papers?'

She frowned. Apart from the two she had placed in the bank's safe deposit in her own name . . . but they weren't relevant. 'Quite sure.' She nodded.

'Have you searched at home? Gone through your husband's chest of drawers, hunted through his pockets?'

'No-o-o, I haven't. I'll do that tonight.'

'It won't help the situation, I'm afraid, but might explain what has happened.' He sipped his sherry and continued. 'Your husband's businesses are grossly over-capitalised, but added to that is the fact that the bank holds bonds on both the hotels.'

'You mean that Cam has borrowed money against them?'

'Yes. And the bank is demanding interest on the loans as well as repayment. In fact I doubt they will wait more than another month or two at the most. What you need is to find someone who will purchase the hotels, quickly, and for enough cash to write off the debts and leave you with some working capital in hand for the other businesses.'

'What do you think the hotels will sell for?'

'Nothing like as much as if they were in first-class order and showing a good profit margin – which they are not. But I can't give you a figure, only an approximation. You'll have to have a professional assessor.'

'Will you be able to find one for me? If the figures are reasonable I think I can find a buyer.'

He looked up, startled. 'You think so? Well done!'

She smiled, and he smiled back. Her legs felt like water. Good Lord! This is ridiculous, she thought frantically: they had exchanged very little conversation on their private lives but she had to presume he was married . . . as she was. And she was thirty-six, not sixteen. None of which altered the fact that after twenty years he had an even more devastating effect on her.

239

She cleared her throat. 'Now, hadn't we better look at the viability of the other companies? The grocery shops are still showing a little profit. . . .'

He brought a pile of papers round to her side of the desk and placed them in front of her, holding the back of her chair and leaning forward to point out the figures. She felt the warmth of his jacket against her arm – and desperately tried to concentrate on what he was saying. His fingers traced down the columns, occasionally swerving left to underline the legends, came to the bottom of a page and stopped.

She waited for him to turn to the next sheet, but he didn't move. She looked up, and he was gazing down at her, his face pale and serious. Their eyes held together. Her pulse was racing violently, her breath coming only in short gasps as his hands touched hers, drawing her up into his arms. They clung tightly together, feeling the pounding of each other's hearts.

Janthina felt her breathing slowly return to normal, all the knots of tension in her neck and shoulders, all the stress and misery of the past twenty years, washed away by an overwhelming sense of peace and safety.

At last she looked up.

His mouth was waiting to caress the line of her hair, her brows, eyelids . . . and then she felt his cool breath on her mouth. The soft kisses became more passionate and her arms crushed him against her, trying to fulfil the frantic need to be part of him, lose herself in him, utterly and forever.

Then with unspoken understanding they parted, to sit facing each other across the desk again, fingers touching.

Roland was shaking his head. 'My dearest darling Janthina: how the hell could I have been so careless as to lose you? I should have visited you in France when I returned from South Africa – but I thought you didn't want me.'

She shook her head. 'No, no. It wasn't that I didn't want you. I . . . oh, it was so difficult to reply to your letter. You see . . .' she closed her eyes. 'I didn't want you to know that I was expecting a child. . . .'

He frowned. 'But I didn't know that you. . . .'

'No,' she interrupted. 'I wasn't married.'

He sat in silence, gripping her hand as she told him the story; there was no way she could hold back anything from him now.

When she finished, he got up to refill their glasses. He shook his head. 'My darling, you could have told me. I was hopelessly in love with you. I would have married you before the child was born.'

'Don't, Roland, please don't,' she gasped, squeezing her eyelids, shaking her head. 'It is too . . . awful. I try desperately not to think of what might have been. I had no idea you felt so strongly, after just a few days at sea. I imagined that when you got home to all the memories of your wife. . . .'

'Understandably. But let me explain about Mary and me. She was a childhood playmate. We never actually fell in love. Our eventual marriage was just something assumed by both families over the years. We liked each other very much, but . . . I must confess I was not as devastated by her death as maybe I should have been had ours been a passionate love match.' He smiled, and reached across for her hand. 'You are the only woman I believe I have ever truly loved. I won't pretend I have led a pure and celibate life, but I never met anyone else that I wanted to marry.'

She stared into his eyes, hardly able to believe, not sure she wanted to believe the tragedy of all those wasted years. 'And what about your son? How old is he? What is he doing?'

'Michael is nineteen, and reading law and commerce at Cambridge.' They sipped their sherries.

'You remained in France for several years, then?' he asked.

'No, I didn't, actually. My friend in France forwarded your letters and Christmas cards. I didn't want you to know I was in England or what had happened. I was so ashamed.'

He clasped her hands. 'I loved you, Janthina. Nothing you did could have changed that.' Sadly he stared into her eyes. 'I love you still,' he whispered.

She stared back. 'I think I love you, too. But it's all right for you, you're a widower, whereas I'm supposed to be a respectable married woman.'

He paused a moment before asking, 'Do you love Cam?'

'No. I hate him. I never even liked him.'

He frowned. 'Did you have any more children?'

'Four. Angus and Flora are at school in Brighton. Ian is only nine. Alexandra would be twelve now, but . . . she died in the fire that destroyed the Excelsior three years ago.'

'Oh, God, how awful!' He sat looking infinitely sad. So many things to say – yet nothing meaningful. It was all too late. Eventually he looked at his watch and stood up. 'I must go. I promised Michael I'd be home for the weekend. I'll be back on Monday.'

'Better make it Tuesday. The children will be home from Brighton this evening, and I'll go back there with them on Monday. I must attend to some business of my own there.'

He hunched into his overcoat, turned to face her . . . then opened

241

his arms. She ran into them, her hands sliding inside the coat to hold him close. When they had kissed she stood watching him straighten his tie and button his coat.

He picked up his briefcase and hat. 'Till Tuesday,' he whispered, and was gone.


Janthina wondered why she hadn't thought of checking Cam's pockets before. The evidence was in a little pocketbook in the suit she had brought home from the hospital. It contained a list of unfamiliar names alongside two columns of figures: one headed 'W' and the other 'L'; the 'Ls' far outweighed the 'Ws'. Some of the figures in the 'L' columns corresponded with amounts she recalled from the list of unspecified bank withdrawals. She sighed in exasperation. Wins and Losses. She had never realised he had taken to gambling as well.

The drawers of the bureau downstairs had revealed nothing – nor did his chest of drawers in the bedroom. She was about to go downstairs again when she remembered the old steel deedbox, sitting out of sight on top of the wardrobe. She tried several keys from Cam's ring before the lid was released and she could sift through the pile of papers, all to do with a Mr Johnson. Copy invoices for goods supplied to him by the Cameron Companies; a list of figures on two pages torn from an exercise book, yellow with age. There were two letters addressed to Cam from Mr Johnson, begging his patience, and one from Mrs Johnson apologising for her husband's tardiness and explaining that the man was sick in hospital . . . and at the bottom of the box a roll of stiff papers tied with frayed green ribbon. It was the deeds of a house, this house, and the legal conveyance of the property from 'Mr and Mrs Johnson' to 'Mr J. Cameron, in settlement of debts incurred. . . .'


The wind was north-easterly, dry but icy cold. Janthina hurried into the office early on Tuesday morning to light the fire before Roland arrived – and to think. There was so much private thinking to be done and so little time to herself in which to do it. Thoughts of her successful visit to Brighton the previous day made her smile to herself as she heaped coals on the fire; everything had worked out so well, though her heart pounded at her own daring.

Why had it taken so long, till she was thirty-six years old, before. . . . How would one describe the change in her? Transformation? No, she still looked the same. Perhaps one could say she had at last become a whole person in her own right. At long last she was asserting herself, making her own decisions. She was doing what she wanted for the first time in her life. And why not? Had she been born with the misconception that all her life should be governed by men? An idea instilled in her by her parents, she supposed, and look where it had got poor Mama. Oh, poor Mama, her life must have been hell on earth. But so had her own, at times. Only the support of Ruth's independent thinking had improved things for her while she was living with them, after which Cam was in such an appalling state . . . and now there was Roland.

The shop bell tinkled and she heard his voice and approaching steps. Her pulse quickened; what might his feelings be after a weekend at home in which to think?

He stood with his back to the closed door, intense, unsmiling eyes holding hers. Then he was striding across the room, tossing his hat on the desk as he came to grasp her, hold her against him as their mouths met.

A long time later he said, 'I couldn't wait to get back.'

He looked down at her. 'So much of our lives has been wasted by being apart, I don't want to be without you a minute more than necessary. Did you miss me, or were you too busy?'

'I can never get enough of you,' she whispered.

He held her away and looked questioningly into her eyes. 'Do you mean that?'

She flushed, knowing he had read more into her reply than she had intended. But she couldn't bring herself to deny the truth, and, still holding his gaze, she nodded, a warm rush of sensuous feeling flooding her body.

'I want you, Janty; all of you.'

She nodded again.

'When?'

'Soon.'

'Where?'

She hesitated. 'We have a Ford Trojan in the garage. I was wondering if you could teach me to drive?'

'You? Women don't drive motor cars.'

'This one is going to.'

'I don't see the connection.'

'I thought we might drive along the coast this afternoon,' she said pointedly.

He kissed her nose. 'Scheming woman. But it's going to be jolly cold out on the cliffs.'

'Who said anything about cliffs? If I'm going to break my marriage vows it will be in style and in the comfort of a big, soft double bed . . . or not at all.'

The morning dragged by very slowly after that until, having telephoned to tell Susan to give Ian his supper and put him to bed as she would be out of town on business until tomorrow, they were free to walk out and collect the car.

Roland returned from the bathroom with a large towel fastened round his waist, and laid his clothes over a pink velvet chair. The room was all pink and cream with frilled net curtains, the best that Bognor Regis could offer.

Janthina was standing by the window wrapped in the quilt, watching the gale whip up white crests on the breakers.

'Changed your mind, sweetheart?' Roland asked, seeing she was not in bed.

There was little chance of that, but she was reluctant to rush this moment – as though they were not both rushing it anyway. It had been their intention to order drinks in the residents' lounge and sit warming themselves by the log fire until dinnertime, but when the bellboy had left them standing in their room, feeling slightly embarrassed by their inadequate luggage, and they had embraced, she had known that the need which had been building in her for the past week – if not years – demanded immediate fulfilment.

Roland obviously felt the same way for he had said, 'My love, I'm afraid dinner is going to be a sadly rushed affair unless. . . .'

She had laughed and nodded; yet once she had undressed she found herself gazing out, unseeing, at the foaming seas, wondering if events had gone full circle in her life and now she was about to start anew with her original beau – the man she should have married. . . .

'No. Just thinking,' she smiled, and slid modestly between the sheets so that he had only a glimpse of her naked back, before he dropped his towel onto the floor.

She loved him with all the pent-up emotion of years: watched shamelessly as he lifted the bedclothes to swing his long legs in beside her own, heard his breath quicken as he encountered her warmth. As they kissed, their eyes spoke the years of loneliness, of yearning for their true soulmate, of life passing by in loveless tones of grey.

The hardness of his wanting pressed against her, but he held back, not realising that her need, her readiness, matched his own. Impulsively she rolled onto her back, pulling him with her, arching up to receive him, crying with the joy of holding him there. They wanted to wait, make the

244

sweetness last – but it was impossible. Breakers surged and ebbed on the distant shore to match their passion. Her head rolled from side to side, moans of ecstasy drawn from her lips by every movement until, toes curled and tingling, and faint with excitement, she took from him the accumulated love of nearly twenty years.


Sedate and cool, they entered the hotel lounge watched by a number of elderly residents. Exchanging polite nods here and there, Roland and Janthina selected a pair of armchairs some distance from the group near the fire and waited in silence for a waiter.

Dinner was unremarkable, except for the presence of each other. They acted out a cool indifference for the benefit of curious eyes, while murmuring a quiet toast to the belated consummation of their love . . . the single most exquisite experience of their lives.


The sale of the hotels was completed in less than a month. Roland and Janthina both signed the conveyance of shares in each company, with two nominee directors signing on behalf of the purchasing company.

'I think you have been incredibly lucky to find a buyer so quickly,' Roland remarked on the way back to the office, 'and for such a good figure. He was being very generous, though I must admit I'm always a bit dubious when these contracts are handled only by lawyers and nominees. Why can't we meet the man? We don't even know his name, only the name of his company. . . . Shell Holdings Limited is meaningless to us.'

'Not to the owner, though.' Janthina led the way through the shop and unlocked the office door. 'Normally I would agree with you but not in this instance, as I do happen to know the owner.'

Roland's brow furrowed. 'You do? And you never told me! Who is he?'

Janthina placed four brand-new ledgers on the desk and sat down. 'I didn't tell you because I thought you might raise some objection.'

'Why should I do that? Is he an unsavoury character or something?'

'For a start it is not a man, and I will leave you to judge whether or not she is of suitable character. I must confess I know her to be committing adultery quite frequently.'

He stared at her, unbelieving. 'You? What are you talking about?'

'I'm trying to tell you, in a roundabout fashion, that I am the new owner of the Dolphin and Grand Hotels.' She was quite unable to suppress a grin of satisfaction.

245

He collapsed, mystified, into the opposite chair and waited.

'I explained to you some time ago how Cam founded the business on money belonging to me – intended for Caroline's upbringing. But he avoided having my name on any deed or shareholding as joint owner, though he assured me at the time that I would be. Even the house is in his name alone. Well. . . .' She sat back, green eyes flashing. 'Two can play at that game. When I inherited money I omitted to tell him, simply invested it – well. And now, perfectly legally and for a generous price, *I* have purchased *his* hotels. Fair enough?'

He gaped at her, slowly shaking his head, then pushed back his chair and bellowed with laughter. 'Janty, my love, you are wonderful! Absolutely wonderful! But have you any idea of what you have taken on?'

Much relieved by his reaction she opened one of the new ledgers. 'No, I haven't. I am relying on you to start my new accounting system, right now.'

'Of course I'll do that, but there's much more to running hotels than merely keeping the books.'

'Don't worry, I've learned a great deal about the practical and physical side of hotel management in the past decade. One of the first things I intend to do is fire the manager from the Grand and replace him with someone well trained and competent. Several of the staff are very slack – they will need shaking up or replacing.'

'What about the Dolphin?'

'I've plans for that as well.'

'You must have inherited a great deal of money,' Roland commented.

'Thirty-eight thousand pounds, altogether, but I had excellent advice from my bankers and it was well invested during the war. It has now increased enough to make me a reasonably wealthy woman. However, I may well need overdraft facilities for the refurbishing and restaffing.'

His eyes narrowed. 'Are you sure that's wise?'

Janthina's chin came up. 'Quite sure. Now let's get down to business.'

Interviews, endless interviews: with electricians and plumbers, interior designers and decorators, prospective managers and staff. She bargained and haggled with the owners of furniture warehouses, harried workmen and seamstresses who were machining dozens of pairs of curtains. Striking but genteel advertisements appeared in fashionable magazines, recommending the hotels, while she ate incognito at London restaurants, sampling meals prepared by chefs who had applied for her vacancies, ticking or crossing off names from the list in her handbag.

Meanwhile, the managers of Cam's grocery shops were summoned to account for their inattentions and warned of dire consequences if matters did not improve immediately. The shifty old fellow whom Cam had left running the wholesale company and who failed to appreciate the lady's efforts to reverse the losses, was dismissed on the spot.

Roland was staggered. He watched with alarm at first, gradually relaxing into increasing admiration. He was with her on the evening she swooped on the Dolphin, unannounced. Without one word being said, the barman was made amply aware of her displeasure with his spotty jacket, and the empty tables strewn with sticky glasses and full ashtrays. The unhappy man read the explicit message in the one look she gave him before passing through to the kitchens.

And all the while Roland loved her. Loved the determination that drove her on from day to day, week by week, coping with the petty irritations and frustrations, restraining her anger with the men who openly displayed their reluctance to take instructions from a woman. He knew that despite the frustrations and weariness, this was the most exciting, stimulating period of her whole life – and his.

They returned to Bognor, as well as visiting Arundel and Seaforth and hotels in other towns and villages sufficiently removed from Whitehaven. But it didn't matter where they were – they loved. At least twice or three times each week her long, white limbs twined round his naked flesh and she nestled under his vast length and width, determinedly oblivious to all the looming, impossible tomorrows.


Janthina continued to visit the hospital daily. She felt no sense of guilt: the man who lay helpless on the high, white bed surrounded by sickly green walls had been her husband for sixteen years, but only in the sight of the law. Otherwise their union had been a travesty, a means whereby he had obtained ownership of her body, put her to work for him, and abused her. There had been no love, therefore theirs could not have been a true marriage in the eyes of God – at least, not God as she understood Him. And every time she saw him she was bitterly reminded of Alexandra.

Cameron continued to look a pathetic shell of a man, even when he awoke from his coma, even when his organs began their slow recovery from alcohol poisoning. Each day the nurses greeted his apparently devoted wife, took from her his clean linen to be placed in his locker, and handed over the bundle of soiled nightshirts. They answered her questions regarding his progress, remarking amongst themselves on her sweet attentiveness and concern. They quite misread her interest, misunderstood the reason for her wanting his recovery. How could they guess that this charming, beautiful woman was only waiting for the day when he was well enough to take his punishment, when she could have her revenge.

Progress was slow. There were setbacks, just when the doctors thought he was mended, but by mid December he was pronounced fit enough for his family to prepare his homecoming for Christmas.


Janthina often felt exhausted by the pressures, physical, financial and emotional. The meetings and interviews, flying visits to London, attendance at the hospital, passionate secret escapes with Roland and the resumption of duties as mother at weekends, made continuous claims on her time and mental energy. Fortunately, Angus and Flora seemed to entertain themselves quite adequately, and even included Ian in their various pursuits, much to the boy's delight. Caroline she seldom saw. The tall, blonde young woman graciously accepted her 'aunt's' invitation to dinner at a Brighton restaurant to celebrate her eighteenth birthday, asking if she might include two friends in the party. Janthina had been delighted to comply – until she met the friends. They were silly gigglers with painted faces and gowns cut offensively low, who eyed all the male diners in the room, their conversations and giggles emanating from their observations. It was disappointing that Caroline had taken up with this type and Janthina hoped soon to have the opportunity to discuss the friendship with her daughter . . . but as always, the opportunity failed to present itself and she was far too preoccupied to worry about it once she returned home. Maybe during the Christmas holidays. . . .


Christmas was approaching fast.

The boutique window was decorated with tinsel and coloured glass bells, attracting the attention of happy window-shoppers. A vase of chrysanthemums stood on the office filing cabinet, but failed to dispel the huge cloud of choking sadness which hung over the room.

Nothing had been said between them, but they had both known from the start the impossibility of their love. Now it was time to speak, to state the obvious – say goodbye? Forever?

They stood beside the office fireplace, eyes fixed on the flames, unfocusing. The four new ledgers containing her revised accounting system for the hotels stood on the shelf, their spines neatly labelled, beside those of the grocery and the wholesale companies. All outstanding accounts had been dealt with, invoices filed, customer accounts dispatched, letters replied to or filed, and orders, in and out, listed. Roland had been a good tutor and Janthina clearly understood how everything should run. Now all she required was a clerk to assist her . . . and Roland could depart to resume work in his office in London.

'I will always love you, Janthina.'

'And I will always love you.'

'You have a right to do it to Cam, to divorce him.'

'Yes. But I won't. At least, not in the foreseeable future. Not for his sake, of course. But the stigma of divorce may have a bad effect on the children – and on myself as a businesswoman.' She sighed. 'If Cam had not survived. . . .' Subconsciously her fingers played with the waxy flower petals. 'Will you ever come back?'

'I . . . I don't know. Can we ever see each other again without . . . pain?'

'We could try.' Anything rather than a final goodbye. 'Is it possible, I wonder, for two people loving as we do, to meet regularly and yet never touch? Would it be very wrong to try?'

'According to the Bible, sin is in the mind. I doubt I could ever meet you without committing mental adultery.'

She glanced up to see the sad grey eyes fixed on her. 'I will dream of making love with you for the rest of my life, whether we meet again or not.'

They both laughed.

'I suppose you're right. But actually to meet, deliberately, see each other regularly – wouldn't that be asking too much of ourselves?'

'You mean could we resist the temptation to emulate our thoughts? I wonder. Perhaps.'

'And if we fail! The devil has very subtle ways of twisting our thinking into the belief that what we want is good, not bad. We would soon find ourselves taking what we believed to be our God-given right.'

'Women are the reverse of men: we are more emotional than physical. I think I could handle it . . . but if you can't, I will quite understand.'

'These past weeks have not been long enough to burn out the urgency of my need of you, my darling.' He dropped to his chair, elbows on desk and head in hands.

'Is there a God? A devil? Is there a heaven and hell?'

'I was brought up to believe in God,' he mumbled, 'but we have no

249

proof, who has? But as for heaven and hell . . . well, I think we find them here on earth, in our own lifetimes. We were tempted and succumbed, tasted our heaven – and now our hell begins.'

'So? Goodbye?' She choked.

He thought for a moment. 'I suggest that you should seek the advice of your legal and financial adviser. . . .' He paused, gazing at her. 'Next March. Then the situation can be reviewed.'

'March! Three months!' She swallowed hard. 'Yes, Roland, I agree.'

He reached up to catch a tear from her cheek with his forefinger. 'That's my beautiful, brave Janthina.'


It was impossible to believe that his weekly visits to Whitehaven were over; they had lasted forever – yet flashed by in one fleeting dream. She lay in the darkness picturing his face above her, smelling his man-smell, feeling the weight of his body. How many times had they made love? Perhaps only a dozen; she'd never counted. Not enough; it could never have been enough. They had always registered in the hotels as Mr and Mrs Griffiths – why Griffiths she had not bothered to ask. She had learned to drive the Trojan, still a little nervously but she did enjoy it, and enjoyed seeing the expression on people's faces at the sight of a woman at the wheel.

She and Roland had talked endlessly – there was not a detail of their lives, their thoughts or feelings, omitted – but for one: Alexandra's death. That secret had to remain buried up on the hillside behind St Mary's.

Now Roland was back in London, the children would be returning for the Christmas holidays tomorrow, and in a few days Cam would be home from hospital. She had prepared one of the spare bedrooms for him, bought a new bed and had Susan install all his clothes in the wardrobe and drawers. Everything of his was removed from her room. However her feelings towards him might swing between hatred and indifference on the one hand and pity on the other, she would never share a room with him again, let alone a bed.

The alarm shrilled beside the bed and she rolled over to reach and turn it off. It was only six o'clock and still pitch dark, but life was too short to lie abed after waking, even when there was no Roland to greet any more.

Angus, Flora and Caroline filled the house once more with their chatter, exchanging news, telephoning friends and discussing the parties to which they had been invited. Even Ian noisily entertained friends in his bedroom, adding to the bedlam. Janthina was thankful for the two days they had to get over the initial excitement of their freedom, pointing out to them the need to be reasonably quiet when their father arrived home.

The difficulty of starting to walk again had been eased for Cam by the considerable amount of weight he had lost during his illness. The nurses had given him a great deal of help and encouragement so that he was able, with the assistance of a walking stick, to step over the threshold and walk quite steadily to his armchair in the drawing room, followed by his family. The children had all visited him in his green-walled room on weekends, but were excited to have him home at last, rushing about offering their services, waiting on him with a will. Like Janthina, he was well aware that their mood would not last and grinned at them as he made the most of his opportunity.

Preparations for Christmas, daily visits to the hotels, and overall control of the wholesale and grocery shops left Janthina with little time to agonise over Roland's absence – for which she was thankful, although there were times, especially in the evenings, when, with a mask of total happiness on her face, the suppressed misery struggled to surface. Then she was forced to close her eyes momentarily to obliterate the utterly impossible vision of Roland sitting opposite her in Cam's place. Then she would turn her attention to her children, interested to compare their development from one Christmas to the next.

Flora was now making great efforts with her appearance, sleeping, heaven knew how, with metal curlers screwed into her hair each night. She was still painfully thin and totally flat-chested, but was being consistently and sweetly attentive to her father.

Angus was at least two inches taller than Cam, serious most of the time behind his spectacles, yet given to outbursts of fun and laughter, and Ian was now growing fast, losing a little of his puppy-fat, still slow-thinking and enjoying his mother's affection when no one else was around to see.

Now that Giles no longer spent his holidays at Whitehaven, Janthina was reluctant to allow Caroline to attend any but the most assuredly respectable parties, unescorted. No longer a child, stunningly beautiful and with a full, mature figure, it was surprising that she did not appear to have formed any attachments among the young men in the local set, though Janthina could never be sure – Caroline avoided confiding in her. Only recently, another letter had arrived from Joseph asking if the girl had been told the facts surrounding her birth yet; it lay in the drawer of her dressing table, unanswered. She longed to reply that Caroline now knew everything and was thrilled and excited to have

251

'found' her mother at last – but the fact was that the subject had been shelved over the past year. How could one really concentrate on planning such an important matter when one's emotions were in turmoil, first over Cam's behaviour, then his illness, then discovering the truth about Alexandra's death. . . . And now Roland. However, she excused herself, it would be impractical to attempt an approach to the subject during this holiday; there were too many people about all the time, demanding her attention – and anyway, she never had wanted to say anything until Caroline left school. Maybe during a weekend in the spring term, or at Easter. . . .

From the day of his return home, Cam nagged to be told about the business. Janthina repeated the assurances she had given him in hospital, that everything was under control and he wasn't to think about it until the doctors declared him fully recovered. But her assurances only made him nag the more, pester her with questions, and she knew she would be unable to hold out much longer. The doctors helped with good-humoured banter, quietening his exasperation when Janthina hurried out of the house, day after day, to visit the hotels and inspect her young clerk's work in the office; he was good, willing and reasonably well turned-out, but needed her constant supervision. The grocery shops were picking up trade again, and orders were rolling into the wholesale department for goods required for the opening of next season. She studied the buying of liquor and wines, bought well and offered stocks at highly competitive prices – with excellent results.

'I don't know how you've done it but I have to say there is a marked improvement,' Cam admitted, when she allowed him to examine a ledger she had brought home. 'What I don't follow is why you've changed my method of book-keeping.'

'Because Mr Burrows, who was sent down from London by your Mr Williamson when you were very ill, recommended it. He said this new method is much easier and more efficient.'

'Hmm,' had been the only comment.

Ruth, Freddie and Giles had driven over from Brighton to spend Christmas with the Camerons, a busy, happy holiday commencing with the Watch Night Service at St Mary's on Christmas Eve. Cam was already in bed when the family left in two cars late that night. All eight of them managed to squeeze into their one long pew, gazing around at the beautiful flowers heaped on the window ledges and at the foot of the pulpit, lit only by hundreds of flickering candles; they sang favourite carols and took part, at midnight, in the communion celebrating the Holy Birth.

Janthina was pleased that Miss Entwhistle had been able to arrange a brief service of baptism for Caroline in the school chapel, so that she could be confirmed and she was now taking her place at the altar rails alongside her, to receive the sacraments. The details registered on the baptismal certificate regarding parentage were, of course, false – but did it matter so long as the girl was accepted as a member of the church?

It proved to be a very exciting Christmas for Janthina, the first ever at which she felt she was truly in charge of her own life as well as that of her family. Thoughts of Roland had frequently invaded the preparations but were easily forced to the back of her mind as the children decorated the tree from the big box of tinsel and baubles, while she stood on chairs pushing drawing-pins into the picture rails to hold festoons of paper chains in place.

Christmas morning was a riot of noise. Though even Ian had known the truth about Santa Claus, Ruth and Janthina had filled stockings for all the children and were amazed to find the children had secretly made up stockings for all four adults. Even Cam, who had grumbled to his wife, privately, about extravagance, laughed as he drew handkerchiefs, cigars, bananas and nuts from one of Giles's rugby socks.

Leaving coloured papers and ribbons well scattered over the drawing room floor, they had trooped through into the dining room where Cam insisted that he was strong enough to carve the giant turkey. Crackers were pulled, glasses filled, and toasts drunk.

Caroline looked happy. She had hugged Janthina, briefly, in thanks for the gold bracelet she had found in the dainty parcel tied with red ribbon, joined in the evening's party games and obligingly helped to entertain friends invited to the house on Boxing Day, but her mother had been disappointed when she asked if she might return to Brighton with Giles and his parents for a few days, acutely aware of the widening gap between them.

It had all passed too quickly without an opportunity to speak with Ruth, tell her about the hotels and the coincidence of meeting Roland again, although, as at Glenfalk years before, she did not intend to reveal all that had happened during his visits. So she had waited until now, during a slack period in February when it was possible to leave John, the clerk, for a few days, to drive in to Brighton to stay with Ruth, sit

253

by a roaring fire and a tea tray and launch into a long tête-à-tête.

Ruth squealed with delight on hearing of Roland's reappearance. 'Janty! You must have been shocked out of your mind! What is he like? How did you feel, seeing him again?'

'He looks older; going a little grey. As for feelings. . . .' She shrugged. 'It's been a long time. People change.' How difficult it was to be non-committal.

'What did he say about the business?' Ruth asked.

'That the hotels should be sold as soon as possible.'

'Difficult, I should think, they are so run down. Do you think you've any hope?'

'They were sold in November.'

'Good heavens! That quickly? To whom?'

'Me.' Janthina tried vainly to suppress a smile.

Ruth goggled at her. 'You! Are you crazy? You must have had to borrow a huge sum of money to get them.' Memory of Cam's fatal gamble to buy the Grand loomed at her.

'No, very little. Mr Hudson, the Brighton bank manager, gave me very good advice on investments for both inheritances. I made a lot of money.'

'You must have! But what do you know about hotel management? How on earth are you going to cope?'

Janthina spent the next half an hour convincing her sister that she was going to cope very well, then Ruth pulled the bell rope and asked the maid to bring fresh tea.

'What does Cam say about it?'

'He doesn't know, yet. I'm waiting for the doctors to pronounce him fit before letting him get back to business.'

'He'll need to be fit to take that news!' Ruth laughed. She was undoubtedly pleased for her younger sister.

'Now that's enough about me and my news; what about you and yours? No need to tell me you're happy. I can see that.'

Ruth sighed contentedly. 'Yes. Freddie is wonderful. I never really believed I could replace Ben – but I have. Truly, Jan.'

Janthina leaned forward to squeeze her sister's hand. 'I can't tell you how happy that makes me.'

'There are a couple of pieces of news I have to tell you,' Ruth went on. 'First of all, right out of the blue, I had a letter from Uncle William.'

'Uncle William! Golly, I haven't even thought of him in years, I'm afraid. He left the Navy to start sheep-farming in Australia, didn't he?'

'Yes. Grandpapa told us about it when we were at Glenfalk, but frankly, I'd forgotten all about him, too.'

'He's younger than Uncle Andrew, isn't he? I wonder if that's why he didn't want to go back to Glenfalk? Perhaps he preferred not to play second fiddle to his older brother and decided to start off on his own.'

'It seems so. Did you know he had married and has two sons?'

'No! Bit old to start, I'd have thought.'

'Look, he's sent some photos. He married late, and his wife is a lot younger than him.'

Janthina examined the sepia-coloured prints. 'Mmm. The boys are huge. They look a real couple of toughs.'

'Uncle wants us all to keep in touch. He's asked for your address and wants us to send photos of ourselves and our families.'

'I suppose I should write to him. He provided Mama and Papa with a name for me, remember?'

'Yes, vaguely. You must read his letter later.'

'I will. And have you any other news?'

'Yes.' Ruth paused and waited for Janthina to look up at her before announcing, 'I'm going to have a baby.'

'Ruthie!' Janthina left her armchair to give her sister a hug. 'How absolutely wonderful! I bet you're both madly excited.'

'Yes, though I feel a bit old to be starting again.'

'Don't you believe it. They say you're as young as you feel.'

'Well, you're certainly looking younger than you did ten years ago.'

'I feel like it.' How she longed to tell Ruth why. 'Are you hoping for a little girl, this time?'

Again Ruth paused. 'I don't know,' she said seriously. 'Giles has been so easy, like Angus and Ian. . . .'

'Yes,' her sister agreed. 'And in all honesty I can't say I've had much success with my girls. I do wish Flora had a less waspish disposition. A pity she couldn't have been more like Alexandra,' she said wistfully. 'And as for Caroline, I don't know why but she really bothers me. How did she behave when she stayed with you after Christmas?'

Ruth gazed into the fire for a full minute before answering. 'I must admit I was disturbed – and so was Giles.'

'Really? Even Giles? Why?'

'She seems to have some rather – well – odd sort of friends in Brighton.'

'Yes, I met a couple of them once and they struck me as being exactly the type I wouldn't want Caroline to know.'

'Quite. And the young men are much the same.'

'I didn't know there were any.'

'Yes, lots. Caroline whisked Giles off to meet them all the first night

255

we got back from your place and he didn't like them at all. He tried to talk her out of joining them again the following evening, offered to take her to a theatre, anywhere . . . but she insisted. He wouldn't let her go with them alone, so he went along too, and confessed to me later that he hadn't enjoyed it. I hate to say this to you, Janty dear, but I'm afraid we were thankful when she returned to Whitehaven.'

Janthina leaned her head against the high back of her chair. 'Don't worry about telling me, for heaven's sake; I've known for some time that she was drifting further and further away from us – away from me. I know I've been burying my head in the sand for the past two or three years, telling myself this was just a phase she was going through and she would eventually get over it; that's why I've been delaying telling her the truth, waiting for the gap between us to narrow – when all the time it's been widening.' She closed her eyes. 'Oh, Ruthie! What am I going to do? I do love her so; I so want her love, and now I'm terribly afraid I've lost her.' Salt stung behind her closed lids. Pictures of the tiny red infant placed in her arms on the day of its birth, of the curly blonde toddler cuddling on her lap, of the little girl in her first school uniform, flashed through her mind. She remembered how, as the child grew, the happy grin had faded, the exquisite features had become solemn. Oh God! 'It's my own fault, I should have fought Cam harder, stood up to him long ago.'

'There's no point in blaming yourself. There was nothing you could achieve except more rows and frustration. Cam is far too stubborn a character ever to give in.'

Not any more, Janthina thought to herself; he won't ever get the better of me again. But she couldn't say so out loud because she could never tell Ruth – or anyone – why. Instead she struck the arm of her chair with her clenched fist and said, 'I vow I will tell Caroline at Easter, come what may. I've waited far too long as it is.'


Two weeks later, the doctors told Cam he was now fit enough to return to business, issuing only a mild warning about over-tiring himself.

Flora and Angus had just returned to school after a weekend visit, and Caroline had been invited to stay by the parents of one of her school friends. Janthina had remained home from the office to hear the doctors' decision.

Cam returned to the drawing room after seeing them out. 'Well, that's that. I'll come to the office with you straightaway. Go and get your hat on.'

At last the moment had come: the moment she had planned for months, the moment she almost dreaded.

Hats in place and coats buttoned up against the chill wind, they climbed into the Trojan, which Cam insisted on driving. While Janthina poked up the fire which had been lit earlier by John, Cam poured them a sherry each and went round to sit behind the desk.

'Been cleaning up, I see, in my absence. I'm glad you've been making yourself useful.' His tone was thick with condescension.

Little do you know, yet, how useful I have been, she thought. Aloud she said, 'I'll get out the books and balance sheets.' Before sitting down she hesitated beside the door to the outer office, opened it, and told John to go out for an early lunch today.

'Why did you do that?' Cam asked.

'Privacy,' she replied, and plonked the books down on the desk.

He sipped his sherry, and waited.

'You were aware, I've no doubt, of the catastrophic state the whole business was in when you were taken ill,' she started.

'I wouldn't have said catastrophic. Certainly there were problems.' He looked rather annoyed.

'I repeat – catastrophic. The bank and the other creditors were about to foreclose.'

'Nonsense! I could easily have talked them out of that. They probably panicked when I was incapacitated. . . .'

'No. As a matter of fact they breathed a sigh of relief.'

'What the hell do you mean?'

'Simply that you had not only grossly neglected everything for the past three years, but you were also drawing out money we didn't have to pay your gambling debts.'

'Gambling! What the hell are you talking about?'

'Don't make a fool of yourself by trying to deny it. . . .'

'You!' He pointed a forefinger at her. 'You've been snooping, prying into my private papers while I was at death's door. . . .'

'Yes, Cam, I have.'

'You despicable bitch!' he shouted, purple with anger.

She took a deep breath. 'At least I'm not an arsonist and a murderer,' she said quietly.

The purple slowly faded to a sickly yellow. He stared at her, swallowing hard, trying to guess how much she knew. He closed his eyes, swaying in his chair.

Janthina watched and waited in silence.

'I didn't know. For God's sake, how could I have guessed she was there?' His voice was scarcely more than a whisper. Then he sat up straight and stared at her. 'Anyway, what do you imagine you can do about it? You've no proof.'

'Indeed I have. I found it all there in the safe.'

He pulled viciously at his key chain and got up. 'We'll soon see about that!' He jabbed the key into the safe lock.

'Don't waste your time. I have sorted out everything that was in there and the evidence is in my safe-deposit box in the bank,' Janthina said, and, seeing murderous fury contort his features, added, 'where they have instructions that if anything should happen to me, the contents must be handed over immediately to the police.'

He saw her watching his struggle to remember just what evidence had been locked in his safe, averted his eyes, and tried to control his breathing. 'So,' he hissed through his teeth, 'what are you going to do about it?'

'Nothing, for the moment.'

'In that case perhaps you'll get out.' He spat the words.

'No, Cam, because there are certain conditions to my silence about your crime. Please sit down quietly, and listen.'

He opened his mouth to deliver a scathing retort, saw the cold, calm determination in her face, closed it again and sat down.

'As I told you a few minutes ago, the overall situation was catastrophic when you were taken ill. In particular, the Grand and the Dolphin were losing money daily through gross mismanagement and staff dishonesty. The thieving and waste was phenomenal. You had mortgaged them both to the hilt, creditors were pressing, and there was no way of paying them, let alone finding working capital for the following season. In agreement with the bank and your lawyers from London, an independent valuation was made of both hotels and a buyer found who was willing to pay that amount. Thus the mortgages and creditors were paid off and a little was left with which to salvage the three shops, the café, and the wholesale and wines and spirits businesses.'

'I should bloody well think so,' he mumbled. 'And now I imagine I'm supposed to feel grateful that you've left me even those.'

'Well, only in a manner of speaking,' she replied.

'What do you mean?'

'I mean that everything was being grossly mismanaged. You cannot fail to be aware that you were neglecting all facets of the business. There was an endless stream of complaints even from our most faithful customers, and the less faithful had already abandoned us.'

His eyes narrowed. 'Go on. Criticism has always been your forte.'

'In the past five months I have worked very hard overseeing, managing, hiring and firing.' Cam's eyebrows shot up but she ignored him. 'Here are the quarterly balance sheets for each separate company, from which you will be able to see the steady improvement.'

'I suppose you want me to thank you,' he said sarcastically.

'No. I'm not asking for thanks. I am asking you to hand over the entire operation to my management.'

'Wh-a-t!' he roared, leaping to his feet.

'I will allow you to remain as titular head of these companies, though I wish to be made joint owner, immediately, but, although I will allow it to be assumed that you are still owner of the Grand and the Dolphin, they are actually mine, as will be the New Excelsior, which I intend to build on the old site. . . .'

'You? What are you . . . ? You're lying! Where could you find that sort of money?'

'My grandfather left me five thousand pounds. He apparently felt guilty for foisting me off on a liar and a cheat – little did he know those were the least of your sins – but I also inherited thirty-three thousand pounds from my father. I invested it very well during the war. . . .'

'You never told me. . . .' He drained his sherry.

'Certainly not! By then I knew you were not to be trusted. I daresay that . . .' she pointed at his empty glass '. . . had contributed to your problem considerably, which is why I must insist that you either control your drinking to purely socially acceptable limits, or become teetotal – and the doctors have told you that to drink heavily again will certainly kill you. Anyway, to continue. . . .' She held up her hand to quell the retort on his lips. 'You may remain head of the business but in name only. No one but you or I, and the lawyers and Ruth, will know the truth. Your friends and associates in Whitehaven will continue to believe you own and control everything. You may sit on your committees, etcetera, and play the clever fellow to your heart's content. I repeat, no one will know differently, not even the children. And only I will know about the arson.'

He stared at her for a moment in utter disbelief, then pushed back his chair and roared with laughter. 'You must be mad! You can't imagine for a moment that I'd agree to. . . .'

'Would you prefer imprisonment? It's your choice.'

'You wouldn't. You couldn't!' His lip curled.

She smiled coldly. 'I most certainly could, and would.'

'You sadistic, grasping bitch!'

'After the treatment you've dished out to Caroline and me all these years, I suppose one could say I've had the best possible training. Oh, and another thing,' she added. 'I want to change houses. I don't think either of us needs to be reminded of the way in which you obtained the one we have. I have chosen a new one; it's a little out of town but with marvellous views. In it we will continue to have separate bedrooms; as you can imagine, I never, ever, want you to touch me again.'

He sat opening and closing his mouth, shocked and speechless.

Janthina stood up. 'Think about it. I will expect your decision by tonight.'

# 2

JAMES CAMERON stood in front of the full-length mirror in the spare bedroom and brushed an imaginary hair from the sleeve of his dinner jacket. The suit was immaculate, a present from his wife. He stroked his beard carefully so that the coarse hair jutted evenly from his chin.

Did he hate her? he wondered. Certainly he was still furious with her, at the way she had manipulated the business away from him during his illness, though there was no doubt it had been in dire straits at the time. But would she be capable of running it and supervising the management of the hotels? Perhaps. He had obviously grossly under-estimated her up to now. He remembered the laird's beautiful granddaughter who had attracted him so much from the moment he first saw her on that Christmas Day, 1901 – and who had been offered to him once it was discovered that she was not only no longer a virgin but had actually mothered a child and was therefore unacceptable as a wife to anyone of her own class. God! How he had resented that offer, hated himself for desiring her too much to refuse, and then hated her that he was not the first to possess her, that he was her social inferior, that she was so tall and could look down her aristocratic nose at him. He smiled to himself remembering how much he had enjoyed seeing her on her hands and knees cleaning and scrubbing his first shop, and then hated her again for her good humour and willingness, her eagerness to please. The reason he had evaded adopting Caroline had been partly to torment her and later as a lever to get his hands on her money – until Angus was born; then, as he had told her, he was not prepared to adopt a child who would be senior to his own.

That five thousand pounds had made all the difference in the world. The business, their lives, had really taken a great upswing once she had allowed him to use it. He had earned the respect and friendship of every worthwhile person in Whitehaven. Of course, he had taken a big gamble in buying the Grand, but he couldn't have guessed that the country would be plunged into war so suddenly. That was when the rot had set in. He had watched the half-empty booking charts and half-empty dining rooms and bars, and the declining wholesale and retail trade with growing despondency. Reducing the number of staff had only lowered the standard of service which added to the problem rather than easing it, until the September of 1917 when he knew he couldn't hold on any longer, and. . . .

For the millionth time he closed his eyes in a vain attempt to blot out the picture of Alexandra's terrified face at that window. She had been brave enough to smash the glass when the window proved too heavy for her to open, so that they might hear her calls. . . .

Janty had every right to feel bitter and angry when she had learned the truth . . . but would she really go so far as to turn him over to the police, publicly denounce him for what he had done? What a damned fool he had been not to destroy those books, erase the evidence of his thoughts. . . .

He sighed, pursed his lips, and left the room.

Janthina was waiting in the drawing room. She had replaced the heavy old brown curtains and much of the Victorian furniture with lighter colours and more delicate pieces, making the room look much brighter and more feminine. He noticed she was wearing a new jade green evening gown, and with it those old imitation pearls she had bought for the opening of the Grand. She was even more beautiful now than when he had first seen her – which was a pity in a way: he might have found this situation less uncomfortable if she had become fat and ugly.

'How nice you look in that suit, Cam. You should always wear good clothes, they are very flattering. Do you want to help yourself to a drink? I already have mine.'

She's being extraordinarily polite and charming, he brooded, as he removed the decanter stopper; is this the sugar on the pill?

'Do you like my new gown?' Janthina revolved to show him the low-cut back.

'Beautiful, yes. But those pearls are not up to the standard.'

'No, I agree. I thought perhaps you might give me a good set for my birthday, this year,' she smiled sweetly.

He lifted one eyebrow.

'Oh, don't worry, I'll give you the money.'

Ian came in; he had had his supper and wanted to be with his parents until they went in to dinner. The three talked until Susan announced the meal, then Ian kissed his mother goodnight and went upstairs.

Janthina had hired a cook-housekeeper some months ago, who proved not only a very capable manager but also an excellent chef. Susan carried in a tureen of delicious soup followed by fried fillets of plaice served with mashed potatoes and green vegetables – simple fare but beautifully prepared. Finally the maid served Cam's favourite plum pie with custard and left the coffee tray on the sideboard before returning to the kitchen.

They ate in silence until Janthina's plate was empty. 'Well, Cam, have you come to a decision?'

He dabbed his mouth with his napkin and sat back. 'What I would like to know is, why, if you would consider reporting me to the police, you haven't done so already?'

'I very nearly did. I must tell you that when I discovered what you had done I was bitterly angry. I wanted to make you suffer as you had made Alexandra suffer.' He winced, but she ignored him. 'I thought it only fitting that you should be punished in accordance with your crimes.'

'What changed your mind?'

She left the table to carry the empty plates to the sideboard and pour the coffee. 'Pity.'

Pity! How could she know. . . .

'I'm sorry for you, Cam. I believe we all do have our limitations – unfortunately we too often fail to recognise them. You exceeded your limit when you bought the Grand. It was not only a financial gamble, it was a personality gamble, too.'

He raised an eyebrow. 'Go on.'

She set his coffee cup beside him and returned to her chair. 'It's all very simple. You were gambling that your personality growth as well as your ability was infinite; that you would be able to handle the status of multi-millionaire businessman. . . .'

'If it hadn't been for the war. . . .'

'There would have been another excuse. Some people know when they have over-reached themselves and are able to retract, re-consolidate in time, while others are not mentally big enough to do this: they imagine it is a matter of losing face and insist on backing a losing situation in the vain hope that something will turn up.'

'I tell you, if the war had ended as quickly as it started. . . .'

'It wouldn't have altered the fact that you had done a mean and despicable thing ejecting those elderly residents from the Grand.'

Cam frowned. So she knew about that as well.

'That fact in itself, like your method of obtaining this house, betrays how inadequate you are to conduct business fairly and honestly.'

He peered at her, eyes narrowed. 'Are you suggesting that you can handle big business better than I can?' There was a sneer in his voice.

She stared straight back at him. 'No, I'm not suggesting it: I am categorically stating it. Perhaps being a woman has some advantages. Women are less concerned with face, better able to seek and accept expert advice.' Watching the muscles twitching in her husband's face as he willed himself to survive, to win this confrontation, Janthina knew the anger and misery, the mortification he was feeling. It was what she had worked for, for months, what she wanted. Yet . . . she couldn't help but feel for him in his bitterness; after all, she had felt the same for years. 'I can sympathise with the way you feel. . . .'

'Sympathy! Pity! How understanding and generous you are!' he sneered. 'I suppose you think you are in a strong enough position to show compassion, now.'

'Please don't let me mislead you. I still get moods of anger and bitterness in which I want to wipe you right out of our lives, the children's and my own, but I do know you loved Alexandra. I know you've suffered. The only question is whether you've suffered enough.' She leaned forward with her elbows on the table, fingers templed, staring into his face. 'Have you, Cam? Have you been hurt enough to do as I ask? Let me run the wholesale business, the restaurant, and the shops?'

Cam stared back for a full minute, then, reaching into a pocket for his leather case, slowly withdrew a cigar, clipped the point and removed the band before sucking smoke through the tobacco until the end glowed in a complete circle. He leaned back to exhale smoke to the ceiling. 'I am quite willing for you to have a more active role. I'll put you on the mandate. . . .'

'I am already on the mandates, and I am not just seeking more control. I don't think you are quite understanding what I am asking: perhaps I haven't made it clear that I want fifty-one per cent of the shareholdings in all companies and properties transferred to me.'

'No! Dammit, no! That's going too far!' His fist hit the table with a crash.

The impassive expression on Janthina's face remained unchanged; she said nothing, just waited for his temper to calm.

'I know damn well you wouldn't go to the police. You wouldn't do that to the children,' he challenged.

'You're wrong, Cam. I will do it tonight, if you force me. Then, while you are in prison, the shops will be sold to repay me what they owe me already, and I will sell off the hotels and the site of the Excelsior and move away from this district, perhaps to Eastbourne. I will never take you back, and you will have nothing when you are eventually free. Nothing. No home, no family, and no business. . . .'

'You wouldn't, Janty! I don't believe you!'

'Try me.' Her voice was barely audible. Would she? Could she? Even now she was uncertain, but it didn't really matter. All she had

264

to do was convince him that she would. . . . Frighten him. . . . The green eyes were lowered to her coffee cup, and seeing it empty, she carried it back to the sideboard, a tall, very graceful woman, hair elegantly coiffed, the imitation pearl earrings swaying as she moved. Her mouth was soft and full-lipped, but firm, and her beautiful jaw line was strong.

How she has changed, he thought, watching her. She is no longer the confused, emotional, biddable girl I married, nor the sad, weary hag whose life I controlled absolutely. In the back of his mind he knew he had failed, made too many stupid mistakes, drunk, gambled . . . committed arson . . . and murder. He closed his eyes to shut those thoughts out of his mind. So what was she offering him in return for his controlling interest in his companies? His freedom. His position, in the eyes of society, as a leading businessman and hotelier; as head of his family, and. . . .

'More coffee, Cam?'

'Yes, please.'

Her long fingers removed the cup and saucer, her perfume drifted round his chair. His friends would continue to envy his ownership of this beautiful creature; he sighed, they wouldn't know that in fact she owned him and that he was never allowed to touch her. His eyes followed her movements as she replaced his cup and returned to the far end of the table. The full breasts, narrow waist, and slightly swaying hips attracted him now more than ever and he moved in his chair to ease the tightening in his trousers. God, how he wanted her! Wanted to feel that soft, white flesh under him, fill her, possess her. . . . Supposing he agreed? Just supposing he gave in to all her demands and played the role she'd planned for him? If he was careful never to get drunk, never to be rude or cross her, tried always to please her, might she soften towards him eventually? Might she forgive and forget, give herself, and perhaps even his companies back to him?

What was the alternative? He wasn't absolutely sure she would denounce him – but she had suddenly acquired a new forcefulness and determination which it might be foolish to challenge. It wasn't worth the risk; the choice was obvious . . . but he would have to be clever, use plenty of the old Cameron charm on her for the first time.

'Well, my love, you seem to have been very successful in controlling the businesses in my absence, and if it gives you pleasure and perhaps increases your confidence actually to own the controlling shares, then I shall be happy to comply.' He raised his glass. 'I give you a toast – to a most exceptional and beautiful wife – Janthina!'

She smiled graciously, despite her awareness of his insincerity, and raised her own glass. 'Thank you, Cam. And shall we also drink to our new life together?'

Roland received Janthina's call next day.

'Mr Burrows?' she asked formally. 'Would you, or someone from your firm . . .' she had to give him the option of not returning '. . . come down to Whitehaven as soon as possible, please? My husband has expressed the wish to transfer a major part of the shareholdings in his companies to me. We would both appreciate your assistance.'

'Yes, of course, Mrs Cameron, I will arrange it. Would Wednesday be convenient to you both?'

'Excellent. We will be waiting for you at the office at three o'clock.'

'Very good, madam. Thank you for calling. Good morning.' He put down the receiver and glanced across the room, wondering if the flush on his face and neck were noticeable to Mr Finey; but the older man's head was bent over the documents on his desk. Roland took a white handkerchief from his breast pocket to dab at the tiny beads of perspiration on his face, angered that the sound of her voice should have such an effect.

Hell! It wasn't as though he was a gangling youth feeling his first surge of manhood, knocked silly by his first love. He was a middle-aged man with an almost adult son, a qualified and respected lawyer . . . but Janthina was his first love – his only love; he had loved her all his life and always would.

He picked up the Memorandum and Articles of Association of the company whose problems he was currently attempting to solve, read the first paragraph, and sighed; he had no idea what the words had said, had even forgotten why he was reading it. Eyes, green as jade, flecked with brown and amber, stared up at him from the typed page. He rubbed tense fingers over his closed lids, as though to blot out the vision . . . only to feel the warmth of her white skin against his in the darkness.

God alone knew how hard he had fought the urge to abandon everything and return to Whitehaven. And after all these weeks, months, he had only just begun to control his thoughts, concentrate on work . . . and home. And now, the sound of her voice had totally scrambled his brain again. He desperately wanted to go to her on Wednesday, but dare he? Wouldn't that only cause his life to relapse again into miserable confusion?

\*     \*     \*

266

Janthina returned the receiver to its rest, heart pounding, mouth dry. It was three months since she had heard his voice – and its effect was devastating. She wanted to clap her hands and sing with excitement – and collapse into tears, because she knew their love was impossible. Utterly impossible. She longed to know what was going through his mind at this moment. Was he suffering the same torments as herself or had he got over his passion for her? Had the months back in the old routine healed his pain?

The next two days passed painfully slowly. Every task, every thought, every hour of darkness, was invaded by the question – would he come, or would he send someone else instead? Could he face meeting her, and her husband, be polite, professional, offer them his advice and then just walk away . . . without touching her, without his eyes betraying him?

Could she face him and keep the love out of her eyes, the persistent flush from her cheeks?

During those two days she rehearsed the scene so frequently in her mind – Cam sitting at the desk while she busied herself about the office, waiting, and the door opening and Roland walking in . . . or perhaps Mr Williamson – that on Wednesday afternoon she had the strangest feeling of déjà vu. It was exactly as she had imagined. Suddenly he was there, shaking Cam's hand, smiling politely, distantly, enquiring after his health. She tried not to look at the curl of hair over his ear, the movement of his lips as he spoke, the tremendous width of shoulders as she passed behind his chair.

'I understand, Mr Cameron, that you wish to transfer some company shares to your wife. Is that correct?'

Cam felt, rather than saw, the two pairs of eyes on him, his own not leaving the papers in front of him. He nodded, 'Yes.'

'A wise decision, I'm sure, after such a serious illness. You will always be able to rely on Mrs Cameron's exceptional ability to handle your affairs. She has turned previous losses into most commendable profits in the past five months. . . .'

The stiffness and formality of his speech caused Janthina to turn her head away so that the men might not see the smothered laughter in her face. It was all so proper!

She had hoped Cam would like Roland: it would be an advantage if he were to approve, or even welcome, repeated advisory visits, and Roland obviously had the same idea. Gradually he relaxed, made flattering observations about the rapid growth of the business due to Cam's remarkable ability – even complimented him on having found such a beautiful and clever wife.

Cam relaxed, too, and by five o'clock was asking where Mr Burrows intended staying the night. 'We have plenty of room at our house, haven't we, dear?' He smiled adoringly at Janthina. 'Why don't you stay with us, Mr Burrows?'

Janthina's heart leapt. 'Yes, Mr Burrows, please do.'

She watched the doubts cloud his face, waited anxiously until he smiled and nodded.

'Thank you very much. I do appreciate your offer and would be delighted to accept, if you are quite sure it won't be inconvenient.'

So when Roland had finished making notes for the legal documenting of the transfers with which he was to return next week for signatures, the three drove back to the house together.


While Susan served dinner, Cam suggested they should drop formalities and use Christian names. 'We hope this is only the beginning of a long and friendly business relationship.'

Coffee was served in the drawing room, after which they discussed the after-effects of the war on the British economy – until Susan announced that Mr Cameron's hot water was ready in his bedroom. 'Ten thirty already? The evening has flown. Will you excuse me, Roland, if I retire now? The doctors are still very strict about my bedtime,' he explained, adding, 'Fussing old hens.'

'Of course, of course. I do apologise for keeping you up so late. You too, er . . . Janthina. We should all go up, now.'

'No, quite unnecessary. Janty never goes up till at least eleven thirty. Real night owl, my wife. She'll give you some more coffee.' He picked up his newspaper and spectacles. 'I'll see you in the morning. Good night.'

They sat listening to the crackle of the fire in the grate and the sound of Cam's footsteps receding up the stairs.

'Everything all right?' Roland asked.

Janthina nodded. He was sitting in the corner of the sofa with his arm along the back, invitingly, and she had to will herself not to move, not to take up the invitation. 'How has it been with you?' she asked.

His eyes drifted away to the dying embers in the grate, then back to her face. 'Pretty grim,' he sighed.

'Then why did you come?'

'I couldn't help myself. I love you.'

'Has coming made it worse?'

'No. Eased it, rather.'

'And for me.' She got up and grasped the poker. 'Shall I stoke up the fire, a little? It's getting chilly.'

'Here, let me.' He tried to take it from her hand but somehow missed . . . and instead they were in each other's arms.

They kissed long and hungrily, holding, caressing, while all the time Janthina held the poker behind him, not wanting to break the magic moment by bending to replace it.

Roland laughed as they separated, seeing the weapon still in her hand. 'Come, give me that.'

'Do you really still want to build up the fire? Wouldn't it be warmer upstairs in bed?' she asked, shocked by her own boldness.

'Oh, God, darling, don't! How can I, in the man's own home?'

Janthina gave a cynical smile. 'The house he took from a sick man in payment of debts he, Cam, had encouraged the man to run up.'

'Really! But still that doesn't give me the right to. . . .'

'Cuckold him? Personally, I don't think we need give that another thought.'

'Why? What do you mean?'

'I've told you about his breaking his word over adopting Caroline – and cheating me over the five thousand pounds with which he built up the business; but there was something else, something enormous and horrible about which I have given my word to say nothing to anyone. That thing he did was appalling and criminal and the only reason I have not handed him over to the police is because he has suffered worse punishment over it in the past three years than anything a judge or jury could inflict. I only discovered the truth after he was taken ill. I was shocked, angry, bitter and terribly distressed . . . I will never get over it. Certainly, as I have explained to him and as he has accepted, I could never be a wife to him again – not in the full sense. I will never share a bedroom with him again, let alone a bed. I refuse ever to let him touch me. But we will continue living in the same house, appear in public together and present a united front for the benefit of the children and society in general.' The mystified expression on his face made her add, 'I'm sorry I can't tell you more. I have promised faithfully I will never tell another soul, not as long as he conducts himself properly, within the bounds I have set. And I intend to keep that promise.'

'And it was something bad enough for him to transfer a major block of shares to you from each of his companies?' Roland asked incredulously.

'Yes. I have evidence, of course, in a safe-deposit box in the bank, with instructions that the contents be handed over to the police if anything untoward were to happen to me.'

Roland gasped. 'You think he might . . .?'

'A man who has done what he has might consider anything.'

'My God!' He sat down again, heavily.

'Would you like a hot chocolate or something?'

Slowly he shook his head. 'No thanks.' He reached up to take her hand and hold it against his face. 'My poor darling – I had no idea. You always appear so serene and unruffled.'

She stroked the hair over his temple. 'So would you like me to build up the fire?' she asked, archly.

'Why bother?' He stood up again. 'Let's go to bed.'


It was heaven to be back in his arms again. They fell asleep, limbs twined together, after making love, and in the early hours of the morning they woke to make love again before he crept away to the spare room.


Trade picked up remarkably quickly as Easter and the opening of the new season approached. Orders for canned and bottled merchandise, dry goods, and wines and spirits were canvassed and taken by a personable young representative Janthina had hired for the purpose on a small salary and large commission. It was an arrangement which worked admirably, even earning favourable comments from Cam and, eventually, grudging appreciation from the managers of the wholesale and liquor companies and the grocery shops. There had been a pleasing response to advertisements in a variety of journals and newspapers, recommending the Grand and Dolphin hotels, and she watched the bookings chart with growing excitement.

The relationship with Cam was strange. Their attitudes towards each other ranged, for differing reasons, from anger, irritation, bitterness and resentment, through polite indifference to occasional muted appreciation or pleasant comments on one or the other's latest contribution at home or in the business.

The deposed husband and businessman was obviously making great efforts to impress his wife as well as their acquaintances. He worked in the office, carried out her requests on visits to her hotels and to the other companies and played the charming husband and host at Janthina's fortnightly dinner parties. She chose her guests with care, mixing good friends with political and business acquaintances, often stepping back to allow Cam the limelight. Her scheming worked wonders. Soon he was invited back onto a committee he had abandoned two years previously, and he was delighted to be asked to canvas for one of the contenders for the next mayoral elections. It was very satisfying that, whatever her private opinion of him, their children could once again have a respectable and respected father . . . in place of a drunken gambler.

As the Easter holidays approached, thoughts of Caroline were uppermost in her mind. She was now determined to reveal the truth to the girl – she had prevaricated long enough. Caroline was talking about a career in art, asking if she might go on to art school after leaving Brighton at the end of the summer term . . . time was running out.

Ruth and Freddie and Giles came to stay with them for Easter, which was wonderful but time-consuming. It allowed little chance of a tête-à-tête, and Janthina found herself becoming more and more tense as days passed by without the opportunity she sought. So it had to be created.

'Caroline, dear, will you come down to the office with me, please? The pastrycook at the café has made us a Simnel cake and hot cross buns and one or two other goodies for Easter. I would appreciate your help in collecting them.'

'Of course, I'd be delighted, Auntie. Shall we ask Giles to come too?'

'I'd rather not. We will need all the back seat for the food. Anyway, men are not very good at handling delicacies,' Janthina teased the boy, who was walking down the hallway, hopefully.

They drove in silence, parked outside the boutique, and once inside, Caroline headed straight for the stairs.

'Would you come into the office for a moment, first?' Janthina asked, and led her through, unlocking the doors as she went. She knew John would be with Cam at the Grand for the whole day and they would be entirely private. She closed the door behind them. 'Come and sit down for a few minutes, will you? I've been wanting to talk to you for ages but we never seem to have the chance at home, and you are away so much, now.'

Caroline sat on the edge of the chair in front of the desk, looking puzzled and rather apprehensive. 'Y-es? What did you want to talk about?'

'Your parents.'

'I thought I had been told all there was to know about them.'

Janthina avoided the big desk chair . . . it would make the situation seem too formal, so instead she perched on the corner of the desk itself. 'Don't look so worried! Just sit back and relax; this may take some time.'

271

Caroline sat back, but looked far from relaxed.

'It has been very difficult for me to decide when to tell you all this and you may think, when you hear what I have to say, that I have waited too long. However, I hope you will understand my difficulties and appreciate why I have delayed.' She took a deep breath. 'Caroline, I am not your aunt. . . .'

'Well, that doesn't matter too much,' Caroline smiled. 'No one could have been kinder to me.'

'You must prepare yourself for a shock. You see, the fact is . . . I am your mother.'

Her daughter continued to stare at her, almost as though she thought her aunt was developing psychological problems.

'Your Aunt Ruth and I are sisters,' Janthina continued, 'but there never was a third sister, really. She and her husband were invented purely to give you a surname other than mine.'

'You mean Morton isn't really my name at all?'

'No.'

'Then what is it?'

'McKenzie. You see, your father and I were never married.'

'My . . . father? Then he wasn't Uncle Cam, either?'

'No.'

'Then who was he?'

Her mother hesitated. Should she tell, or not? She had turned this question over in her mind dozens of times without making a decision.

'If I tell you, will you promise me faithfully that you won't breathe it to a soul? You are eighteen, now, and old enough to keep a confidence.'

'I promise,' Caroline said impatiently.

'The man who is the present Earl of Frey.'

'Who?' It was all too incredible for belief.

Janthina's heart pounded with excitement. This was the moment she had waited for, for . . . how many years? Over fifteen. Waited to re-establish the mother-daughter relationship she had been forced by Cam to relinquish . . . the beloved little girl she adored.

Caroline continued to stare at her in blank amazement.

'It is true, my darling. You ask Aunt Ruth.' She waited for the girl's expression to soften into joy, longed to hold her in her arms and say all the things she had reluctantly held back for so long.

But Caroline's expression remained coldly incredulous.

I must give her time, more explanation, Janthina decided, and launched into the story. There were many details it seemed more

272

prudent to omit, but the outline and necessary facts were recounted.

Caroline didn't move a muscle throughout, just sat and stared.

'I so longed to acknowledge you as my legal daughter, show you all the mother love and affection I feel.' She sighed again and reached impulsively for her daughter's hand. 'You can understand my dilemma, can't you?'

'No!' Caroline shouted, snatching her hand away. 'No, I cannot! How could you? How could you be so cruel and unfeeling all these years?'

'Cruel? Unfeeling?' Janthina whispered, horrified.

'Yes! Cruel! Why, it could almost be described as mental sadism!' Her face was twisted with anger.

Janthina shook her head in disbelief. This couldn't be happening. 'Caroline! I don't understand. I don't know what you're talking about.' She felt sick and dazed, unable to think.

'I'm talking about a mother who deliberately rejects her daughter, who subjects her to the miserable upbringing I've had, who makes her daughter feel like an outsider, an orphaned outsider, not belonging to the family, the household: who allows her to be subjected to all the meanness and cruelty of her half-brothers and sisters . . . no, sister. Alexandra was never cruel.' The girl paused for breath, panting and crying.

'Caroline! Stop it! I did no such thing. You're imagining. . . .'

'I'm not. Flora and Angus were horrible. . . .'

'I was never aware. . . .'

'You must have been blind, then! I can remember when I was quite little coming to you for love and affection and being pushed away by Flora. She said you were her mama, not mine. I didn't have one.'

'I knew Flora was jealous of the affection I showed you, from time to time, and I scolded her when she was. . . .'

'Precious little good that did!'

'Caroline! Don't. Please don't go on like this. Try to understand that I love you. . . .'

'Love me! Love me! Yet you've sat back all these years and allowed me to be teased and tormented and bullied. Don't you realise I was always living on charity? I had no right to the bed I slept in, the clothes you bought me, the very food I ate? Flora and Angus claimed the right to walk into my bedroom whenever they liked, they took my key, but I was never allowed to set foot in theirs. Flora would take anything of mine she fancied, because I had no right to it, and they would both take my sweets and chocolate. They loved to make a fool of me. Remember that party you gave for Uncle Joseph and Uncle Simon?

273

Didn't you know that Flora and Angus had deliberately tripped me and made me fall with the salver of canapés? Weren't you aware of the hell they gave me if I allowed them to see you give me any affection?' Caroline was shaking and sobbing, her lovely face swollen and reddened with tears and misery.

Janthina stood beside her daughter's chair, held the unresisting girl in her arms. 'My darling! I can hardly believe it. Why did you never tell me? Why were you always so cold and distant?' She was sobbing too.

'Cold! Wouldn't you be cold if you had always been totally denied love and affection? I've had to grow up without them while watching *your* children being kissed and petted every day.' Caroline blew her nose on an inadequate lace handkerchief, ignoring her mother's closeness.

'But I couldn't let it be known that you were my daughter, that you were illegitimate,' Janthina argued, desperately. 'I had to keep it a secret . . .'

'Well, I'm afraid you kept your secret too well.' The girl stood up, pushing her mother aside.

'Caroline! Please don't go,' Janthina pleaded. 'Wait, let's talk. I am dreadfully sorry I have allowed you to be hurt so much. I had no idea. Please, darling. Give me a chance to make it all right.'

Caroline stood with her hand on the doorknob. 'You're joking! How can you possibly make anything right, now? I've just been one big embarrassing mistake to you, haven't I? Ever since the moment of my conception. The greatest pity is that you didn't allow me to be adopted. At least I could have grown up in a household with people I could call Mama and Papa instead of Aunt and Uncle. People who really wanted me and would have treated me as a daughter on equal terms with their own children, whether or not they were adopted, rather than letting me feel like a leper.' Seeing the tears on her mother's face she paused in the doorway. 'You may be feeling miserable now, but just try to imagine the years of misery you've given me.' Then she walked out, not bothering to close the doors behind her.

Janthina stood staring at the empty doorway, unblinking, the salty moisture drying on her face.

No more tears came. She was too numb to weep.

# 3

THE SUMMER of 1921 proved to be a record season for hotel visitors to Whitehaven. Every room in both the Grand and the Dolphin was booked throughout July and August, the peak months, and even after the Easter rush was over, May and June were busy. Most of the other hotels were doing well, too, thereby increasing the turnover of the other Cameron companies.

Janthina, Cam and John were kept very busy overseeing each operation, and Roland came down from London once a month to keep an eye on the book-keeping. They all knew this was not really his field, but his visits were accepted by Cam as a friendly and helpful gesture; he apparently suspected nothing.

Meanwhile, Janthina remained terribly disturbed by the now open conflict between Caroline and herself. Everyone noticed it, even Cam who overheard a petulant jibe from the girl when she returned for her first weekend exeat of the new term.

'Do I understand that Caroline is not as enchanted as you had hoped, to find she has you for a mother?' he asked with a grin.

'She is finding the relationship hard to accept,' Janthina admitted, adding irritably, 'for which I have you to thank. I think I had better tell the other children while they are here this weekend.'

'Why? What for? They don't need to know.'

'Of course they do. They must know and accept Caroline as their sister eventually.'

'They are my children and I don't wish them to be told.' Cam glared at her aggressively.

'Because it follows that they will find out what a worm you've been? I understand your reluctance but you should have thought about that more than sixteen years ago.'

It was the first topic of conflict they had had for some weeks, apart from business, and he was suddenly aware of the way she looked at him. The savage retort died on his lips.

'I suppose, as always, you will have to have your own way,' he grumbled, 'but I intend to be there when you tell them.'

*     *     *

Apart from Caroline who, as usual, had remained in her bedroom, the family were all together in the drawing room before dinner.

'There is something important I wish to tell you children. May I have your attention, please?' Janthina's face was slightly flushed and her mouth dry.

Ian left the table in the window where he was repairing a wooden model of a battleship, to come and sit on the arm of the settee. Flora and Angus looked up from their reading, saw Janty's eyes on the open books on their laps, and closed them.

'It concerns Caroline,' their mother began.

Flora's tongue clicked and her eyes rolled up to the ceiling. 'We are having to put up with a lot of peculiar behaviour from our cousin, lately,' she remarked.

Janthina was nettled. 'This is the point. She has only just recently been told that she is not your cousin . . . she is your sister.'

'Sister!' The three young people chorused.

'No,' Cam snapped, 'your half-sister.'

'What do you mean?' Flora demanded, looking from one to the other.

'She is my daughter,' Janthina replied.

'But . . . then who is her father?' Flora persisted, 'I didn't know you were married before.'

'I wasn't. And it doesn't matter who her father is.'

The sharp-featured girl turned to grin at her brother. 'Oh,' she murmured with unnecessary emphasis, 'so that means she's a bas. . . .'

'It means that she is my eldest child and therefore senior to all of you,' Janthina interrupted angrily.

Cam opened his mouth to retort, saw Janty's expression and closed it again.

'I don't believe it!' Flora's eyes flashed. 'It's not fair!'

'I think it's very fair and just, considering how grossly unpleasant you have been to her all these years.'

'Unpleasant?'

'Mean. Despicable. Hateful. Call it what you will, you have succeeded in making her life a misery. But I assure you it will never happen again.'

'Papa!' Flora appealed. 'Say something.'

Cam shifted uncomfortably in his chair, feeling his wife's gaze on him. 'Your mother is right. Caroline is your step-sister.'

'Then why were we always told she was only a cousin?' Angus asked.

'So that people wouldn't know she was a bas. . . .'

'Flora! Stop it! I want you to understand that this matter is strictly confidential and you are being told now because I think, and hope, you are old enough to keep it that way.' Janthina looked hard at the girl and went on, 'Of course, if I ever discovered that you had breathed a word of this to anyone, Flora, your pocket money and dress allowance would cease immediately and you would be removed from school and put into a clerical job to earn your own living.'

'Papa! You wouldn't let her!' Flora flung herself onto the carpet at her father's feet.

'Don't be silly. There's no question of that happening because you're not going to tell anyone, are you?' Cam gave Janthina a look of pure vitriol as he spoke.

Flora's thin lips pressed tightly together as she peered from face to face through narrowed lids. 'I see!' she said significantly. Slowly she got up, glared at each parent in turn and walked out of the room.

'Don't see what she's on about. I'm glad Caro is our sister; wish we'd known before, don't you, Angus?' Ian was clearly mystified by his sister's exit.

'Can't see that it makes any difference,' Angus shrugged. He picked up his book, 'Is that all you wanted to say, Mama?'

Janty sighed. 'Yes dear, that's all.'


Twice during the summer term Caroline asked if she might invite a boyfriend from Brighton College for the weekend. Janthina was reluctant to have him, partly because it 'just wasn't done' and also because she had never met the boy. But she was afraid of upsetting Caroline even more, so agreed. Stephen Lewis proved to be a very nice boy, far nicer than Janty had dared to hope. He was very grateful for the Camerons' hospitality, explaining that at the end of term he would be leaving school and going out to spend two years sheep-farming with his godfather in Australia. Stephen was enthusiastic about Caroline's art and when he learned that the pictures of Château de Berenac and of Caroline as a small girl were painted by Janthina herself, he exclaimed that the talent obviously ran in the family and Caroline should definitely go to art school.

Even a blind man could tell that Caroline was highly infatuated with Stephen, and he with her. She was delighted by his encouragement and Janthina was happy to agree that Caroline should continue to study the subject.

Once, Janthina found them kissing passionately when she returned to the house unexpectedly early, and she wondered if she shouldn't ensure that they were always chaperoned. But as it was Stephen's second visit and he would soon be leaving the country she decided to do nothing that might antagonise the girl. This Caroline seemed to appreciate, and the tension between them eased slightly throughout the summer holidays.

During the summer they moved into the new house. It was a lovely old Tudor manor, low and rambling, with leaded windows, high-pointed gables and beautiful oak beams and floors. The huge hallway with vast granite fireplace was panelled in natural oak, but the panelling in the drawing room and dining room had been painted white, making the rooms brighter, setting off the gay chintz covers and moss-green carpets. French windows led out into rose gardens beyond which, through the ancient pines, waves could be seen breaking at the foot of the headland. Upstairs, Janthina had her private suite – a turquoise and white bedroom with a matching bathroom and small sitting room where she hoped, one day, she might have time to sit in the window, sewing, watching the gulls wheeling across the garden and down to the sea.

The overall success of the Cameron companies encouraged Janthina to think of the New Excelsior, and at the end of September work proceeded on site clearance, while a team of London architects, recommended by Roland, drew up plans for a new construction. The Dolphin remained ideal for visitors who enjoyed old-world charm, dark-stained beams and studded leather, who liked to sit by the light of old ships' lanterns in the bar and swop stories with local characters. The Grand appealed to a different type: people who enjoyed dressing and eating well, liked to be seen in smart surroundings but without having to pay too highly. So Janthina decided that the new hotel must be of top-class luxury for those visitors who wanted only the absolute ultimate and were prepared to pay any price to get it. The décor and fittings in every room should be exceptional, every bedroom being complete with its own private bathroom en suite.

Cam was horrified. 'Really, my dear, that is going too far! One bathroom to every four bedrooms is more than adequate.'

'I'm not aiming at adequacy, only total luxury. I know it will be expensive both to build and to maintain, but I intend this hotel to be far, far better than anything Whitehaven has seen before.'

Plans were spread across the office desk, and Cam and herself bent over them discussing details with the architects, when the phone rang in the outer office.

John answered and then called, 'It's for you, Mrs Cameron.'

'Who is it?'

'Mr Gordon.'

'Ruth!' Janthina squealed and rushed to take the phone. 'Yes, Freddie, yes. Oh, good. I'll drive over right away.' She returned to the three men. 'I'm sorry, but I'm afraid I must leave you. Cam, I'm driving over to Brighton. Ruth is in labour.'

He smiled and nodded. 'Splendid. Drive carefully and give them all my regards.' He was quite happy to be left in charge, for once.

Ruth and Freddie's little girl, Maxine, was born on September 19th, 1921. Considering she was only her second child, and Ruth was now thirty-nine, the birth was not too troublesome, though her mother was very weary afterwards. Giles came down from Sandhurst to meet his half-sister and congratulate his mother and step-father, while Freddie himself was so overwhelmed with excitement that when Janthina finally returned to Whitehaven, two days later, she left him still popping champagne corks.


After a tearful farewell to Stephen when he sailed off to the southern hemisphere, Caroline settled happily into her London art school and when she came home for Christmas, Janthina noticed how much she had quietened down, seeming almost reluctant to go out with her old crowd of friends; her time was divided equally between drawing and writing to Stephen, though she appeared to be penning far more letters than she received.


The New Excelsior grew at amazing speed, Cam and Janty visiting the site nearly every day. Cam presumed everyone accepted him as the owner, and was quite happy to accept the situation though he learned to be wary of taking decisions not previously approved by his wife. But he was being over-presumptuous. Although everyone from the architects to the stonemasons treated him with the respect his titular position demanded, for some reason all major problems were referred to Mrs Cameron, and, between themselves, the work force always spoke of her as 'the boss'. They preferred her cool-headedness and clear analysis of each situation, whether financial, structural, or purely aesthetic, and after their initial reluctance to accept a woman employer, soon came to appreciate her businesslike approach.

Likewise in the Grand, Dolphin and the shops and wholesale companies. Everyone was aware when Cam was taken ill that his drinking and neglect had brought his business empire to its knees – as they were aware of who was responsible for saving it. The new manager at the Grand was strict but popular and the staff knew Mrs Cameron had appointed him. They enjoyed her almost daily visits. A chambermaid, summoned to a bedroom for which she was responsible, knew that if the room had been cleaned thoroughly she would be praised and thanked; if it was not, the need for more thoroughness and how to achieve it would be kindly but firmly explained. If she had already received such an explanation and Mrs Cameron was still dissatisfied, there would be a firm but gentle warning; and where a warning had already been given, then Mrs Cameron would quietly explain that she felt the job needed someone with more strength and application and would thereupon instruct the manager to pay her off and replace her. This method applied to cooks and clerks, waiters and doormen – everyone – and the managers of the hotels and shops knew it applied to them as well. Hotel guests enjoyed her visits and enquiries as to their comfort, and welcomed the whole Cameron family for Sunday lunches at the Grand or Dolphin each week. They appreciated the tall, dignified woman's uncanny memory for names and faces, and felt quite honoured by her attentiveness.

The roof was completed on the New Excelsior by late March and as the exterior work was finished and the doors and windows closed out the elements, so the detailed work on the interior began. It was fortunate that Janthina had had the previous season with which to establish a good working relationship with the various company managers so that she could rely on them during this period of increased involvement with the new hotel.

Roland's visits continued to be a great joy; it was strange how well they had both adapted to the restrictions of their relationship, anticipating and enjoying their monthly reunions, learning to bear the separations without anguish.

Angus had no doubt in his mind about the career he wanted. 'I will be in the Lower Sixth next term,' he told his parents, 'and I will have to study very hard for the next two years so that I can go on to university to read law.'

280

'For heaven's sake, Angus,' Cam exploded. 'Haven't you got over that silly idea yet?'

'Silly? What do you mean?' Janthina demanded.

'Well, isn't it silly for the boy to waste all that time and effort when there's a ready-made business waiting for him to step into? We want him to study accounts and hotel management, not law!'

'It's not a matter of what we want, at all. It's a matter of what Angus wants,' Janthina said, quietly.

Cam saw the uptilt of her chin, a flash of green in her eyes – warning signs. But this time he was not going to give in. He had always set his heart on having his son in the business; she could not expect to have her own way in everything. 'I agree, if what he wants is sensible. But there is no sense whatever in his turning his back on the massive opportunity offered in the Cameron Companies, just to do something he happens to fancy more.'

Angus sat uncomfortably on the edge of his chair, looking from one to the other. He had always known his chances of doing what he wanted with his life were slim.

'Law is sensible. Whoever you are and whatever your parents might wish for you, that fact is indisputable. Angus is quite adult enough to understand that whilst the business would be easier to step into, and more lucrative, that is not everything. Law is a fascinating study in which he has always been interested. Therefore I think that is what he must do.'

'Rubbish. I don't agree.'

'Angus, I think it might be a good idea if you left us to discuss this matter alone.' Janthina's voice was calm, but there was an icy look on her face which both man and boy recognised.

'Yes, Mama.' Angus got up and left the room. A few years ago he would have despaired, but for some time now, things had changed between his parents. . . .

Cam opened his mouth to speak as soon as the door closed, but Janthina held up her hand. 'No, Cam, there is nothing more to be said. . . .'

'There damned well is!' he snarled. 'I didn't send that boy to an expensive school so that he could just turn his back on me and go off on his own. He owes it to us. . . .'

'He owes us nothing! No child owes its parents anything. He didn't ask to be born, or for an expensive education. That was our choice. He is an individual in his own right, not an extension of ourselves. He has a God-given right to choose his own career, order his own destiny, as, in due course, he will to select a wife.'

'The cost of his school fees was an investment . . .'

'The price of slavery?'

'No!' he shouted.

'Then what else if, having accepted that standard of education, he automatically becomes your creature to command, allowed no free will of his own?'

'There's no point in having children, in that case. Certainly not in giving them a costly education.'

'Quite,' she acknowledged. 'I couldn't agree with you more. Any man, or woman, who only wants children for enslavement or to satisfy their own egos should never have them!'

'Stop talking about enslavement. That's ridiculous.'

'On the contrary, it's ridiculous to dress up the situation with any other term. If, by use of mental, physical, financial or emotional pressure, or any other means, one is forced to act against one's will, that is enslavement.' Janthina got up and went to the cocktail cupboard. 'Anyway, I don't intend to discuss it any further. I've told you I would like our son to go to Cambridge University, which is what he wishes, and I think we should discuss it with his headmaster at the beginning of next term. Will you have a sherry?'

The famous Cameron charm was swept away by anger. 'Bugger you, you arrogant bitch! What am I, if I'm not your slave?' And he slammed out of the room.

She supposed he did have a point there!

When Angus returned to the drawing room later, his mother smiled up from her book.

'Hello, darling, come and sit down.' And in answer to the unspoken query on his face she added, 'Don't look so worried! Of course you are going to Cambridge. Why don't you have a chat with Mr Burrows, next time he's here? He is our lawyer, you know, and he may be able to offer some useful tips.'


A letter from Uncle William arrived shortly before Angus, Flora and Ian returned to Brighton. Janthina, who had maintained an occasional correspondence with him, read his letter aloud at the breakfast table. In it he described the farm, measured in square miles rather than acres, the people, his wife, sons and employees and neighbours, and eulogised about the beauty of the Australian countryside and its wealth of wildlife. He believed there was a lot in Australia to interest young English people and also felt that young Australians should know about life in England. He finished by suggesting that one of Janthina's children

282

might like to correspond with his eldest son, Bernard, who was not that much older than them.

Cam and Janty looked dubiously, first at each other, then at their sons, who stared significantly into their porridge.

It was Flora who spoke up. 'I'll write to him. Lots of the girls at school have pen friends.' At fifteen she remained flat-chested and sharp-tongued and although she could make herself quite attractive when she made the effort to curl her hair, dress prettily, and smile, she all too often forgot. Which may well have been why she was painfully lacking in young admirers and spent so much time alone. From time to time Janty had initiated 'cosy chats' during which she attempted to explain the 'do-as-you-would-be-done-by' principle, but Flora was not a good listener, and continued to nip promising friendships in the bud with her acid remarks. Here was an opportunity for a friendship to develop if only her pen could be better controlled than her tongue.

Her first letter to Bernard was posted before leaving Whitehaven. In it she told him about herself, her school, her family, even mentioning her 'Cousin' Caroline and her boyfriend, Stephen Lewis, saying that one day they might meet, as he was now 'down under'.

Months later, on receiving Uncle William's Christmas letter, when all the family were back from school for the holidays, Janthina asked if Bernard had replied.

'Of course,' the girl answered airily. 'I gave him my school address and he, er . . . wrote me a very nice letter. In fact, he sounds like a very nice person. He says they hope I will go out and visit them, one day.'

'Would you like to?' Caroline asked.

'Rather! I'd love to. Oh, and by the way, I told him we knew someone called Stephen Lewis who'd gone out there. By an amazing coincidence, Bernard says he has met him, and was actually invited to Stephen's engagement party. He said that apparently there was some girl all lined up for him who he'd been corresponding with for years, and they fell for each other immediately. Oh! What's up, Caroline? Didn't you know?'

Caroline was white as a sheet.

Janthina could have wrung Flora's neck. She knew darned well that she had planned to give the announcement maximum impact. Meant it to hurt. 'Are you sure you're not mistaken? May I see the letter?'

'Of course!' Flora left the dining room to fetch it from her bedroom.

Hope was reflected in Caroline's face as she watched her mother glance over the pages to the appropriate paragraph, but faded as she read Janthina's expression. She excused herself abruptly and left the room, watched by her smiling half-sister.

'Flora!' Janty snapped as Caroline's footsteps receded. 'Why are you so nasty? You know jolly well that she was keen on Stephen.'

'Really?' Flora exclaimed innocently. 'I had no idea. I thought he was just one of the crowd.'

'Flora!' Janty shook her head sadly. 'Why? Why do you so resent Caroline?'

'I don't know what you're talking about, Mama. I think I'll go to my room.'

'A good idea,' Janthina retorted, unable to contain her anger.

Flora made a dignified exit with a pinched and pained expression on her face.

Thereafter, Caroline emerged from her room for meals only, often red-eyed and sullen. Even on Christmas Day, when they were joined by Ruth, Freddie, Giles and little Maxine, she could scarcely raise a smile. The phone kept ringing and Janthina overheard her refuse invitations; she was heavy-hearted and longed to comfort the girl.

As the Gordons were staying over until after the New Year, she enlisted Giles's help to persuade Caroline to go out and enjoy the festivities, and Caroline succumbed. Looking beautiful and unnaturally cheerful she sailed out of the house escorted by her favourite cousin.

Watching them go, the tall, gorgeous pair of youngsters so dear to her heart, Janthina had no indication of the disastrous effect her interference was to have.

There were other people, other things to think about. Ian wanted to tell her about the sports scene at Brighton College; Angus chose a private moment to discuss the subjects he would take for Cambridge entrance. And no sooner had they all returned to their respective studies than Roland arrived – to make love to her.

Builders and architects required directions, the various managers needed guidance in anticipation of the coming season, and the exquisite New Excelsior, with its marbled floors, gilded mirrors and specially designed carpets and furnishings, risen resplendent from those fatal ashes, was finally ready for opening at the beginning of Easter week.

Janthina was sheathed in stiff cream satin, with a matched suite of emeralds gleaming from neck, ears and wrist. Her rich, soft hair was set in waves close to her head with not one wisp out of place as she helped Cam with his bow tie, fastened Flora's necklet, and re-made the parting in Ian's hair. She was proud of her family; they all looked splendid and the only disappointment was Caroline's failure to arrive home in time for the opening reception. It was difficult to imagine where she might be; she had been expected hours ago.

They were assembled in the drawing room when Cam remarked on the girl's absence.

'What on earth are you talking about, Papa?' Flora exclaimed. 'Caroline arrived this morning. She's been here for hours.'

'She has? Well, why haven't we seen her? Where is she?' Janty demanded.

'In her room. And she's locked the door,' Flora replied, dramatically.

Janthina sighed. 'I'll go up to her. If I'm not down in five minutes, you go on without me. It will be a bit of a crush in the car, anyway. Perhaps you could drive back to fetch me, Angus? And be sure you don't let them start the proceedings until I get there,' she added. She left her gold filigree evening purse and blonde mink stole on a chairback, and went upstairs.

Reluctantly, Caroline turned back the key in the lock, and Janthina gasped with horror at the sight of the girl's blotched and swollen face.

'My dear! What is it?'

Caroline shook her head and turned away.

'Please! It won't help if you refuse to tell me. Are you in trouble? What is it? You know there is nothing in the world you can't tell me.'

The blonde head moved slowly until the sad, violet eyes met her mother's. There was a shuddering gasp before she said, 'I'm sorry, Janty. I'm afraid history has repeated itself. I'm going to have a baby.'

Janthina's arms encircled her daughter immediately, the girl's tears soaking the shoulder of her cream satin gown. After a few minutes the sobbing ceased and she said, 'Come, blow your nose and wash your face, then you can tell me all about it.'

'No. Not now. You mustn't miss the opening ceremony. I'll be all right. Have you got an aspirin or something? My head is bursting.'

'Have you eaten today?'

'No.'

'Then I'll pop down and fetch you something. The opening can wait.'

'I think it would be easier if you were angry,' Caroline said seriously.

'Sorry I can't oblige. Remember, I've walked this path myself.'

'You're wrong. You, at least, were in love. I wasn't.'

Janthina stood by the door. 'When did it happen?'

'On New Year's Eve. I got drunk.'

'Who with?'

'Roger Sands. He'd had a row with Betty and was in much the same mood as myself.'

'Does he know?'

'Yes. He says he'll marry me.'

'What did you say?'

'Yes.'

'But you don't love him!'

'No.'

'Then why . . .?'

'Because my child is not going to be brought up without parents,' she snapped savagely.

Her mother winced. 'I see. Well, I'll go down and get you some food,' she said, and left the room, mind reeling.

She smiled and nodded, shook hands, endless hands, graciously accepting adulatory comments and congratulations, for although most people still assumed that Cam owned the hotels, everyone was aware that she was responsible for the magnificent surroundings in which they now were.

This was her finest hour. The moment when Janthina the Shell emerged from the storms of her life, having changed, adapted, strengthened her will and determination, now heading a string of thriving companies and hotels, the single most successful business person, male or female, in the county. Lights flashed as photographers jostled and the lump in her throat was swallowed again and again as she maintained her happy pose.

'Are you all right?' Roland had sidled up, smiling, so as not to betray his concern. Only he recognised the trauma behind her pose as she nodded and said, 'Fine, thanks.' She was grateful for his presence, though she could confide nothing yet. He, and everyone else, would know in due course.

Having decided against pseudo-French grandeur, Janthina and her architects and interior designers had followed a theme of contemporary elegance for the New Excelsior, with examples of Ancient Egyptian art giving an exotic atmosphere. The floor of the foyer was chequered in large squares of black and white marble, the central carpet bordered in Egyptian frieze, and black, sharp-eared dogs lay en couchant on tall marble pedestals guarding the main entrance. It was pure luck. No one could have guessed how popular the Egyptian theme would prove to be when, later in the year, the Egyptologist Howard Carter stunned the world with his discoveries in the tomb of King Tutenkhamen.

After the opening ceremony and speeches, as everyone milled through the rooms eating, drinking, and gossiping, Janthina told Cam she had a bad headache and would retire.

At home she hurried upstairs.

Caroline's eyes were dry, and once again masked by the old, hard, icy stare that chilled Janthina to the bone.

'Did you manage to eat your supper?'

'Yes.'

'Feeling a little better now?'

'No.'

She sat on the edge of the bed. 'Have you and Roger discussed any details about when you intend to marry?'

Caroline's shoulders lifted slightly in a shrug. 'As soon as possible, I suppose.'

'What does Roger do for a living?'

'His uncle is an accountant and Roger is his articled clerk.'

'Then he isn't earning anything! What will you live on?'

'Charity, I suppose.' Her voice sounded hopelessly indifferent.

'I'll help, of course.'

'Thanks.'

'When does he hope to qualify?'

'Next year.'

Instinctively Janthina moved towards her daughter to demonstrate her love and understanding. 'Darling. What's done is done. There is no point in crying over spilt milk.' She reached out for Caroline's hand – but it was quickly withdrawn.

'How come you're home so early? I can't believe the reception is over already.'

'I was worried about you.'

'Forget it. I'll survive. Why don't you go back?' Lying back against her pillows she picked up a magazine and started turning the pages. It was a pointed dismissal.

Janthina persisted. 'Please don't hide away in your shell. Talk to me. Tell me what happened – everything.'

Caroline managed a cool smile. 'What is there to tell? Stephen has fallen in love with someone else. I allowed myself to be persuaded out on New Year's Eve where everyone was being fearfully jolly . . . except Roger and me. We drank our sorrows together and . . . well . . . we just finished up in bed in one of the rooms at the Grand.'

'Was that your first time?' Janthina dared to ask.

Caroline didn't seem to mind. 'No. I had slept with Stephen. It had felt so normal and natural a thing to do, feeling the way we did, or rather, as I thought we did, about each other.' She buried her face in her hands. 'With Roger it was meaningless.'

287

They were silent until her mother asked, 'What is he like? I've never met him.'

'A cross between a Teddy Bear and a puppy. Sweet and cuddly but when he ought to make up his mind about something he'll sit down and scratch.'

Janthina laughed. 'Nice, in other words.'

'Yes. I suppose I should be grateful for that.'

'Did Stephen write, eventually, and tell you about his engagement?'

'No, rather rotten of him, don't you think? I should have suspected something, I suppose, when his letters got shorter and less . . . affectionate, and fewer.'

'Did you write to him again, after you knew?'

'Only to tell him not to bother to write and explain. I said I'd burn anything I got from him, unopened.'

'My poor Caroline.' Janthina was close to tears.

The girl turned her head away, eyes closed. 'For God's sake don't start me off again,' she sighed.


The wedding took place in Whitehaven Registry Office at the end of April, soon after Angus, Flora and Ian returned to school. Cam, predictably, had said, 'Like mother like daughter' when he heard the news, passing on the information to Flora who had enjoyed making endless quips on her half-sister's condition. Cam and Janthina, and Roger's parents, were the only people present, other than the registrar, and as there was to be no honeymoon the unhappy couple moved into the two rooms in an unfashionable area of town which was to be their home.

Caroline's bitterness increased with the size of her abdomen. She was too resentful and angry to spend any time with Cam and Janty, and Roger was too embarrassed, so they stayed at home, replacing tired paint and wallpaper, preparing for the unwelcome event.


The New Excelsior was an immediate success. Even Cam had to admit that his wife's decision to aim at the top was a good one, especially when the hotel booking clerk told them how many would-be residents asked for private bathrooms.

Janthina, busy as ever during the holiday season, regretted seeing so little of Caroline. She didn't want to force herself on them with repeated visits to their home, but did ask that they come to dinner once a week. Before one such dinner at the beginning of the school holidays, Janthina lectured her three younger children, particularly Flora, threatening them with dire consequences if there were any unkind remarks made to either their sister or Roger. Conversation was restrained throughout the meal, but tended to relax over coffee as Janthina fed in a succession of 'safe' topics for discussion. Later, she could have kicked herself for unwittingly mentioning her latest letter from Uncle William. It prompted Cam to ask Flora if she still corresponded with Bernard.

'Oh, yes, regularly. In fact,' she added to Caroline, who was standing at the sideboard refilling coffee cups, 'I meant to tell you that Bernard said he met Stephen Lewis at a wedding at Easter. Remember he said last year that Stephen was engaged?' Janthina frowned at Flora, trying to get her off the painful topic, but the girl didn't appear to notice. 'Well, he says he'd got the name wrong. It was a chap called Steve Davis who'd got engaged, and it was at his . . .'

There was a crash of breaking coffee cups as Caroline fell.

Again history repeated itself . . . Janthina's daughter had fainted.

And all over a stupid mistake.


Jonathan arrived in October. He was adored by his maternal grandmother from the start, but she was constantly upset by his petulant crying, sure it was due to his parents' indifference. He was not getting the loving he needed.

The marriage never stood a chance. Roger pined for Betty; Caroline just resented everything and everybody, including her son. It was an insoluble, tragic situation, forever distracting Janthina from her work, causing grief to etch deep new lines in her lovely face.

Cam regarded the situation as a sort of Divine Retribution for what Janthina had done to him, and sometimes she wondered if he wasn't right. Her only solace was in the comforting arms of her lover – and that was so seldom, now.

Roland's professional services were in increasing demand in Whitehaven, friends and associates of the Camerons requesting his assistance until he found himself needed more in the seaside resort than in London.

The spring of 1924 was hard and cold. Janthina nestled into Roland's arms as the night winds shrieked under the eaves, hurling intermittent hail and sleet at the windows. There was obviously something on his mind, judging by the lack of response to her stroking fingers.

'Come on, tell me. Get it off your chest,' she teased.

He kissed her hair. 'My gauge has given me away, has it?' He sighed and sat up, bunching the pillows behind him.

She sat up too, and waited.

'Events have rather overtaken us, I'm afraid, which are going to change things rather, some to the good, some bad.'

She looked at him, but said nothing.

'I have mentioned several times how much business has built up here in Whitehaven since I have been visiting you regularly.' He paused.

'Yes. Go on.'

'The senior partners have asked me to open up a branch office here – come and live here.'

'Oh, Roland! How wonderful.' She sat up in bed, eyes dancing.

'We-ell, in a way. We will certainly be able to see a lot more of each other. But there is another less pleasant aspect. . . .'

'What?'

'I will no longer have an excuse to come and stay with you, once I have a house of my own, here.'

'But how else can we . . .?'

'Quite, we can't.'

'Surely we can work out something.'

'I don't see how it is possible without starting tongues wagging.'

A few months later they lay side by side whispering through the brief darkness of a July night which they realised could be their last foreseeable one together.

'Can you bear it?' Janty asked.

'No. But I suppose I will.'

'Perhaps we could arrange to meet abroad, some time.'

'Perhaps. But if we hope for that we will find ourselves just living on dreams. Better if we adapt to the situation, and enjoy, day by day, what we can. Then, if an opportunity arises, we'll take it.'

'I love you.'

'I love you, too.'

'It will be a terrible exercise in self-discipline to see you and never touch you.' Her head was on his chest, listening to the steady throb of his heart, while her fingers sifted through the hair on his groin, to grasp him and feel the hardening response.

'Yes,' he sighed, a cool breath against her forehead. 'We'll only be able to shake hands and kiss under the mistletoe at Christmas.'

'Not quite the same.' She gripped him fiercely, moving her hand, feeling the thrill shuddering through him.

'Will you go back to sharing a room with Cam?'

She sat bolt upright. 'No! I've told you. I won't ever let him touch me again.'

'And you still won't tell me why.'

She hesitated, then said, 'No, I promised him I would tell no one.'

'Fair enough.'

The moon was full that night and the air still and warm. They lay naked, with the bedclothes thrown back, enjoying the magic and mysteries of each other's bodies in the pale silver light. Neither could bear to sleep, to waste a single moment, luxuriating in almost continuous love-making until the early sunrise forced them apart.

Roland and Michael moved to Whitehaven in early September, and it was Cam who suggested that Janty arrange a surprise house-warming party for them. Roland had already established a number of local friends and the party was not difficult to organise. Everyone took a present, a bottle of wine and a contribution to the evening's banquet, and the Cameron cars – Janty now having her own – arrived laden with people and parcels, jugs of soup, a huge ham and a bowl of trifle. Even Caroline had been persuaded to come, leaving Roger baby-sitting with little Jonathan. Everyone was talking at once, laughing, leg-pulling, and kissing in welcome as they trooped into the house, a seemingly endless stream of cars disgorging passengers behind them. Roland and Michael were delighted by the gesture, produced glasses, mugs and even cups, in which to serve wine to all the guests.

Having done all the organising, Janthina was content to sit back and watch the party swing. Caught out in old clothes fit only for unpacking crates, Roland was quite unabashed and Michael, whom the Camerons were meeting for the first time, collapsed with laughter as he removed the lid from a shiny new dustbin to reveal dozens of toilet rolls. The young man was incredibly like his father, as tall, broad and handsome as Janthina remembered Roland at that age. Funny, she mused, to think that he could have been her son – and Caroline Roland's daughter – if things had been different. She watched the two of them chatting together as they unpacked a plate of sliced tomato salad, and attempted to arrange all the food in some semblance of order on the table. What an extraordinarily handsome couple they made. And there was Flora, moving across the room towards them: what might she be going to contribute?

\*   \*   \*

The arrival of the Burrows household in Whitehaven did bring a big change in their lives, as Roland and Janty had known it would. Suddenly, instead of meeting only once a month, they saw each other, professionally, or socially, two or three times a week . . . which was wonderful, except that at forty years old, in her mental and physical prime, Janthina desperately wanted more. So did Roland – but they knew it was impossible. Neither wanted a frustrating and nerve-racking relationship of deceit, clandestine meetings in the dark, dodging neighbours for fear of recognition; an affair based on guilt and lies; that would be to turn their love into something sordid and sly. When he had lived in London, that had been different. Now. . . .

The Gordons, Camerons and Burrows spent Christmas Day of 1924 together. In fact, they had shared several festive occasions like birthdays, during the previous months, and only the addition of Joseph made the covers on the long mahogany table up to unlucky thirteen, but as little Jonathan was with them in his high chair he was counted as the fourteenth, and nobody worried.

Susan's sister and niece had come in to help with the preparation and serving of the vast luncheon. Cam carved the turkey with great expertise at one end of the table while Roland massacred the ham at the other, crumbling it into pieces which Janthina laughingly scooped with a spoon. Freddie, having only one hand to contribute, poured the wine. The McKenzie sisters were delighted their brother was with them; he was quite bald now, stiff, proper, and tending to be reserved, but he was clearly happy to be with his family, handing out beautifully wrapped parcels containing inappropriate gifts for which he was hugged and kissed by his 'womenfolk' – as he fondly called them.

Caroline and Roger were seated well apart, theirs being the only discordant note at the table. She looked drab and colourless, with discontent marring her beautiful features. Roger at least made some effort to be pleasant to his in-laws, but Caroline almost snubbed them. She tried to be affable with Ruth and Freddie, and with Roland, actually laughed with Giles and Michael, but Janthina was hurt when the girl pointedly avoided kissing her 'Happy Christmas'. Time, far from healing the rift between them, only seemed to widen it.

There was a repeat of the same gathering on New Year's Eve at the Grand Hotel. Maxine and Jonathan were put to bed upstairs while the rest of the family gathered round a table loaded with festive hats, whistles and crackers, and for the first time, Ian was with them, tall and athletic for his fourteen years, looking splendid in tails and white tie.

When the orchestra struck up, Giles, the jovial, kilted giant, led his mother on to the floor for the first dance; Angus asked Janty, Cam partnered Flora, and Roland smiled enquiringly at Caroline, who immediately stood up to take the floor with him, after a slightly wistful smile towards Michael. The Reverend Joseph McKenzie looked down the table at Roger, wondering whether to move to a chair next to the unhappy young man and make conversation with him, but suddenly noticed the expression on his face as he gazed across the room at a young woman in another party – who gazed sadly back. There was no question about the message passing between them. Thoughtfully, Joseph turned to talk to Michael.

When midnight struck, everyone kissed everyone . . . or nearly.

'Happy New Year, darling,' Janthina said to Caroline who was dancing with Michael.

'What a hope,' the girl replied, quietly so that only her mother heard, before she danced away.

Suddenly Janthina was angry. She had tried, dammit, tried hard. Caroline was behaving like a spoilt, belligerent brat, creating an unpleasant atmosphere and unhappiness at every family occasion.

The anger, refuelled by another discordant brush two weeks later, finally burst out. Janthina had called at Roger and Caroline's home with some baby clothes Ruth had passed on from Maxine, and was hurt once again by her indifferent reception. When she suggested Caroline should telephone Ruth to thank her, Caroline made a sarcastic remark about charity for the poor.

Janthina remonstrated and the girl told her to mind her own business.

'Caroline! Will you stop it? That's the outside of enough! For heaven's sake, what has your Aunt Ruth done to deserve your nasty remarks? And what's more, I will not tolerate your impertinence any longer. I know you've been hurt and I've tried to make allowances, but it seems I've made too many. Perhaps a damn good thrashing would have done better. As for minding my own business . . . discord within my family *is* my business and I will do my utmost to eliminate it. You've made your mistakes and you're paying for them – as I have paid for mine. The difference is that I do not spend my time trying to make everyone's life around me miserable. For God's sake pull yourself together and try to behave like a rational adult.'

Caroline stood in front of her, shaking with anger, eyes blazing. 'It's you who should stop it,' she snarled. 'Just you try to remember that I'm not only having to pay for my own mistakes, but for yours as well. I've had enough, too. Enough of the Camerons and the McKenzies . . . enough of everyone. The hurts just keep piling up and up. I don't know why I bother to go on living! I've never been really wanted by anyone – Roger doesn't want me, he's in love with Betty, but we're stuck with each other . . . thanks to me being forced out to a party on New Year's Eve with a lot of jolly people when I was miserable. . . .' She gave an extra hard stare at Janthina as she said it. 'Jonathan is the only person in the world who needs me. If it wasn't for him. . . .' She sobbed and shook her head angrily. 'Oh . . . please go. Don't come here any more. Leave me alone.' She ran into the other room, slamming the door behind her and waking the baby.

Janthina sat listening to him cry, to Caroline talking to him, and to the silence that followed. Instinct made her stay. Though she thought she should leave, she couldn't bear to walk out on such a miserable scene.

Some time later Roger walked in, swaying slightly and smelling of beer. He looked at his mother-in-law and then at the closed door to the other room. 'Oh, Christ! Has she been having another of her tantrums?'

'She is very unhappy.'

'Aren't we all? I'm sorry.' He sank into the armchair opposite her. 'Christ! The price you pay for one New Year's Eve . . . er. . . .'

'Fling?' Janthina suggested.

He grinned at her and shrugged. 'A rose by any other name?'

She smiled back. 'I suppose I'd better leave; I was ordered out over an hour ago.'

'Join the club.'

'I'm so sorry, Roger, it's all so sad.'

'Yes. It's Jonathan I worry about most. It's going to be a rotten life for him.'

'Yes.' She thought she should add something useful and profound, but nothing came to mind. Instead, she stood up and Roger helped her into her coat and opened the outer door for her.

'Goodbye,' she said softly.

'Cheerio,' he replied.


Caroline telephoned her at the office next day. 'Janty? I just want to say I'm sorry for saying the things I did last night. I was feeling particularly sorry for myself. I know that's no excuse, I don't have an excuse, but I think it might be better if we don't see each other for a while, don't you?'

Janthina closed her eyes and sighed. 'If that's what you want.'

The phone was silent.

294

'Is that what you want?'

'I think it would be better. We're only upsetting each other.'

'Very well. I'll wait to hear from you.'

'Right.'

'Au revoir.'

'Au revoir, Janty.'


Roland was in the office when Janthina walked in a few weeks later.

'Feeling better?' he asked.

'Much, but still rather shaky, I'm afraid.' She had had a bad bout of influenza lasting two whole weeks and her legs were still feeling like rubber.

'You've been working far too hard, you know. You're constantly overtired nowadays, and that's why you're catching so many bugs. Why don't you ease up a bit? Can't Cam do a bit more than he does?'

'He's never been quite the same since his illness. I know he's only fifty but he has definitely slowed down. He seems to tire so easily. The main trouble is the circulation in his legs.'

'Then why don't you get an assistant?'

'I would if I could find the right person.' She hesitated, then added, 'I know who I'd like to have.'

'Who?'

'Michael.' She watched him closely for his reaction.

He glanced at her and shook his head. 'Nice of you to say so, but I doubt if there's any chance. He's trying to get away from Whitehaven.'

She dropped into the chair opposite him, frowning. 'Why? I thought he loved Whitehaven and wanted to settle. What's changed his mind?'

He stared at her incredulously. 'Do you mean to tell me you honestly have no inkling? You can't guess?'

'Guess what? What on earth are you talking about?'

'God, darling, I really thought you must know . . . about him and Caroline. They've fallen for each other. Isn't it sad? They are so miserable.'

'Michael and Caroline?' Her mind reeled. Oh, no! How awful. Impossible! Her eyes closed and she bit her lip. 'I had no idea. Have I been very unobservant?'

'I don't suppose so. You don't see as much of Caroline as I see of Michael. He was moping around the house, day after day, so I eventually tackled him, asking him what was up, and he told me all about it.'

'She'll probably blame me for this disaster, too.' She was only speaking her thoughts aloud but Roland frowned.

'Blame you? Don't tell me she thinks you are responsible for her troubles?'

'Indeed! She regards herself as the greatest, unwanted, mistake in my life.'

'Janty, my darling.' He left his chair to stand beside her and place a sympathetic hand on her shoulder.

She leaned her cheek against it. 'What a pity we seem unable to learn by the mistakes of the previous generation.'

She tried to settle down to some work but found it impossible to concentrate, so went home early. Susan brought her a tray of tea in the drawing room and she sat staring into the log fire, then up at her painting of Château de Berenac. Sipping her tea she thought back to the tranquillity of the Dordogne, the contentment of sitting on the river bank beside the little girl with the golden curls – all the miseries of the months prior to the birth forgotten, erased by this new joy in her life. Joy that was to be destroyed by Grandpapa and Cam, by all the petty inhibitions and false moral dictates of society.

If.

If only those inhibitions had not stopped her from telling Roland the truth in her letters, from claiming Caroline as her daughter as soon as Cam refused to adopt the child.

The picture which hung upstairs in her bedroom, of Caroline sitting beside the river holding a posy of wild flowers, was clear in her mind's eye: the plump cheeks swept by long, curling lashes, the sun lighting a halo in her curls, soft lips widening in a baby smile to show her milk teeth. A happy, innocent smile . . . now grown hard and thin. Was Caroline's life now set in a pattern of successive miseries, as her own had been?

Had been! Yes, but not any more. She had adapted, developed new attitudes and thinking to suit her circumstances. So why couldn't Caroline do the same? Only do it now, not wait until she was in her thirties.

She paced the room, saucer in one hand and cup half full of cold tea in the other. How? Was it possible, tied to a man who only wanted another woman, but who was, at the same time, decent, honest and kind? Surely it was just as much a tragedy for Roger, being fettered by a marriage that should never have happened.

So why shouldn't they divorce?

But what would happen to Jonathan? What would society do to them?

'Damn society!' she exclaimed out loud, and setting her cup and saucer on the tea tray, she picked up her handbag and car keys.


Jonathan was in his cot, flushed and fractious and being nursed by his mother. The young woman's hair was lank and greasy, as were the dishes left on the table from the last meal.

'What do you want?' she asked ungraciously when she opened the door.

'I want you and Roger to divorce.' Janthina was waiting on the doormat to be asked in.

Caroline gazed at her, dumbfounded, then beckoned with a tilt of the head as she returned to the howling child. 'What the hell brought this on?' she asked, bending over the cot.

'Are you in love with Michael?'

Caroline's back straightened. She didn't look round as she whispered, 'Yes.'

'Are you sure? After all, it's not very long since you thought you were in love with Stephen.'

'I'm sure. Stephen was just a girlish pash.'

'Does Roger still love Betty?'

'Yes.'

'Then what are you waiting for?'

Jonathan's wailing ceased.

'I think he's asleep. Let's go into the other room and sit down.' She closed the door softly behind them. 'Sorry about the mess.'

Janthina grinned at her. 'Would I be putting my foot in it if I said "I know this feeling well"?' Her arm swept over the disordered room.

Caroline's reply was a thin smile as she sank into an armchair.

Janthina sat in the other, and took a deep breath. 'Did you know that Michael's father and I love each other?'

Caroline's mouth fell open. 'Since when?'

'Since I was seventeen.'

'Seventeen! But. . . .'

'He had been visiting relatives in Canada. We met on the *Campania* crossing from New York some months after his wife died. We only knew each other a few days, but it was long enough.' She launched into the story, not omitting a single detail, and when she had finished Caroline gave her a puzzled stare, and asked, 'Why are you telling me this?'

'Two reasons. One, because I love you and trust you not to repeat it to anyone, and two, because I want you to benefit from my mistake. You see, if I hadn't been frightened by the thought of Roland's

297

reactions, Roland being part of the decent, moral society to which I no longer belonged, I would have told him about you . . . about my mistake. He swears he would have married me and adopted you. You and Michael would have grown up together.'

'I think I would still prefer him as a husband than a brother.' Caroline leaned her head back against the chair and added gloomily, 'If I had the choice. But what . . . are you trying to tell me?'

'For years I made the mistake of allowing myself to be pushed around by the false values and stupid moral stances of the family, and of society. I wept and felt sorry for myself – and did nothing. I looked exactly as you do now . . . no, worse! I had three children and we lived in rooms in the Dolphin Hotel attic. There was not an ounce of flesh on my bones and I remember that every time I combed my hair it came out in handfuls; my hands were calloused and my nails broken down to the quicks.'

Caroline looked at the elegant creature sitting opposite her, cool and cross-legged and immaculately dressed, in obvious disbelief. Her eyes travelled down from the pearls to the black patent leather shoes and back again. 'I remember living at the hotel, vaguely. But . . . what happened to change you?'

'I decided to take charge of my own destiny. Rather too late to be of much good to you, I'm afraid. I used to be too hidebound by the Victorian dictates of my upbringing.' She leaned forward. 'Caroline, don't let the same thing happen to you. Stand up for yourself, now, before it's too late; before Michael goes off to London or somewhere to try and forget you, and finds himself a wife he doesn't love; and while Betty is still free to marry Roger. Don't let your chance of happiness escape as I did.'

The clouds of misery in Caroline's tired eyes seemed to lift. A hopeful smile played round her lips as she started to lean forward. Then she sank back again, eyes closed, while a shudder ran through her body. She shook her head. 'How can we divorce? What about Jonathan? And what about all the sordid newspaper reports? Roger and Michael and I would be hounded by gossip for ever more. And Jonathan, too. We would be ostracised. No one would want to know us.'

'Nonsense! As far as Jonathan is concerned, you'll have to sort out custody with Roger, but I believe he would agree to any arrangement you cared to suggest, just to untie this tangle. I know he hates the thought of the little one growing up in this atmosphere. And as for the rest, well . . . anyone who ostracises you will have to ostracise the Camerons, and they won't, believe me. We are too wealthy, too powerful in the community. No one will risk losing our goodwill, for fear of losing our business.'

Caroline sat up straight. 'You'd stand by us?' Her face was white and drawn.

'Of course. I'd do anything.' Janthina longed to take the girl in her arms, reassure her . . . but it was too soon. She mustn't spoil her chances.

'What about Cam? I bet he won't agree.'

'He will.'

'How do you know?'

'Because I will tell him to, order him to, if necessary.'

Caroline raised her eyebrows. 'You can do that?'

'Yes.'

There were more questions she wanted to ask, but she was too tired to bother.

'When is Roger due home?' Janthina asked.

The clock on the mantelpiece showed a quarter to five.

'About half past.'

'Go and wash, fix your hair and put on a decent dress. You'll feel better. I'll tidy up in here and we'll be ready to talk when he arrives.' She had no intention of leaving Caroline, in her present negative frame of mind, to put the proposition to him.


'Great Scot!' Roger stood in the doorway, blinking at the tidy room and his immaculate wife. 'What the hell's happened? Is it somebody's birthday?' Then he saw Janty. 'Oh! It's you. You've been busy, I see.'

'Hello, Roger. Cup of tea?' She held the pot poised.

He nodded. 'Thanks.' And raised an eyebrow at his wife.

'Hot, buttered toast?' Caroline held out the dish.

He took two pieces and placed them in his saucer, licking melted butter from his fingers. 'Will someone please tell me what's going on?' he asked with a grin.

So they did.


Three weeks later Roger and a red-haired Irish girl from London were photographed at a Brighton hotel *in flagrante delicto*. When the photographer had departed they climbed out of bed, virtually fully clothed, and put on their hats and shoes. Roger counted out a pile of banknotes and handed them over, for which the girl thanked him, and

299

when he had paid the bill at the cashier's desk, they went their separate ways.

Caroline had moved back into the old Tudor house above the town where her husband was now a frequent and welcome visitor, coming mainly to see his son, but now on friendlier and more relaxed terms with his wife and in-laws than ever. Sometimes he even brought a shy and pink-faced Betty with him.

Roland had recommended a good divorce lawyer to Caroline . . . and now it was only a matter of time.

Michael, too, was often at the house, a gentle, patient husband-to-be. Happy and confident that soon he and Caroline would be free to marry before the end of the year. No longer wanting to leave Whitehaven, he agreed to Janthina's request and discussed with her the possibility of working in the Cameron Group, as the overall operation was now known. But there was one worry on his mind.

'What about your own sons?' he asked. 'Angus may well change his mind and Ian won't be involved with sport all his life. I don't want to join you only to find I am either usurping them or they are promoted over my head, leaving me in a comparatively minor position.'

'I understand your doubts, but I can assure you that at the rate the Group is expanding there is going to be room at the top for as many energetic young executive brains as I can find. Angus has chosen his career. The only thing that might change his mind, as you put it, is if he fails in his law studies – in which case I must tell you that I am not going to employ failures in executive posts. It would not only be fatal to the business but also I have seen too many sons destroyed as people after they have been pushed into an executive position in a family firm for which they knew they were inadequate. Everyone must find their own level in life, doing a job they can feel confident and successful in. Also, you must realise that the whole operation was really launched on money intended for Caroline. Cam was bankrupt when I bought the hotels with my own money and rescued the grocery outlets and wholesalers. Added to which, Caroline is my eldest child. I am delighted by how much interest she shows in the Group and I hope, if you agree, to involve her more and more. I see no reason why we shouldn't expand continuously, buy more hotels in other resorts and even in London.'

'What about the grocery and wholesalers? Do you intend to expand them?'

'Perhaps. We need their turnover, certainly, and they will continue to show a profit even when the economy heads into recession, as I believe it is doing now. But as a continuing investment we must move into property. The values may temporarily drop from time to time, but in the long run they will always increase.' She paused and looked into his face. 'Now tell me honestly, do you think you can cope with working for your mother-in-law?'

Michael laughed. 'I have thought about that point very seriously. I know most people would advise against it, but in your case, Janty, I have no doubt at all that I would love every minute.'

Janthina beamed. 'You are very sweet to say so.'

'I mean it.'

'Good. Well, let's get down to discussing the details like training, responsibility, and salary. Your law and accountancy qualifications will be invaluable, but there is a great deal more to learn.'


On the surface, everything seemed to be going so well, yet Caroline could not relax. She couldn't believe that the pattern of being a misfit in life would ever change; that the divorce would go through or that, if it did, Whitehaven society would ever acknowledge or accept them, that the wagging tongues would ever leave them alone. She thought that Janthina meant well, but was not convinced that this latest interference would bring any less disaster than the last. She was polite and friendly with her mother and tried to be helpful in the house, but the cook-housekeeper Mrs Bates, and Susan, could manage perfectly well without her and in fact they frequently offered to look after Jonathan as well.

'Could I be of any use at the office?' she asked Janthina one day.

'Why not? Come in tomorrow with me, if you like. We can do the hotel rounds together after going through the ledgers.' Her voice was cool and casual, but inside she was quivering with excitement.

Caroline's previous spasmodic interest immediately flared into enthusiasm, prompted, no doubt, by Michael's eagerness to discuss business affairs with her whenever they were together. She was particularly keen on the whole theory and practice of hotel management, pouring over the individual accounts and balance sheets and noting every detail of each hotel's efficiency – or otherwise.

Her mother was elated. She knew she would have to be cautious but it was clearly possible to foresee the fulfilment of all her plans over the next few years. Gradually more and more responsibility would be handed over to Michael and Caroline until, in the long run, she would be able to retire. The future was hazy, as always; nothing was ever certain, so she must make a will. Angus, Flora and Ian would benefit, handsomely, from dividends, though they would own very few shares outright; they would inherit all Cam's remaining shares between them, but the hotels would belong to Caroline . . . and her issue.

One thing still bothered Janthina. Flora would be leaving school at the end of the summer term, in a few weeks, in fact, and had told Cam some time ago, she was interested in the business. He was naturally keen for the girl to join the Group, but this would inevitably lead to conflicts between the step-sisters. However, she need not have worried.

Flora had made her own plans.

Home for a weekend only two weeks before the end of term, she announced at dinner that she wanted to go to Australia. 'Bernard and Uncle William have asked me several times and I'm sure I should like it. The farm is huge and they have an enormous house. Look, they've sent photos of it, and that group of people, there, are all the house servants. They have lots of horses, carriages, and motor cars, and see here. . . .' She passed her father another photograph. 'This is Bernard. Isn't he handsome?' There was no doubt in anyone's mind of her intentions. 'Please may I go?'

Cam was disappointed, reluctant to see his only daughter leave for the other side of the world, possibly never to return. But he gave in to her cajoling.

Janthina was relieved. She had long felt guilty that she loved this child less than the others, but she had found it hard to forgive Flora for the pain and misery she had caused Caroline throughout her childhood and continued to mete out at any given opportunity. She was sure it would be easier to love the girl as she should from a distance, and perhaps this tough-looking Australian boy would knock some of the sharp edges from her abrasive nature.

'Do you think that Uncle William should be made my legal guardian whilst I'm out there?' Flora asked, concentrating on peeling her apple.

Cam and Janthina exchanged glances. They knew this was so that she would gain quick permission to marry if she wanted. Cam frowned but Janthina spread her hands. He shrugged and nodded.

Flora wrote off to Bernard in great excitement and her mother wrote to Uncle William. Enthusiastic replies were received and after some hurried shopping Cam and Janthina drove Flora down to Southampton with her two smart new suitcases at the end of August, to wave her goodbye on the SS *Canberra*.

'Strange,' Janthina remarked as they drove home, 'I had expected Flora would be the most difficult of our children to settle; now it seems she will be the easiest.'

'Let's hope that if she does wed the boy this marriage is more successful than Caroline's or ours,' Cam sighed, little guessing the humiliations and hardships in store for the girl.

Despite all Caroline's fears, the divorce hearing went through very smoothly in May and certainly no one showed any sign of being less than friendly. But she socialised very little. Jonathan was growing fast and she spent most of her time with him when she wasn't at the office or in the hotels. Her life was in limbo. Not daring to believe that all the dreams and promises Janty had made could possibly come true, she remained cool and distant, still protected by a feigned indifference. She was politely attentive in her mother's company – but never relaxed and warm. As for the wedding arrangements, she was content to allow Janthina to organise the family for a get-together following the brief ceremony, after which she and Michael could slip away to the little house they were to rent until they could afford something better.

Janthina herself had other ideas. Caroline needed convincing that she was not a social leper, and she knew exactly how to achieve that conviction. Three hundred and fifty invitations were printed saying:

Mr and Mrs James Cameron
request the pleasure of your company
at a reception to be held at
THE NEW EXCELSIOR HOTEL
at noon on December 23rd, 1925
following the marriage of their niece
Caroline Morton
to
Mr Michael Burrows

RSVP

Caroline was told only that the meal would be held at the hotel to save Susan and Mrs Bates extra work.

'I hope the decree nisi is through in time,' was her only comment.

Janthina and Roland agreed there should be a honeymoon, and with great secrecy they shopped together for the additional wardrobe the couple would need and packed it all carefully in a large trunk. Tickets were bought on the Golden Arrow to Paris and Janthina reserved a suite at the Georges V.

Janthina also persuaded the nervous bride-to-be to drive up to London with her to choose a gown.

'Just something simple that will come in useful later,' Caroline said as they made the arrangement. And was shocked by the price of the first ensembles they were shown.

'This is my show, remember,' Janthina argued. 'It is the bride's parents who will foot the bill. Your first marriage was a non-starter from the beginning, but this one, with your beloved Michael, is going to be different. You just pick out anything you think might make him swoon.'

Caroline laughed. It was a genuine, giggly laugh, as happy as her tensions would allow, causing Janthina a sudden lump in her throat. They were talking quite openly now, the old animosity having disappeared, but . . . loving? There was no touching or affection, just a pleasant form of communication – and that laugh.

Janthina saw it first. Slim, low-waisted in palest aquamarine, a combination of heavy lace panels stitched with tiny matching beads, set in the same shade of stiff satin. It was a two-piece, the short sleeves and boat-shaped neck of the dress concealed under the high-collared jacket.

'Oh, no, Janty, it is far too dressy for such a quiet occasion.' Caroline shook her head.

'Try it on, though, just for fun.'

She stepped out of the drab, biscuit-coloured crêpe de chine which had done nothing for her figure or colouring, and allowed the assistant to ease the luxurious aquamarine dress over her head.

It was perfect in every detail. A smile spread over Caroline's pale features as the jacket was fastened at the neck, the collar framing her face.

'Isn't it wonderful?' Janthina murmured.

'Fantastic,' Caroline breathed. 'But don't you think. . . .'

'In my opinion it could not possibly be bettered, but if you don't like it. . . .'

The assistant had slipped out of the changing room and returned with a pair of high-heeled matching satin slippers, complete with diamanté buckles. The ankle-length skirt revealed them to perfection, and Caroline sighed a happy, 'Oh, ye-es.'


Only the Camerons, Gordons and Burrows were at the short ceremony. Caroline looked lovely, but subdued, still not daring to believe that total happiness could be hers. Michael was calm and confident. He and Roger were on friendly terms, Roger having agreed that Caroline should have custody of Jonathan, knowing that he was welcome to visit the child at any time. It had been his suggestion that his son grow up calling Michael 'Daddy', relegating himself to the role of 'uncle'. It was a sweet and generous gesture, but then, as Caroline had originally explained to Janthina, Roger was that kind of person. He and Betty were excitedly preparing for their own wedding in a few days' time, and were delighted to be amongst the invited guests waiting in the ballroom of the New Excelsior for the wedding party to arrive.

'Which room are we in?' Caroline asked as she smoothed her skirt and waited for the men to dispose of their hats and gloves.

'In here, darling,' Janthina told her, as the huge double doors were flung open and the hotel orchestra struck up the Mendelssohn 'Wedding March' with all the zest and gusto they could muster.

The crowd parted to form an aisle and old Reverend Cooney stepped forward to greet the couple and lead them to the low dais. Roland and Janthina followed as far as the foot of the dais, arm in arm, with Cam and Ruth on their heels and the boys, Joseph and Freddie behind them.

Champagne had already been served to the guests and the family were now given theirs as the rector of St Mary's began his speech. He said he had known the Camerons since their arrival in Whitehaven over twenty years ago; praised their achievements and their children. He spoke of Caroline's beauty and Michael's brains and the courage of this couple, and that of others concerned – looking directly at Roger and Betty – daring to fly in the face of social and religious dogmas so as to correct their youthful mistakes and achieve happiness. 'I only wish I could have performed the ceremony myself, but I can at least offer them my personal blessing and wish Michael and Caroline everlasting joy. I give you Michael and Caroline,' he called, raising his glass.

There was no hesitation. Every glass was held high, their names repeated over and over again. People cheered and put down their glasses, so freeing their hands to applaud, and Janthina noticed Joseph clapping loudest of all. Roland passed her his handkerchief and squeezed her arm. For a moment their eyes met. There was no need to speak the words. Both knew this moment might have been theirs, years ago, if . . . and maybe, before many more years passed. . . .

Standing back, watching the scene, Cam, too, saw the message which passed between his lawyer and his wife, and knew he had lost her, irrevocably. Lost everything. His shoulders drooped and a great leaden weight filled his chest. He had gambled – but the stakes had been too high.

Roland and Janthina turned to smile again at the newlyweds, their son and daughter who would perpetuate their love through the next generation. Caroline was smiling, but her lower lip quivered and everyone could see tears splashing into dark patches on the smooth satin as she looked down at the friendly, loving, smiling faces, listened to the congratulations and good wishes. Not one face lacked warmth, or was turned away.

Michael put a comforting arm round his wife as he made his brief reply, and, as there were no bridal attendants to thank and toast, Caroline herself stepped forward, holding up her hand for silence. Tears still streamed down her face as she spoke. 'I would like to propose a toast, please.' She took a deep breath. 'To the most wonderful lady in the whole world, my dear, darling Janty.' She raised her glass to her lips, then stepped off the dais to rush into her mother's arms. 'I love you, Janty. Thank you so much for having me,' adding in a whisper, 'Please forgive me for all the pain I've caused you.'

'There's nothing to forgive,' Janthina whispered back. 'You were hurt through my own mistakes, and in pain you hurt back. Dearest Caroline, I do understand.'

The two women embraced, then stepped apart to dry their eyes while Michael stood beside them waiting to reclaim his bride, a huge smile on his face.

Suddenly Janthina noticed Cam at her side, his eyes over-bright. He looked at her sadly and said, 'Janty, I'm sorry, truly sorry, for having denied you your daughter all these years.' He shook his head. 'But words are meaningless. I can't expect you to believe me. And anyway . . .' he looked pointedly at Roland '. . . it's too late to say sorry, isn't it?'

She saw the sadness in his face and knew it was genuine. Her eyes followed the line of his gaze and returned to his face. 'Yes, Cam, I'm afraid it is far too late,' she murmured gently.


Outside the hotel the young couple sat in the back of the Rolls Royce hugging each other excitedly, firmly clutching their surprise honeymoon tickets. They were showered in confetti and laughed as the tin cans and balloons bounced behind them as they set off towards London.

Unnoticed among the waving crowd left on the pavement, Roland's hand held Janthina's, lovingly. They allowed their eyes to meet, expressing all the love and joy of the years to come.